BLOOD BROTHERS

"John Taylor? You in there? You asleep?"

Jacob waited. The radio continued to play.

When he carefully, slowly swung open the door, he immediately saw the gleaming red dots—the eyes of someone lying on the floor in a nest of straw—but before he could say or do anything, the figure raised itself and hissed, the eyes flamed, and warm, putrid air gusted into Jacob's face. Suddenly the radio popped and crackled as if it had been hit by an electrical surge, and the ensuing silence was thick and heavy.

But Jacob could not move.

The shadowy figure was holding him with some mesmerizing power stronger than any grip Jacob had ever felt. The figure—the features of its face visible in the eerie glow of its eyes—clearly resembled John Taylor. But something had seized the body of his brother, something had possessed it and was now staring at Jacob as if he were prey.

It hissed again.

Then the figure rose and began gliding toward him.

Jacob's nightmarish paralysis continued; he could not even scream or lift his arms to protect himself from the penetrating glare of those red eyes and the advance of fangs. . . .

IN THE BLOOD

Stephen Gresham

PINNACLE BOOKS
Kensington Publishing Corp.
http://www.pinnaclebooks.com

A special thanks to Rod Smith, the only true poet I have ever known, for graciously allowing me to "borrow" the Hollow Log Lounge from his marvelous collection of poems, *The Hollow Log Lounge*, 1985 *Texas Review* Poetry Award Chapbook.

Rod, I think maybe you know as much about vampires as I do.

—Stephen Gresham
July 14, 2000

Look at them and see what they are
like.

They move as though a wind were
pushing them.

They rest as though a hand had stopped
them.

In their eyes is the oncoming darkness
sweeping across summer's fields
before the storm.

—from Rainer Maria Rilke's
"Betrachte sie und sich, was ihnen gliche"

Chapter One

The Darkness
Before the Dawn

Trackers stand by blood.

Always have. Always will.

As Jacob Tracker broke open a new roll of quarters, he did not know why those thoughts should have stuck in his mental filter. They came out of nowhere, just the way customers occasionally did on this, the graveyard shift at Jimmie Jack's, a combination gas station and convenience store in Soldier's Crossing, Alabama. What he did know was that those words, or words to that effect, belonged to his father, Clarence Tracker, who said them a few months before his sixty-second birthday—his final birthday, dying a week later of a massive heart attack in the front seat of his pickup in the parking lot of the local textile mill, where he had just completed an overtime shift. That was five years ago. To Jacob, it seemed like yesterday.

His father died having failed to clear the Tracker name from a cloudy legacy extending back to the

War between the States and even before, to a time when the Trackers became infamous for the ruthless and violently effective ways in which they pursued and recaptured runaway slaves. It was a cold business. These earlier Trackers were bounty hunters, and they accumulated a small fortune for their efforts. The inglorious defeat of the Confederacy changed all that. But the attendant "bad name" haunted the family like the proverbial ghost of the proverbial Southern mansion.

Folks said the Trackers suffered under a family curse.

No one truly knew the source of it, though many speculated. Some, for example, believed the gods of social justice were punishing the Trackers for the years of mistreating slaves and harboring an antipathy toward the black race in general. Others whispered of the Trackers having been involved in a conspiracy to assassinate President Lincoln—hadn't Jefferson Jackson Tracker, himself an aspiring actor, befriended John Wilkes Booth? they reasoned—the family receiving, justifiably perhaps, a sentence of inevitable doom or at least dissolution. Still others passed along for decades a dark rumor that when Sweet Gum plantation, the once elegant home of the Trackers, had been converted to a Confederate hospital very late in the Great Cause, something vile had occurred: unspecified acts of violence so horrid and perverse as to stain the Tracker family forever. No Tracker since that monumental war had gained more than modest success financially or otherwise, and over the years some Trackers had been shunned as outlaws, murderers and reprobates.

Most, like Clarence Tracker, simply never amounted to much. As his son Jacob was painfully aware,

Clarence had fallen short of making his mark, of making a name for himself as a building contractor. His heart had been set upon Jacob and his two other sons, Daniel and John Taylor, known as "J.T.," joining him to form Tracker & Sons Construction. It didn't happen. A father cared; his sons were indifferent. So the man harbored just one final request: help your blood. A Tracker should always be there for another Tracker.

His elbows propped on the cash register counter, Jacob embraced his father's call. But he could not shake the feeling that, like his father and other Trackers before him, he, too, seemed destined to be a failure, his future as bleak as the empty tarmac beyond the glass door of Jimmie Jack's. He was twenty-four, had earned an associate degree from the local community college, and was not without ambition. Yet, he was unmarried, lived with his mother—an ageless beauty filled with melancholy and secrets—and had virtually no career prospects. Jimmie Jack's was not even the bottom-most rung on anyone's corporate ladder. Nevertheless, Jacob did have two ambitions: to be a successful country-western songwriter in Nashville and to win the love of Brianna and live happily ever after with her.

Brianna. Lovely Brianna.

His niece.

There was a forbidden stirring in Jacob's blood. But he couldn't help it. Brianna, divorced from her abusive husband, Spence McVicar, drove Jacob crazy with desire, and her sweet little daughter, Emily— dear, tiny "Em"—ripped his heart up as easily as if it were made of Spanish moss or camellia blossoms. God, he adored that elfin creature. And she was the light of her mother's life. So hopelessly and emotionally loyal was Jacob to Brianna that he dated no one, thus causing him to have to deflect suggestions that he was gay—like his cousin, Franklin Tracker.

Sadly, Brianna's heart was off limits, and Nashville might as well have been on the moon.

Jacob felt trapped. Unfortunately, it was little consolation that all his blood relatives lived in and around Soldier's Crossing, including his brothers and their families, his uncles Douglas, Winston, Calvin and Warren, his cousins Roy Dale, Mattie Lee, Janie and Royal, his nieces Sharelle and Brianna and his nephews Benjamin, Josh and Tyler.

Tracker blood was everywhere. Family. Jacob needed it, of course. But he needed something more. On a chilly January night, one deep and dark and lonely, Jacob needed to be galvanized by something. He needed to feel alive. But there were deadening cleanup chores to do: fresh coffee to make, rest rooms to mop, gas pump tallies and cash register totals to record. And any second his cousins Janie and Mattie Lee would be wheeling in with a morning delivery of the Montgomery and Birmingham newspapers, and his Uncle Douglas would be at the back door with the day's supply of milk—whole, nonfat and chocolate "goo-goo"—as well as cream and other products from the Good Neighbor Dairy, an inefficient enterprise that Uncle Douglas operated, managing somehow to avoid going bankrupt over the years. Invariably the man would remind Jacob that he needed a partner to run the dairy—"I'm gone give first shot at it to blood," he would often say.

Jacob started to change the tape in the store's video camera and thought of Brianna.

My God, she was so beautiful: her thick black hair

and ice-chip green eyes and full, young breasts and world-class bottom and legs, and the package was especially tempting when tightly contained in her Mr. Pancake waitress outfit, white with gold and black trim. Jacob glanced at the clock. In another hour she would be off her shift; he had agreed to give her a ride home because her worthless old Chevy needed a new alternator. He couldn't wait to see her. But he would have to.

Wind rattling the glass doors pulled him from his pleasant reverie.

Janie Tracker slammed through one of those doors and tossed a bundle of the *Montgomery Advertiser* toward the counter.

"You ever seen anything like this wind?" she cried. "Warm one like the middle of summer. Strange as can be. Came up all of a sudden. You want to know what I think it is?"

Jacob could feel some of the sudden and curiously warm air. He knew Janie would hold forth regardless of his response. She was loud and opinionated, a large-boned and not particularly attractive woman. Like her sister, Mattie Lee, she was in her late thirties and unmarried. Both lived with their father, Winston, who in thirty-five years of service had not risen above the position of assistant meat department supervisor at the local Piggly Wiggly. Both women, however, doted on him, long ago concluding that no other man could possibly caress their heart like their daddy. Jacob knew that Mattie Lee, shy to the same degree as Janie was forward, would be waiting for her sister, sitting out in their rusting SUV, with a loaded revolver in her lap, much too timid to ever use it, but somewhat comforted by its presence. She believed all manner of wicked men were afoot in the wee hours of the night.

"Janie, I think computers are responsible for it," said Jacob.

She grinned.

"No, it's not that." She paused for effect. "It's that global warming—that's it. Mattie and I watched a thing about it on *Oprah* yesterday. Weather's gone go crazy, they say. The polar ice caps gone melt and flood New York City and Miami, and Charleston and New Orleans gone be lakes you can sail a boat on." She turned to face the glass again. "Look at that wind kick up dust. You hearin' it howl?"

He was. It was an unnerving sound. But he went on about the routine business of counting Janie's copies of the papers and duly recording them, and as he was doing so, his Uncle Douglas swung in from the back room with a dozen quarts of milk.

"Mornin', Jake," he said. "Your aunt Mollie and I aren't gone claim our offspring no more. We give up on 'em." He typically had a friendly twinkle in his eyes even when serious.

Janie hollered a good-bye to Jacob and exchanged a "hey" with Uncle Douglas before clambering away. "Global warming," she added. "Y'all see if the whole dang planet don't wash on away." She braced herself for the wind and then was gone.

Jacob turned his attention to his uncle Douglas.

"You got problems with your boys?"

They weren't boys, of course. Franklin was approaching thirty and Roy Dale was Jacob's age, though shiftless and unable to keep any kind of job, including one helping his father at the dairy. Roy Dale was married to Jessie, whom everyone knew ran around on him. She was a barmaid at the Hollow Log Lounge, a questionable establishment owned by Jacob's uncle Calvin. Jessie and Roy Dale had a boy, Jeremy, who had yet to speak a word, though he had started kindergarten. Franklin was another matter entirely. Despite the fact that his parents frowned on his homosexual lifestyle, Franklin was at least more responsible than Roy Dale. He lived with an older man, Myron Florence, who was his lover, and together they ran the town's only antiques store, a place they called The Treasure House.

"Mainly it's Roy Dale," said Uncle Douglas. "He's done been influenced too much by your brother John Taylor. I mean, what good can come of that?"

Jacob wasn't sure that *any* good could come of it. His older brother was a drunkard and mean to boot. Jacob had always feared him and constantly felt sorry for his sister-in-law, Miriam, a saintly woman, and their two boys, Josh and Tyler.

"I heard Roy Dale's helping John Taylor rake down Sweet Gum," said Jacob. "You sorry to see the old Tracker homestead destroyed like that?"

Uncle Douglas scratched at his graying crew cut and squinted at Jacob, and yet there was an unmistakable glint in his eyes. "Not one damn bit," he said, and finished stacking the quarts of milk in the refrigerator section before heading back to his truck.

Thankful his uncle hadn't brought up the subject of a possible business partnership, Jacob scribbled a note for his boss, Jimmie Jack Bonner, regarding a need for a larger milk order during the middle of the week. Jimmie Jack would amble in around six o'clock with a report on how his latest diet was going. At a pound or two over 400, Jimmie Jack had decided within the past year to lose 200 or more and, accordingly, had tried on diets the way women try on shoes—one right after another. To mention only a few, he had experimented with the Grapefruit Plan, the Protein Power Plus, the Green Tomatoes and Okra Slim Down and the current system: the Fried Catfish Once-A-Day Guaranteed Loss Plan. None had worked. Not yet. Mostly because Jimmie Jack was not willing to forego his daily six-pack of beer, claiming he needed it to keep from getting dehydrated. But he was a pretty decent boss, and he positively envied Jacob's tall, thin physique.

Jacob heard the wind shriek again. He glanced up. The tarmac looked desolate, like something from an end-of-the-world movie. It was time to load up his clipboard and check the pump numbers for each of the three types of Southern Star gas. He heard his uncle Douglas banging around bottles and cartons out in his truck before the din suddenly and curiously halted. Dawn was approaching. Maybe with it the peculiar wind would die down—or so Jacob reasoned.

Brianna was suddenly in his thoughts again. This time, an image of her from summer wearing a black bikini at the Tracker picnic out by Moon Lake. Dear God, she filled that bikini deliciously. Above each cup of the bra and the edges of her panties, there was a filigree of lace; the sight of it had given Jacob an erection despite the subsequent blush of shame he had felt for lusting after his niece. A mouthful of his aunt Mollie's potato salad had soured on his tongue and he had ended up drinking too much beer in an attempt to drown his salacious thoughts.

The memory of Brianna's bikini dissipated like the head on one of those beers. . . .

The wind was pushing someone across the tarmac toward the door.

Jacob blinked. It was almost as if the person—a man, a stranger—weren't taking steps as he hurried to the doors. It was almost as if he were generating the wind himself. The man wore a long, dark coat with the collar hiked up around his face as if he were very cold. Jacob played his usual mental game of trying to anticipate what this customer wanted: cigarettes or snuff, or maybe a loaf of bread or a six-pack of beer. Or condoms.

Meeting a new customer was always fraught with inscrutable possibilities.

Especially on the graveyard shift. Jacob knew there was also, of course, a chance he'd have a gun pulled on him and be robbed. Jimmie Jack had repeated the same advice like a litany: "You get in that sitchee-ation, best give up the money, son. Ain't worth gettin' all shot up—you know what I'm sayin'?"

Jacob did.

The wind screamed loudly. The man stood at the door as if something prevented him from entering. It was unsettling to see him just standing there with the wind buffeting him. Jacob lowered his clipboard and stepped out from behind the counter. He felt hot needles of discomfort thread down one leg. He suddenly thought he recognized the person, but wasn't certain.

"Josh?" he called out.

Yes, it certainly appeared to be. Yes, Jacob's nephew, Josh, a young man of sixteen. He was trembling or perhaps shivering—Jacob couldn't determine which.

"Josh, come on in."

When the young man slipped inside the store, the wind calmed.

Then ceased completely. The hair on the back of Jacob's head stood up.

There was something wrong with Josh. That was obvious. Jacob recognized the coat as being John Taylor's. Then he noticed something more.

The coat glistened slightly in the fluorescent light because it was blood soaked.

"Jesus, what happened to you?"

Josh quickly raised a hand to keep Jacob away. But he did not speak. He had a cigarette lighter and raised it and started mechanically flicking it on and off; he appeared to be fascinated by the small flame. The lighter was out of place, because Jacob knew that Josh didn't smoke, that he had tried, in fact, to get his father, John Taylor, to quit, often going so far as a younger boy to hide the man's matches and lighter.

In momentary shock, his thoughts racing, Jacob studied his nephew, a bright, sensitive kid who had aspirations of one day becoming a doctor. Jacob, who had read some of Josh's dark and brooding poetry, liked him and his younger brother, Tyler, and often went to the movies with them—fantasy and science fiction being their favorites.

"Stay right there, Josh. Just stay right where you are."

Jacob ducked his head into the back room and hollered, "Uncle Doug, get up here quick. There's trouble." He didn't wait for his uncle's response, and when he turned around, Josh was at the counter staring up at the ceiling at the video camera. He continued flicking on and off the cigarette lighter. When the young man spoke, his voice was tinged with fear, though otherwise flat and even slightly disembodied.

"Can it see me?" he said.

"Josh, my God, are you hurt? There's blood on that coat."

It blazed through Jacob's thoughts that it could be the blood of a deer John Taylor had forced Josh to help him dress out.

"Can it, Jacob? Can it see me?"

"Sure it can. The tape's about to run out, but it can see you. What's with you? What's wrong, man? What's happened?"

The young man leaned forward conspiratorially. His breath reeked.

"It was in the walls, I think."

"What was? What's happened? You and your dad have been raking down Sweet Gum, haven't you? Where'd that blood come from? Did you cut yourself? I can take you to a doctor, Josh."

When it looked as if the young man might faint, Jacob started to reach for the phone, but then stopped as he caught sight of the video monitor trained on the counter area. Something clicked in his throat.

The monitor did not show the presence of Josh.

"Jesus Christ," Jacob whispered.

He looked at Josh and was almost crushed by the expression of sadness in the young man's eyes.

"Jacob, I think it was in the walls." The young man hesitated and drew even closer to the counter, and Jacob found himself mesmerized. The cigarette lighter flicked on and off twice more, and Josh said, "Daddy's dead and he's up walking around and he did something to me and I think this is about blood and family. You got to help, Jacob. You have to help blood. Save Tyler and the others."

Jacob was gasping a bit for air. He called out once more for his uncle, but still received no response. He then managed to calm himself slightly and to speak slowly and in a controlled voice. "Josh, it's OK, man. We'll get help and—"

Jacob gave out a grunt of surprise.

The transformation squeezed all the air from his lungs.

It began with Josh's eyes—the sudden eerie redness, like eyes caught in a camera flash—and then the teeth, the canines spreading into fangs and then the trickle of blood from one corner of the mouth, like innocent drippings from a kid's melting Popsicle. Then the fingers—the nails suddenly growing an inch or two and sharp as knifepoints. And then the voice, lower, raspy—not Josh's voice at all.

"Jacob, do you know what's out there?"

The silence was palpable.

Jacob grunted again.

Josh, or what was once Josh, turned to walk away. Incredulous, Jacob suddenly could not move, could not speak. He could only watch as the young man hesitated, then wheeled around and reached for the hard countertop, slicing a fingernail into it and leaving a deep gash. Jacob stumbled back away from the counter and then continued watching, terrified, as the young man used the same finger to cut open his own forearm and suck hungrily at the blood.

Jacob could feel his knees start to buckle.

In the next instant an invisible force seemed to push the young man through the glass doors without breaking them. Then Jacob heard the young man speak, not aloud, but telepathically: *I'll save myself. You save the others,* said the voice.

Staggered and shaken beyond anything he had ever experienced, Jacob moved out from behind the counter as the young man continued to advance to the pump area and settled there beneath the overhead bank of lights at #4 lead-free regular. At the glass doors Jacob, quaking so badly that he had to grasp one of the door handles for support, stared at the young man. The wind rose again and a sickly yellow light filled the air like an unnaturally long stroke of lightning.

The young man lifted the pump nozzle and with an eager attentiveness began to douse himself with gasoline, finishing the process by sticking the nozzle in his mouth and filling it until it splashed out like someone drinking from a water hose on a hot day. And then with preternatural quickness, the young man flicked on the cigarette lighter and held the flame to his lips.

Much too late, Jacob yelled at the top of his lungs for the young man to stop.

And one word filled Jacob's thoughts as he watched an incredible scene unfold.

Dragon.

A flame spewed from the young man's mouth, like one from a fire-breathing dragon. And then the dragon burst into a ball of flames, and Jacob began running toward the back room, knowing it was already too late to switch off all the other pumps. He ran out of the rear of the store and into the darkness, and behind him the night thrummed with heat and a chain of fiery explosions.

Parked behind the store was the Good Neighbor Dairy truck.

Behind the steering wheel was his Uncle Douglas. But there was nothing friendly in his eyes; they matched the eerie, glowering redness of Josh's. He was staring at Jacob. Then he spoke and his voice was thick with blood.

"Know what's out there?" he said.
Losing consciousness, Jacob crashed to his knees.
And the night continued to roar.

Chapter Two

The Aftermath of Morning Down

Soldier's Crossing made the news in big-time fashion.

Film crews and reporters from Montgomery and Birmingham, and Columbus, Georgia, swooped down like scavenger birds drawn to roadkill. After the fire had been brought under control, Jacob, still recovering from shock but refusing medical attention, answered questions directed to him by the local police and fire chiefs, but ducked from the scene when a television camera was pointed at him and a microphone was jammed in his face.

He sought refuge at Mr. Pancake, where he called his brother Danny and pleaded with him to come talk immediately.

"Jake, you tellin' me you haven't told the whole story of what happened?"

It was midmorning at the restaurant and busy as usual. Much to Jacob's disappointment, someone else had given Brianna a ride home. Jacob and his brother sat in a booth, and yet they were close enough to the counter to hear a clutch of men talking about the explosion at Jimmie Jack's and how, miraculously, only one person had been killed. Jimmie Jack's had been closed indefinitely. On the jukebox Reba McEntire was singing a country-western ballad.

"I couldn't," he said in answer to his brother's question. "Didn't think anybody would believe it."

Feeling empty, as well as distraught, Jacob had ordered an egg over easy, grits and biscuits while he waited for Danny's squad car to pull in. But now that the hot food was on a plate in front of him, he knew if he ate any of it he would lose it. He looked up from the plate and stared into Danny's face. He felt confused and very, very scared. His hands were shaking too much to lift his cup of strong coffee to his lips.

"Jake, damn it, fella, you got to tell us exactly what happened. You know that."

Danny Tracker was a smooth-faced, somewhat heavyset man; his police officer's uniform strained to hold in his wide back and chest and ample stomach. His eyes, no matter the situation, seemed always to hold sadness, as if sadness were a color instead of an emotion. That sadness had been stamped there for the past half dozen or so years following the loss of his wife, Bonnie Gayle, to ovarian cancer. And at times Danny fell into a deep depression, becoming a walking dead man of sorrow, oblivious to work and family. When on top of things, he was more concerned about being a good father than being a good cop, and yet his professional record was respectable. He had no desire to become chief one day; he did hope, on the other hand, to one day have more grandchildren and to become a great-grandfather. He loved Brianna, his eldest, and Sharelle, his "flower child," and Ben, his rebellious teenager, more than his own life.

Jacob nodded. "What did they find?" he said.

"What do you mean?"

"About Josh. I mean, his body. What did they *find?*"

Danny frowned and shook his head.

"Hell, Jake, they aren't gone *find* anything. The body burned up to where it'd fit in a peach basket. What'd you think they would find? That kind of fire—my God." He shook his head several times before continuing. "You say there's more to the story. What are you keepin' to yourself?"

Jacob closed his eyes.

Dragon.

Images of Josh poured through his thoughts like a creek after a hard rain. Jacob didn't know where to begin. And worse, he was starting to doubt what he had seen. So much of it seemed impossible. No one could believe it. When he opened his eyes, he suddenly thought of his uncle Douglas and asked whether anyone had checked on him.

"Mollie claims she hain't seen 'im, but that don't mean much. He could be off hunting and won't be back till dark. Are you sayin' Uncle Douglas saw what happened, too?"

"No," said Jacob. "No, I was the only one who saw it. I saw some things . . . that I can't figure out."

"Damn it, Jake, I know all this has been upsetting. Hell, of course it is. Our nephew deliberately taking his life like that, and most of Jimmie Jack's bein' blown to kingdom come, but if there's something more to the story, you got to tell me, tell me now."

"I'm worried about Miriam and Tyler," said Jacob.

And he knew that his words sounded freaky. It was not *his* voice. "Josh was worried about them. And he told me something happened to John Taylor. Something happened at Sweet Gum."

Digging into his breast pocket for a pen and notepad, Danny said, "Why in the hell didn't you tell us that earlier? We can't find J.T. nowhere. Miriam, she's flat on her back with grief, and Tyler's there with her. Mollie's at her side and so's Mother and Aunt Ruby. Now what are you sayin' 'bout J.T.?"

Jacob took a deep breath and squeezed hard at his forehead. Reeling through his thoughts was the memory of Josh slicing open his forearm and sucking at his own blood. Lowering his hands out in front of him, Jacob studied his fingers and fingernails.

"It wasn't suicide, Danny. Not exactly. I don't know what it was, but Josh—what I saw . . . it wasn't even him no more. And it's not Uncle Douglas no more, either."

Danny glanced around apprehensively to see whether anyone was trying to listen in on their conversation. He blew out his breath in a small gust.

"Jake, goddamn it, I want you to start from the very beginning and tell me everything that you saw and everything you know, and let's get this all out on the table. You understand?"

And so Jacob reluctantly began.

And felt relieved when he had finished.

At the outset of Jacob's narrative, Danny took detailed notes, but midstream he stopped writing and started staring at Jacob as if his younger brother had completely lost his mind. At the end of the account, Danny's professional self emerged and he pressed Jacob on whether he or Josh had been using drugs or drinking beer or sniffing glue or engaging in a number of other potentially aberrant and consciousness-altering activities.

"Because otherwise," Danny continued, "you got to see how this is the bugshit craziest story any sane or sober person could ever come up with."

Jacob nodded again.

"But it's the truth."

He suddenly felt sorry for Danny, an older brother who had, unlike John Taylor, tried always to be a decent brother to him, and now he had made it extremely difficult for Danny to do anything but send him to a shrink.

Jacob waited for his brother to say something. To offer advice. To point to the next thing. But for a minute or longer, Danny simply gazed out the window, apparently lost in some jungle of thought Jacob would never know or explore. Finally he sighed heavily and looked at Jacob. He held up a finger as if to lend emphasis to his comments. His voice was grave and tired.

"Little brother, we're gone keep this a family matter. You hear me? I could get myself in a shitload of trouble and probably will, but what I see right now is simply a family matter. This is a Tracker matter. We're gone keep it down home. I'm fixin' to find J.T. and I'll find Uncle Douglas—you just shut yourself up 'bout any of this. Stick to the first story you gave. Josh was depressed about something and went out of his head and set himself on fire. End of deal. You hear me, Jake?"

"I do. But—Jesus, I'm scared, you know, scared something more's gone happen."

Danny slid out of the booth and put some bills on the table.

"We just have to help blood," he said. "This is Tracker business. Let's keep it that way."

But all Jacob really wanted to do was see Brianna. No, what he really wanted to do was lose himself in her arms, in the press of her body against his, her lips upon his. He didn't want to think about what his nephew had done or what was behind the tragedy.

He didn't want to think about blood.

Out of the corner of his eye, he saw Danny swing out of the parking lot, and he had decided to leave as well when someone bustled in across from him.

"Guess our finest eggs aren't too appetizing, what with all you've seen this morning."

The voice was couched in a gravelly, deep Southern drawl, scratchy and breathy as if the speaker were suffering from laryngitis. Jacob smiled despite his depression.

"It's not the eggs, Bo," he said.

"Glad to hear it, son. Glad to hear it."

Orpheus Beauregard Smith, known to everyone in Soldier's Crossing as "Bo," laughed his sandpaper laugh. Jacob knew what the man was doing—he was trying to ease his emotional load, and Jacob appreciated it. He had known Bo for years and had liked him most of that time. Bo owned Mr. Pancake and on busy days took charge of the grill. A lifetime resident of Soldier's Crossing, he knew more about the town and the county than any other living soul, and had even penned a history of the area, taking the historical narrative all the way back to 1832.

"You ever seen somebody burn to death?" said Jacob.

He looked into Bo's flushed face and let his eyes wander to the man's small, piggy eyes, which were brightly expectant, his alcoholic nose and the ragged scar on his chin, and suddenly he was very glad that his old friend was there.

"No, sir. I hain't never seen nothing like that. Seen a few men shot in Korea and 'Nam, but none burned like what you saw. I'm real sorry it was your nephew. Seemed like a real good boy."

"He was."

A silence fell before Bo shifted uncomfortably, then hollered something at one of his waitresses. He raised his hands out in front of him as if he were holding an invisible football.

"Jacob, there's something I need to tell you, and maybe this has got nothing, I mean absolutely *nothing*, to do with what your nephew did, but all's the same, I got to get if off my chest, you see."

His interest piqued, Jacob leaned forward. "Bo, do you know what made all those changes in Josh?"

Bo shrugged. "Don't rightly know what you mean. What I got to say is about J.T. and about Sweet Gum."

"Josh said something about the walls. Like maybe they found something in the walls. And he said his dad was dead but up walking around."

Bo pitched back a few inches and studied Jacob.

"Holy shit," he whispered. "I'm maybe closer on this than I thought."

"I think I definitely need to hear you," said Jacob.

Bo took a deep breath before he began to speak. "Long and short of it is this: last evening about twilight I was out at Sweet Gum, you know, taking what might be a final look at the old place. Just a crying shame folks didn't go ahead and vote to have it preserved for posterity. Anyway, J.T. and Josh were working, getting ready to quit. Roy Dale had done gone home—hard to say whether he'd worked any."

Bo chuckled and Jacob shared the response.

"Uncle Douglas says he and Aunt Mollie don't claim him as their own no more."

"I bet that's right," said Bo. "Well, anyway, I sorta cornered J.T., and I asked him if he'd turned up anything interesting—you know, maybe old papers, who knows what. And that's when he told me they'd found bodies in the wall."

"Bodies?"

"Well, bones at least."

"Did you see them? Do you think he was just shittin' you? Which wall was it?"

"Way it sounded, and as far as I can tell, it was that thick wall between the entrance hallway and the big dining area. But here's the thing: he wouldn't let me see for myself. Fact is, he acted strange—even for J.T., you know. He told me to get the fuck away from there. Got real agitated, and I was afraid he might punch me in the face or get his gun. So I left."

Bo folded his hands together and drummed them on the tabletop.

Jacob thought about Danny's request to keep the matter among blood, but he knew that in some ways he was closer to Bo than he was to his brothers or any other relatives.

"You wanna hear the whole story of what happened at Jimmie Jack's?"

"I think maybe I do," said Bo. "If you're up to tellin' it."

When Jacob had completed his spiel for the second time that morning, he felt exhausted. But he needed to get Bo's reaction—he needed to hear something that would make sense of it all. However, the only immediate response was Bo muttering to himself, which caused Jacob to press him to share what he was saying.

"Maybe there really are such things," said Bo.

"What? Such things—what things?"

The sounds of dishes clattering and orders being shouted out filled most of the restaurant, and yet in the booth Jacob occupied with Orpheus Smith, it was almost, for a few moments, preternaturally quiet.

"Vampires," said Bo. "Honest-to-God vampires."

"You mean, like in the movies? Bo, that's fucking nonsense."

Bo was shaking his head.

"I can't quite hardly believe it myself," he said. He sighed, not as if he were sad or tired, but as if he had suddenly confirmed some long-held belief. "Sweet Gum plantation has secrets. That old manse has held them for many, many years. Tracker secrets. There's something buried in Tracker blood. Something J.T. should have gone and left alone."

"Bo, when Josh said that J.T. did something to him—what do you think he meant?"

Their eyes locked.

"I think maybe he took his life," said Bo, "and gave him a different one. A life like you and me don't know about. A life that's got to have blood to live—it lives on blood. Human blood. And maybe Tracker blood has to feed on its own kind."

I'll save myself. You save the others.

On Brianna's sofa Jacob started to doze off, and in a rocking chair nearby, Brianna held her daughter, Emily, and both of them appeared to be settling into a nap. Josh's words echoed in Jacob's thoughts with an eerie immediacy. And while Jacob believed that all of Bo's conjectures were preposterous, he was glad he had confided in the man. In doing so, of course, he had broken his agreement with Danny, and yet if J.T. and Uncle Douglas now posed a threat to others, then wouldn't it be irresponsible not to tell someone outside the family? And shouldn't the authorities be informed?

Fighting to keep his eyes open, Jacob glanced over at Brianna and Emily.

He loved them. It was as blood simple as that.

Brianna's eyelids looked as delicate as rose petals. Jacob wanted so much to step over and kiss those eyelids that he ached. Nestled against Brianna's shoulder was the doll-sized body of her daughter, Emily, still holding the package of cheese- and peanut butter crackers Jacob had brought her after leaving Mr. Pancake. To Jacob, the scene—beautiful mother and divine child—breathed of a certain holiness.

He knew how much Brianna loved her daughter. Little Em was something of a miracle, being born six weeks premature and weighing less than two pounds. Her doctor doubted that she would live. Perhaps it was Brianna's love or perhaps it was some innate desire to survive on Emily's part, but the medical profession witnessed the wonder of the development of a primordial dwarf, one of no more than a dozen in existence. And so after she left her husband, Brianna tended lovingly to her oddity of a child, fitting her out for the first several years of her life in infants' clothing and the shoes of dolls from Wal-Mart.

Little Em was now six years old and two and a half feet tall, weighing in at an even dozen pounds—a dozen pounds of heart-tugging angel, filled with a ton of energy and an endless supply of love and affection. Jacob admired the way Brianna handled the situation. She insisted on Em's life being as normal as possible, including school and going into public places despite the incessant cruelty of strangers who stared and asked ugly questions and looked upon mother and child with pity. Yet, Brianna, as Jacob observed, never pitied Em and never treated her as a freak of nature or anything abnormal.

Little Em was her child of forever love.

She had Tracker blood, and Brianna was proud of her.

"Hey, guy, did you ever get anything to eat?"

It was Brianna. She had jostled awake and was smiling at Jacob as he looked on lovingly at Em.

"No. No, I guess I'm just not hungry."

"You sure? I can fix you something. Boxed macaroni and cheese? Or a peanut butter sandwich? Em has a new container of peanut butter—about the size of a gallon of milk. You know how she loves peanut butter."

"I do," said Jacob.

Warmth flooded his throat.

"Jacob," said Brianna, "It was horrible, wasn't it? It's just so hard to _____ _____ _____ was going to be such a fine your____

Jacob nodded we____

"Yeah, he might ____ made something of____

Brianna smiled a____

"Hey, I think *you*____ the rest of us pro____ will play on that ____ and I will be sittin____ Jacob."

He hated for he____ No, she couldn't ____

he hoped she wasn't too aware of his feelings for her. She wasn't blind to them, though, and there had been moments, delicate and fleeting, in which it seemed she might have feelings for him—feelings beyond those of a niece for her uncle. Only two years separated them in age, and yet propriety separated them light-years.

"Maybe it'll happen," he said. "Don't hold your breath."

"You're welcome to get some sleep if you'd like. Does your mom know you're OK and where you are?"

"Yeah, I phoned her before I came over. Apparently, she and Aunt Mollie are planning some kind of wake for Josh tomorrow evening."

"We need that," said Brianna.

Jacob began to feel exhaustion hold sway. He closed his eyes and pulled Brianna's beautiful face with him into a realm on the edge of sleep. And then he let go of her image and he slept.

And he dreamed.

Of blood.

Blood flowing from the walls of Sweet Gum. Tracker blood. And of shadows gathering around im, threatening to pull him down. He dreamed he running from Sweet Gum, running from some monster and turning as he ran to see the e mushroom up in flames, and suddenly the swell of the fire, was a dragon flying flagration and burning the night, and ing down, down, a predator intent prey.

's face.

ster cowered in fear of the

And Jacob fell and rolled onto his back and braced himself for the dragon's attack, but as it extended its talons to claim him, the creature burst into flames and hovered above him as it burned and burned before falling onto his chest.

Jacob slammed awake.

He heard giggling.

Before he could shake himself fully conscious from the nightmare, he grabbed at the thing on his chest—something barely larger than a small dog—a thing he had convinced himself was the charred remains of Josh.

But then more giggling and a squeal of delight.

Jacob blinked, and there in focus was Em, a smile as wide as the carved smile on a Halloween pumpkin.

"You want one of my crackers, Uncle Jacob?"

He swallowed and closed his eyes and loosened his grip on the tiny girl.

"Oh God," he whispered. He was trembling, but he managed to open his mouth as Em pressed a broken cracker into his upper lip.

"Peanut butter crackers are my favorite," she said. Then she giggled some more and applauded as Jacob began to munch on the cracker.

Brianna entered the room, and when she saw her daughter, she said, "Emily, are you being a pest? Uncle Jacob was trying to sleep, sweetheart."

Jacob pushed himself up. He choked down the bite of cracker and said, "It's OK. I need to be going anyway." But he couldn't shake off the residue of the dream. And something more: there with Em and Brianna, he was suddenly frightened that he, too, might somehow become a Tracker monster and be driven by a mysterious force to do them harm—those two: the most precious people in his life.

At the door Em hugged his knees, and Brianna reached up and touched his cheek tenderly with the back of her hand.

"I'm worried about you," she said.

Jacob smiled down at her gorgeous eyes and wanted to say, *I love you,* because he did. He loved her and little Em and wondered if they were safe; he wondered if there were any way to *keep* them safe.

Know what's out there?

No, he did not. Vampires? Trackers gone crazy? He did not know.

He felt deep sorrow over the death of Josh, and he wanted to help Danny with his determined stance regarding family. This was a Tracker matter. But Jacob knew that for his own peace of mind he had to find out more: he had to see John Taylor and Uncle Douglas. He had to know exactly what had happened to them, and to Josh, and why Josh had needed to save himself by destroying himself.

And he had to know what darkness loomed ahead.

Chapter Three

Twilight Songs

"Trackers have always had secrets. Why I 'spect
every family has them. Trackers have more than
most, and, yes, Sweet Gum has them aplenty."

Jacob's mother spoke those words as she watched
her son try to eat cowpeas and a slice of ham and
some warm corn bread. She was holding the Tracker
family Bible open to the genealogy page, and Jacob
knew that she had already recorded the death of
Josh. As a child Jacob had believed that the family
Bible, well over a hundred years old and the property once of his great-grandfather John Jacob Tracker,
who had lived to be ninety-eight, possessed almost
supernatural power. Its thick wooden cover, ornately
carved, and its crinkled pages and Gothic lettering
had cast a spell over him that had lingered until he
was a teenager. He longed to feel its power again
because he sensed that some kind of evil had entered his life and that only tools of goodness could
be wielded against that evil.

He had shared with his mother a version of what

Bo had alluded to regarding the Tracker family history. He was aware that his mother and Bo had been good friends over the years and that she also harbored an interest in the legacy of Sweet Gum plantation. Putting down his knife and fork, he said, "I have to go see if I can find John Taylor."

His mother gazed away.

"He's always been the kind of boy got into things he shouldn't. Same now that he's a man. He's got no respect for secrets."

"Does he know them? I wonder if he does, because I don't. Just like you, Bo says the Trackers have them, but I don't know what they are. Do you?"

His mother looked down at the Bible in her lap. He couldn't read her thoughts. She looked sad and distant; she looked as if she knew things she wasn't ready to tell.

"Take Orpheus with you if you go out to Sweet Gum," she said. "Would you do that for me?"

"I will."

"We'll all remember Josh tomorrow evening. A special remembering. Remember him in a way so we won't never forget him."

Jacob nodded soberly.

He got up to leave because it was late afternoon. Twilight came with a sudden rush in the South in winter. For reasons that did not fully make sense to him, he wanted to avoid being at Sweet Gum after dark. He said good-bye to his mother, and a few minutes later as he was going out the door, he heard her singing snatches of a hymn—something touching upon the blood of the Redeemer and promises of life everlasting.

* * *

Bo's old blue van, a road warrior of a vehicle that had passed 200,000 miles in cross-country treks, was parked at the Hollow Log Lounge as Jacob drove by in search of his friend.

He won't be no help now.

Jacob reasoned that Bo would be in the homestretch toward the finish line of being seriously drunk, and so he kept driving, determined to find J.T. or Uncle Douglas or both on his own. There were too many questions hanging in the chilly air—some curious matters of blood that needed to be confronted.

Sweet Gum plantation lay five miles west of town. The country around it was flat and dispossessed, with a scattering of cotton and peanut fields, but mostly scrub pasture and an occasional copse of pines or white oak and a sprinkling of cattle. Kudzu vines rioted wherever they had gained a foothold. The whimsical notion that kudzu vines were the vampires of the Southern plant world slipped into Jacob's thoughts—he smiled momentarily through his near exhaustion. When he turned through the rusting gates down the crushed white shell road to the old mansion, the western sky was ablaze with fiery swirls of pink and orange and blue, stunningly beautiful. No hint of horror. No suggestion of evil in the dying day. Jacob followed the meander of the road for a hundred yards and then, quite suddenly, there it was—Sweet Gum, decaying and yet still maintaining an arresting presence.

And Jacob found that he was holding his breath.

What, he wondered, had always captured his fascination here? It seemed as if something had always drawn him to this house, a pull like the siren song of some melancholy tongue tender beyond words. Sunset was bathing the old manse, washing it half in shadow and half in the living light of mystery.

Did some secret and innominate life inhabit Sweet Gum? Was there something in its walls that transcended ruin, something animated by a potential for cruel metamorphosis? Was there something ghostly that would haunt Trackers forever? Jacob was trying hard not to think of Brianna and Em and the fears he harbored.

He saw Roy Dale's camper truck parked in the shadows.

He got out and, as he had over the years, stood in front of the looming, paint-chipped Tuscan columns and felt virtually the same awe that he had felt as a child in eyeing this behemoth. He could almost imagine it as it might have looked in the 1850s, a freshly painted monument of grace and elegance and architectural splendor, the classic coldness of Greek Revival tempered by the Georgian influence showing in the deep arched windows and doors. He could almost imagine the gaiety within and the rich trappings gained through the Trackers' ill-gotten accumulation of wealth.

But it was gone now. All of that life, all of those images.

Sweet Gum was coming down.

And was it taking the Trackers with it?

Standing in the front entranceway, Jacob could hear someone singing a twangy George Jones tune, singing it quite wretchedly at the rear of the house. As he walked down the long hallway, he noticed that black plastic sheeting had been taped over a large portion of the wall separating the hallway from the once-formal dining area. He felt his pulse quicken as he passed it; he wanted to look behind that sheeting.

It was in the walls, I think.

Josh was there and gone in a blink of memory. Jacob shuddered and then called out, "Roy Dale? It's your cousin Jake."

The singing ceased.

Jacob found Roy Dale sitting on a heap of wood and plaster drinking a can of Coke. He was thin and dark and appeared indifferent to Jacob being there.

"What the hell you want?" he said. "I heard you 'bout got your ass blowed off this morning. That right?"

"Something like that. Yeah."

Roy Dale belched after another swig of Coke. He wiped a sleeve across his mouth and shook his head.

"That crazy bastard nephew of yours fried himself, didn't he? Fuck, I knew he was crazy. Too damn smart for his own good. Readin' books and shit all the time. Kinked his fuckin' brain is what it did. Don't surprise me none what he ended up doin'."

Jacob took a deep breath and glanced around.

"Where's John Taylor?"

Roy Dale shook his head.

"Why's ever'body wanna know that? Your brother, the cop, was out here while ago askin' for him, and I told him, shit, I don't know where he is. I need to find 'im myself 'cause he owes me money."

"Danny was here?"

"I already said he was—and he wanted to know what J.T. did to Josh, and I said I didn't know and he kept after it, and so I got pissed at all the questions and told him to fuck off, and then he started to rough me up, you know. The bastard. I told him Josh was just a weird, sissy-ass kid with fucked-up brains. I mean, your brains have to be fucked up to set yourself on fire. Am I wrong? Hell, I don't feel one damn bit sorry 'bout what happened. I don't care if he is blood."

Jacob started to walk away, but then stopped when something more occurred to him.

"You seen your dad?"

Roy Dale snorted. "Not if I can help it. Me and him don't see eye to eye these days. He thinks I'm a lazy fuck, and maybe I am, but nobody wants his daddy sayin' it to his face. It'd take a helluva lot for us to ever be close again. You know what I mean?"

Jacob nodded.

He'd been around Roy Dale long enough, and, besides, he thought he might just know where J.T. was. He told Roy Dale he'd be seeing him around; his cousin belched and scratched at his crotch and crumpled the Coke can as if it were made of paper, but he said nothing more. As Jacob walked back through the house, he paused at the plastic sheeting. He realized suddenly that he knew the temptation Bluebeard's wives faced—similarly, he couldn't resist seeing what was being hidden from him. Without giving it too much further thought, he peeled away the tape and let the sheet fall.

He wasn't aware how long he stood looking at the burial alcoves. Six of them hollowed out in the thick plaster. Five of them contained bones—he assumed they were of Trackers dating back over a hundred years—but it was the sixth alcove that held his attention.

It was empty. . . .

Except for several glops of blood that couldn't have been more than a day old.

In his pickup Jacob tried to calm himself, tried to make sense of things.

Tried to account for the blood.

With his thoughts opaque and on the edge of sliding into frenzy, he drove away from Sweet Gum and turned down a red-clay pulpwooder's road about a half mile from the plantation. He knew that at the end of that road J.T. had been attempting to refurbish three repossessed trailers to pick up some extra cash. The sun was on the verge of disappearing, and that fact caused him to drive faster.

At the trio of trailers he studied each one, hoping for some sign that J.T. was there. Then he heard a radio playing from the middle one. He went to the door of it and called out his brother's name, but he got no response. The door was unlocked, so he pushed it open. Shadows rushed in around him. Dust and silence greeted him; there was no furniture. The stench of the place was strong—like the odor of dead animals.

"John Taylor? It's Jake—are you here?"

Hesitating first, he summoned up the courage to follow the sound of the radio—a man on it singing a gospel song—down a narrow, quite dark hallway. The door beyond which the song was coming was shut, and something warned Jacob that it was sensibly shut and ought to stay that way.

"John Taylor? You in there? You asleep?"

He waited. The radio continued to play.

When he carefully, slowly swung open the door, he immediately saw the gleaming red dots—the eyes of someone lying on the floor in a nest of straw—but before he could say or do anything, the figure raised itself and hissed, and the eyes flamed, and warm, putrid air gusted into Jacob's face. Suddenly the radio popped and crackled as if it had been hit by an electrical surge, and the ensuing silence was thick and heavy.

But Jacob could not move.

The shadowy figure was holding him with some mesmerizing power stronger than any grip Jacob had ever felt. The figure—the features of its face visible in the eerie glow of its eyes—clearly resembled John Taylor. But something had seized the body of his brother, something had possessed it and was now staring at Jacob as if he were prey.

It hissed again.

Then the figure rose and began gliding toward him.

Jacob's nightmarish paralysis continued; he could not even scream or lift his arms to protect himself from the penetrating glare of those red eyes and the advance of fangs. All he could do was close his eyes and quake. He lost track of time; he lost track of everything except the sound of his heart trip-hammering.

Then—how much later he didn't know—he opened his eyes.

And the shadowy figure of John Taylor—a much changed John Taylor—was gone.

The sun had set.

Jacob scrambled to his truck as quickly as he could. As he drove, he fought his best instincts. More than anything else he wanted to rush back to town and be with Brianna and Em and erase all the images and sensations of the horror he had just experienced. But he knew that he should stop at Sweet Gum and warn Roy Dale. Because he was blood.

John Taylor had gone mad. He was dangerous.

Why didn't he attack me?

Jacob was confused. He thought about his nephew Tyler and about John Taylor's wife, Miriam—how much danger were they in? And he found himself thinking of Bo's vampire theory and once again rejected it, though he could not deny what the physical presence of John Taylor and Josh and Uncle Douglas suggested. All he could reason was that John Taylor recognized him, and though something had turned him crazy, something else kept him from harming blood.

Jacob roared toward Sweet Gum.

Seconds later, he skidded to a stop. White dust swirled and billowed around his truck.

Darkness held the scene firmly.

There was no moon. The stars were impossibly distant.

He stared straight ahead.

Parked directly in front of the old mansion was a Good Neighbor Dairy truck.

Got to help blood.

He sat for several minutes wishing he had a weapon and debating whether he should find Danny before making any attempt to go into the darkened mansion. When he heard a man scream, he knew he had to investigate. He fumbled in his glove compartment for a flashlight and then headed inside. He kept the light off until he was several steps within the entrance hallway.

He heard someone moaning. And that was followed by another sound: sucking—like the sound of an infant at its mother's breast.

"My God," Jacob whispered.

He moved in the direction of the sounds.

"Roy Dale? Uncle Douglas?"

His voice echoed slightly. He heard another moan, and it seemed a moan of ecstasy.

"Who's there?" he called out, and in the next instant switched on the flashlight.

***

The house was filled with Trackers.

In the living room Miriam Tracker sat on the couch in a black dress and a black hat with a veil; she was ashen and her eyes were teary and without focus, and, more than anything else, to Jacob she looked diminished. She looked as if grief had shrunk her entire body, had deflated it like a basketball. To either side of her sat Jacob's mother and his aunt Mollie, their arms looped gently over Miriam's. Aunt Mollie's bulk caused Miriam to appear even smaller.

Other Trackers stood around the room and on out in the kitchen talking more softly than they would have at any other family get together. They were uncomfortable, and not just because they were dressed up, the men in coats and ties, the women in Sunday dresses. The air was suffused with questions. Why did Josh do it? And where had John Taylor, Douglas and Roy Dale disappeared to? Jacob had noticed that they were the only Trackers missing. Even Roy Dale's wife, Jessie, usually not one to attend family gatherings, was there with her little boy, Jeremy, who was restless and bored, yet eerily silent as always. Jacob's uncle Calvin was at her side drinking coffee and scowling. In another corner was Uncle Winston and his daughters, Janie and Mattie Lee, who were holding on to their father as if he might, at any second, be abducted by aliens or be sucked off into a black hole.

Jacob pushed by them into the kitchen. He was looking for Brianna and Em and maybe also for Danny. Most of all, he was trying to erase the horrid images of what he had experienced at Sweet Gum the night before when his flashlight caught sight of Roy Dale and Uncle Douglas.

"Hell of a thing, wasn't it?"

Jacob turned and there, at his shoulder, was his uncle Warren, who ran an auto salvage on the edge of Soldier's Crossing. As a younger man he had been a Baptist preacher, but he had stepped down from the pulpit when forced to serve twelve years in prison for manslaughter, the details of the crime having remained sketchy over the years. His invalid wife, Ruby, was next to him in her wheelchair. Jacob had seen their son, Royal, who was borderline retarded, outside with Danny's teenage son, Ben, admiring Ben's motorcycle. Ben, a dark-haired double for James Dean or a young Brando, was revving the sleek machine the way one might egg on a bad dog.

"About Josh, you mean?" said Jacob.

The face of his uncle Warren appeared about to crumple. He glanced down at his wife and then back to Jacob. "Did you see it coming? Did anybody know the boy was upset enough to take his own life?"

Jacob shook his head.

"I just don't understand what all's behind this," he said.

Then his aunt Ruby stabbed a trembling finger at him. "Warren and I, we watch for signs that our Royal is thinking of harming himself. I know he's older—a few years older than you are, but he's got the mind of a little boy and he gets blue all the same, terrible blue. I'm just so thankful he has all his dogs for company."

The three of them nodded gravely because they didn't know what else to do.

The kitchen suddenly felt too warm and too close. Jacob's head was starting to swim, so he excused himself and went to the sink to get a glass of water. The cool liquid helped. He ran himself a second glass from the spigot and was drinking it when he heard a softly distant voice.

"Hey, Jacob."

It was his niece Sharelle. She was the only woman not dressed in black, though her old-fashioned, floor-length dress, green with tiny flecks of yellow flowers, seemed respectful enough. She put her head on Jacob's shoulder and whimpered like a lonesome puppy. Her long, dark hair fell to the center of her back. She smelled of potpourri and lilac water and a hint of marijuana.

"It's a sad time," he whispered to her.

She raised her head and brushed at her tears. "Come and see what we made for Josh."

She took his hand and led him from the kitchen through the living room to a side room—a sitting room of sorts—where a high table had been placed with a trident of lit candles on either end. In the center of the table was a large, framed photo of Josh, probably his most recent school photo. Flanking the photo was a small trophy he'd won at the county spelling bee when he was in junior high and a stack of three paperbacks—Tolkien's *The Lord of the Rings* trilogy—Josh's favorite books. Sharelle's too.

"He was so decent," said Sharelle. "A smart and sensitive, *humane* boy."

But Jacob's mind was filled with images of Josh as he appeared at Jimmie Jack's. Suddenly, Brianna was there, too, comforting her sister. To Jacob, she looked staggeringly beautiful despite her being dressed in mourning. Em was with her. He lifted the tiny girl high in his arms and smiled into her face.

"How are you, doll face? That's a pretty black dress you have on."

"I wish nobody would cry," she said in a thimble voice.

"Sometimes people have to cry. They get so sad, they have to."

"Like I did when my daddy went away?"

He hugged her.

"Yeah, kind of like that. We're all sad here because Josh . . . he went away."

"Is he coming back?"

Jacob paused.

"No, sweetheart. He's not."

Over Em's shoulder Jacob saw someone standing with his hands clasped in front of him, someone obviously lost in thought and on the verge of tears. It was Franklin. Jacob wanted to go to him, wanted to say something to him about Uncle Douglas and Roy Dale, but he couldn't imagine exactly what he would say.

Except to warn him.

I think your dad and brother are vampires. Stay away from them.

But was that what he really believed? Jacob wasn't certain. What he had seen at Sweet Gum was nearly beyond comprehension. And yet, it was becoming abundantly clear that every Tracker might be in danger. Bo's unlikely theory could be on target.

I have to help blood.

But should he say something here, at the wake?

He handed Em to Brianna and they exchanged smiles. His thoughts in a tangled knot, he made his way from the area and negotiated again through the living room and kitchen and out the back door into

the chilly night air. And there his mind vividly re-
played the scene at Sweet Gum.

A scene of father and son and an embrace of
blood.

For when he captured them in the light, that's
what he saw: the two men on their knees, shirtless,
with Uncle Douglas tenderly pressing his son's face
into his chest an inch or so above his heart. Roy
Dale had his fangs buried in his father's flesh.

Feeding.

A father feeding his son.

For an instant, to Jacob, it had looked horrifying,
yet innocent and loving.

Father and son. A portrait of blood.

Then fury held sway as Roy Dale pulled free; with
blood dripping from his lips, and blood spilling
eagerly from his father's chest, both men turned to
face the harsh light, both hissing and growling hide-
ously, their eyes flaming.

Jacob didn't even recall dropping his flashlight.

Recalled, in fact, little of the careening drive back
to town to get Danny. They had returned in Danny's
squad car only to be greeted by the silence of Sweet
Gum. No father and son. Yet, Jacob had been able
to show his brother drops of fresh blood. And they
had gone to the repossessed trailers to hunt for J.T.
But again they found nothing except bizarre traces
that something darkly extraordinary was afoot.

Tracker blood had gone strange.

Back at home later that night, Jacob had taken several sleeping pills. He had awakened midafternoon
and found Bo and had recounted everything. And
Bo had said, "After Josh's wake, you and I and Danny,
if he's willing to come, have to do something. We

have to try to stop this; that is, if we're not already too late."

Jacob stood in the darkness and wondered if he possibly had the courage to destroy members of his family. Wasn't there another way? Couldn't they be helped?

I have to help blood.

Someone was sitting in the swing he and Josh had tied up to a large limb of a massive water oak in the backyard years ago. Jacob started walking toward the figure. He suddenly knew who it was.

"Hey, Tyler, you need company?"

The boy, recently turned thirteen, said nothing at first. Then Jacob pressed his hand onto the boy's shoulder and the boy began to weep, quietly at first, then in wracking sobs. Jacob held him tightly, afraid that if he let go the earth itself would swallow him just to relieve the boy's grief.

Minutes later, Tyler said he was OK and wanted to go back inside. Jacob told him that he and his mother were in Josh's final thoughts. Tyler nodded and freed himself. Jacob wanted to say much more, wanted to warn him, wanted to share more of the specifics. Instead, he merely said, "You be careful. All right?"

"Yeah."

Jacob watched the boy walk back to the house. Then he sat down in the swing and wondered how his world had gotten so far from the innocent delights of swinging in a swing and laughing about nothing, nothing at all. Jacob looked down and fought back a wave of tears and made aimless markings in the dust with the toe of his shoe. He wanted to forget himself. And for several more minutes he did.

"That you, Jake?"

It was Danny. And Jacob was glad because he needed to talk with him again.

"I think everybody ought to be told," he said as Danny approached. His brother somehow looked smaller, not being in his officer's uniform.

"Told what? Told three Trackers have gone loony? Gone South?"

"I think they ought to be told they might be in danger. What Bo said about maybe Trackers needing to be violent to other Trackers—and his idea about vampires—"

"Whoa, just a goddamn second here. You or nobody else is gone spread that nonsense around, ya hear me?"

"But, Danny, Christ, what I saw—"

"What you saw, you keep to yourself. Stay away from Bo, and like I said, let's try to keep this a Tracker thing. We can get to the bottom of this without tellin' the whole goddamn world about it."

"The family deserves to be told *something*," said Jacob.

"Told what? You mean, reminded again of the Tracker family curse, of all the shit we've heard over the years. Told how crazy J.T. is? Or how fucked up Roy Dale is? Or how Uncle Douglas reached the end of his rope worryin' 'bout his kids? We all don't need to be reminded that we ain't exactly the all-American family. So tell them what, Jake?"

It was cold and the darkness coiled around Jacob like a giant serpent.

Tell them what? he asked himself as Danny walked away, walked back to the house leaving Jacob more alone than he'd ever been in his life.

Tell them of Sweet Gum and the Trackers in the wall.

Tell them of things changing.

Tell them of darkness and madness.

Tell them of evil.

Tell them of the dragon.

Tell them of vampires.

Tell them of something feeding.

Of something living in death.

Of something forever in the blood.

Chapter Four

Afternoon of the Snakehole

Jacob yearned to go back . . .

To quiet days when, with a mind of summer and the rich taste of the future in his mouth, he had played at writing country-western lyrics the way boys play with toy trucks or girls with dolls. To those happier hours when his guitar was more than an instrument—it was a friend, a confessor, his second self. Not that his life was necessarily going anywhere then, but at least he had known a rough contentment. No fears of blood. Now he wanted to stop time and return to the days before that midnight shift during which his nephew Josh appeared, a darkly, horrifically changed Josh. A nightmare Josh. If only those days before something monstrous happened at Sweet Gum would dawn again, and if only the walls of that old manse could have remained untouched and J.T. and his son could have taken on some other project, could have started raking down some other decaying mansion instead of that one. If only . . .

In Jacob's yearning he longed to hear the voice of Uncle Douglas in the early hours at Jimmie Jack's complaining about federal regulations or President Clinton or something stupid or wicked his sons had done. And Jacob wanted somehow to erase the image of Uncle Douglas and Roy Dale locked in their bloody and perverse embrace and to erase as well memories of J.T. nesting in that vacant trailer like some wild creature hungry to tear at the world.

Jacob yearned.

He yearned to have his family back the way it had been. The Trackers. Broken and yet all in one piece. Now it seemed impossible. And yet, he had to try, had to try to salvage as much of the family as possible before this darkness passing swallowed it up, devoured it whole. He yearned to communicate with Josh, and, most of all, to tell him he was committed to saving the other Trackers from whatever madness had blossomed like poison flowers in the midst of their family garden.

I'll save myself. You save the others.

What had Josh meant when he said that? Several times Jacob had questioned Bo about it and his friend's reading was that Josh knew—he understood that he had become a vampire and understood further that the only way to "save" himself was to destroy himself. Before *he* destroyed others.

I'll save myself. You save the others.

Jacob shut his eyes tightly and forced back a welling of tears.

"I will try," he whispered.

And at his sides he clenched his fists.

"Will try what?"

A woman's voice broke upon his intimate, self-imposed reverie. He recognized it. He wheeled around and there was Brianna. He attempted to mask how startled he was.

"Oh, I thought you were downstairs with Miriam and all the others."

He suddenly felt ashamed of himself even as he was dazzled by her beauty. He felt ashamed of how the flush of his emotions must be showing; more so, he was ashamed that he couldn't be honest with her, this woman he loved and desired. But he had come to agree with Danny and Bo that the truth about the Tracker family had to be hidden. At least, for the time being.

She smiled and stepped toward him. It was remarkable how she could look both sad and breathtakingly lovely at the same time.

"I was. But Em got tired and so I put her down for a nap, and when I joined the others, Miriam was crying again and Aunt Mollie had launched into a hellfire-and-brimstone sermon about how evil has these times in its grip and how the Beast of the Last Days has been set loose and how the Trackers are being punished. I half expected her to conjure up a devil or a dragon right there in the living room."

"A dragon?"

She shook her head.

"You know how carried away she gets. Then I noticed you had slipped away and I wanted to see you. I wanted to see how you were and what you thought of the service."

"I'm fine, I think. The service was good . . . well, a real downer, of course. It was good that just about the whole family came. Real good. And the weather cooperated. You ever see such a warm, sunny day in January?"

Miriam Tracker had requested a graveside service,

family members only. She had specifically asked that Josh not be buried in the Tracker family plot on the Sweet Gum property, choosing instead a quiet corner of the town cemetery. Jacob thought her choice was a good one, and he had made a point of telling her that he and Bo and Danny would find J.T. and not to worry. Things would eventually drift back to normal. Of course, he didn't believe that. Miriam's pinched, tear-wearied eyes seemed skeptical, too. "John Taylor's a good man, mostly," she had said. And Jacob had realized that this small, frail woman would be crushed by the truth. He had spoken virtually the same words of reassurance to his aunt Mollie regarding Uncle Douglas and to Jessie regarding Roy Dale. He hated the way his glib, empty promises tasted; he hated knowing that the men attached to these women had become inhuman creatures.

Brianna was close to him now, nodding, searching his eyes, then glancing around.

"This is Josh's room, isn't it?"

"Yeah. Yeah, it . . . it was."

Star Wars posters and a map of Middle-earth cluttered one wall. Another was splattered with posters of *Dark Shadows, Buffy the Vampire Slayer* and *The X-Files*. Otherwise, the room was unusually neat and well ordered for that of a teenage boy. There was a radio and an inexpensive computer. No television. And Josh had more books than most boys would have collected. Science texts and popular fantasy novels. But a few volumes of poetry, too. There were few personal touches—no photos of girls, none of himself. One each of his mother and his brother, Tyler. None of his father. It was the room of a serious, lonely, thoughtful boy who, in trying to help his father, had accidentally stepped into the path of a terrible, swiftly moving darkness. A boy who apparently knew, as Bo had speculated, how that darkness had changed him and that he mustn't attempt to live with it and place others in danger.

"Jacob, what's happened? What's going on? What's happening to our family?"

He turned away. Blood drained from his face. Blood. It was all about blood.

"I don't know what you mean?"

"Yes, you do."

He shrugged. "I only know that Josh was very upset and . . . maybe it had something to do with him and his dad. Maybe things had gotten so bad, he just couldn't . . ."

Brianna's eyes tempted him to be more forthright. To ward off that temptation, he looked away and didn't finish his sentence.

"Jacob, there seems to be a lot more to this story. Three Trackers are suddenly missing. Daddy says he's handling it as a police matter, but it's just all so strange how it seems to have started with Josh's suicide."

Jacob sighed heavily. "I know. You're right. But I don't want you to be afraid. I won't let anyone harm you or Em. Neither will Danny."

"Harm us?"

He found himself looking into her beautiful face again, and he was dizzied by how close to the edge of truth he was. And how deep the chasm of reality plunged beneath him.

"We'd better go back downstairs," he said. "I have to meet Bo. He and Danny and I are going to find the others. I don't want you to be frightened."

But he could see that she was. Frightened and confused. And all he could do was silently hope that

one day he could share the real story with her—and
that the darkness would end.

Then she said, "I wish I knew what was going on.
But I won't press you. Just one thing, though: be
careful, OK?"

She put a hand on his shoulder and rose on her
toes and kissed him warmly, gently on the cheek.
He felt that kiss like a fountain erupting within him.

"I will," he said. "And you . . . please be careful,
too, and watch after that little angel of yours."

The midafternoon sun speared through the large
panes of glass at Mr. Pancake. Seated across from
Bo in a corner booth, Jacob could feel tiny beads
of sweat breaking out on his forehead. He was only
listening at half attention to what Bo was saying; the
other half of his mental energy was engaged in hero-
ism, or, rather, in a fantasy projection of saving Brianna and Em from the fiery breath and bloody
talons of monstrous, dragonlike creatures.

Each of them with the face of a Tracker.

Then something in Bo's words brought him fully
back to the moment.

"I said, you know who Stromile Greene is, don't
you?"

Jacob imagined he heard the wind whistle and tiny
bells tinkle insistently and the ugly hiss of something
alive and yet dead.

"You mean, the black piano player? The old guy
who rides his bike everywhere?"

"He's the one."

Opened out in front of Bo was a small, spiral-
bound notebook with a red cover, the color faded
because of obvious age and use. Thumb and finger-

prints stood out on it with the clarity of fossils stamped in ancient rock. Near one edge of the notebook Bo's cigarette burned down as it rested in a slotted ashtray. The smoke rose and writhed like a thin, ghostly snake. On the pages of the notebook, Jacob could see Bo's tiny script and what appeared to be drawings or doodles, like the hieroglyphics of boredom. Nothing about the script or the way it was arranged on the page suggested the strangeness of the content. It could easily have been a guide to pruning crepe myrtles or hanging a storm door. But it wasn't.

It was a summary overview of how to destroy a vampire.

Jacob took a drink of his ice water. When he lowered his glass, the cubes rattled like a handful of dice, and he looked around at the other customers sitting in booths or at the counter and he mused about how virtually impossible it was to know the subjects of their conversations. Some, no doubt, were talking of money matters, others perhaps of a basketball game or the political scene, others perhaps of love. But he was quite certain that no one else was entertaining the issue of vampires. And family. And Stromile Greene.

The latter had been a source of fear for Jacob as a child.

Greene was skeleton thin with leathery flesh so black it turned blue at twilight. No one knew exactly how old he was or much about his origins. But he was as endemic to the landscape of Soldier's Crossing as the giant water oak down in front of the high school, and one couldn't walk or drive the streets of the town without, at some point during the day, catching a glimpse of Greene pedaling his old bike, the handlebars festooned with horns and bells and whistles and colorful pinwheels. Most who saw him wrote him off as retarded or nearly so; only die-hard drinkers, in fact, knew that the man possessed amazing musical talents, especially on the piano. On rare late nights at the Hollow Log Lounge, he played, like a virtuoso, everything from ragtime to Mozart.

Jacob, however, remembered the man's "panther."

"He scared the shit out of me once when I was a kid."

Bo looked up from his notebook and grinned.

"That a fact?"

"Yeah. One time when I was about eight or nine, maybe, I was at the Sani-Freeze as it was turning dark. I had bought a chocolate marshmallow ice cream cone, a double dip, and I was licking away at it and didn't notice old Stromile lurking out behind the place. Well, when I walked by that big Dumpster they have, I heard the most god-awful, throaty scream. Sounded like some kind of jungle cat. Only it wasn't, of course. It was Stromile Greene. I shot away from there, my ice cream just a memory in the dust. My heart didn't stop beating fast for days. Damn, he scared me."

Bo chuckled.

"Sure 'nuff, ole Stromile has what you'd call a prodigious ability to mimic all kinds of sounds. He's freaked out more than a few folks, but this time around we might could find he's a heap of help to us."

"How so?"

Bo took an anxious drag on his cigarette and let it dangle from his lip.

"You ever read *Dracula*?"

The cover of the paperback he retrieved from the

seat beside him was splashed in black with a single drop of bright red blood at its center.

"No, but I've heard of it. I've seen some of the movies."

Bo lifted several other books up onto the table.

"I've been going through as much material on vampires as I can get my hands on. These here tell you all the folklore surrounding them—and the conventions, you know—and how to kill one. And this is fine. But, you see, Stromile, he really *knows* about the supernatural and the occult. Why, there's still coloreds out in the county who believe Stromile can change shapes, and cast spells, and heal the sick, and talk to the moon and the devil and every kind of spirit wandering God's green earth. He knows about voodoo and hoodoo and everything in between."

"So you talked to him?"

"He came in real early this morning and I was a mite hungover, but I shoveled some eggs and grits down him—free of charge—and asked him about all this vampire lore."

"Jesus, Bo, you didn't tell him about J.T. and Uncle Douglas and Roy Dale, did you?"

"No, sir, not exactly. I just asked Stromile could it work. Could a body destroy a vampire following what's written in these books—and he said a body could. Not that he actually had. And I've been knowing Stromile for a lot of years and I believe him. And he told me something else."

"What was that?"

"He said we better damn well hurry because if we're on the hunt for vampires we have to get 'em before they start feeding again. Like before night falls. That means you and I got to get our ass in the crack. I've already put some things together. Danny, he was in here at lunch looking for Ben. Came right from your nephew's burial service, and I think he's going back out to Sweet Gum this afternoon. But he don't know all this."

Bo swept his hand across the opened pages of the notebook.

And Jacob said, "If he's going to Sweet Gum, then maybe you and I ought to go to those empty trailers and see if J.T. has come back there. I don't want to cross paths with Danny unless you think he shouldn't be out there alone."

Bo nodded. "Don't know what to think about Danny. Him and me aren't communicating it seems." Jacob could tell the man's thoughts were racing ahead to other issues. "I've got most of what we need," he continued, "but I'd feel better if we had a big ole hunting knife. Something bigger and meaner than the butcher knives I've got here."

"I have one at home."

"Good."

When Jacob made a move to get up, Bo stayed put.

"Well, what are we waiting for?" said Jacob.

Bo smiled grimly.

"Today's lesson."

For the better part of another hour, they pored over Bo's notes. Jacob, his mouth dry and waves of fear-generated nausea pounding his stomach, sipped his ice water while Bo drank hot coffee and smoked and played professor, carefully condensing all he had learned about vampires and especially their destruction. And when he finished, he studied Jacob's expression, and Jacob said, "My God, Bo, are we really going to do this?"

His scratchy voice flecked with fear, Bo said, "The way I see it, we ain't got a choice."

The cargo area of Bo's van was filled with sawed-off broom and mop handles sharpened into vicious stakes, several hammers and sledges, a shoe box of plastic crucifixes, strings of garlic, vials of holy water, Eucharistic wafers, gas cans, shovels, pickaxes, a chain saw and a shoulder holster containing what appeared to be a small-caliber revolver. From the passenger's seat Jacob looked back over his shoulder at the bizarre collection of items.

"This is unreal," he said.

Bo nodded, but he said nothing. Jacob was suddenly aware of how quiet his friend had become, how firmly the man's jaw was set, and how narrowly his eyes had fixed as if looking toward some distant horizon beyond horrors yet to be faced. When they pulled up to the house Jacob had shared with his mother for a number of years, Bo broke his silence.

"Don't let on to her that you're scared," he said.

"I'm not. I'm not scared."

The fix of Bo's gaze caught Jacob between the eyes like a fist.

"Yes, you are. Go head on and get the knife. I'll wait here." And when Jacob hesitated, Bo snapped, "Move your ass."

Once inside, Jacob was relieved that the house appeared to be empty. He bounded up the stairs and riffled through his closet, where he located the hunting knife—a Bowie model—safely sheathed, and at that point he was seized by the dark irony of the situation: he had received the knife from Josh.

And it was J.T. who had given it to Josh in the first place.

Jacob unsheathed the knife and cautiously fingered the blade. It was razor sharp. Josh had explained that his father, hoping his son would be thrilled to have such a weapon, a weapon which, in turn, might fire the boy's desire to abandon his books and his realms of fantasies for the great outdoors and for manly activities like hunting, had given it to him. His father had possessed the knife from his youth—he had cut out the heart of a deer with it and he had smeared the deer's blood on his cheeks and forehead. Blood to blood, the knife was to seal some vaguely mythic bond between father and son. It hadn't worked. Josh hated the knife. And so he had passed it along to Jacob asking him to keep it or sell it or whatever. Josh had told his father that Jacob was borrowing it. Both of them understood that it was J.T.'s knife. Only a man like J.T. could be comfortable with such a deadly weapon.

Jacob's hands shook ever so slightly as he stared at the knife and whispered, "Jesus, I can't do this."

Although Bo hadn't told him what the knife was for, Jacob knew. It was part of the process: after you stake the heart of a vampire, you cut off its head. But nowhere in the vampire literature Bo had shared with Jacob was there an account of a man beheading his brother.

And with the brother's knife.

You save the others.

"I can't."

Bo would have to. That was the only answer. As mixed as Jacob's feelings about his brother had become, he could not suddenly imagine performing such savagery upon him.

"Jacob, is that you up there?"

His mother's voice rose to him and his first instinct was to hide the knife. And his second was to tell Bo that he wanted out, that he wanted no part of being a vampire hunter. Whatever darkness flowed in the veins of J.T. and Douglas and Roy Dale, he believed that he lacked the courage to expunge it.

Yet, they were family, these changed men.

Family: the unavoidable shadow of one's self.

Jacob was standing in that shadow.

. . . *save the others.*

"Oh God, Josh."

The gossamer threads of a promise held him. Then he heard his mother repeat his name. He gathered himself.

"Yeah, it's me. I'm coming down."

On the drive out of town the landscape scudded by, bathed in a false summer light. The weather was winter perfect: sunny and cloudless, spring hinted on the gentle breeze. Simply being alive on such a day should have been glorious. When Jacob glanced from the passing scene to the book open in his lap, he thought again of his exchange with his mother. Still dressed in her Sunday clothes, a dark suit with a tiny strand of imitation pearls, she looked stunning, her smile warm and convincing as if she had created it just for Jacob and for no one else. But catching sight of the knife, her countenance had changed. Her body stiffened and she pulled within herself, and in her eyes were secrets.

It was as if she knew and it was painful to keep her knowledge from him.

He told her he and Bo were going to find J.T. He

said nothing about the purpose of the knife. It was simply there like a weapon in a Greek drama never to be used on stage, but the audience knew, everyone knew that blood would follow.

"I'm glad you'll be with Orpheus. He's always been close to us. Was close to Clarence. He understands Trackers as much as anyone outside the family can."

"I can't say what will happen," he told her. "I don't know what we'll find."

She understood. She held secrets. She held them as if it were part of her role as woman, mother and Tracker. She embraced them like an affliction she had learned to live with, like a withered arm or a clubfoot. But she wasn't ready to share those secrets; instead, she smiled the smile of someone recalling a pleasant memory.

"You know," she said, "when John Taylor was a little boy, he used to run off and hide if he thought he was in trouble. Oh, he was good at it, the scamp. And I think maybe that's what he's done—gone off to hide. I mean, I know it's not the truth, but it's the way I'd like to think it is."

Jacob suddenly prayed she wouldn't start crying.

"We'll look for him," he said, his heart pumping fire across his chest, "and we'll see what has to be done."

His mother nodded as mothers do when they understand that the worst possible news about their child is likely and no amount of maternal love and concern and protection can change things.

"There's something I want you to take with you," she said, not as an afterthought but rather a comment born of some reflection.

Jacob had accepted the family Bible from her and

tucked it under his arm and not asked why she had wanted him to have it. He embraced her; she held him tightly momentarily and then pushed him away as if she knew he needed to hurry.

In the van Bo glanced at the Bible, but he said nothing about it. They pulled away and Jacob did not look back at the house. When they drove past the turn-in for Sweet Gum, Jacob said, "Maybe we should have prepared Danny for what he's going to run into."

"I tried," said Bo. "He wouldn't believe an ounce of my theory, so I just told him I thought he was making a mistake, and he pretty much told me to mind my own damn business."

"You think he's at Sweet Gum?"

"I'd say he is. If we don't come across J.T. at the trailers, we'll cut back there and see."

Jacob agreed.

At the abandoned trailers Bo stopped the van a good fifty yards away from them. The afternoon continued to be graced by beautiful weather, temperature in the seventies, an eye-watering, intensely clear blue sky, and just a whisper of a breeze. A good winter day for fishing or for kids to be playing on the school playground at recess. Jacob thought fleetingly of Brianna and Em. He hated being where he was. He stared at the trailers; they were ugly and one of them right that second was probably harboring something monstrous.

His brother.

He looked over at Bo and was about to say something when he saw that his friend was holding one long-stemmed red rose.

"What the hell is that for?" said Jacob. "It's not Valentine's Day, is it?"

The rose was the color of pooled blood.

Bo smiled. "You forget part of our lesson?" When Jacob shrugged, Bo added, "Well, maybe you'll remember at the end of things."

"The end of things," Jacob echoed. "I'm having trouble imagining how this will end. I think about J.T., and it seems I should be trying to save him, not destroy him. And I think about how he and I have never really gotten along. I remember once Uncle Winston had given me a pair of goldfish and a big fishbowl for my birthday—I couldn't have been more than six or seven—and I did everything right taking care of them. You know, feeding them and changing their water. But then I came home from school one day and somebody had poured turpentine in the water and killed both fish. He never admitted it, but to this day I think it was J.T. who did it. Just out of meanness. He was like that."

"The man never lost his mean streak, that's for sure," said Bo.

"But, Jesus, Bo, he's my *brother*. He's blood."

Bo's face had gone slack. And Jacob could see that this hard, tough, wizened man was scared.

"Not no more he isn't. J.T.'s not even human no more. You saw him for yourself. Did the thing you saw right there in that trailer look human to you?"

Jacob let out a slow, dry whistle of regret and exhaustion. His shoulders slumped. He held the family Bible tightly.

"But . . . I mean, how can we be *sure*? Bo, how can we know for sure that he's a vampire? I mean, maybe he just went nuts. Maybe Josh's suicide drove him over the edge. Maybe . . . maybe we ought to just bring him in and get him some help, you know, some kind of medical help."

"We been over this, Jacob. I know it's incredible. It all pitches against reality as we know it, but it's plain 'n simply the only explanation."

"But I still don't understand how he got that way?"

"Good Christ, son, I don't have all the answers." Anger and frustration and fear seeped into Bo's voice. "It was something in the walls of Sweet Gum. It . . . it must've infected J.T. and then he attacked his son. He turned his son into a vampire, and Josh, he must've turned Douglas into one out behind Jimmie Jack's, and then Douglas and Roy Dale . . . Christ, Jacob, what more proof do you want?"

One of Bo's hands trembled as it gripped the steering wheel; the other hand held the rose gently as if it were about to be offered to a sweetheart.

Jacob shook his head. He could hear birds singing in the pines beyond the trailers.

"I think maybe Danny should be with us. We should have the police here—I mean, we're talking about killing someone. Could be it's self-defense, could be it's murder. Everything's moving too fast."

"We can't wait, Jacob. We got to do this while there's light. And the thing is, me and you are the ones that need to do this. It could be a lot harder for Danny. Are you ready for this or not?"

"I'm not, but I know I can't just sit here. Seems you're right. I can't just do *nothing*. I promised Josh."

Then, before they got out and loaded up with the equipment and articles they would need, Jacob heard Bo whisper under his breath, "I wish Stromile was here."

At Bo's insistence, they searched the other two trailers first. They were hauntingly empty, but there were scattered signs that a family had lived in each:

a tiny, armless doll, discarded clothing, a calendar on a wall, a few empty beer cans. No vampires.

At the doorway to the center trailer, they paused to take inventory. Bo was carrying a small sledge-hammer, two sharpened stakes, a flashlight and, around his neck, a crucifix. In turn, Jacob had the Tracker family Bible under one arm; in his other hand he gripped the hunting knife.

"Guess we don't need to knock," said Jacob, forcing a weak smile.

Bo tried to return a smile. "Feels kinda like god-damn Halloween, don't it?" And then he shivered.

"Let's get this over with," said Jacob.

The stench was nearly overpowering. The living room, despite sunlight slanting through one window, seemed unusually dark. And the air was warm and thick and oppressive. They moved through it as if they were wading through water.

No radio played.

There was absolute silence.

Suddenly, as they started down the narrow hallway to the room where Jacob had found J.T. before, Bo caught Jacob's arm and whispered, "If he's there, we can test to see if he's a vampire."

"How do you do that?" Jacob whispered back.

"You have to drive home the stake with one hit to kill a vampire. I'll hit twice, and if he's still alive, then we know he's a vampire."

"Shit, won't that be dangerous for us?"

"It will, but we can bring him down. We have to."

"Guess this is the point where I say, 'Trick or Treat,' " said Jacob.

But neither man laughed.

Eyes watering from the stench, they moved to the door. Jacob glanced at Bo, and when Bo nodded,

Jacob kicked it open. And the darkness within rushed to meet them.

"Jesus," said Jacob, "I can't see a thing."

Sheets of black plastic covered both windows in the warm, putrid room. Bo clicked on his flashlight and aimed it at his feet, generating enough light for them to see the reclining body of J.T. resting on his back on a bed of straw. He appeared to be asleep, though it seemed to Jacob that one arm twitched slightly as Bo sprayed the light closer.

"Hold the light for me," said Bo. He put one of the stakes on the floor and moved around to the far side of J.T.'s body. Jacob took the light and then tucked the knife inside his belt. He aimed the light at J.T.'s chest and watched Bo position the stake over the man's heart and raise the sledge.

"No," Jacob cried. "No, Jesus, wait, Bo."

"Jacob, goddamn it, it's the only way. The only way, I'm tellin' you."

"My God, this is murder."

He let the circle of the light spread onto J.T.'s face. It surprised him that it looked so peaceful and serene, flushed with a contentment Jacob could not fathom.

"No, it's not," said Bo. "I'll hit him twice; then we'll know for sure. Be ready to use that knife."

With the stench burning his nostrils, Jacob pressed the Tracker Bible against his ribs and tried to hold the flashlight steady. And he shut his eyes when Bo brought the sledge down onto the end of the stake the first time.

J.T.'s cry of pain tore the darkness as if it were rotted cloth.

Jacob staggered back a few steps. J.T.'s eyes flew open, fiery coals beaming rage, and his fangs gleamed as he bucked against the stake in his heart, but he could not raise himself. Blood spattered out in all directions, then settled into a bubbling, gurgling flow around the wound. Jacob and Bo watched in abject horror as the thing struggled to rise and confront its attackers. It screamed and flailed its arms, and the air swam with the warm, sticky feel of blood. And everywhere was the smell of death in life.

Then Bo struck the stake a second time.

The thing turned its head to look squarely at Jacob, and it was all he could do to keep from dropping the flashlight, for ghosting through the hideous countenance of the thing's face was a suggestion of J.T.'s, and the look it gave to Jacob was a plea for help.

Help brother. Help blood.

"Bo, stop! My God, stop it!"

By degrees, the thing ceased its struggle. It settled back and closed its eyes, but not before staring at Jacob helplessly, reaching out and seeming astonished that one brother had not come to the aid of the other. More than anything else, Jacob felt a need to rush forward and pull out the stake and give whatever aid and comfort he could to his brother.

"Wait!" Bo shouted. "Stay back and we'll see if it's down."

"My God, we killed my brother, Bo. We murdered him."

They were staring at each other as the thing grew still.

Bo was shaking his head. "No. Wait. Just wait."

As seconds passed and the air ticked off the moments of tension like an old-fashioned clock and Jacob kept the flashlight beam on the face of the thing, he began to feel the Tracker Bible generate heat. And then tongues of flame began to lick out from the gold gilt of the edges of numerous pages.

"Bo, do you see this?"

Jacob dropped the flashlight and as he held the Bible with both hands, it opened on its own and the pages flamed up in a nearly lightless fire.

"Christ," said Bo. "And look there."

A pale, sickly yellow light haloed the head of the thing as it continued to bleed. And then it opened its eyes. And the Tracker Bible danced in flames and Jacob tossed it to the floor.

"Bo!" he yelled.

"Use the knife! Now, Jacob, goddamn it!"

The arc of Bo's arm swinging down with the sledge parted the yellow light. The hammer thudded and the thing screamed, and more blood flowed and steam rose from it, and the room began to fill with a chilly, cloying mist. Jacob hovered over the throat of the thing, the hunting knife readied to cut.

"Do it, Jacob. Christ, do it."

Jacob heard himself cry out and felt the blade slicing into the flesh of the thing, and felt its hot, putrid breath and felt its blood gush up and glove his hands, and he felt the anger flashing in its eyes and felt how near its fangs were, and he felt the cold mist fleck onto his face and felt the darkness roar as if it were a living thing.

Jacob was pressing and sawing the blade deeper, cuffing through muscle and bone as the creature thrashed about and spit blood and a sour, burning saliva into the young man's face. Tears ran down Jacob's cheeks and he trembled as he pushed with all his might.

And the final sensation was that of the knife cutting through and severing the head.

Exhausted, Jacob fell onto the creature's body and sobbed.

"We'll make us a snakehole," said Bo.

They had wrapped J.T.'s body in black plastic and tied the ends, and as a chilly wind kicked up around them, they made their way into a thick stand of pines behind the trailers. Barely able to hold up his end, Jacob, puzzled, glanced over at his companion, and Bo added, "Back in the Civil War days, it's what hospital personnel called the hole where they tossed bloody bandages and all their medical trash, including body parts—amputated arms and legs, that kind of thing. We'll dig one and put 'em all in it."

Jacob said nothing. He continued to struggle with the makeshift body bag until Bo found a good spot deep in the woods.

"Don't think of it as your brother," he said. "Think of it as a wild animal that had to be put down. It had to be. Don't think of this thing as human. No way is it human."

They went back to the van and got shovels, and when they returned, they dug a trench and rolled the body into it and covered it with the loose dirt.

"When we've taken down the other two, we'll put them in the snakehole, too."

Jacob nodded weakly.

The intense violence of the episode in the trailer staggered him. His hands were coated thickly with blood, which was drying and caking. The sudden closure of the burial added to the surrealistic mood of things. He hunkered down by the snakehole and watched as Bo reached over the mound of earth and placed the single red rose onto it.

"It keeps a vampire from returning," he said. "At some point we'll drive by the cemetery in town and put one on Josh's grave." Bo paused and looked around. "No one in hell would find this place. Now, you and me gone go back and set that trailer on fire."

Moments later, as Jacob stared at the flames eating away at the roof and licking out from the windows, he tried to think of Brianna and Em, but he couldn't. His entire body quaked, and he wanted nothing more than to lie down and sleep. Sleep forever if possible. And forget.

But Bo was there to shove at him and bring him out of his daze.

"Come on, son," he said. "We've got two more Trackers to put down."

Chapter Five

Dying Light

Danny Tracker was thinking about blood.

He had fallen into the habit recently of whispering aloud in his patrol car whenever he got to thinking about blood—about his three children and one grandchild, that is—whenever he was troubled because he believed he had failed them. In such moments, alone, thoughts stabbing at him and cutting away at his peace of mind, he would talk to the ghost of his wife, Bonnie Gayle, and share with her his concerns. He would imagine her listening sweetly and patiently, and having her there, sensing that she was close, eased his anguish some.

"I don't hardly know what to do about Ben, sweetheart."

Danny slumped behind the wheel and stared at the columns of Sweet Gum. The afternoon was gloriously sunny, though a chilly breeze had kicked up and was keening low as it wrapped around his patrol car. It was the sound of mourners; it made Danny involuntarily shiver. He tried to concentrate, because he had another reason for speaking to his dead wife—he was putting off searching for J.T. and Uncle Douglas and Roy Dale. They were still missing. Missing blood. Where on God's holy creation were they? Something had turned wrong. Gone shadowy. He couldn't figure it out, but he refused to accept Bo Smith's vampire theory and he was beginning to have serious doubts about the sanity of his brother Jacob.

"After the service for Josh I drove by Mr. Pancake 'cause I thought Ben might be there. He didn't show at graveside. Bonnie Gayle, I'm afraid he's become a 'runner' for gamblers in Montgomery and Birmingham. He's been puttin' a lot of miles on his cycle and, God, I'm gettin' scared that he's in with the wrong element. The money's a real temptation for kids these days." He told his wife of his fears that "butcher men"—the hired thugs of gambling operations—would rough up his son for the slightest step out of place or that the law would catch him.

"I can't talk to Ben no more. We just claw at each other—God, I just want to hold him sometimes, like I did when he was a little boy, and then I end up yelling at him and he yells back and takes off. I threatened to chain up his cycle, but nothing seems to help. I can't reach him, sweetheart. In his heart he's gone away from me. And Sharelle and Brianna, I worry about them, too."

He told his wife of going by his youngest daughter's apartment after not finding Ben at Mr. Pancake. Sometimes his son hung out there. The small, ratty apartment Sharelle lived in was above a retro coffee shop called Mixed Bag; it was operated by Jerry Garbo and his wife, Big Eva, both of them long-in-the-tooth hippies who relived the 1960s on some day-to-day dreamy level while selling cups of strong espresso and tie-dyed clothes and beads and used paperbacks.

"I fixed Sharelle's kitchen faucet 'cause Garbo's too damned lazy to. Our daughter drifts through her life like smoke. Hardly makes enough as a waitress to get by. Won't take money from me. While I was there, two of her friends dragged in—one called 'Kitt' and one called 'Cardinal.' My God, Bonnie Gayle, you should have seen them."

He described Kitt as a very tall young man, thin and pale with bushy black hair thick as fescue grass in summer, who wore black leather except for a cotton T-shirt, black with red letters reading, GOT BLOOD? Cardinal had smeared-on black eye shadow and painted-on black lipstick. Even paler than Kitt, she had teased and obviously dyed black hair with a bright red stripe down the middle. She wore a push-up black bra that shoved plenty of cleavage into any onlooker's face. When the freaky pair left, Sharelle had told her father that they were Goths and heavily into role-playing games such as Masquerade.

"They get good vibes from acting like vampires," she told him. "They have nothing else."

And her comment had made him recall what Jacob had related about Josh and the missing Trackers and Bo's crazy-ass notions.

"Bonnie Gayle, the world is gettin' stranger by the day. At . . . at times I don't want nothing more than to join you. But I know you wouldn't like me runnin' out on the kids. And God would probably for sure send me to hell for puttin' a gun to my head."

Danny told his wife that he was also concerned about Brianna and Em.

"That bastard Spence McVicar's back in town. Be just like him to come around and do more harm.

I'll arrest him if I catch him stalking them, but I can't stand guard on their place, and Brianna refuses to move back home. Can't say I blame her. She's trying to make herself a life. Make something of a life for little Em, too."

Danny sighed from deep in his bones.

"Oh Christ, I'm sorry, Bonnie Gayle. I'm not bein' the father I need to be. You were always the parent for both of us. You could always talk to our kids. Knew what to say. Something in your voice—like soft hands or a cool drink on a hot day. God, I wish I could hear your voice, sweetheart."

But he had. That was the strangest part of all. At around four o'clock every morning since Christmas, just after he woke and went to the kitchen and fixed coffee and sat at the table, he would hear his wife's voice. He often couldn't make out her words, but unmistakably, it was Bonnie Gayle's voice. He hadn't told anyone about it. Too embarrassed. Too scared as well.

"Maybe I'm losing my mind, sweetheart. Maybe it runs in the family, you know. The Trackers. Maybe we're all crazy fuckers. Now there's this. Here I am, sweetheart, trying to find blood gone off to the savages. That Tracker family curse come home to roost—hell, I got no idea. I'm here at Sweet Gum, baby, and nothin' makes sense. J.T.'s boy's dead and seems like everything's comin' apart. Comin' all the hell apart."

A gust of wind howled like a frightened animal as it skimmed the hood.

"Christ," he shrieked.

More than a touch shaken, he got out of his patrol car and surveyed the old manse, and then let his eyes swing around the property until he saw something that held his gaze. A hundred yards off to his left, a triangle of white ghosted through the edge of the piney woods. Danny recognized it instantly.

A Good Neighbor Dairy truck.

His mouth went dry. Seemed a very peculiar place for the truck to be parked.

He thought of his father and of Uncle Douglas and how he recalled that his father had loaned his uncle money years ago to start the dairy and that there was always talk of other Trackers going into business with him. But Danny hadn't wanted to work at a dairy, or, for that matter, to work at the textile mill or at construction with his dad; neither had J.T. For a few weeks one summer, Danny, having just graduated from high school, had ridden the daily route with his uncle—even got to drive the truck. He recalled drinking gallons of chocolate milk and putting on some muscle lifting crates of bottles, but more than anything else he remembered "Peaches."

Her real name was Francine Faulk. She was divorced, had hair tinted about the color of a ripe pumpkin, and met the dairy truck every morning without fail. She was talky and, in a slightly over-the-hill way, even sexy, deliberately wearing a housecoat unbuttoned strategically to reveal snatches of a powder blue negligee. She liked Uncle Douglas. He liked her. Danny, more innocent than kittens with their eyes stuck shut, didn't pick up on the natural progression of their flirtatious morning exchanges until one day his uncle turned to him and said, "Danny boy, think I should fuck her?"

And something had closed off in Danny's throat, and his face had reddened like a fiery sunset, and they had driven most of another mile before Uncle Douglas added, "I bet she'd let *you* ride'n her saddle, too, if you want." Then after another mile. "Now, of course, you know your aunt Mollie can't never hear about this. So just keep it under your hat, y'hear?"

Danny had silently assented, too unsettled to say anything. And he never learned whether anything between his uncle and the eager Miss Peaches was ever consummated. Did not want to know. But as he stared at the Good Neighbor Dairy truck, he wondered whether Uncle Douglas had crossed into some dark realm that would make adultery seem like nothing more serious than farting while writing up a speeding ticket. Lost in thought, he walked back to the patrol car, radioed in his location and headed for the truck.

As he neared it, he hoped as hard as he could that he would find Uncle Douglas sleeping off a drunk and maybe dreaming of long-ago steamy moments with willing ladies who wanted more than buttermilk from him. The truck itself was parked on what looked to be a deer run, too narrow for the width of the vehicle. Accordingly, undergrowth had been crushed as the driver—he assumed it was Uncle Douglas—had attempted to park such that he got as much shade as possible from the tall pines. The late-afternoon sun, however, had soon started to spear through and under the pine canopy. The shade was being dispelled.

When he reached the rear of the truck, he called out, "Uncle Douglas, you here? It's Danny."

As a policeman he had, in certain situations, felt cold air snake through his intestines when he sensed danger, when something about a scene, something about the unfolding of a moment, squeezed at his heart to pump up his courage. Suddenly the sight of the Good Neighbor Dairy truck, the looming, forbidding silence of it, roused that snake of cold air.

Everything was too quiet.

"Uncle Douglas?"

This time, a touch of fear was in his voice. He stepped along the side of the truck trying to decide whether to draw his revolver or not. Then at the door to the driver's side, he stopped. And he stepped back. The snake was leaving an icy trail as it climbed into his stomach.

"Good Christ, what's going on?"

The driver's-side window and rearview mirror were completely covered on the inside with black plastic. Danny walked around the front of the truck. The windshield was also covered on the inside with black plastic. He continued walking and the snake slithered into his throat before he swallowed it back. The passenger-side windows were also covered with black plastic.

No light could penetrate the truck.

Danny shook his head. He tried to make sense of the plastic. What were the possibilities? He reasoned that maybe the truck had stalled and Uncle Douglas had parked it and he didn't want his load to get too warm, so he found shade and blocked out all of the light. It wasn't a convincing projection, but it was all Danny could come up with. Unless . . . maybe his uncle was in the truck with a piece of well-worn pussy and wouldn't appreciate a visitor.

Danny stood at the driver's-side door for several seconds listening.

Self-consciously he ran his fingers around his belt, touching first his holstered revolver, then his night stick and then a small flashlight he had started carrying because he had been on so many midnight shifts lately.

He imagined opening the door and shining the

light and seeing the piggy fat, fleshy white of Uncle Douglas's jiggly ass as he humped away on some horny gal who couldn't find anyone better to satisfy her needs. He leaned his head against the door and listened more closely. But there wasn't a sound. No groans or guttural effusions of sexual ecstasy. No sign of the truck rocking to the rhythm of ill-starred love-making. Of course, it was entirely possible that the act had been concluded and they were lying naked in each other's arms.

"Uncle Douglas? You in there?"

On the chance that his uncle was indeed basking in the afterglow of the deed and would require a few seconds to throw on his clothes, Danny called out a few more times. But he got no response. He reached out and grasped the handle to the folding door. He could feel his cold air snake coiling around his organs, intent upon strangling all or most of them.

It then occurred to him that Uncle Douglas might have been robbed and what he would find was a bloodied body left behind after a crime had escalated from petty thievery to murder. The possibility had merit. Except for the black plastic.

He took a deep breath and swung himself quickly up into the darkness of the truck.

The stench hit him like a two-by-four.

"Shit," he exclaimed.

It was a dead animal smell, only muskier.

The darkness was thick, like deep inside a cave.

The air was warm and moist. A fine mist tickled his face.

"Uncle Douglas?"

One hand fumbled for the flashlight. He was trembling uncontrollably, and every police instinct he possessed was shouting for him to head back to the patrol car and call in for backup. But he wouldn't let himself do that. This was family. This was blood. Whatever was going on here was about Trackers.

He held his breath and switched on the small flashlight.

The groan of pain and surprise lifted from the rear of the truck, the refrigerator compartment that was closed off from the rest of the truck by a sliding door. Danny swallowed hard. His saliva tasted sour. He nosed the beam over everything in the front area, but noticed nothing out of the ordinary except for the black plastic. No telling clues to what awaited. He fought back an urge to tear the plastic away.

"Uncle Douglas, it's Danny. You back there? You OK? Damn it all, say something."

He slid open the door.

And something growled and hissed.

"Jesus Christ," Danny murmured.

The snake of cold air was biting hard at his lungs. Danny squinted into the suddenly illuminated darkness.

And a creature that might have been his Uncle Douglas, once upon a time, raised itself and snarled into the beam of light, blood dripping from its lips, its fangs yellow and menacing, and a look in the red-hot coals of its eyes that Danny would never, ever forget.

Crouched at the opening to the refrigerated area, Danny shuffled back a few feet, and with one hand unsnapped his holster and with the other hand tried to hold the flashlight and keep it trained on the creature. Gasping for air, Danny watched, mesmerized, as the creature gathered its feet beneath it as if preparing to spring. It was bare chested and slightly heavy and very pale. There was a trickle of dried blood above one nipple. Its fingernails were small knives.

"Hold it right there!" Danny yelled.

For an instant that seemed to last for an ungodly run of seconds, the creature glared at him. Something familiar ghosted through the hideous masklike countenance—something Danny recognized as his uncle Douglas. And yet too horribly changed to be the man he had known.

"Hold it," Danny whispered.

He held the revolver in his left hand, the flashlight in his right, and waited, poised like a fencer for the charge of his opponent.

Suddenly the creature hissed again and Danny pitched back and felt his trigger finger twitch.

"Stay there. Don't move," he said.

The breath of the creature was hot and the stench of it burned at Danny's face. His eyes began to water, and he was so frightened he wanted to cry, but instead he whispered, "Uncle Douglas, please, my God, what's happened?"

The creature lifted its hands palms up. It seemed a gesture of appeasement or conciliation. And then it spoke, and the voice was also familiar, though deeper and more sinister than Danny anticipated.

"Danny boy, come join us. Do you know what's out there? Tracker blood. Come be with your family. Forever."

Danny could feel the pull of that voice, those eyes, and wanted nothing more in the world than to drop his revolver.

And surrender.

"Come, Danny boy, come on. It's family."

And as the creature spoke, it crawled forward, angry with the light, its eyes searching for Danny's, wanting, needing him.

Needing his blood.

Danny had his back against the steering wheel, and he was sweating profusely and the sweat was stinging his eyes, and he was trying to avoid responding to the creature's call, and yet it was seductive. Oh, so seductive.

"Stop right there, goddamn it!"

But the creature did not.

Just before he squeezed off three rounds, Danny was somewhere else. It was as if his conscious mind had had enough and couldn't allow more. More terror. More horror. And it took Danny to another place, another time. To a moment years ago on some family outing with Bonnie Gayle and Brianna and Sharelle and Ben—and Ben was very small and happy, and they were near some pristine stream that gurgled and purled softly over rounded rocks, and he had experienced such a rush of contentment that he wanted to praise the heavens.

The report of the shots was deafening.

Danny screamed.

Chunks of flesh tore from the creature's throat and shoulder and chest. Blood blossomed. The steering wheel punched into Danny's back and he dropped the revolver and the creature, stunned and rocking on its knees, tapped at the wound above its heart as if it did not understand what had occurred, and blood began to stream from its mouth and nose. Then it threw its head back and howled. Like a wolf in a death throe. It convulsed twice violently before falling forward where it twitched and jerked for several seconds. Then grew still.

Danny, shivering as if he were freezing, kept the beam of light directly on the creature.

He coughed and nearly gagged with the commingling of the creature's stench and the acrid smell of the gunfire. He waited. And he began to cry soundlessly. Tears and sweat formed rivulets down his cheek and off his chin. He waited and he trembled. And when he thought he had waited long enough, he began to relax.

And then he saw the creature's hand move.

In the sunlight Danny knelt down.

From a distance someone seeing him there behind the truck might have assumed he was praying, and perhaps in his own way he was. When cancer struck his wife, it was as if it also struck his faith and diseased it; just as it had taken the woman he loved dearly, so it had taken his faith. Stilled its beating heart.

Danny dry retched. Strings of sour saliva dangled from his mouth. He felt too weak to stand. The sun was setting. A chilly breeze had lifted, but he could hear birds singing in the pines, and it made him hope that everything he had experienced was merely a nightmare, an astonishingly realistic nightmare.

Beyond Sweet Gum plantation smoke danced above the tree line.

And caught in Danny Tracker's mental filter were the words "dying light." They seemed to come out of nowhere, trapped in his consciousness like some unusual fish tangled in a seine or net. "Dying light." He reflected upon the words, but he found them confusing and contradictory, and yet something in the texture of them came near to explaining what had happened inside the truck.

Something about the light.

Danny sat down and draped his arms on his knees and lowered his head until it rested on his hands, and he let the final seconds of his encounter with the creature replay themselves as if he had pushed a VCR button.

At fast-forward speed he relived it: the creature rousing and coming at him. His attempt to scramble away and then sensing that he couldn't turn himself to open the door and escape. Feeling the hot breath of the creature and knowing that its fangs and claws were clutching at him.

And then something miraculous. Or so it seemed.

Flailing his arms and reaching for the door and grasping the black plastic and tearing at it. Pulling it away so that he could find the door handle. Then hearing the penetrating shriek of the creature when the sunlight poured through the glass that had been covered by the plastic.

The creature cowering. The creature dying with the light.

And Danny yanking away the plastic from the windshield so that more light streamed into the truck. And more cries of agony from the creature. And then the face of Uncle Douglas returning, reclaiming itself, a sad and tortured face. And then in a matter of seconds, the body of the creature shriveling up like a mummy's.

Then turning mostly to ashes and collapsing upon itself.

Danny knew what he had witnessed wasn't possible. He knew he wouldn't be able to write it up in a report. It wasn't police business. There could be no investigation. Something beyond natural laws had occurred. Exactly what, he wasn't certain.

Something connected with the Trackers.

Sitting there on the ground, alone, in shock, wondering whether he had lost his sanity, he was relieved to see the approach of Bo Smith's van. He could see that Jacob was with him. Mostly, Danny was relieved because he had someone to tell his story to, someone who was aware of strangeness in the blood of the Trackers.

"You find Uncle Douglas?"

Those were Bo's words as he and Jacob walked up to Danny and the Good Neighbor Dairy truck. Danny saw how bloody they were, but he didn't ask about it. He sensed that they had encountered horrors, too.

"He's in there," said Danny.

"What happened?" said Bo.

Choking back a sudden attack of the shakes and a wave of tears, Danny began to talk, and as he did so, he studied the reactions of Bo and Jacob and found that they seemed not to be surprised by his account.

Bo waited until the narrative was completed and then said, "We brought down J.T. I'm sorry. You've lost your brother, but, you know, he just wasn't your brother, not the person you knew, any more than Douglas was." He paused, and Danny nodded somberly before Bo continued. "Jacob and me, we dug a snakehole out in the woods and buried him there and we set fire to the trailer he was in. What I understand of this kind of thing, it means he won't come back. I think we ought to take the remains of Douglas and bury them with J.T. I think that's what we ought to do."

For several moments they stood, not moving, not looking at each other. It was as if they were strangers, unfamiliar with who they were and this new, bizarre configuration they had been thrown into. Then they broke and seemed to come together and went to the truck and entered it, careful once again not to look each other in the eyes.

Danny couldn't stop his hands from trembling as he helped Bo and Jacob lift and scoop the bones and ashy remains of Uncle Douglas onto a sheet of black plastic. They wrapped the remains in the plastic with care, with a certain degree of respect and awe.

"Let's put this in the back of my van," said Bo.

A matter-of-factness veneered the moment. Then Danny said, "We can't never tell nobody about *any* of this."

He glanced at Bo and then at Jacob until each gestured assent. Then Bo said, "Follow us on over and we'll do like I said."

The trailer where J.T. had nested had burned quickly to the ground. They stepped through the smoking ruins and out into the woods. Bo and Jacob carried the plastic containing the remains of Uncle Douglas, and Danny followed carrying two shovels. When they reached the snakehole, Danny saw the red rose atop the mound of dirt, but he didn't ask about it.

He was thinking about J.T.

Thinking how a brother was gone and he didn't get to say good-bye to him.

It wasn't J.T. no more.

That's what he told himself over and over in a dark litany that seemed to help.

He thought of his mother and his children and the other Trackers, and he shivered.

The second burial finished, Bo again set the rose atop the dirt. No one spoke at first. Danny turned and looked to the west, to what seemed an inappropriately glorious sunset. He thought again of the words "dying light." Then he felt a hand on his shoulder. It was Jacob. They embraced each other hard, and both fought back tears and tried not to show how frightened and shocked they were.

"Now it's Roy Dale we got to find," Bo whispered. "He's out there and we've lost the light."

Chapter Six

The Women of Midnight

The fox was always snarling.

You could count on it. For Jessie Tracker, that was important, because she had found very few things in life to count on. Balancing a tray of empty Miller Lites, she glanced up at the stuffed fox hovering over the bar and recalled how when she first started working at the Hollow Log Lounge—had it been two years?—that fox was so dusty and cobwebby that she pleaded with her boss, Calvin Tracker, to let her clean it. The poor creature had a snotlike cobweb dangling from its nose and dust bunnies nesting under its tail. She had wiped them away with motherly concern and continued serving the lounge every possible way she could: in fact, within six weeks she had spread her legs for Calvin to satisfy his lust and to earn herself a buck-fifty-an-hour raise.

She and Roy Dale and Jeremy had needed the money.

Besides, poor ole Calvin, sad and morose, had a rough, quietly needy way about guiding her into his back office and locking the door and cupping her bottom and sort of snarling like a horny teenage boy—or like the fox over the bar—and Jessie simply found it irresistible, though the man was old enough to have been her father. Yet, it wasn't as if Calvin were *her* blood. Not exactly. On top of that, her husband, Roy Dale—Calvin's nephew—wasn't shit for a lover. And zero for a father.

Jessie smiled up at the fox as sexy as she could, but the fox held its snarl.

Friday night—no, officially Saturday morning, as it was ten after midnight, the period, she had been told, in which evil spirits hold sway—and business at the Hollow Log Lounge was unusually slow. Randy Bucklin, a regular, was at the bar putting a move on some floozy, and back at the pool tables Ben Tracker—Danny's boy—was hustling some redneck who was so drunk he could barely hold his cue. While Ben was not old enough to drink legally, Jessie had seen that he was plenty old enough to pick fights. She also saw that he was cute in a throwback juvenile delinquent manner and well hung, but she drew a line in the sand on pursuing her attraction, figuring one illicit Tracker affair ought to be her limit. A few other nameless, faceless customers were drinking and smoking and talking low in that tone audible only in seedy bars. Because the jukebox was on the fritz again, Calvin had coaxed Stromile Greene with free beer to come pound on the piano. As Jessie slid her tray onto the bar, Stromile was tickling on an old Joe Williams's favorite, "When Did You Leave Heaven?" It was about as out of place at the Hollow Log as a man in a tuxedo or a lady in an evening gown. But Jessie liked it. Hummed it. It was mellow and sultry and romantic all in the same key. Made her wish some dark and mysterious and dangerous man would waltz in and one-two-three her off to a mattress heaven somewhere. Roy Dale sure as hell wasn't going to.

It had been a tight-fisted evening for tips, so Jessie unbuttoned one more button of her blouse so that her lilac camisole peeked out. Calvin saw her do it, set his jaw disapprovingly and turned away. He didn't really have a claim on her. Neither did Roy Dale for that matter. No one did. Except Jeremy.

"Hey, sugar, you doin' OK?"

She stole away from the bar to a shadowy corner table where her son, Jeremy, was clumsily shuffling his Pokémon cards, pausing only to drink two-handedly from a huge, ice-choked glass of Pepsi, the glass itself guarded by *Star Wars* action figures. Three empty candy-bar wrappers and a half-eaten Zinger completed the scene. Jeremy had Jessie's blond hair and somebody else's eyes.

She hunkered down where she could look her son square in the face.

"Sweetie, now if you get sleepy, Uncle Calvin has a cot in his office and you can sleep till Mama finishes her shift. Will you tell Mama when you get sleepy?"

The boy did not respond. She might as well have been speaking to the fox.

She leaned over and pressed his head against her throat and whispered, "Sorry, baby, I'm such a bad mama. I can't afford a baby-sitter. If your daddy was home like he's supposed to be, he could be looking after you. I'm sorry. Now don't drink all that Pepsi or you're liable to wet on Uncle Calvin's cot, y'hear me, sweetie?"

She hated his silence. Would he ever talk? Doctors told her he should be able to.

She also hated, for an instant at least, the image of putting Jeremy down on the same cot where she and Calvin had made the beast with two backs. This was her reality. She was where she was. And just what the hell else could a woman like herself count on?

Besides the snarling fox.

Which was snarling because it had to. Because, to Jessie's way of seeing things, the whole fucking world was just one big fucking hound chasing after that poor little bastard of a fox—and that being the case, who wouldn't snarl?

With the sleeve of her blouse she wiped Pepsi drool from Jeremy's mouth, gave him a tiny wave and scooted back to her beat. Out of nowhere she thought of Josh Tracker. And she tried to imagine pouring gasoline on herself and lighting that final candle. Jesus. Was the kid's life really so bad that he saw flames as the only way out? J.T. had, no doubt, been a real bastard of a father, but . . . *is Roy Dale any better?*

She tossed a glance back at Jeremy.

Dear God, she wondered, will he one day bring himself all the way down?

She shuddered.

Then someone called out for two more beers and she was back in her harness. She was waiting for Calvin to hand her the beers when she happened to catch movement and a flicker of light through the diamond-shaped glass cutout in the front door. Someone just standing there? Someone just standing there flicking a cigarette lighter? She really couldn't see anyone, but there was something unnerving about the small flame dancing, hovering there like a moth to fire.

"Do we got ourselves a Peeping Tom?" she said to

Calvin, and gestured toward the door. When he strolled over to investigate, Jessie kept one ear on the unfolding moment even as she delivered the beers. She sucked in her breath hard when she heard Calvin say, "Roy Dale? Don't just stand out there. Come on in."

He did. He was flicking that cigarette lighter off and on like someone lost in the night or very confused midway through life's journey. Jessie ignored him. But she noticed that when Roy Dale crossed the room over to the far end of the bar, Stromile Greene stopped playing and stared a trail of apprehension after him.

Jessie thought Roy Dale looked like hell: very pale with dirty, stringy hair and wearing some kind of dark trench coat that she imagined perverts or exhibitionists would wear. She waited until she had taken care of all her customers before stomping over and demanding of him: "Just where in the hell have you been the last couple of nights?"

When he worked his lips into something like a smile, she saw his fangs. Or thought she did. That end of the bar was always the darkest. It was unnerving waiting for him to respond. Frightening too, and Jessie wasn't sure why.

"Know what's out there, Jessie Sue?" he said in a voice with more bass than she was accustomed to. He looked past her, and it was almost as if he could see through the walls of the lounge into the deep recesses of the night. Jessie hated being called "Jessie Sue," and she knew that Roy Dale knew that. He smelled to high heaven, and yet there was something about him, something very different, something oddly alluring. And even as Jessie's anger was rising, she felt a hot finger of desire probing at her private parts.

"Where have you been? You've been gone, and I didn't know where you was," she said.

He flicked the cigarette lighter on and off once more and paused as he stared into her eyes and siphoned off some of her anger.

"I was walking around inside the night," he said.

She had no idea what he meant. She wanted to sound furious, but she was softening. She could feel it.

"Roy Dale, I'm serious. I had to bring Jeremy here tonight because we can't afford a baby-sitter. What have you been doing? Why haven't you at least called me?"

On the edge of bewilderment and frustration, she watched as he swung around and flashed a smile at Jeremy, then returned his attention to her. His eyes beamed red.

"Been out tryin' on a new life."

There were the fangs again. Jessie swallowed. Thought she was seeing things.

She was about to insist that he take Jeremy home and put him to bed, but something instinctive, something motherly, stopped her. She fixed a hard gaze on her husband, or this man who resembled her husband, and said, "What's happened to you? Are you on something?"

She stepped back from the uncomfortable warmth and stench radiating out from him.

"Just something in my blood, darlin'," he said.

She felt herself start to tremble. Here was a dangerous man. Here was a man who at once repulsed her and attracted her more than her Roy Dale ever had. Her voice softened another notch. "What do you want? What are you doing here?"

His pauses were brutally seductive.

"Waitin' for my brother."

"You mean Franklin?" Jessie stifled a nervous chuckle. "Franklin Tracker's never been in this place and never will be. He knows a fag would get his head bashed in here. Franklin won't never come in here. It'd be dangerous for him."

She could hear Roy Dale's ragged breathing. There was an animalistic, predatory rhythm to it. It excited her and scared her.

"He'll come," he said. "He'll come because I called him. I reached right into his head."

Jessie backed away a few more steps. She heard Calvin ask if there was anything wrong. She turned and shook her head and then pulled herself away from her husband and started to check on her customers. She noticed that Stromile Greene couldn't keep his eyes off Roy Dale. Someone was hollering for him to start up the piano. "Play 'Sweet Home Alabama,' " someone else called out. But the old black man was frozen in his attention to Roy Dale.

Calvin reached across the bar and caught Jessie's arm. He gestured with his head toward Roy Dale and said, "You sure he ain't givin' you trouble?"

At first she muttered, "No," then quickly followed with, "Yes, yes . . . it's fine."

Apparently wanting to check on things himself, Calvin ambled over to Roy Dale. Jessie stayed within earshot.

"You brought trouble in with you?" said Calvin. "I just need to know."

Roy Dale raised his index finger and the nail snapped up like a switchblade.

"*I* know you've been fucking my wife, dear Uncle. But I've found something better'n sex, better'n drugs or beer. Something money can't buy. Something better'n love. Better'n life."

Calvin didn't press the matter.

Jessie spun away, her face burning, her heart beating much too loudly. But when she looked again at the dark end of the bar, Roy Dale was gone. Her heart racing ever faster, she cut her eyes to where Jeremy was smearing a Zinger around his mouth and she felt instant relief.

"Hey, motherfucker, you messed up my shot!"

That shout silenced everything else in the lounge.

Roy Dale was standing by the pool table licking his lips as he stared at Ben, who, in turn, was holding his pool cue as if about to ram it through Roy Dale's stomach. But the young man had fear in his eyes— Jessie could see it from thirty feet away.

"You owe me for the game," Ben continued, his voice losing steam.

Roy Dale continued staring. To Jessie, it looked like a hawk eyeing a field mouse.

Nothing happened. No fight. Though everyone in the place expected something. Stromile Greene was up off his piano stool with a surprising burst of movement. He grabbed the pool cue with one hand and Ben's shoulder with the other and gently pulled him back the way someone might pull a barking dog away from a coiled rattlesnake.

"The motherfucker's messed up my shot," said Ben, but he wasn't giving the old black man much resistance.

Jessie watched Roy Dale turn from Ben and the pool table and stride over to Jeremy. Her mind screamed for her to run and press her boy into her arms, but her body wouldn't move, and it remained paralyzed until something absolutely bizarre occurred.

Roy Dale hunkered down in front of Jeremy and whispered something inaudible.

Jeremy opened his mouth wide.

And screamed.

"Mama!"

His first words ever.

Jessie tore from herself and had the terrified boy in her arms in a heartbeat. She and everyone else in the lounge followed Roy Dale as he glided slowly toward the end of the bar nearest the front door. He stopped not far from the stuffed fox and stared at it, then sat down as if intent upon waiting for someone.

It took Jessie a minute or so to calm Jeremy.

She told Calvin she wanted to go home and he nodded that he understood.

With Jeremy in her arms, Jessie gazed up at the fox, and maybe it was because her eyes were teary, maybe it was a trick of the light, but it seemed that the fox was no longer snarling.

It seemed scared.

It seemed, in fact, that Death had that fox cornered.

Mollie Tracker could not pray.

And that was very strange because praying was what Mollie did best. She could pray while frying chicken or slicing green tomatoes, or while shopping at Piggy Wiggly or sitting on the toilet, or even while having sex with Douglas—the *only* man with whom she had ever had sex. But now, much to her distress, something kept burning her words to ashes before she even got them formed.

She had awakened, after midnight, sweating, and having gone to the bathroom, she waddled into the front room where she eased her wide, heavy body into an overstuffed chair and dabbed at her sweaty jowls with a cold rag.

She had dreamed again of Roy Dale. And Jesus.

Same dream two nights in a row: a good dream as it started out. There was Jesus freshly crucified, His wounds bleeding freely, and He was approaching her boy. Her Roy Dale. And Jesus wore that enormous martyrdom on His brow and extended His huge forgiveness to Roy Dale, who was a lost sinner and had been for years, and Mollie's heart had leaped with joy at the sight of her son meeting the Son. What a glorious moment.

But then . . .

Well, the dream took a strange and wicked turn. There was Roy Dale speaking words that ought to have been spoken by Jesus. There was Roy Dale kneeling before Jesus and saying,

"Feed my lambs!

Feed my sheep!

Feed my sheep!"

It wasn't Roy Dale's voice. It was a voice filled with blood. But Jesus didn't seem to mind that someone else was using His words. With His lordly grace He lifted Roy Dale to Him and offered Himself. Offered His wounds.

And Roy Dale fed upon them—the nail holes, the spear wound, the trickle made by the crown of thorns.

Mollie woke both times with a piercing cry.

And now she hugged herself and trembled. She

couldn't pray. She couldn't even recall where in the
Bible one could read the injunction against eating
blood. It was there. Jesus knew where. Jesus knew
about the mysterious flame, too. Perhaps He had
sent it because she hadn't suffered enough—a missing husband, a missing son, and yet . . . Perhaps her
burdens needed to be heavier. More crosses to bear.

The flame flickered at the back of her throat.
That's what she imagined. It flickered on and off just
about where her tonsils were. It was the tiny flame
which kept her from praying. But when she checked
her mouth in the bathroom mirror, there was no
flame. Nothing. She sensed the hand of Satan in this.
Jesus, after all, wouldn't play cruel tricks on her. She
called her other son, Franklin, and asked him to
come over. His mother needed him. She would sit
and wait for him. She would send Franklin to find
Roy Dale and Douglas. And when he found them,
she would be able to pray again.

Mollie knew, of course, that Franklin was a sinner,
too. He lay with another man. He lived ungodliness.

But he was blood.

Mollie sat in her chair by a meager light and listened to the darkness tick away. Waiting. Fearing
that she might never be able to pray again. And terrified that she would fall asleep and dream of Jesus
feeding His sheep. The Son feeding the son.

The night lulled her.

Her head nodded. Her puffy hands relaxed. Her
eyes fell shut.

Minutes later, she woke to a knocking.

Death at my door? The Holy Ghost?

This time, during her brief snooze, she had experienced a pleasant dream or not even a dream at

all, but rather a vision. Something more certain than a dream and much more reassuring.

She welcomed her son Franklin.

"Mother," he said to her, "why did you want me?"

His voice was too female—it annoyed Mollie, and yet he was blood of her blood and flesh of her flesh from the seed of her man missing now, and in this night of dreams and visions, of small flames and of ashes for prayers, she needed him. Needed all her men.

"Oh, my Franklin," she gushed. Then hardened. "You didn't bring *him* with you, did you?"

Franklin grunted. He gave his mother an obligatory embrace and knelt at her fat knees.

"If by *him*, you mean 'Myron'—no, you'll be relieved to hear that he did not accompany me."

"You know, hon, we got several new young pretty women in our church. Very pretty and nice—if you'd throw down your ways, I know some of them would like to meet a handsome young man."

"Mother, don't. If that's what you called me here for, then I'm leaving."

"No, no, please. Please don't leave your mother. You see, I've just had a vision. It just came to me from the Lord. It must be from the Lord. And now I know that your daddy is at peace."

"Have you heard from him?"

"No, it was a vision. Like I said. And I couldn't tell where he was—it was dark—but he was with John Taylor and they was at peace, and I'm gone tell Miriam her husband's at peace, and now I know mine is, too."

"So is that why you wanted me?"

"No, it's about Roy Dale. Your brother, Roy Dale. I dreamed about him being with Jesus, but I don't understand it. I want to know where he is. Has he gone off somewheres, you think?"

"Mother, I believe I know where he is. It came to me—like he was speaking to me—while Myron and I were watching a movie. I believe I know where to find him."

"Maybe he's calling because he needs you."

Franklin shook his head.

"Hard for me to imagine that Roy Dale would ever need me. We're as different as brothers can be."

"But you'll go to him?"

"Yes."

"And bring him back to his mother?"

"If he wants to come back, I will."

Tears rolled down Mollie's round cheeks.

"You know, this could be your father's doin's. I mean, I pray he's at peace like what I saw in my vision, but it was his ways, I think, that brought on our family trouble. He got off the right path and it broke our family, you see, what with Roy Dale being wild and irresponsible, and you—you slapping the Lord in the face with your behavior."

"Mother, I won't listen to—"

"Hush, now," said Mollie. "Hush and hear me out. You might well not know this, but your father, he strayed; he smashed up one of the holy commandments." She paused and gathered herself before heaving her upper body in one impressive convulsion. "He sought out other women—that's what he done."

She stared into her son's face; her lips trembled. Franklin nodded.

"I know about all that, Mother. And it didn't make me what I am. Nature did that. And I'm not sorry I'm the way I am. I wish you could accept it, but I don't believe you ever will. I'm still a Tracker no matter what, and I'm going to meet Roy Dale and find out where he's been and what has happened to him."

Her son continued to kneel before her; Mollie forced a smile. She reached out and cupped her hands over her son's ears as if to block out the voices of evil.

"You'll help my old heart if you do it. I'll try to pray for you."

Then, after a moment of hesitation, she asked Franklin to look into her mouth to see whether he could see a small flame burning there.

"Mother, are you serious?"

But she insisted. He saw nothing. She felt a surge of relief. She looked into his face lovingly, and he responded with something of a smile, and yet as she continued gazing at him, his facial features seemed to change—something hideous beneath the surface began to emerge and his lips worked into the snarl of a wild beast.

Miriam was at the kitchen table holding one of J.T.'s dirty shirts. It was after midnight, and she had fixed herself some coffee because she hadn't been able to sleep. On the table she had placed a framed photo of her son, Josh, and she volleyed between staring at that photo and lifting her husband's shirt to her nose. She had thought the familiar smell of him would make her feel better, would help her to believe that he was all right, that no harm had come to him.

She felt there was a huge hole in her life and she would never be able to fill it.

"Mama? Mama, why are you up?"

Hearing the voice of her son Tyler, she stuffed the shirt in her lap and smiled.

"Hey, why aren't *you* asleep? You need a glass of milk or something? You're not sick, are you?"

Tyler sat down at the table. He shook his head. Suddenly he looked scared. His chin quivered and he was fighting back tears.

"Mama, I think Josh has been trying to talk to me. Talk in my head."

Miriam reached across and took his hands.

"Honey, you've had a bad dream. That's all. I'll get you some milk and then you can go back to bed. Things will be better in the morning."

The boy shook his head.

"No, Mama, listen. It wasn't a dream. It's Josh. It's his voice, I know it. Only . . . only I can't understand what he's saying. I can't make out the words. It's like when you're watching TV and the sound's too low and the words—you just can't know what they're saying. Josh is saying something to me, Mama. He is, and I don't think I'm crazy or nothing like that."

"Tyler, honey, what do you want Mama to do?"

She felt her heart quake like a leaf in the wind as she waited and watched his face contort as some new sadness or terror tried to shake free there. Finally he spoke, his voice laced with tears.

"Could we go see him? Could we go see him right now?"

Gladys Tracker hoped against hope that the approaching headlights might be her son John Taylor. It would make sense that having missed his son's burial, having gone off somewhere to grieve alone, he would sneak into the cemetery after midnight and pay his respects. But as she raised the single long-stemmed rose to her nose, she told herself to stop hoping.

She had read the book of moonlight and knew how the story ended.

In fact, she knew the moment, earlier in the evening, when Orpheus Smith brought Jacob home and helped him to the door and then on inside. She had given her son a hug and told him to go get a hot shower. He said nothing and obeyed.

"Your boy's had a bad shock," Orpheus told her.

"By the looks of things, so have you."

Both men were dirty and smelly; their clothes and skin showed traces of blood.

"We tried to wash up best we could."

"Some kinds of stain you can't clean away."

Orpheus had stared at her, weariness glazing his eyes and causing him to slump.

"Don't ask what we've been doin'," he said.

"You really think I don't know?"

His voice filled with regret, he replied, "I'm sorry. You know I'd like to be with you. Now more'n ever."

"I know that," she said. "We've talked that all out before."

And then he said, "Well, if you know what's been goin' down, I've got something in the van for you, and a favor to ask of you."

He had returned with the rose.

"It's for Josh's grave," he said. "I'm gone go get drunk, 'less you'll reconsider and give me a different kind of evening."

"No," she said. "I just won't. I just can't. I still have Clarence everywhere I go. He lives in my heart too strong."

And then, in a poetic afterthought, Orpheus had smiled wearily and said to her, "Roses climb your life like you was a trellis, my dear." She had giggled and squeezed his wrist. He had driven away, and she had imagined him stopping at a convenience store for two six-packs. *By now he's blissfully passed out,* she told herself.

She leaned down and placed the rose on Josh's grave.

She prayed that its power would work.

On the narrow asphalt road the approaching car stopped and killed its lights. Two people got out. Again she reminded herself that John Taylor wouldn't be one of them, and something in the moment made her think back to the brief period she and Clarence had lived at Sweet Gum when they were first married and how they had big and foolish plans to one day return the place to its former glory.

She remembered believing something was in the walls.

She remembered cleaning the bloody streaks on one area of the wall—like tears of blood. And she remembered Clarence wanting to claw into those walls, but she wouldn't let him. They moved back into town and left Sweet Gum to whatever shed blood in its walls. She also remembered that Caleb Tracker, Clarence's father, had left Sweet Gum, too. Before he died, he told her that he'd seen something like a ghost there. He said he feared being "called to darkness." Those were the words he had used.

Miriam and Tyler came up on her, Miriam carrying a flashlight. Gladys momentarily thought it odd that neither woman was surprised to see the other. Something about the shared bond of grieving for blood.

"What a beautiful rose," said Miriam.

While Tyler knelt at the grave and listened for his brother's voice, the two women talked softly of things surrounding Josh's service. But before long they turned their attention to John Taylor and the unspoken comparisons between losing a son and losing a husband, and Gladys could not keep grim acceptance from entering her tone.

Miriam read it well.

"He's gone then," she said. "That's it, isn't it?"

The woman suddenly buried her grief in her hands, and when she finally raised her head again, it seemed her suffering was so great that her face had been erased.

"I'm not holding out hope. It's a thing a mother knows," said Gladys.

She watched as Miriam went to Tyler and knelt by him and whispered something, and the boy wept. When he had finished, he said, "Mama, I won't never see Josh again. He's not coming back."

Gladys walked aside, out of earshot, and to herself said, "I pray to God he won't."

Chapter Seven

Daybreak of the Damned

The winter fog settled in like a hangover.

Jacob sat alone in a booth at Mr. Pancake wishing he could see the sunrise, but the fog, thick and gray and suffocating, closed over the parking lot and rubbed menacingly at the windows, allowing him to see the ghostly approach of headlights from the meager traffic on Soldier Road. But nothing more.

Except for one very unsettling sight.

A gulp of coffee calmed him somewhat, enough for him to get a hand on the darkly fleeting moment he had experienced a few minutes earlier. It had unfolded innocently. A flock of breakfast-hunting crows landing on the asphalt beyond the glass, beneath the fog, hopping, cawing noisily, brashly—an in-your-face attitude about them, or so it seemed to Jacob. They were the final breath of night. Then, as seven or eight of them took flight, one stayed, a large, handsome brute, parading a black silkiness that soaked in any hint of illumination nearby. Jacob watched the bird through the patches of fog that rolled in, and he continued watching it when it hopped twice, flung its wings up as if it were wearing a cape, and exploded from the asphalt. It winged magnificently. It winged as if it belonged in its world more so than any other creature possibly could. It landed across the road, far enough away to make it difficult to see precisely what happened next.

But Jacob suspended his disbelief. The events of the day before demanded that.

When the crow found solid ground again, with its elegant wings raised high, the change came like a magician's sleight of hand. Blackness swirled and the creature welled up and the fog embraced it, and as the gray mistiness parted for a heartbeat or two, Jacob saw a man materialize and reach his stare across the road at him.

It was Roy Dale.

Jacob couldn't swallow. Could barely breathe.

A car passed, momentarily blocking his vision. In its aftermath Jacob squinted to see again the figure of Roy Dale. But he was gone. Gone somewhere to escape sunrise.

Because all vampires must.

Belief had entered Jacob as invisibly and forcefully as a bad cold. It was still incredible in so many ways, but he had to admit that he now believed in vampires. Tracker vampires. He rubbed his hands and discovered that he couldn't keep from closely examining his fingers and palms; he couldn't accept that they were clean—hadn't he washed them a dozen times?

He kept seeing blood on them. Faint shadows of blood.

His brother's blood.

Tracker blood.

He and Bo had murdered J.T. They had murdered his brother.

No, damn it, it wasn't . . .

The creature Bo had staked in the heart, the creature Jacob had beheaded, the creature they had buried in the snakehole, could not have been his brother. His brother's body had been stolen by that creature—a vampire—and now J.T. was at peace. As was Uncle Douglas. They would not feed upon the night again.

Or upon family. But Roy Dale was still out there.

"God help us," Jacob whispered over his coffee.

He looked again across the road. He knew he should get up and find Bo or Danny or both and go after Roy Dale. Finish the job.

Go hunting.

After one more vampire. During the daylight hours.

Then it would be over.

But exhaustion held sway. And he knew that Bo was sleeping off a killer drunk, and he had no idea where Danny was.

"More coffee, sir?"

Her smile was both sympathetic and teasingly sexy.

"Hey," he said, glancing up into the most beautiful face he could imagine. "No, I drink any more of this and my kidneys'll be swimming in it."

Brianna slipped into the seat across from him and set her coffeepot down.

"I'm glad business is slow," she said. "Of course, it'll pick up in an hour. Bo switched me to the six-to-two shift. Seems to think working here late at night isn't safe anymore."

Jacob surveyed the surroundings: two customers

at the counter, one in a booth on the opposite side of the restaurant. Someone he recognized.

"Bo's right. Hey, is Stromile Greene becoming a regular?" he said.

"Oh, he's a sweet ole guy, really. Came in early and seemed upset about something, though."

"Did he say what?"

"No. Just that he wanted to see Bo. But Bo's sunk pretty far deep in himself."

Jacob smiled at the image. It was one that fit the way he looked at Brianna—he sank into her beauty, wanted to surrender to his desire for her. Wanted to tell her how he felt. Wanted a life with her away from all the blood. But it seemed borderline crazy and certainly insensitive to be thinking about such things when he had just lost a brother and an uncle.

"I need to talk to him," said Jacob. "And to your dad, too."

"Daddy came by last night. He acted real strange. It was so . . . I don't know, he was so grim. He acted like a zombie, you know. There was this look in his eyes—like he was one of the damned."

Jacob nodded.

"Yeah, I can understand that."

She reached across the table and took his hands lovingly into hers.

"You've got that same look in your eyes, Jacob."

"I know."

He was trying hard not to meet her eyes. He didn't know how much she knew. He didn't know how much any other Tracker knew about the horrors that had been taking place.

Brianna's voice was laced with concern. "All I can figure is that this is about J.T. and Douglas and Roy Dale, and whatever the story is, it's not good. When your mom came by this morning to baby-sit Em, I could tell she was hiding something. I prodded, but she wouldn't say much. Daddy wouldn't tell me anything, either, so I was hoping maybe you would."

"No." He sank deeper in her eyes. "No, I can't, except that . . . maybe real soon things can somehow get back to normal. Meanwhile, you have to promise me again that you'll be careful. Especially after dark."

She shook her head.

"You're scaring me, Jacob, and I don't even know what I'm supposed to be scared of."

Jacob swung his eyes back to the glass and the fog beyond. He paused a moment and then said, "The dark. You need to be afraid of the dark." And his breath caught high in his chest, and then he added, "I am."

Every Tracker should be.

That's the rest of what he wanted to say.

New customers called her away. She carried worry on her shoulders. She appeared thinner than usual, and Jacob feared that before the Tracker nightmare ended she would become like a dress on a hanger—empty, ghostlike, terrible. And he feared that his love for her couldn't change things.

He closed his eyes and waited, and Brianna succeeded in winning him over to two more cups of coffee, but not even his usual sexual fantasies about her could blot out yesterday's images: the blood, the burials. The deep red rose.

He had nowhere to go. Jimmie Jack's would not reopen for weeks, and though Bo had offered to give him work at Mr. Pancake, Jacob seriously wondered whether he could concentrate on an honest day's work while the vampire threat existed. Roy Dale had to be found and destroyed.

Another twenty minutes passed before Brianna swept by again and whispered that Bo was up growling and snarling and demanding coffee. Jacob saw him sit down in a booth with Stromile Greene. He considered joining them, but he decided he would let Bo report to him. Besides, Jacob continued to feel uneasy around the old black man—more fears that would have to be buried? And what about the survivors? He was suddenly awash in thoughts of Miriam and Mollie, wondering what their lives would be like without husbands, and wondering when and how they would be told the news. Only distractedly did he notice Bo making his way over. Jacob shifted his thoughts to his mother, to how she had made a life without her husband, and it struck him as never before that she was strong. And he tried to imagine telling her that he had recorded the names of J.T. and Uncle Douglas in the Tracker family Bible. She had lost a son. Did she know somehow? She seemed to understand so much.

"Mornin', bright eyes," Bo mumbled as he joined Jacob.

"Jesus, your corpse will look better than this," Jacob responded as he scanned his friend's red eyes and puffy face.

Bo chuckled.

"Yeah, well, tough night. How's it hangin' for you? What I'm seein', you ain't exactly settin' the world on fire."

Jacob's voice fell.

"I just can't get yesterday out of my head, you know. My God."

Bo gritted his teeth.

"Well, son, I'm tellin' you, you got to. There's at least one more out there. We got to finish what we started."

Jacob nodded, and before Bo could continue, he said, "I saw him."

Bo ritched back.

"Saw who?"

"Roy Dale."

"When? Where? You sure?"

Jacob pointed through the dissolving fog to the point across Soldier Road where Roy Dale had appeared. He described in full what he had seen. "Could be I was seeing things. But I don't think so."

"Shape changing," Bo muttered, "it's somethin' they're capable of. But get this: Stromile Greene just told me he saw Roy Dale last night. He was at the Hollow Log Lounge and seemed to be waitin' for someone."

"Just a minute," said Jacob. "You said 'at least' one more out there—who else you talking about?"

"That's what I'm gettin' to. Stromile said Franklin showed up and sat with Roy Dale. Had a few drinks. But they didn't leave together, and Stromile thinks maybe that's a good sign."

"Hard to imagine Franklin at the Hollow Log Lounge, you know."

"You're right, but we have to check it out. Here's what I'm thinkin': why don't you go on out later this morning to Sweet Gum and look for any signs of Roy Dale. Wouldn't hurt to see if Jessie's seen him. While you're doin' that, I'll go on by The Treasure House and have a talk with Franklin if he's around. This has me scar't."

"What about Danny? Shouldn't he be in on our plan?"

"A good cop oughtta know how to find us. Thing is, I ain't sure your brother believes us yet, despite what he saw with his own eyes. But I think he'll come around, and the way he's set on keepin' this a family matter, he ain't likely to open up to nobody 'bout J.T. and Douglas."

"I suppose you're right. Most of the time I hope nobody else ever knows the truth about what's happened."

"Keepin' this kind of secret won't be easy."

The hardness of the moment sank around them.

"Do you think my mother knows?" Jacob asked.

Bo set his eyes on the ever-diminishing fog.

"Son, the thing about women is, most of them have a powerful intuition. Some of them just know things out of nothin'. But most of them are a damn sight better at keepin' secrets than men are."

He winked at Jacob and started to get up.

"Wait," said Jacob. "What about the rose? Remember, you said we were going to put a rose on Josh's grave."

Bo's smile was deep enough to drown in.

"It's been tended to, "he said.

The late-morning air was unseasonably warm, the sun startlingly bright. Well beyond the Sweet Gum mansion, at the far edge of the plantation property, Jacob waded into a muddy, nameless pond he had known of for years. Most of the Trackers, in fact, knew of it, but he thought of it as his private body of water, though nothing as impressive as Moon Lake or other bodies of water in the county. It was a good spot to come and sit and pluck at his guitar and scratch out pieces of lyrics on a notepad; it was not, however, a good place to fish, turtles having claimed so much of the territory.

Jacob had come for cleansing.

Birds sang in the pines as he leaned down and rubbed and splashed his hands in the red-clay-colored water. But no matter how thoroughly he scrubbed, shadows of bloodstains returned. Under his breath he hissed, "Goddamn it."

And he thought suddenly of a play he had been required to read in high school. *Macbeth* by Shakespeare. One dramatic scene in particular in which Lady Macbeth—the ambitious woman who had aided her husband in taking the throne—bewailed the imagined presence of spots of blood she couldn't wash away. A king murdered. Bloody daggers of the mind. The blood had driven her crazy. Jacob couldn't keep from wondering whether a similar fate awaited him.

He wiped his hands on his jeans. Discouraged, he waded back to the bank. He had brought the Tracker Bible, and with it in hand he sat under a small willow and pondered how many other names would need to be recorded before the family curse ended. Would the darkness really pass once Roy Dale was brought down? That's what Bo assumed. Earlier, when Jacob had first arrived at Sweet Gum, he had cautiously wandered through the old manse, and he had been intrigued again by the mystery and strangeness of the burial alcoves in the wall. The experience sent him to wondering, as he had before, about what (or who?) had been responsible for J.T. becoming a vampire in the first place. He sensed that Bo knew something more, something he might share in time. Something more about the Tracker family: its dark history, its intimacy with vampires.

"Looks like you got the right idea, little brother. Sit under a tree and let the world go by."

Jacob hadn't heard Danny approach, but he was glad to see him.

"I just came out to see if I could find any signs of Roy Dale. What are you up to?"

His brother appeared to be so weary that he nearly staggered. The bags under his eyes looked like pockets of dough. He, too, was one of the damned. When he sat down beside Jacob, he groaned from carrying around much more than his physical weight.

"I had Uncle Douglas's truck impounded. Officially filed a missing person's report on him and J.T. Thought that was the best way to handle it. Beyond that, I'm doing the same as you. Any trace of Roy Dale?"

Though he hesitated to do so, Jacob told him of the morning sighting.

"Bo thinks it'll all end with Roy Dale."

Danny listened thoughtfully. To Jacob, he seemed a man who had entered a realm of disbelief that he couldn't have prepared himself for. He, too, had learned of Roy Dale's appearance at the Hollow Log Lounge, and he seemed somewhat reassured that Bo would be checking on Franklin. There was an air of police business about their approach to locating Roy Dale and stopping the spread of the vampires, and yet this territory was so unfamiliar that rational language failed to convince either man that their world could be sane ever again.

"Have you taken a look at the grave?" said Danny.

Jacob shook his head. "You think we should?"

"It would ease my mind, yeah. All I want to see is that it's not empty."

In Danny's patrol car they rode in silence to the

trailers beyond which the snakehole had been dug. Jacob avoided the charred ruins of the one that had housed J.T. At the site of the snakehole they were relieved to find the earth mounded and the rose, though wilted, still atop it.

Danny hunkered down by the grave.

"I hope to God I never have to try to explain to anyone what's happened with this. There's no way we could ever deal with it beyond our family. Beyond blood, you know."

Jacob hunkered down beside him.

"I'm afraid for all of us," he said. "No Tracker's safe."

"You really believe whatever's happening here only affects family?"

"I guess I do. Bo thinks that's the case. That's the pattern so far."

"Yeah. So far."

Sunset found Jacob knocking on the door to the trailer Jessie Tracker shared with Roy Dale and their boy, Jeremy. The worse-for-wear double-wide was anchored in a corner of Tarp's Trailer Court not more than fifty yards from Brianna's trailer.

It had not been a good day.

Not in terms of locating Roy Dale. Jacob and Danny and Bo had hunted for him everywhere they anticipated he might be. But the obvious fact was that Roy Dale had secured a dark lair somewhere to lie in wait for the darkness when he would walk about again, when he would feed again if the hunger for blood drove him to do so.

The single bit of good news during the hours of searching came when Bo reported that he had talked with Franklin Tracker who, in turn, explained that, yes, he had met with Roy Dale at the Hollow Log Lounge to buy him a beer as a gesture of thanks for helping him and his companion, Myron, move some heavy antique furniture they had purchased. Roy Dale had been appreciative. No, Roy Dale seemed fine, except that he was not getting along with Jessie. He thought he might have to end things.

There were no signs that Franklin had become a vampire.

On another front Jacob's plan to steal away somewhere for a picnic with Brianna and Em had to be scuttled because Brianna was tired after her shift at Mr. Pancake and Em had the sniffles. Downcast, Jacob had made his way home, where he found a note from his mother informing him that she would be having supper with Miriam and Mollie. So he had fixed himself a sandwich before following through on Bo's suggestion that he talk with Jessie: "See if she's seen our boy," as Bo had put it. Then Jacob was to meet Bo at the Hollow Log Lounge on his hunch that Roy Dale might return there. At some point Danny was to join them.

As Jacob stood at Jessie's door, the wind kicked up, an unusually warm wind that seemed to want to shove him inside when Jessie greeted him with a friendly smile. She was wearing tight jeans and a see-through blouse, a dark blue push-up bra clearly evident beneath it.

"Hey, Jacob, whatcha need?"

She took his wrist and guided him in, closing off the gusty twilight wind. Though he had never found Jessie to be as attractive as Brianna, he could understand why other men might desire her. She had a way of touching a man's arm that, together with the way she could touch a man with her eyes, broke down those initial barriers to intimacy. If she liked a man, she could make him feel that he was the only sexual interest she could possibly have. She wasn't just easy like Sunday morning, she was easier; she was easier than a handshake or blowing out a candle.

"I'm looking for Roy Dale."

She gestured for him to sit in a stained rocker recliner, though to do so, he had to step over Jeremy and dozens of toys scattered on a dirty carpet like land mines. As usual the boy was quiet, fascinated at that moment by a brightly colored model car.

"You want something to drink?" she said. "I've got beer, soft drinks, coffee."

When he declined, he got herself a can of diet soda and one for Jeremy as well. The boy took it without a word. Then Jessie sat down, Indian style, at Jacob's feet. She was wearing lipstick almost as pink as a spoon of Pepto-Bismol. Jacob suddenly didn't want to be there, but he knew that Bo would ask whether he had checked out what she knew.

"I heard Roy Dale was at the Hollow Log last night. Do you know where he went when he left? Have you seen him today?"

She shook her head.

"The bastard—yeah, he came around to the Log, but I took off with Jeremy because he was acting freaky and I thought he was going to get ugly. I don't know where he went. He hasn't been here. I'd just as soon he didn't show. He can stay away for good, for all I care."

The wind, gaining strength, rattled the siding and cried across the roof.

"Did he seem—different?"

As if the move were instinctive, she reached for her son and pulled him to her side.

"Like I said, yeah, freaky. I thought he was on something. And the weirdest thing happened. You know that my Jeremy here has never said a word in his life, but last night—I think Roy Dale scared him hard—well, last night Jeremy said something. He said 'Mama.' He was upset and scared, and that's when I told Calvin I had to leave." She kissed her son on the top of his head. "Jeremy's not talking again. But I think he knew his father was, you know, dangerous. And it's like a switch went off in his head and he needed his mother and called my name."

"You think Roy Dale will go back to the Hollow Log again tonight?"

"I've got no clue. Like I said, I don't care—as long as he stays away from me and Jeremy."

"We heard that Franklin met him there. What do you figure that's all about?"

He was testing her, just checking to see if some useful, overlooked detail might slip out.

"Shit if I know. You ever see two brothers more different? Like roadkill compared to sirloin steak. Franklin, he's a classy guy in his own way. I mean, I know he's gettin' boinked by that older guy he's with—or maybe he's doin' the boinking; hell, I don't know—but I always say that somebody's sex life is their own damn business and who the hell can say what's right and what's not. I know Mollie would get her panties in a wad hearin' me say that, but I don't give a shit what she thinks. Did you know she won't even baby-sit with Jeremy here because she thinks maybe he's got a demon in him or some such shit? You ever hear of a little boy's grandmother who wouldn't even baby-sit with him, for Chrissake?"

Jacob looked down at his hands.

"Has Calvin said anything about Roy Dale? You think he would know where he is?"

"Calvin doesn't want Roy Dale hangin' at the Log. There's trouble written all over that. We almost had a fight last night—Roy Dale and Ben."

"Ben Tracker was there?"

"Shootin' pool. Sneakin' beers when Calvin looks the other way. Well, anyway, I don't know what started it, but Ben was fixin' to jam a pool cue down Roy Dale's throat when Stromile Greene stopped him. I guess the old nigger thought Ben would get his ass kicked."

Jacob nodded. "Yeah, at least that."

He continued looking at his hands until Jessie scooted up closer to him. He could smell her perfume, some combination of floral and cinnamon, and he could feel the heat of her body.

"Tell me something, Jacob. What do you know about what's goin' on with Roy Dale? There was this weirdness about him I hadn't seen before. Like I said, I don't really care as long as he leaves us alone—I'm just maybe curious. That's all. You know what he's been up to, don't you?"

"No," he said. "No, not really."

"But it has something to do with J.T. and Douglas being missing, doesn't it? I mean, this whole fuckin' family is turning very strange. First, Josh frying himself and then—I don't know, it's all freakin' strange. You know I don't really give a shit about the Trackers, but this little guy here . . . my Jeremy, I'll fight right into Hell to protect him."

The room fell silent. The wind slammed into the side of the trailer a few more times and then died down as if the sound were mechanical and had suddenly been switched off. Jacob pushed to his feet.

"I better be goin'."

Silence filled in around his words.

The boy stood up, and Jacob saw that he was trembling. Jessie saw it, too. He stood that way for several seconds longer. Then, as the diet soda can slipped from his grasp, he screamed, "Mama!"

And a voice whispered through the front door, whispered into the room where they were gathered, a whisper and yet loud enough to batter them with its intensity.

"Jessie! Jessie!"

"Mama!"

Jessie scooped up Jeremy and held him. She looked at Jacob. He raised his hand, a gesture to signal he was listening and trying to determine the source of the voice.

"It's Roy Dale," he said.

"Jessie!" The harsh whisper ran through the trailer like hands sweeping up and down the keyboard of a piano. "Jessie, I want to come in."

"Don't," said Jacob. "Whatever you do, don't let him in."

"He just gone tear down the door." She held her son more tightly. "I've got a gun in the bedroom. In the top drawer of the nightstand. Go get it. Hurry."

"No. No, it'd be useless. You can't shoot him, Jessie. You can't stop him that way."

"Jessie! Jessie! Know what's out here?"

"Mama! Mama!"

Jessie tried to soothe the frightened boy, and Jacob glanced around frantically, searching for anything that might work as a stake. He chided himself for being unarmed.

"Know what's out here, Jessie?" The voice shook the furniture and dimmed the lights.

"We gotta call the cops," said Jessie. "Get the phone and dial nine-one-one. Jacob, get us some help."

Jacob grabbed her by the shoulders and pressed his face close to hers.

"You don't understand. The police can't help with this."

Suddenly Jessie tore away to the door.

"What do you want?" she shouted.

"I want Jeremy. I want my child."

"I've got a gun, Roy Dale, and I'll blow your fucking head off if you come through that door. Y'hear me?"

"It's about blood, Jessie."

Jacob pulled her and her son away from the door.

"I'm telling you, he can't come in unless you ask him to. Just stay back."

"Do you know about blood, Jessie?"

She was crying, and so was the boy, his head shaking uncontrollably. Jacob tried to touch him, tried to calm him. But his crying suddenly welled up into a scream, a scream so penetrating that all other sounds snapped into silence.

The scream drove Jacob back a few steps, and in the ensuing quiet he stared down at the carpet by the front door. His breath caught. And he murmured, "God, what is this?" He guided Jessie and Jeremy into the center of the room.

"What's happened?" said Jessie.

Jacob glanced at the windows and around the door frame.

"Oh Jesus."

Then Jessie cried out.

Jeremy very softly started repeating, "Mama, Mama, Mama."

Blood seeped in under the door. It seeped in under and around the window frames and door frame and trickled down, and a cool mist formed in the room.

A fine mist of blood.

Before it thickened into cold, icy droplets, Jacob tried to move through it, but it was like walking neck deep in snow.

Jessie was sobbing hysterically and Jeremy was lost in his terrified litany.

And Jacob thought that it was the end.

Time swung out beyond his reach. Minutes passed in which he could not move. Wrapped in the icy womb of blood, he could faintly hear Jessie and Jeremy. He called their names. He wanted to reassure them. Or say good-bye.

Then he heard something tapping on the roof. It sounded like rain or tiny feet skittering along. Jessie heard it, too. She turned, and Jacob could see her breath and that of the boy. It had to have been below freezing in the room.

"He's up there," said Jacob, pointing at the ceiling.

The wind returned, gusting, and its warmth began to worm its way into the room and to dissolve the thick, icy flecks of blood.

"Look at this," said Jacob, this time pointing at the door and the windows where the rivulets of blood had stopped flowing and were magically fading, disappearing totally from sight.

"Jacob, what's happening? What's next?"

He shook his head and gestured for her to stay still and listen.

Again, the skittering on the roof. Then a flapping of wings.

And, finally, a loud, shrill cawing.

The wind ceased.

The world was stone silent.

Jacob waited.

He turned to Jessie and said, "It's gone. He's gone. Roy Dale."

"How do you know?" she demanded.

"I just do," he said. He reached within for words of assurance, but what he found rang hollow and he knew it. "You'll be all right now," he offered.

She stood away from him and stared around the room as if she had never seen it before.

"No," she whispered. "No, I won't be."

Chapter Eight

The Trance of Sunrise

The fox was snarling as if cornered.

Jacob shared the feeling. He looked away. Try as he might to convince himself that he and Bo and Danny were the hunters in this case, he felt nothing of the emotional surge of pursuit. Instead, he kept hearing the threatening voice of Roy Dale and the cries and screams of Jessie and Jeremy. They had been trapped in her trailer, and only the vampire's inability to enter where it was not invited had saved them. And though he regretted leaving the woman and child, he intuitively sensed that Roy Dale would not return that night.

He could feed elsewhere.

Find more willing victims.

Jacob glanced up again at the stuffed fox above the bar. Bo was sitting with him at a table near the juke-box and was already into his third glass of beer from the pitcher they had ordered. Three beers and the night so young—it didn't bode well. Bo appeared to be carefully mulling over all that Jacob had described about the episode at Jessie's trailer. A female voice filled in around them; Jacob recognized the singer as Faith Hill, the second, most beautiful, sexiest woman he had ever seen. Too bad she was married to that McGraw fellow, he pondered. Why are all the gorgeous women off limits?

Bo took a long swallow of his beer and pitched back on the legs of his chair.

"You shoulda told Jessie not to leave her trailer. She and her boy are targets."

"If you'd seen how upset she was, you'd know she wasn't about to leave. I checked around outside. Didn't see any sign of Roy Dale."

"What makes you so sure you would?"

Jacob shrugged.

"Hell, I don't know. This is all new and incredible to me. Seems like it's just dumb luck if we happen on to where he's going to be. For that matter, we don't know that he's coming here."

"What I'm countin' on is that he could be drawn to where we are. Don't ask why. I'm just slidin' on the ice, too. But he was here last night—could be he'll be back."

"Have you seen Danny?"

"I talked to him, yeah. He's comin' once he's had a visit with Mollie. She's pretty upset apparently. Bad dreams about Roy Dale or somethin'. Says she thinks Franklin's not acting himself. But I told Danny he seemed fine to me. And, of course, she wants to know if he's heard anything on the whereabouts of Douglas."

Faith Hill was holding her final note when Jacob said, "When is all this going to blow wide open? I mean, how in the hell will we ever keep this just in the family, just among you, me and Danny? Hiding the truth about J.T. and Douglas and Roy Dale—and now what about Jessie? She's bound to talk to somebody outside our circle, and then what?"

"Could be the rumor mill's gone help us out."

"How you mean?"

"Well, I was talking to Calvin earlier and what he said is that folks think they got the missin' Trackers pegged. What they're figurin' is this: J.T.'s got in hot water over bad debts or some kinda money trouble and had to light out for the territories as Huck Finn would say. And Douglas, well, speculation is he's been chasin' skirts and caught one he wanted to hang on to. That he's skipped the scene to be with his new lady, leavin' Mollie with her Bible and her obesity, and sayin' to hell with his dairy, too."

"But what about Roy Dale?"

"Nobody gives a shit about Roy Dale. He's not even worth startin' a rumor over."

"He will be if he keeps making public appearances."

The jukebox traded Faith Hill for Garth Brooks crooning, ironically, about friends in low places, as if he personally frequented the Hollow Log Lounge. Jacob put a fresh head on his beer as he prepared for Bo's next observation. Back at the pool tables Ben Tracker was laughing maniacally, a sign that he was winning, or so Jacob guessed.

"Mind if I join you boys a minute?"

The intruder was Calvin Tracker. He looked stubbed out like a cigarette butt. Jacob and Bo gestured for him to join them.

"Slow night for a Saturday, ain't it?" said Bo. "I was hopin' ole Stromile would be here bangin' on the piano."

"He got spooked last night. I'm not expecting him back anytime soon."

Bo nodded.

Jacob could tell Calvin's thoughts weren't on business. Not exactly.

"Got a call from Jessie," he said. "She's real upset. Not coming in to work." Then he turned to address his remarks directly at Jacob. "She claims Roy Dale's stalking her. Wants to know should she sic the police on him. She asked 'cause I'm blood and she didn't know if it would get under my skin, and I told her Roy Dale's never been nothin' but a no-count son of a bitch as far as I'm concerned. She seems to think that Jacob here knows what's goin' on with him."

"He's no count," said Jacob. "I'll agree with that. But look, Danny's been told about this, and so we can let him take care of it. I don't know much."

Jacob was surprised at how easily the lie slipped out from him. He silently vowed that at some point he'd tell Calvin the truth.

Blood ought to know the truth even if it's unbelievable.

Calvin appeared to be thinking over the exchange. Jacob surveyed the man's wrinkled face, a surprisingly old face, though Calvin was only in his early fifties. It was clear that Jessie's call had put a few more years on his heart.

"Maybe you're right," said Calvin. "Thing is, I'm awful fond of Jessie and that little boy, and if that bastard husband of hers is trying to get rough with her, I'll get a gun and blow the sucker's head off— don't matter that he's blood."

"Jessie will be fine. She's strong. She can take care of herself."

But Jacob wasn't sure he believed his own words.

The incident at the trailer had shaken her badly. She was vulnerable, and she had a son to protect and a monster lurking at the edges of her life.

Above the roof of the lounge thunder rolled. Two tentative flickers of lightning seemed to usher someone through the front door. A soft, misty rain was evident before the door was swung shut.

"Good," said Bo. "Here's Danny."

He wasn't in uniform, but as always he carried an invisible badge. He walked like a cop and could not help eyeing everyone suspiciously when he entered a room. As he joined the threesome, he rubbed moisture from his hair.

"Not a good night for man or beast," he said. "Hey, Calvin. How we doin'?"

Calvin repeated his concerns, and Danny, after shooting a questioning glance at Jacob, played along as if he knew what had occurred. Then he tried to assure Calvin that someone would be checking on Jessie and her son, adding that until Roy Dale actually did something more than hassle his wife, there wasn't much the authorities could do. Dissatisfied, Calvin trudged off. The storm shoved closer; the thunder made the walls quake; the lightning dimmed the smoke-shrouded lamps over the pool table. And the fox sank deeper into his snarl.

Danny's attention had been drawn to his son's laughter and what sounded to be the onset of some kind of disagreement the boy was having with his opponent or his opponent's friends. Jacob glanced at Bo as if searching for some signal regarding what to say or do next. He decided it was better to share what he knew than to keep it between him and Bo.

"Danny," he began, "there really was trouble earlier at Jessie's trailer—it's not Calvin blowing smoke."

"Sort of figured that. What kind of trouble? Does Calvin have the story straight?"

"Some of it. It was Roy Dale. I'm sure of that much. I was there with Jessie and Jeremy."

Jacob believed the account gained more of an incredulous air each time he retold and relived it, and he could tell that Danny was suspending his disbelief to the breaking point as he listened. When Jacob finished detailing the incident, Danny pressed at his forehead as if massaging a stubborn headache.

"Y'all think maybe we should let Calvin in on the whole truth?" he said. "I mean, if he takes it upon himself to play protector for Jessie and Jeremy, he may walk into something he sure as hell can't handle."

"Danny, you're the one who's wanted from the get-go to keep this under wraps as much as possible," said Bo.

"I know. I know. But . . . it's gettin' to be too damn complicated and too damn dangerous."

Shouting suddenly erupted from the pool table. Danny sighed and pushed up from the table.

"Excuse me, fellas, while I see what yellow jacket's nest my boy's stuck his hand in."

Jacob watched as Danny pulled Ben aside and they began talking, Danny poking a fatherly finger into Ben's shoulder, the expressions on both faces lined with seriousness.

It began to rain hard. The roof rattled like marbles on metal. The group Alabama had to strain on the jukebox to be heard over the storm, and at the front door a new customer entered, curiously dry somehow. Jacob continued to follow the scene between Danny and his son until Bo rapped on the table.

"Look what the night just dragged in."

It was Franklin Tracker. To Jacob, he seemed nervous and unusually pale with dark circles under his eyes.

"Talk about somebody being out of his element— he's a stranger in a strange land. You think we should invite him over?"

"No. Leave him be," said Bo. "Could be he's waitin' for someone."

Jacob knew what his friend meant.

Franklin sat at a table by himself near the door. He gave no indication that he was aware of Jacob and Bo or anyone else for that matter. When the barmaid subbing for Jessie came over to get his order, he waved her off. Unnerved, but determined not to show it, Jacob returned to his glass of beer and thought about how wonderful it would be to spend the evening with Brianna and Em watching television or playing games, then tucking Em into bed and slipping under the sheets of paradise with her mother.

But none of it was going to happen. It was time to focus on reality.

Saturday night at the Hollow Log Lounge began to percolate.

A few more customers wandered in. A confusion of noises rubbed at Jacob's ears: laughter, a loud voice or two, the jukebox giving play to the Dixie Chicks, who were longing for wide open spaces and the embrace of an audience they couldn't see. And Bo continued to guzzle beer and Danny continued to act as referee in the pending bout at the pool table.

The fox looked down on the scene, still snarling but going nowhere.

Jacob was feeling a buzz from his beer and the

thrum of the place coming alive when Bo, his eyes cutting to the front door, said, "Holy Christ in a cotton field!" Jacob glanced that way in time to see Franklin letting someone in.

Roy Dale.

"Why the hell didn't we bring some kind of weapon in with us?" said Bo. He leaned across the table. "You and me's got to get him out to the parking lot so I can hustle up what we need from the van."

"Shit, Bo, it's pouring down rain out there. We need to bring him down here inside."

"What with? A goddamn chair leg?"

"If we have to."

People noticed Roy Dale. Tables where the talking had been animated and the smiles plentiful fell silent as the vampire disguised as a man came toward Jacob and Bo with his brother, Franklin, in tow. His easy gait was animalistic, smooth and sure and predatory. Eerie. The already dimmed lights took on a sickly yellow cast, and Roy Dale seemed to darken as he approached. It was as if his shadow preceded him.

He stared at Jacob with eyes not of anyone's world. Anyone living, at least.

"You wouldn't let the bitch ask me into my humble abode," he said. "I wanted to see my boy. I wanted to be with my family. I wanted to be in the bosom of my wife and child in the life I used to know."

"Leave Jessie and Jeremy alone," said Jacob.

But his tone carried no threat to the creature standing over him.

Roy Dale smiled. Fangs glistened into view momentarily, then appeared to retract.

"Know what's out there?" he said. He raised his

voice so that everyone in the place could hear. "Does everyone know what's out there? My brother here does. What's out there is all the darkness and all the life you could ever want."

Franklin put a hand on Roy Dale's shoulder and Roy Dale patted it warmly.

Brothers. Best friends. This was not the relationship Jacob had witnessed over the years. The two men had never been close. Their exchange made Jacob very uneasy.

From behind the bar Calvin, holding a shotgun, called out, "You're not welcome here. Get on out. Take your brother, too."

Roy Dale wheeled and waved one hand aloft and the lounge plunged, for a heartbeat or two, into darkness, and when the dusky lights came on again, customers, amid surprised whispers and nervous murmurs, began moving to the door to stay out of harm's way, and Jacob saw that Danny had drawn near.

"We have business with you," said Danny. "Jake and Bo and I—on the part of the Tracker family—so you're goin' nowhere till I say so." He shifted his gaze away from the vampire. "And Calvin, the Hollow Log as of right this second is closed. You folks that are here, y'all go on. This is a police matter. Sorry. This is a police matter. Y'all go on home. Call it a night."

No one seriously protested.

Before another minute had passed, the only ones remaining were Trackers except for Bo.

To Jacob, Roy Dale appeared pleased at what had transpired. It was as if something preternaturally dark and confident welled up from deep within him, as if he held the moment suspended in time, with no one capable of challenging his command of the scene.

And in that moment Jacob found that he envied whatever it was Roy Dale possessed. Or whatever Roy Dale had become.

"You are my blood," said Roy Dale, as if he were speaking directly into everyone's thoughts, and his voice was mesmerizing. "Even our ole friend Bo. We'll call him our blood brother, won't we, Jacob? Won't we, Danny?"

"You're not *my* blood," Ben shouted suddenly from near the pool table. He came at Roy Dale with his pool cue raised like a lance or a spear.

"Stay the hell out of this, son," said Danny. "We'll take care of this. You and Calvin and Franklin need to go on. Jake and Bo and I'll take care of this."

Ben, anger roiling in his face, jabbed the cue at Roy Dale, who immediately raised his hands as if in a gesture of surrender. Franklin quickly stepped in front of him, offering himself as a shield. He spoke in a soft, reassuring, effeminate voice.

"My brother means you no harm. He wants all of us to be closer. Blood ties. Blood bonds. Tracker blood. Don't you see?"

"What I see," Ben shouted, "is a crazy bastard. I shoulda kicked the shit out of the motherfucker last night."

When the boy jabbed the cue at Roy Dale a second time, Danny grabbed it.

"Ben, goddamn it, I said stay out of this. You don't know what you're getting into."

But the boy tried to jerk the cue free of his father's grasp, and when he did, it broke so that he was holding a wickedly pointed shard perhaps a yard long. Jacob and Bo got up out of their chairs and Calvin swung around from behind the bar and leveled the shotgun at Roy Dale's chest.

"What I have to say is this: I better never hear of you laying a hand or so much as a finger on Jessie or her boy, or so help me God I'll fill you so full of buckshot you'll sink right through to China. Y'hear me?"

The eyes of Roy Dale reached out to each of them. Jacob felt an unaccountable wave of shame. It seemed that Roy Dale was somehow generating feelings of guilt within him—*you're being unjust to this man*. That was the thought that suddenly haunted Jacob. He watched as Roy Dale turned to face Calvin. But it was Franklin who said, "You misunderstand. As I said, my brother doesn't want to hurt anyone."

"I understand plenty about him," said Calvin, though he was shaking and his voice threatened to crack. "I understand that he's a son of a bitch. Ben there's right—he's a crazy bastard, and I want him out of my place right now."

Danny took a step toward Calvin and put on his domestic-squabble tone.

"Y'all, we're just gone cool down. Calvin, here's what gone happen: you gone put away your shotgun, and Roy Dale is gone go quietly. No trouble. He and I and Jacob and Bo gone go out back. We've got things that need to be done. Franklin, you and Ben, y'all not gone be in on this, either. So let's cool down here a second, and we all gone be fine. Ever'body follow me on this?"

"Yes, we do," said Roy Dale. "Families should express love. We should fill the night with it. No violence. Just blood. I mean no violence to Calvin or anyone else. In fact, I'd like to be closer to Calvin. I'd like for us to get to know each other better."

He began moving very slowly toward Calvin, though it didn't appear that he was taking steps—

simply a gliding movement that defied all natural laws. But Calvin held the shotgun on Roy Dale as he approached. The lights flickered again. There was a loud clap of thunder, and then a flash of lightning that slashed blue light across the scene.

"Shoot the bastard!" Ben exclaimed.

He raced forward and Danny jumped in front of him and Franklin shouted, "No!" Then the Hollow Log Lounge roared as it had never roared. Two shotgun blasts slammed into Roy Dale's chest. He staggered backward, looking down at the blood instantly soaking his coat and the torn material. He reached his fingertips into the wound just below his heart and then raised them to his mouth and sucked at them as if they were covered in chocolate icing instead of blood. He closed his eyes. It appeared that pain froze his face. He groaned once, and blood pulsed from his mouth. Doubling over, he reached out for Franklin, who was screaming and beginning to cry. Then Roy Dale convulsed and crumbled forward, and Franklin howled like a sad beast.

"Goddamn it," said Danny. "Oh, goddamn this." He wrenched the shotgun away from Calvin who was trembling and had to steady himself with a hand on the back of a chair to keep standing.

Everyone gathered over Roy Dale's body and the figure of Franklin hunkered down near it, weeping softly. Jacob was stunned. He couldn't think. He couldn't feel.

"He deserved it," said Ben, his tone bitter and defiant.

His words hung in the air. The only other sound was Franklin's weeping.

No one moved.

Thunder rumbled low, trailing the rapidly passing storm at a distance.

Nothing more occurred until the creature that was Roy Dale gasped and shook free of the grip of the violence and the death wound it had experienced.

And rose to its feet.

And Jacob heard Calvin mutter, "Jesus God almighty."

The creature stood, unsteady at first, with Franklin locking his arms inside its elbow. The creature's wounds had miraculously stopped bleeding. It appeared to be staring at Calvin.

"I forgive you," it said.

"Danny," said Calvin. "Danny, my God, what is this?"

"Go on to your back room," said Danny. "Go on. It's gone be all right. Go on."

Calvin obeyed, scrambling away hurriedly, banging into chairs and tables as he fled. But Ben was there, close to his father, and obviously amazed at what he'd seen.

"What kind of fucking monster is he? He oughtta be dead. What is he?"

He was in his father's face, but Danny, weary, frightened, unsure of himself, looked away from his son to the creature.

"We can't let you live," he said. "We got to put you down all the way. It's what we have to do." He turned then to Bo and Jacob as if for some signal that they agreed, and Jacob couldn't decide whether Danny was the most stupid or the most courageous soul on the planet.

The creature embraced Franklin and whispered something inaudible to him, and Franklin stood aside.

"I'll go with you," said the creature to Danny. "We'll go out into the night where we can know each other better. The night is a song of blood. Darkness lives. It can live within you—each of you—forever, if you'll surrender to it."

The creature moved past them, moved out through the back door, stepping through it as if it did not exist. Jacob glanced at Danny, who gestured that they should follow, so Jacob and Bo were at his shoulder and Ben and Franklin lagged behind. Ben continued to clutch the broken cue as if it were his one contact with reality.

Franklin whispered inaudible lines that might have been a prayer.

Once out in the back lot, puddles of rainwater dotting the asphalt, and one meager light casting everyone half in shadow, Bo told Danny, "I've got the tools we need in my van."

"Wait," said Danny.

"We can't," said Bo. "We got to do this."

The creature was calm. To Jacob, it seemed that the creature held the totality of its being as naturally as a mother holds her infant.

"No, wait," Danny continued. "I want to say something here. I want to give Roy Dale a chance to give himself up. Keep all that's happened in the family. No police reports or nothing like that." He turned to the creature. "If you'll do that, I'll promise to get whatever kind of help you need. That's my sacred promise. Just give yourself up."

Jacob felt fire brand across his chest.

"Danny, my God, this isn't somebody who's robbed a convenience store. He's gotta be destroyed or he'll destroy others."

The creature smiled at Jacob.

"Why do you talk of destruction when you can talk of life?"

At the back door Ben suddenly burst through, still carrying the pool cue.

"Why's everybody afraid to do something?" he said. "I'll take him on. I'm not afraid of him."

And before Danny could head him off, he tore at the creature as if to run him through, but the creature grabbed him by the shoulders and tossed him to the asphalt as if he were a child.

"Goddamn you," said Danny, and Jacob saw something break in his brother's face as he crashed into the creature like a linebacker blitzing a quarterback. In the next instant Jacob and Bo were on the creature, too, bringing it down with Franklin calling out for them to stop.

The creature possessed physical strength that Jacob could not believe.

And even as the three men wrestled it with all their might, the creature managed to struggle to its feet, its face a mask of rage, its fangs gleaming and ready to enter flesh. It easily tossed Bo aside and then hugged ferociously at Jacob and Danny, and Jacob smelled blood and as he battled to hang on to the creature, he heard a voice, one long battle cry and the racing steps of someone charging in a concentrated desire to kill.

The scene ignited like a bomb. A cry of surprise and pain.

Jacob twisted away as he heard something thud into the creature.

He stumbled and fell and then turned to look again. . . .

To see the creature standing alone, a pool cue jammed through its heart and passing out of its back a few inches where blood glistened from the razor-sharp point.

The creature, locked in the trance of night, the trance of darkness, held the shaft of the cue and shuddered for several seconds before it closed its eyes and lowered its head as if it were surrendering to sleep rather than death.

And then mortal time stopped.

Hours later found Jacob locked in the trance of a nearing sunrise like no other.

Found him wanting to believe that when the sun rose he would break free of that trance and feel joy and relief. He had come to Mr. Pancake because he didn't know where else to go. After he and Bo had loaded Roy Dale's body in Bo's van, they had taken it to the snakehole and buried it there.

"I'll get new roses later," Bo had commented, and the words had seemed unreal to Jacob. Another Tracker had gone down. Talk of roses made no sense. Except in this new and very dark world he was a part of. Jacob had gone home to clean up. Had said good-bye to Bo. Danny had left the back lot of the Hollow Log Lounge to try to find Ben, who had raced away on his cycle after the bloody incident.

Franklin had disappeared.

At home Jacob had not been able to sleep. So he had sought out humanity in any form, knowing, most of all, that he wanted to hear Bo say that it was over. The Tracker nightmare had ended with the destruction of Roy Dale. No more blood on his hands and blood in his thoughts.

As a light fell, Jacob sipped at his hot coffee and willed himself to think about something pleasant.

Somewhere in the wilderness of exhaustion and shock following the death and burial of Roy Dale, he had promised himself one thing: he would tell Brianna that he loved her. He knew it was wrong to desire her—a blood sin—but he couldn't keep his feelings to himself any longer.

He was wrestling with the difficulty of that promise when Bo joined him.

"We did it, friend," he said. "Jakey boy, the Trackers are free."

Bo looked like a man resurrected from the worst kind of death. But Jacob was cheered by the man's sentiment and wanted to believe it as he had never wanted to believe anything else in his life. Still, there was one point that had lodged like a thorn in his thoughts.

"What about Franklin?" he said. "How could he have been with Roy Dale like that and not become a vampire, too?"

"Who gives a shit how? We know that Franklin's been up and about during the day. We saw him come into the Hollow Log on his own—nobody invited him in. All we know about vampires says he ain't one. So stick that worry where the sun don't shine and let's celebrate. At least have some fresh coffee."

Jacob forced a smile. Yeah, Bo was right.

The long night of the Tracker curse was over.

Minutes later, Danny joined their quiet celebration.

"You find Ben?" said Jacob.

"No, but I will. I'll try as best I can to explain things, and y'all may need to help me. I think he'll come back around. I think he will."

The threesome talked over coffee of the end of things. They were too tired and still too held in the grip of disbelief to be cheerful. They wanted to believe that their lives could go on with some semblance of reason and sanity. Three members of the Tracker family had gone down. Their fate had to remain unknown to the world. On that they agreed. And when they had finished sealing their bond of secrecy, they fell silent.

Nighthawks waiting for a better dawn.

Chapter Nine

In Memory of Darkness

The three red roses, fresh from the only florist in Soldier's Crossing, brought color to an otherwise gray, raw morning, one sunless and gloomy and unpromising. Bo placed the roses on the snakehole mound, and to Jacob, it appeared that he was about to say something as he did—final words of some kind. God rest the souls of these Tracker men or some such sentiment. But instead the man merely cleared his throat, glanced at Jacob and forced a smile.

"Maybe we can start gettin' us some sleep now," he said, his voice even more filled with sand and grit than usual. His face looked as if it had been punched and battered like a boxer in the twilight of his career. He moved stiffly and tentatively as if fear continued to reside in his bones.

"I want to believe we can," said Jacob. "I really, with all my heart, want to believe it's over."

"We got the three of 'em. We stopped it."

"Jesus, Bo, I just want to be absolutely certain. I still wonder about Franklin, and I wonder what's back there at Sweet Gum—what's in those walls that started all this in the first place."

Bo wet his lips to respond. He was hunkered down and appeared to list to one side as if he might faint. Jacob guessed that his mind was too exhausted to think it all through clearly and yet he was determined to try.

"Franklin doesn't show the signs," he said. "And whatever's at Sweet Gum, it ain't fixin' to go nowhere or it would have years ago. Maybe it ain't like a regular vampire—hell, I don't know. Leave it be. Or maybe the best thing would be to burn the place down, you know. That could be best. The Tracker family ought to consider it."

Jacob agreed.

But it would need to be hashed over another day, for he had other plans for this one. While Bo was intent upon getting lots of sleep and then getting very drunk, Jacob planned to rest until late afternoon and then pick up Brianna and Em to take in a carnival at the mall. She had asked him earlier at Mr. Pancake if he would be interested in going with them and a definite "yes" had leaped from his throat.

And yet Jacob needed more closure on the events of the night before.

"What about Ben? You think he's going to be all right? I mean, he's out there somewhere and he assumes he's a murderer. We didn't get a chance to explain things before he roared away."

Bo shook his head. "He's young. If he wudn't so bitchin' wild, a body could help him. Danny's tried, you know he has. He'll come around is what I'm thinkin'. He'll turn hisself in, and when he does, Danny can tell him the truth or somethin' like the truth. Don't worry about him."

"I suppose you're right. So I guess this is it. This grave is our secret. We've buried the truth. I just wish I could blank out the memory of it, you know, the things we did. My God."

Bo got to his feet and put a reassuring hand on Jacob's shoulder.

"We gave 'em the best burial we could. We did what we had to. Bein' here is what we're doin' in memory of darkness and, God willin', it's a darkness passed on into the earth where it'll stay. Far as our own memories of it, they're what we got to live with. We ain't cold-blooded killers. Nothin's gone make me believe that."

"You're saying we *can* move on?"

"I am. I truly am. And I'm standin' by my offer if you've a mind to become a workin' man again. Now, I ain't talkin' just about being a dishwasher or a cook or a busboy. I need a shift manager and one day soon I'll need somebody to take over the whole shebang. We can talk money any day you're ready. You think about it."

"I have. Mr. Pancake would be a pretty good place to work. Better than Jimmie Jack's probably."

Bo squinted at him and grinned. Jacob didn't know what was on the way. "You think you could work all right with Brianna around?"

Jacob flushed. "Sure—I mean . . . she's blood. She's a good waitress."

"That ain't what I mean and you know it."

Bo's smiling face was a sticky trap. "Jesus, is it that obvious?"

Bo chuckled. "If ever I saw a man hot for a woman, it's you for Brianna."

"But damn, she's my niece. Sounds like something

you'd see on *Jerry Springer.* I just can't help myself. I'm serious."

"Hey, you don't have to tell Bo Smith 'bout desirin' a beautiful woman. I've been there many a time." He hesitated as if he had more to say. Then he stopped, grinned and shook his head. "I'm fall-down tired," he said. "Let's beat it back to town."

"I'm with you," said Jacob.

And so they gathered themselves and slowly left the snakehole.

And neither man knew that they were being watched.

Jacob bought a single red rose for Brianna and Em.

And won a kiss on the cheek from each for doing so.

"Just had roses on my mind," he offered as an explanation.

It was the richest, warmest of fantasies for Jacob: nestled with Brianna and Em in the front seat of his pickup headed for the mall. He could imagine them as a family on this outing, enjoying each other's company, the scene glazed with talk and laughter on a metaphorical road that could only be called "forever" or "happily ever after."

Em chattered on about a bracelet of colored glass Jacob's mother had given her, something old but not an antique and not valuable except for the priceless connection created when one blood relative offers any kind of gift to another. Jacob played along, acting as if the bracelet were made of sapphires or rare blue diamonds. Delicate lines of concern around her mouth, Brianna interrupted them.

"I've heard that there was trouble at the Hollow

Log last night and that Ben was in the middle of it."

"Some. Yeah. Everything's OK. Don't worry about Ben."

"But I do. And I'm also worried about Jessie."

"Jessie? What about her? What's wrong?"

"Maybe nothing. I called her to see if she and Jeremy wanted to join us for the carnival and, I don't know, she sounded nervous and out of sorts. Mentioned something about Roy Dale. He's likely the cause of whatever's bothering her. Anyway, she said maybe she'd see us at the mall. Has there been any word on where Roy Dale is?"

Jacob shook his head. "Well, Roy Dale's kind of a mystery." And that was all he said. He made sure he didn't meet her eyes. It was best, he reasoned, not to be more specific. Bo was probably right—let the town gossip carry the narrative.

The truth would have to wait.

And Jacob was only too willing to put off talk of any kind regarding the missing Tracker men, for he was rolling along with the two people he loved most on the planet. Why entertain dark thoughts when such precious creatures were near? He was going to enjoy every moment with them. No ghosts of conscience were going to spoil this.

But they were trying—the ghosts, that is. Or one haunting notion at least. By degrees, Jacob was beginning to draw an uncomfortable parallel between his love and passionate desire for his niece, Brianna, and the Tracker vampire curse. It was a stretch—yes, he realized that, but it got its hooks in him and he was starting to feel helpless to fight it. It seemed to him that the world, were it aware, would see his illicit love as perverse or sinful—as something gone wrong in the blood. And wasn't that akin to vampirism? Something gone wrong in the blood? In the case of the Trackers, vampires feeding off family blood, desiring it, consuming it and turning other Trackers into vampires.

Was he, too, a vampire of sorts to want Brianna's love?

Wasn't his desire an unforgivable trespass?

The dark and savagely guilty thoughts faded, however, as he pulled into the parking lot of the mall and Brianna and Em belted out a golden oldie by the Judds—"Mama, He's Crazy"—and Jacob slipped into the warmth of their mother-daughter duet, miles from the cold earth where vampires slept, dreaming dreamless dreams.

The food court of the Soldier's Crossing mall was alive with the upbeat thrumming of calliope music and the swirl of a real, honest-to-goodness, old-fashioned merry-go-round replete with painted horses jerking against invisible reins, which did not hold them, and snarling their paralyzed snarls. The throng of visitors moved in a slow, aimless procession, stopping at various booths for food and games and signing up for drawings and prizes. The public-address system offered a garbled play-by-play of events directing folks first here and then there and promising ever more enthralling developments as the late afternoon evolved into twilight, and the dominant mood was one of release.

Jacob welcomed it.

He hoisted Em onto his shoulders and smiled at her giggling, and just when he thought the moment could not possibly get any better, Brianna reached out and took his hand and squeezed it, and the three of them waded into the crowd, into the aroma of hot grease and the swirl of music, and approached the never-ending image of the merry-go-round. Brianna continued to hold his hand, and Jacob could not resist falling into the fantasy once again of them as a family: husband, wife, child; father, mother, daughter awash in the blood of caring and closeness and love.

Brianna was easily the most beautiful woman there. Jacob longed to tell her so and might have had Em not suddenly exclaimed, "I want to buy something right here!"

"Oh, Em, those are just trinkets," said Brianna. "Wouldn't you like to find something nicer?"

Then it started.

It was the part of being out in public with Brianna and Em that he disliked the most—all the stares, the gapes, the whispers and even the bold and curiosity-generated questions as he lifted the tiny girl to the floor in front of a stand selling cheap jewelry: earrings, bracelets and necklaces. It made Jacob want to lash out at the gawkers or, worse, to smash in their faces, obliterating their frowns. *Stop looking that way! She's not a freak, Goddamn it! She's my child!*

Except, of course, that she would always be seen as a freak.

And she wasn't really his.

"I want this one. Mama, look. See how pretty this one is!"

When Jacob saw what she had selected, he felt the odd light-headedness one sometimes experiences as a striking coincidence occurs: Em had chosen a crucifix.

Brianna lifted the small cross from the bin of trinkets. It was covered in pieces of blue glass and was attached to a necklace made of white glass beads. It was cheap, but it twinkled and Em was enchanted by it.

"Oh, Em," said Brianna. "Honey, are you sure this is what you want?"

"I think it's cool," Jacob heard himself say. "Here, let me get it for her."

Em was delighted; Brianna chose not to protest, and as Jacob slipped the crucifix around the little girl's neck, he experienced a sensation of calm and serenity. He felt suddenly that she was protected— *protected from what?* he asked himself.

From what might be still out there.

The dark thought came and went with the same rhythm of the ebb and flow of the crowd. Jacob was determined not to dwell on the horror he and Bo and Danny had confronted. Move on. That's what he was intent upon. Enjoy the company of these two angels. Yes. The blood of love, not the blood of violence and a living death.

Over the course of the next half hour, the threesome sampled everything except the merry-go-round (for they were saving it for last) before ending up at a table in the food court for cold drinks and slices of pizza and cups of ice cream. Em adored her crucifix, and Jacob adored her, and, as well, he could not keep from occasionally glancing at Brianna with a different kind of adoration. Twice she met his glance and he blushed. She knew. She had to know. His feelings were out there, evident and as difficult to hide as a third arm.

Brianna's sister, Sharelle, stopped by their table for a few moments. Jacob found himself smiling at how much Sharelle seemed a lost child from a fairy tale, and with her long dress and beads, she could have been an extra in a movie about the 1960s—she was her own mixed bag of innocence and intelligence and hope, a creature far removed from the darkness that had befallen several of her Tracker relatives. And yet, accompanying her were her Goth friends, Kitt and Cardinal, attired in black clothing, sporting exquisitely pale skin—playing at all things vampiric. Seeing them angered Jacob.

He wanted to get in their faces and shout at their naïveté.

Vampires are not a fucking game. They're real. I know what they're like.

But he let it pass. The threat, or so it appeared, had been buried.

The earth held Tracker darkness. And there it would stay.

"I wanna ride the ponies!"

It was Em who ushered him away to further release.

"Me too," he exclaimed.

"You're not leaving Mom out of this," Brianna added.

And so at the next opportunity they rode off together, Em was seated on the same horse with Jacob, clutching the pole and insisting that she wasn't afraid, Brianna rode next to them on the matching horse, looking beautiful and desirable. The music thrummed gaily and the world rose and fell around him in a gentle rhythm.

"See us? See us? There we are!"

Em was ecstatic, pointing at the slanted mirrors above them; they waved at their reflections and Jacob squeezed the little girl lovingly. She giggled as if life could not possibly get any better.

Maybe it can't, thought Jacob.

The movement, the music—it was the stuff of some kind of dream vision, an endless journey through an enchanted land that could not possibly contain snakeholes and shape-changing creatures of the night. Awash in the good vibrations of the moment, Jacob stole a glance at Brianna. She was looking at him, smiling, and though he reasoned that it was only wishful thinking, he believed he saw love in her eyes.

For me?

He returned her smile and felt his heart fill.

Em chortled.

And the family of Jacob's imagination circled out of the swing of reality.

Until he saw Franklin.

Clad in a long, dark coat, he was standing between two of the horses, one of them being ridden by Sharelle, the other by the Goth girl. Jacob felt a chill spread up his back, and he wasn't certain why. He suddenly didn't want Franklin on the merry-go-round.

He didn't belong.

Then Jacob looked away. He hugged Em and wished that he could hug Brianna as well.

But he couldn't keep from glancing again at the figure of Franklin, at his pale hand draped onto the head of one of the horses. And at one thing more: the mirrors above him.

Void of any reflection except that of Sharelle and the Goth girl.

When the merry-go-round eased to a halt, he excused himself, saying that he needed to go to the men's room. He desperately felt that he had to locate Franklin and . . . and what? He wasn't certain.

To see for myself.

The lack of reflection, he reminded himself, could

have been a trick of his imagination. Or it could have been that he had viewed the mirrors from the wrong angle. As he pushed his way through the crowd searching for the stark figure of Franklin, he could make out the public-address system drowning in static. The merry-go-round started up again, and Jacob slowed his search. He stopped and felt all alone in the crowd.

A voice broke through on the public address.

"Know what's out there?" it said.

Jacob panicked.

"Brianna! Em!"

He began to backtrack, fighting his way through people, shoving, drawing angry looks and indignant whispers from them. Harried seconds passed as he scanned the crowd until, with a flood of relief, he saw Brianna. But her pretty face was frowning.

Em was not beside her.

Jacob began to run toward her.

And that's when he heard, above the murmur of the crowd, the scream of a little girl.

Brianna's trailer was quiet and, even better, it felt safe to Jacob.

The scream had not come from Em. She had merely strayed for a moment from Brianna, and by the time Jacob came onto the scene, they had been reunited. The screaming had erupted when a girl had her cup of ice cream stolen by two boys—a mother had stormed into the mini-chaos and the matter was quickly resolved.

Jacob had been relieved to get away from the mall.

Too much noise, too much eagerly meaningless movement.

And then the presence of Franklin.

"I'm putting Em to bed, but you're welcome to stay and watch television if you'd like."

Brianna's eyes washed over him. He wanted to surrender himself, and yet what could such a move amount to? It would be inappropriate, he reasoned, and might lead to her shutting the door on their closeness.

"Yes, I'd like that if you don't mind. If it's OK."

Her smile warmed even more. Then Em was rushing into his arms to say good night.

"Thank you for taking us to the mall," she said, a sincere line, but one that Brianna had probably suggested. "Thank you for my cross."

He held her. It was like hugging a pillow.

"You're welcome, my dear," he said. "Now you wear that cross all the time because . . . I think it looks real pretty on you."

"I will."

She kissed his cheek; warmth flooded him and he wanted desperately for no harm ever to come to her. She flitted away like a fairy. He could almost imagine wings sprouting from her tiny body.

My God, she moves me.

When Brianna returned from bedding Em down, she made popcorn and they settled on the couch for small talk and an old movie, and Jacob fought the impulse to tell her, right then and there, how he felt about her—how he would do anything for her and Em. The movie proved to be boring or at least not interesting enough to draw their attention away from each other. Jacob could tell that Brianna had something on her mind.

"It's Spence." she said after Jacob prodded. "I wish he didn't have visitation rights. Every time he comes, it's upsetting for Em. I don't want him in her life. He's like some kind of shadow always sort of lurking near, and I don't trust him."

"Do you think he might hurt her?"

"No, not really. I can't say that. I just . . . I don't know. I'm sorry. I shouldn't be dumping my problems in your lap."

He looked at her. In that moment he knew what a trapeze artist must feel like as he stands on the cusp of swinging out into space to somersault and then, trusting his catcher, to reach out to be snagged and swung safely home. Home was in Brianna's eyes and in her beautiful face.

"I'd like to help," he said. "I'm not sure what I can do. I know that Danny's aware of Spence being back in town and how he can turn mean, and he'll be here for you. But so will I. I want to be. Please know that."

He could hear the quaver in his voice. Could hear blood pounding in his ears.

Brianna leaned forward and kissed him on the corner of his mouth and thanked him and nestled close. He put his arm around her and wondered about boundaries. He was losing his way. Losing his emotional balance.

Her head on his shoulder, they sat and talked about Em and then talked about nothing in particular. Together, they sank warmly into the night until Jacob could hear relaxed breathing and the heat of her body, on the edge of sleep, annealing his soul.

It was bliss.

But he couldn't allow it to last. He roused her and told her he had to go, and he imagined that she didn't want him to. At the door they embraced, and she whispered to him, "I'm glad you're in my life."

"Me too," he said.

He stepped out into the night and felt that every star in the heavens was watching him and knew what turn his life would take next—into the light or back into darkness.

But, if they knew, it was a secret he felt they would not share.

Chapter Ten

Veil of Dusk

She planned to kill her son when he woke from his nap.

It was the only humane thing to do, she reasoned.

Jessie Tracker loaded the small-caliber revolver Roy Dale had given her over a year ago when there had been a spate of break-ins at the trailer court. "For protection for you and the boy," he had told her, and he had shown her how to handle it. The irony that the gun came from Roy Dale was not lost on her; in fact, the attendant strangeness fit everything in her life lately, the dark chariot of her existence racing out of control. With no meaning.

And she was grasping so desperately for meaning.

Worst of all, she was haunted.

And the ghost was in her mind.

She couldn't exorcise it, and so . . . and so she was waiting for her son, Jeremy, to wake up. The only question was whether to fix him some supper before she did what had to be done. The boy liked potpies. Any kind of potpies.

You could put a fucking dead rat in a pie and that kid would eat it, she mused.

But she loved him.

And, no, he wasn't Roy Dale's child, and though her husband had always been suspicious of the matter—mainly because Jeremy had blond hair and no other Tracker male did—he never pressed her on it. Never accused her. Perhaps because he'd done his share of running around. Tit for tat or whatever.

And yet, hadn't Roy Dale gotten some kind of revenge? He had changed into some kind of creature—Jacob had witnessed what he was like and so had Calvin and others—and he had returned from wherever he'd gone to scare the shit out of her and her boy. Scared Jeremy into speaking. Made blood run down her walls. And now she thought she knew what Roy Dale wanted: he wanted to take from her what she loved most.

Jeremy.

The realization had come to her at work the previous evening. What struck her as curious was that she hadn't planned to go to work, having decided, instead, that she would take Jeremy to the carnival at the mall, where they would join Brianna and Em and have a good time and start moving on with their lives. She took Jeremy to work with her, and it actually felt good to be sloshing pitchers of beer and snarling back at the snarling fox and flirting with all the male customers and enjoying Calvin's barely concealed desire.

Except that Calvin was also worried about her.

About Roy Dale, she guessed. He knew that Danny and Jacob and Bo had escorted her husband from the lounge the night before—to set him straight, maybe to rough him up, Calvin wasn't certain. He just hoped Roy Dale wouldn't show up. And so did Jessie.

In a way.

That was the strange part: throughout her shift, she kept thinking about him, about how weirdly attractive he had become to her, a sexiness in him she hadn't seen before. Part of her wanted to get closer to it; part of her was scared of it. She was scared she might not be able to resist him.

What really scared her was the possibility he would grab Jeremy and never return him.

Her son. Her love.

Her reason for living.

She had no idea that Roy Dale was buried in the snakehole.

Once home from her shift, she tried to sleep but couldn't. Jeremy had slept some, played some, and had hovered near her. He seemed fearful that she might run out the door and leave him and never come back. She held him most of the day, and then when she put him down for his nap, dark realities began to sink in.

First, that she was alone. Her parents had passed away. Her only brother was in jail in Texas. The man who had fathered Jeremy—who knew exactly where in the hell he was? She didn't, in fact, care to know. He was probably dust in the wind blowing across Kansas or maybe the Land of Oz—she'd heard he'd kept on the move. Calvin Tracker loved her, yes, but he could never offer her enough. And she didn't believe he could protect her. Or that any of the other Trackers could, either.

The second reality was even darker.

She would sooner kill her son than let someone— or some *thing*—take him from her. She would rather

die than face life without her son. It was as simple
as that.

Revolver in hand, Jessie went to the kitchen and
fingered open a slit in the blinds: the dusk was
ghastly. The sky was a brownish pall shot through
with menacing swirls of gray and black. A chilly wind
stirred, scraping up leftover leaves from fall. It was
as if the dusk were a veil covering the face of some
strange force out there.

She sensed that her trailer was being watched.

Whatever was out there was waiting for the right
moment.

Jessie's fingers trembled. She choked back a sudden threat of tears. It was time to do what had to
be done. She closed the blinds on the dusk. She
jammed the barrel of the revolver down the front
of her jeans. She liked the feel of it there. She liked
how decisive it made her feel. Methodically she went
about the trailer and switched off every light. She
waited. It irritated her that Jeremy was sleeping so
long.

So she went to wake him.

When she lifted him from his bed, she could feel
his body trembling. Gossamer threads of sleepiness
held him. She pulled him free and he continued to
tremble. She patted his back and he whispered to
her, "Mama, Mama . . . what's out there, Mama?"

"It's gone be OK, baby. We're not gone stick
around to see."

"What's out there, Mama?"

"Sh-h-h, darlin'. Don't talk about it. You hungry?
You want a potpie?"

The boy shook his head. She held him so that she
could look him squarely in the face. She smiled to
keep herself from crying.

"All right, then," she said. "Let's go in the bathroom so we don't make a big mess."

"No bath, Mama. No bath, please."

"We're not takin' a bath, baby. No, not that."

She took him into the bathroom and closed the door and locked it. The wind gusted; windows and doors rattled. The small room quite suddenly was warm, and an unfamiliar and unpleasant odor wafted out of the vents. Something rotting.

She sensed that someone had come into the trailer. And so did Jeremy.

"Who's out there, Mama?"

Jessie, shaking so badly she had to set her boy on the edge of the bathtub, listened for footsteps, but she could not hear any. Yet, whisper soft and shadow silent, someone came closer. Someone was standing just beyond the locked door.

"Get down in the bathtub, honey."

The boy giggled. "With my clothes on?"

She nodded, fighting back tears. She helped him down into the tub. Then she took the revolver out of her jeans.

"I can't let nobody take you from me, baby. Don't want to live without you. You're my precious baby, you see?"

The boy studied the revolver as she gripped it, her trigger finger twitching.

"Don't aim it at somebody, Mama. Remember, you said don't aim a gun at somebody."

"I know, baby, but this is different. This is what I have to do. It's OK this time."

She raised the revolver and, momentarily, instead of pointing it at her son, she angled it so that she was staring down its barrel. She was tempted to put it in her mouth—it seemed crazy to her, but the temptation was strong. Then she thought of Josh Tracker. And she thought that possibly she understood why he had destroyed himself. *It's what he had to do.* It made sense to her, and she didn't care whether it made sense to anyone else. But she knew, of course, that if she allowed herself to be seduced by that barrel into slipping it between her lips and pulling the trigger, Jeremy would be at the mercy of . . .

. . . of whoever was outside the door.

She turned the revolver and aimed it at Jeremy's head.

He looked more puzzled than frightened.

"What's out there, Mama?"

She heard her boy's voice in her head where it mixed with other voices—Roy Dale's and other voices—darkly seductive voices telling her what she must do. She fought through a welling of tears; she fought through the trembling of her body.

She didn't know what was out there.

But she was determined to be calm. She forced herself to concentrate on a single image in her mind: the snarling fox above the bar at the Hollow Log Lounge. Yes, she began to concentrate.

"Mama?" said the boy.

She adjusted the position of the revolver.

Someone continued standing outside the door. And Jessie wished she had the courage to throw it open and see who was there. She shook her head as if to shake off every other thought except squeezing the trigger.

She saw the fox snarling and she snarled back.

The wind suddenly howled a long, high-pitched, mournful note over the roof of the trailer, muffling the roar of a single gunshot.

* * *

Calvin Tracker did not like the looks of the sky.

Evening was coming on as he stepped from his tiny silver-colored classic Airstream trailer tied down directly behind the Hollow Log Lounge. His living quarters satisfied him, serving as a *temenos*—a safe place—from dark memories that often rose from the past, memories of 'Nam and of the day, thirty years ago, he killed an enemy soldier and spent several minutes kneeling over the young, delicately small man he had shot in the throat. Stunned that he had snuffed out another human being's life, Calvin had studied the man's face and could not help wondering about the man's family—did he have a wife? Was he from a small town? Did he have brothers and sisters?

Calvin knew that other soldiers had taken souvenirs from their first kill: a scalp, a finger, an ear, but he found that he couldn't do that. Instead, he had dabbed one finger in the man's bloody neck wound and he had smeared the blood on his dog tags. Because the war was about blood. He was fighting for blood, he had told himself. Fighting for family. Fighting for the Trackers back a million miles away in Soldier's Crossing, Alabama.

Those dog tags, still hanging in his trailer, ever so faintly held that bloodstain.

So that Calvin would not forget. Blood and wounds.

But now he could not forget shooting another man. Images of the shotgun blasts into the chest of Roy Dale Tracker would not dim. Would not die. How, he wondered, had Roy Dale survived the point-blank shots? They should have killed him; they would have killed any other man. What had they done with

Roy Dale? Danny and Jacob and Bo—what happened
in the back parking lot? He could not find out. All
he knew for certain was that he was scared, frightened to death. More frightened even than he had
ever been in 'Nam.

And he knew one thing more: he was going to
take Jessie and Jeremy away.

If she would have him, he would encourage her
to divorce Roy Dale and he would sell the Hollow
Log Lounge and they would leave Soldier's Crossing
and start a new life somewhere else. Florida maybe.
Or somewhere out West. Montana or Idaho. It didn't
matter as long as he could be with Jessie and Jeremy.
He would take care of them. He would love them
like blood. More than blood.

Tonight when Jessie came to work, he would tell
her what he had in mind.

He would have a life after so many years of living
alone, a living death.

Glancing once more at the ominous sky, Calvin
went inside and opened up the lounge. Fran, his
other barmaid, slipped in through the front door.

"Some guy's waiting to talk to you," she said, and
went about setting up for business while Calvin
walked to the door and gestured for the stranger to
enter.

"You need to see me?"

Myron Florence looked like a life-sized Raggedy
Andy doll, only with curly hair and fewer freckles.
He was round shouldered and his pink jowls glistened and his lips were too large, but he had sad,
pretty eyes and a warm handshake.

"I live with Franklin Tracker," he said, "and I'm
trying to find him. I've heard he's been coming in

here lately. You wouldn't know where he is, would you?"

Calvin propped his elbows on the bar as Florence squished onto a stool.

"Not a clue," he said. "You thinking he met with, you know, foul play?"

"I don't know what to think."

"Tell you what," Calvin suggested. "My other barmaid should be checking in for work anytime now. You could ask her. She's married to Roy Dale Tracker."

"Oh, that would be Jessie. I've never met her, but Franklin has spoken of her."

Calvin offered to buy the man a beer, and when he declined to accept, a silence closed around them until Calvin broke it.

"Seemed odd, you know, Franklin all of a sudden startin' to show up here. And with Roy Dale—I mean, what I've seen before, they didn't get along much. But now it's like they're buddies."

Myron studied his hands a moment before beginning his response. It was the tone and the narrative voice Calvin, as a bartender, had heard hundreds of times before, its rhythm halting until a certain boundary had been crossed and the confession poured through.

"Something's happened to Franklin," said Florence. "He's . . . he's changed. My God, he never sleeps. Never eats, it seems. Personal habits . . . I mean, he's like a different person. I still care for him. He's a decent, intelligent, warm and gentle man . . . or, at least, he was. Now, the very few moments I see him or talk with him, he's distant."

The man's face reached out to Calvin for sympathy, compassion, for *something* Calvin wasn't at all sure he could return. More so, he suddenly stopped listening to the man's story and excused himself to use the phone. He called Jessie's trailer.

On the fourth ring he hung up and bolted from the lounge, fear surging up from the pit of his stomach. Two words flashed like neon across his thoughts doubling the terror of the moment. Two words.

Too late.

The front door to Jessie's trailer was open.

It was dark throughout.

"Jessie?" he called out.

Then he sensed it: someone other than Jessie and Jeremy had just been there. He knew it. He continued calling out her name and searching room to room until he came to the locked door of the bathroom. When he slammed his shoulder into it, it popped open. He switched on the light.

The sight of all the blood froze him in the doorway.

The boy was sitting near the bloodied body of his mother.

He wasn't crying. His eyes did not blink.

It appeared that he was too deep in shock to utter a single word.

He merely picked up a revolver from the floor and handed it to Calvin.

Jacob had been sitting in a booth at Mr. Pancake since dusk.

Several hours had passed since then, with Jacob having eaten the patty melt special and a piece of chocolate pie and having consumed numerous cups of coffee. He was glad to see the weird dusk fade and gather into a more normal darkness, a star-laden darkness. The wind had died down and the restaurant, midevening, was not busy. It was just the way Jacob liked it.

On a yellow legal notepad he had written a song title: "The End of Just Begun." It was part of his ritualistic process for writing a new lyric: he had to have a title that grabbed him first; then the song would come. But this time, only the title had materialized. Nothing more. He stared down at the title pleased at how the words captured what he had in mind, and yet he didn't know how to express the full story. How to find a tune, how to generate the necessary words to narrate his love for Brianna.

"The End of Just Begun."

How do you express that kind of love? Love for a blood relative—not just the warm, accepting love of one family member for another. Not just love according to one's bond. But, rather, passionate, romantic love. The potential lyrics would sound forbidden somehow. Maybe even perverse. Nashville wasn't ready for that kind of song. And Jacob admitted to himself that maybe he wasn't ready to write it. At least, not for other eyes to view or other ears to hear. Maybe it would just hurt too much to get the words out.

My God, I love her.

He had the Tracker family Bible open at his left elbow. He had recorded in it the name of Roy Dale, hoping that would be the final name until natural causes claimed others. It felt good to have the old, sacred book near him. It spoke of blood. It spoke of the potential holiness of family. And he continued to believe that the book possessed some kind of power—he had seen that power evidenced. His mother believed in it; so did Bo.

The evening waitress assigned to booths was a fetching young woman named Cissy, a touch overweight but with a pretty face and a creamy complexion that many women would die for. She was friendly and flirtatious, especially when Jacob showed up, and he was aware of her interest and tried not to be rude to her. He did, however, smile to himself at how she would, no doubt, be shocked to know that he was hot for his niece, her coworker. Or could it be that others already knew? Bo had certainly noticed.

"The End of Just Begun."

If he ever got around to writing it, that song would be a real tearjerker. He fantasized, momentarily, about sitting with his guitar in the presence of Brianna and singing it to her. How would she react? Hadn't he seen in her manner, her words—her *eyes*—something of his love being reciprocated?

Only my imagination?

He chastised himself for his projections. They were dead ends.

"Have you seen Bo or Danny?" he asked Cissy when she swung around on her frequent trips to see whether he needed more coffee.

"Bo is on a killer drunk, a coma drunk, is what I hear. Danny, yeah, he's been in. He was asking about his boy." She smiled her best smile and pressed him about what he was writing. He told her it was a song and then told her she would be the first to hear it when he finished. She hugged the lie to her ample breasts and waltzed away.

Now why did I say that?

He thought about Danny trying to find Ben and about how scared shitless Ben must be, hiding from his own shadow, on the run believing he'd committed murder or manslaughter at the least. What color is Ben's fear? he asked himself. The answer seemed easy: it was the color of blood.

Jacob glanced out into the night. In the plate of glass he could see his reflection, his long, thin, haggard face, his sunken eyes—*damn I look like hell*—and wondered how he could ever hope for someone as beautiful as Brianna to be attracted to him—even if she weren't his niece. Still staring at his reflection, he raised one hand and shaped a finger-thumb gun with it and playfully fired.

"Bang, bang, you're dead!"

Jacob wheeled around.

Franklin Tracker stood smiling down at him. Jacob tried not to seem unsettled.

"Oh man, I guess I didn't see you or hear you walk up."

"May I join you?" asked Franklin.

"If you like . . . sure. I'll warn you: the coffee's lethal tonight."

Jacob kept his eyes on Franklin as he slipped into the booth, his long, dark coat soiled and dusty. But what Jacob wanted to do was catch, out of the corner of his eye, another glimpse of the plate glass to see what was reflected there. If anything.

"I've stopped drinking coffee," said Franklin. "I can keep going fine without it."

And Jacob suddenly knew that his blood relative had sought him out. It was not an occasion for small talk. No pleasantries about family, etc. Too much darkness had passed. The horrible episode at the Hollow Log Lounge—there was no way to erase it. Franklin's relationship with Roy Dale, the closeness that had evolved so rapidly, and Jacob's suspicions about Franklin despite Bo's pronouncements—the unspoken, perhaps the unsayable, hung there between them like an invisible dagger. Not just a dagger of the mind, but one of the soul.

"We had to do it," said Jacob, and the instant those words escaped his lips, he didn't know where the conversation would lead. He didn't know whether he was inviting trouble, whether he was about to wade into a flowing stream of new horror, wade so far that returning to the stream bank would be too difficult. The tension was there, swirling, capable of pulling one under.

And there was something more.

Franklin Tracker was beautiful.

Like a beautiful, dark fallen angel.

Those thoughts flickered in Jacob's mind as he waited for his cousin to respond. The delicate features, the eyes, the sensuous lips, the long, pale hands—he seemed Christ-like and yet there was as much potential for terror as for gentleness in his gaze.

"I forgive you," said Franklin. "You were like a child who unwittingly destroys a butterfly or a lovely blossom. John Taylor and Douglas were becoming beautiful creatures, whole and powerful—you didn't know what you were doing. But Bo, he's an ugly man who can't understand blood, and what he can't understand, he kills. He's dangerous. Be forewarned. And so is your brother Danny. He believes he's protecting our family, keeping the truth hidden. He's wrong. But in time, he'll join us. And so will you."

The eyes were impossible to stare down. Jacob felt himself resisting the pull of those eyes and the mesmerizing, effeminate tone of Franklin's voice. He was becoming detached from his body like a balloon on a string. And he wanted to ask the one question he already knew the answer to, but he needed to hear that answer from Franklin's lips. He suddenly clenched his fists and forced himself to speak, though the words came out in a soft whisper.

"Are you a vampire?" Even as he asked the question, he could feel his body quivering. It would be obvious to Franklin; no doubt, it would please him. "Are you?" Jacob persisted. "Are you one of the living dead?" It sounded silly and melodramatic, but it *had* to be voiced.

Franklin shook his head as if he pitied Jacob.

"I'm more alive than you are."

Shortness of breath pressed Jacob back in his seat. His mind was protesting, reeling.

"But the signs—all that Bo has told me about vampires—how can you walk around during the day? We thought we had stopped the curse. We thought we had buried it."

"Your little ceremony sickened me. Your roses. I watched you bury Roy Dale, my beautiful brother. I know about your snakehole, where John Taylor and Douglas lay, too. You destroyed them, but you won't be able to destroy every Tracker, Jacob. Josh destroyed himself, but I'll see that others don't." He leaned toward Jacob with compassion and tenderness. "And there's so much you don't know about this new life I have. You see, I've always been different. Society doesn't approve of the likes of me. I've had to create rules for myself. I walk in the beauty of this life, and I walk both day and night."

"Why didn't you stop us? If you're a vampire, if you have powers, why did you stand by and let us take down Roy Dale?"

"Violence is not my way. It's not your way, either, Jacob. And that's why I've come to see you. Because I want you to join your real family. Be on our side.

You're not like the others. Not like Bo and Danny. You're sensitive." He paused to extend a sharp-nailed finger at Jacob's legal pad. "You write songs. You love. And, most of all, you *yearn.*"

Jacob could feel something stirring within: a desire to listen to more of what Franklin had to say; more so, a desire to surrender to a darkness in his blood, to a vibrant Fate filled with unspoken promises. But he fought what was happening. He reached out with his left hand and lay it in the crease of the opened Bible. Franklin merely smiled. Jacob closed his eyes and gritted his teeth.

"No," he said. "I've seen what they became—J.T. and Douglas and Roy Dale and Josh, too: something savage, something inhuman. If that's what you want me to become, I'll fight it. I'll fight you right here. I'm a Tracker. So if Tracker blood is what you're after, try it now."

Fear radiated throughout his body. But he stood up defiantly and readied himself for an attack. One that did not come. Franklin chuckled.

"Sit down, Jacob. People will notice. Don't be foolish."

Jacob glanced around. Cissy had shot a questioning look their way, so he sat down. He hated feeling helpless, hated feeling that he was at the mercy of this creature who was slowly siphoning off all of his resolve.

"I don't want your life," said Jacob. "I don't want other Trackers to have it, either. I'll fight you, and Bo will fight you, and so will Danny and anyone else we can get to join us."

"So unfortunate. You really don't know what this life is like. I'll tell you: it's a strange and wonderful adventure. It's moment-to-moment beauty. It's going home to a place you've never even dreamed of. It's an intimacy you would die for."

"I don't want to die," said Jacob. "I want to live. Live a normal life and love—love my family, love a woman."

"You can have more. Jacob, you can have much more. And you can have it *forever.* I know. Before you destroyed him, my brother gave this life to me as a gift, the most precious gift imaginable. The night I met him at the Hollow Log he took me to Sweet Gum and he held my hand and he undressed me and then he kissed me so tenderly. He kissed me . . . *here.*" When Franklin raised a hand to his throat, Jacob could see a blue vein pulsing across a scar there on the porcelainlike skin, and part of him wanted Franklin to stop talking, but part of him did not. "And then my brother took my blood, and he filled me with eternity. He led me into the walls of Sweet Gum and we walked around in them, and the spirit of the Trackers—our family, our blood—annealed me. Set me free from all my earthly restrictions. Made me totally the creature I'm meant to be. Don't you want that, Jacob? Don't you want to be completely who you're meant to be?"

Jacob looked away. He was shaking his head. He wanted to respond, but his thoughts weren't clear. He closed his eyes, and for a score of seconds he could imagine what having peace of mind would be like. He could imagine himself riding across the road of night on the back of a magnificent dragon. He could imagine his blood singing the most glorious song ever written. He could imagine Brianna and Em there with him.

Then he shook free.

"What do you want?"

"I've told you. Be on our side. Be on the side of blood."

"And if I don't?"

Franklin sighed.

"Jacob, I'm going to finish the work that John Taylor started."

"Meaning, you're going to turn every Tracker into a vampire. What about everyone else close to the family?"

"They are in the way, and they will suffer."

"I don't believe you. I don't believe you'll do it. I'm a Tracker, goddamn it, so do it right here. Take my blood. Change me. I don't believe you will."

Jacob's head was roaring; he could feel his heart hammering in his chest. And it pleased him that Franklin looked, momentarily at least, surprised.

"Patience, Jacob. Patience is everything. When I'm ready, you'll meet your destiny. And if you choose death over life, I'll hunt you down. Without mercy. You see, the end of the Trackers as you know them is at hand. I have a mind of winter."

"I won't join you."

"Very well," said Franklin. He extended a sharp nail and raked it across the pages of the Bible, shredding them. "But you will make a *grave* error," he added, smiling, "if you try to stop me. If you get in the way of blood. The blood of winter is about to flow, Jacob. It started this evening with Jessie."

"Jessie? What happened to her? You filthy bastard, what did you do to her?"

"Nothing. You see, she did it to herself."

Franklin rose from the booth, and Jacob sucked in his breath.

"We put the others down," said Jacob. "We can bring you down, too."

Franklin smiled again; his fangs flashed and his eyes burned. And then, as he began to glide away, he said, "Winter's coming, Jacob. Get ready. I can bring ice, and I can also bring fire."

From a distance then, the vampire wheeled and pointed at Jacob's booth, and the Tracker Bible burst into flames.

Chapter Eleven

Prelude to the Night

"I'd sell my soul for you to be here so you could hold me in your arms. That's the truth, sweetheart. I need you. I need how strong you always was."

Twilight lowering on the day, Danny Tracker drove along like a man with a knife in his heart. He was looking for his son and talking to the ghost of his wife, Bonnie Gayle, and trying to figure out just how in the hell things had gotten so out of control. The night before he had been called in to investigate the apparent suicide of Jessie Tracker. He had received the news from Calvin Tracker, who, for God knows what reason, had left the scene and had called from the Hollow Log Lounge. Claimed he just had to get out of that trailer—away from all the blood. He was seriously distraught, but he also seemed jittery in a suspicious way.

And one thing more: Jessie's son, Jeremy, was missing.

It wasn't shaking down, and Danny was baffled. He had gone to the Hollow Log Lounge the next morning to question Calvin a second time. No, the man wasn't a suspect—not exactly—for all indications were that Jessie had taken her own life. The real hell of it was that evidently the boy had been in her presence when she shot herself. Had he simply run off and was hiding? The trailer court had been searched. Neighbors, including Brianna, had been questioned. Nothing turned up. So it looked pretty clear as though someone had snatched the boy. Roy Dale was the immediate suspect in that regard—except that Danny *knew* Roy Dale had been no part of it. A midnight drive out to the snakehole to make sure it hadn't been disturbed assured him of that fact. Roy Dale hadn't returned from the grave.

More unsettling shit had come to him from Jacob.

About Franklin Tracker.

Danny didn't want to believe what Jacob had told him.

Because it meant that the Tracker nightmare wasn't over.

And it would become increasingly more difficult to keep it all in the family.

And that wasn't all.

"Ben's still gone, Bonnie. He thinks he took a man's life, but he's wrong. It wasn't no man. I've got to find him. He's crazy wild, but he's our boy, and I got to find him and straighten this all out. But, God, sweetheart, I don't feel strong enough to."

He hated how empty his house had become. Several times he had found himself sitting on Ben's unmade bed thinking about all the arguments they had had and forcing himself instead to think of better moments: coaching Ben's baseball team when the boy was nine, and taking him fishing on Moon Lake—the three-pound bass Ben had caught and

Danny had mounted for a birthday present. But those better moments seemed to have occurred in another lifetime.

And to some other father and son.

What lately had generated so much anger in Ben? Something in the blood?

He drove on and listened. And imagined his wife's soothing voice. Imagined her touch on his arm. Imagined the warmth of her body near. Imagined her strength pouring into him like a transfusion.

The sky continued to darken behind him as he drove east, passing to his right the turn-in for his uncle Winston's place, which he shared with his daughters, Mattie Lee and Janie, and then, a quarter of a mile farther on and to his left, the turn-in for Uncle Douglas and Aunt Mollie's and the now out-of-business Good Neighbor Dairy. The image of Douglas dissolving into a skeletal corpse flashed through his thoughts. He winced and swallowed back the memory of being in that dairy truck, and he forced himself to think of Aunt Mollie and to make a mental note to stop by to check on her on his way back to Soldier's Crossing. Would her faith be enough for her these days and in the days to come? She had lost a husband and a son and was not even aware of it. And her other son—no, it seemed beyond the limits of what could possibly happen to one family.

"The world's one damn cruel place, Bonnie," he whispered.

He listened for her to remind him that for every ounce of cruelty it offered the possibility of a pound of love. He imagined that he heard those words, and then he braced himself to turn left into a sea of bashed-in and rusting cars and trucks, some festooned with kudzu vines and to be met by mushrooming clouds of dust and an eager chorus of barking dogs.

Welcome to Uncle Warren "Brother Man" Tracker's Auto Salvage.

Warren had built a one-story clapboard house, white and modest and almost homey, on a rise over-looking his salvage operation. Danny pulled his pa-trol car up to it and got out and was instantly surrounded by a dozen or more dogs ranging from small to large, from mutt to what appeared to be bor-derline pure breeds—one a chocolate Lab, another a German shepherd. Over the barking he heard a shout that sounded much like a gigantic yellow jacket's buzz. He wheeled around and caught sight of Royal, Warren's son, standing atop the dented-in roof of a wrecked and rusting Ford Taurus.

"Hey, Royal," he called out.

The young man shouted at the dogs a second time and they began to back off their barking, shifting gears from tongue to throat. Though it was a mild winter day, Royal Tracker was wearing a heavy coat and a stocking cap and gloves. His face was red from shouting, and he did not seem inclined to come down from his perch to talk, so Danny tried to be friendly.

"How many dogs you have these days?"

When Royal began to count them out loud, much as a child would, Danny held up a hand and said, "That's OK. I can see you have plenty." And he knew that, quite likely, not one had a city license and tag and a current rabies shot. He had cautioned Warren about the matter, but he had gotten only an indifferent response. So, Danny had let things slide. As long as the dogs weren't vicious—as long as they didn't raid a neighbor's chickens or bite a customer, things would continue to slide. "Hey, Royal, have you seen Ben? My boy, Ben—has he come out here in the last couple of days? Have you seen him?"

"He rides a cycle," said Royal.

"Yeah, he sure does. Have you seen him?"

"I saw him once. I did. He took me for a ride on his cycle."

"Did you see him yesterday or maybe today?"

The young man looked up in the twilight sky and pointed at something. The planet Venus maybe. Then he looked back at Danny and shook his head before climbing down from the roof of the car and disappearing into the vast collection of derelict automobiles. He slipped effortlessly into his own world, a kingdom of twisted metal, and broken and torn rubber, and kudzu, his companions an entourage of dogs that just might—if urged to—attack anyone who tried to harm their innocent master.

At the house Danny was ushered in by his aunt Ruby, who switched on a smile when she saw him. Both wheels of her wheelchair squeaked as if they were in pain. There was pain in Ruby's face, too. Years of it. She offered Danny coffee, but he said he didn't have time for it. Thanks anyway.

"Aunt Ruby, your boy out there's ready for a cold snap. He know something the weather channel doesn't?"

The woman laughed softly. "Isn't he a sight? Up and told Warren and me this morning that he saw snow dropping down from Heaven or the North Pole—he didn't know which—and a snowman walking through the air on fire. Ever heard the likes?"

"He has a good imagination is what I'd say."

"He worries me something awful. Warren says angels watch over him. I wish I knew for sure. Those angels need to be watching over every Tracker, don't they? We heard from Mollie about Jessie—just a horrible thing. Another suicide, my Lord. And nobody's found that sweet little boy yet?"

"No. 'Fraid not. Thing is, I've lost my boy, too. He's gone off somewheres, and that's why I stopped here. Just thinking maybe you folks had seen him."

"I sure haven't, but then I don't get out much. Go run down Warren and see if he has. You'll probably find him in the Blue Bird this time of evening." The scowl that had been in control of her expression released its hold so she could smile and ask, "Your girls are doing fine, are they?"

"Yes, I'd say so. Thanks." He suddenly felt awkward. Perhaps because Ruby looked so helpless in her wheelchair. Perhaps because he could see that she had something more she wanted to ask. Whatever it was, it made him want to excuse himself quickly. "All right, then," he said. "I'll see what Warren knows."

Even as he started to turn for the door, Ruby was reaching out, not to grab him, but reaching out into the confusion and fear that hovered like a fog around every Tracker.

"Don't be such a stranger from now on, Daniel," she called after him.

But he felt like a stranger in that realm of broken vehicles, that graveyard of transportation. He passed through a high-roofed welding shop, where skeletal frames waited to be mended. Out beyond the shop a worn path parted the encroaching kudzu. Danny followed it. He knew where it led, for he was familiar with his uncle's "church"—a large Blue Bird school bus, its orange and black paint fading as it slumped on four flat tires and could not protect itself from the daily ravages of weather and the grim advance of kudzu vines, some of which had fingered tendrils into the broken back door.

Twenty yards from the bus, Danny could hear his uncle preaching.

To an imaginary congregation? Or was it a congregation of ghosts?

Hesitating when he reached the steps leading up into the driverless bus, Danny heard his uncle speak in a clear, resounding voice: "Then he showed me the river of the water of life, bright as crystal, flowing from the throne of God and of the Lamb."

"Brother Man?" said Danny. "You got room for one more sinner?"

His uncle Warren, whom he and many others had always called "Brother Man," was a short, dark man, solemn and yet with a glint of hopefulness in his eyes that one had to look closely to see.

He beat a man to death, Danny reminded himself as he reached out to shake his uncle's hand and meet his tight smile.

"Daniel Tracker, as I live and breathe God's good air. How you been, son?"

"Didn't mean to interrupt your sermon. Go on with it—it sounded like a winner."

A touch embarrassed, Brother Man, his coveralls seemingly soaked in grease and coated with dust, glanced away from Danny to his invisible congregation.

"That was Revelation—isn't it a pretty passage? The river of the water of life—I love the ring of the words. It's like birds singing or a sunrise or a cool rain on a hot August day. Something lately's been sending me to Revelation to read again about those who are written in the Lamb's book of life. Most times I don't see my name there, Daniel. The Lord hasn't forgiven me yet, you see. But I think some kinds of men don't deserve to live. All right, then, maybe I haven't walked all the way through darkness, but when I do, I'm gone wade in that river of the water of life and so is my boy, Royal, and so is Ruby—and she's gone walk. That's right: *walk* on legs made whole."

"Amen to that, Brother Man," said Danny. "Amen to that."

Brother Man gestured for him to sit in one of the seats, directing him to one that hadn't been ripped up too badly. They sat across from each other and Brother Man closed his Bible and said, "What you need, Daniel? If it's to tell us about Roy Dale's Jessie, we already heard. It's darkness, is what it is. The Trackers have taken on fellowship with darkness, and no way is that gone please the Lord."

Danny nodded.

"Well, I come lookin' for my boy. My son, Ben. He thinks he's in trouble, so he's hidin' out. Can't find him nowhere. And I thought maybe your boy had seen him or maybe you or Aunt Ruby had."

There was confusion and something like hurt in Brother Man's faraway gaze.

"Our Royal—he worships Ben. He does. Would follow him like the better disciples followed Christ. But, Daniel, I'm gone tell you something—and I wouldn't tell nobody else, not even Ruby—but I'm scared, you know."

"Of what?"

"Of Royal losing his mind all the way."

"You mean this thing of him wearing heavy clothes and talking about snow coming down from Heaven? Ruby told me."

Brother Man reached out suddenly and caught

Danny's wrist, and the movement sent hot needles of fear prickling up his arm. His uncle speared him with a stare that cut deep, a stare he couldn't possibly pull away from.

"More than that, Daniel."

Danny could hear his stomach growling from too much coffee during the day, and he could feel the saliva drying up in his mouth.

"What else?" he said.

"Well, it's this: I caught Royal preaching to his dogs this morning, and what he told them scared me like being dangled on a thread over the mouth of hell."

Jacob hated it that Brianna was upset with him.

It wasn't really about the crucifix he'd bought for her and encouraged her to wear, or the precautions he'd advised, and certainly not about the holy water he'd secretly sprinkled at each corner of her trailer. No, it was the issue of the truth.

And Jacob's unwillingness to share it with her.

Jessie Tracker's suicide had Brianna on edge and that was understandable. She wanted to grasp why Jessie would have felt compelled to do it. And where was Jessie's boy? And perhaps one unspoken question: how deep was the Tracker darkness?

How far would it reach?

Twilight had sent Jacob on a moody, self-pitying drive out to Sweet Gum and on a stroll to the banks of the muddy pond that gave him pieces of solace. Later that evening he was to meet Bo back at Mr. Pancake to plot strategy—mostly, to try to anticipate Franklin Tracker's next move, for he had broken vampire rules and operated outside of vampire conventions, and that had Bo especially frightened.

Bo and Jacob agreed that Roy Dale's attack on Jessie's trailer probably led to her suicide, but neither could quite imagine what had happened to her son. When Jacob thought of that boy, he instantaneously thought of Em and how he longed to protect her and her mother. Perhaps he had stepped over the line in urging Brianna to move back in with her father, where she and Em would be safer.

Brianna had bristled at that.

"Why can't you tell me what's going on, Jacob?"

"Because I don't fully know," he'd said.

And that, ironically, was the truth.

They ended their conversation mutually confused, mutually hurt.

Sitting on the bank gazing at the reflection of a rising moon on the surface of the pond, Jacob also thought about his encounter with Franklin. *Be on our side.* There was something bewilderingly irresistible about the creature Franklin had become. A moon pull on his blood. A desire to have a different life, one free of restrictions and impossibilities.

A desire to draw a new circle.

But then he thought of Josh, too: *you save the others.*

And he thought of the Tracker Bible exploding into flames.

He lowered his head, fearing at the central fire of his soul that he lacked the courage to fight against powers of darkness—powers of his own blood—that threatened to destroy his family and special members of it he loved so dearly.

When he raised his head, he saw a shadowy figure approaching, aiming a gun at him.

He automatically started to get up, but the figure

called out, with anger in his voice, "Who told you I was here?"

In a reflexive gesture Jacob lifted his hands as if he were being robbed. He could see that the man with the gun wore a black leather jacket and jeans and heavy boots, and though the twilight hid most of his face, it was not enough to keep him from being recognized.

"Ben? Hey, it's Jacob. You don't need that gun. I'm not after you. Fact is, no one's after you."

"Don't give me that shit."

The young man edged closer, gun still firmly in hand, though aimed at Jacob's stomach rather than his head. He looked defiant yet scared. His shoulders sagged as if he were nearing exhaustion, and Jacob assumed that he probably was—both a physical and an emotional exhaustion.

"No, it's the truth. You don't understand."

"Fuck that. I know what I did. But it's too late to do anything about it. You tip my dad off about me being here?"

"No. No, Ben, honest. I didn't come out looking for you or looking for anybody else for that matter. Sometimes when I've got a lot on my mind, I come to this pond. It helps clear my head."

Suddenly the young man hunkered down.

"Goddamn, I'm tired." He bowed his head, then quickly looked back up at Jacob. "You're not shittin' with me, are you?"

"No. No, I'm not. I swear. Listen, Roy Dale—I know you think you killed him, but that's not the way it was. You gotta believe me. If your dad or Bo Smith were here, they'd tell you the same thing. Nobody thinks you're a murderer, Ben. I mean it. You don't have to run and hide."

Jacob could almost literally see how disbelief seized the young man's body and how it warred with his physical exhaustion, leaving him shaken, forcing him, after a few more seconds, to sit down hard and let the gun dangle from his fingers.

"Why should I believe you, man? I jammed that pool cue right into his fuckin' heart. You telling me that didn't kill him? You saw it. You were there. I had to do something about him, you know."

Jacob crouched down in front of him.

"I know," he said. "I saw it, but I know something about Roy Dale that you don't. Bo and your dad know it, too. And I'm not sure why you should believe me except that what I'm sayin' is the truth. Beyond that, the only reason to believe me is that I'm your blood. We're Trackers. And I'm telling you that you didn't murder Roy Dale."

Jacob waited for Ben to say something. He could hear the young man's ragged breathing and see the hand holding the gun tremble so much that at last the weapon fell from his fingers to the ground.

And then the young man wept.

Jacob went to him and leaned into him and held his shoulders as he sobbed.

"Ben," he said, "I've got something to show you, and then I've got a very strange story to tell you— you probably aren't going to believe it. I probably wouldn't if I were you. But it explains everything. You need to hear it because the Tracker family needs you right now."

They stood together minutes later with Jacob shining his flashlight on the snakehole and the faded roses atop it. He took Ben's arm, but at first the young man pulled away.

"What the fuck is this? Somebody buried here? This is what you wanted to show me?"

Jacob persisted, and after a few seconds more, both were sitting on the snakehole mound.

"Ben, the creature you killed is buried here. What was once Roy Dale." Then, anticipating Ben's reaction, he held tight to the young man's wrist. "Don't get up. Don't leave. Not until you've heard every word I have to say. When I'm finished, you go find your dad. He's looking for you. He loves you, Ben. But the Tracker family is in deep trouble. Blood has to come together now. We have to be on the same side."

Jacob took a long breath and began his narrative.

At Mr. Pancake later that evening—the first day of February—Jacob sat in a far corner booth with Bo Smith recounting the episode of meeting and talking with Ben Tracker.

"So I thought I *had* to tell him. No way around it, was there?"

Jacob looked into a face carved upon by a wicked diet of coffee, cigarettes and alcohol. Not a pretty face. In fact, it wouldn't take many more miles before it was a death mask. Mr. Pancake was virtually deserted except for a sprinkling of students from the junior college up studying or perhaps eating for the first time that day. Several truckers sat at the counter talking low over coffee and cigarettes—talking about the vicissitudes of the road and the rising price of fuel, and wishing they were home.

Bo shook his head.

"How'd he take it?"

"Didn't believe me. But I think maybe I convinced

him to trust me enough to go find Danny. You think Ben'll be a problem for us in hunting down Franklin?"

"Jakey, you ain't seein' things clearly."

"What do you mean? We're going after Franklin, aren't we?"

Bo hacked coffee and phlegm until his eyes watered.

"Not without some help, we ain't."

"Help? You mean, we're going to tell the cops the whole story?"

"No, I mean help on more the same level as the vampires."

"I'm not following you."

"Finish your coffee. We're gone go see Stromile's sister."

"What for? She know something about vampires?"

Bo nodded. "She's a palmist. And she reads tarot cards. Her name's Prophetess Zammie."

Jacob chuckled. "Prophetess Zammie? You're shittin' me, right?"

"No, sir, I'm not."

"Bo, why you think we need a goddamn fortune-teller all of a sudden?"

"Because she has visions."

"Visions? Visions of what, for Christ's sakes?"

Bo sipped the dregs of his coffee and stubbed out his latest cigarette.

"Vampires, my friend," he said through a veil of smoke. "Vampires."

Jacob thought it was the wrong move. All the way to the curious abode of Prophetess Zammie he complained to Bo that they should be on the trail of

Franklin Tracker instead. What Jacob couldn't fully admit to Bo was that he was worried about Brianna and Em—had he protected them enough? Crucifixes. Holy water. Did that shit really work?

The drive took them into the savage, rural territory where the piney woods ended and the edge of the Night Horse Swamp began, and there, perched on stilts, was a shotgun shack with a crudely painted sign welcoming visitors to the residence of Prophetess Zammie, who promised help with love and death and money.

Jacob reasoned that he and Bo hadn't come for love or money.

Stromile Greene ushered them into a dark, bare room, the only furniture being a card table and a single chair—nothing on the walls, nothing hanging from the ceiling, no crystal balls, no beads or bangles, no skulls, no cards, no black cat or voodoo dolls. Stromile told them to wait as he stepped into a completely darkened adjoining room. Jacob could hear him talking with someone momentarily. Then he returned and whispered that his sister would be right out.

Then he left the premises.

"Jesus, Bo, how is this going to help?"

Bo shrugged. "Stromile seems to think it will. Gist hold on—see what this gal knows."

Ten long, anxious minutes passed before a short, pear-shaped black woman with closely cropped hair dyed blond waddled out. She had a light-complexioned face and had painted her thick lips heavily with red lipstick. Despite the fact that her eyes were crossed and appeared somewhat milky, she was rather pretty and possessed a charming smile. She offered that smile as she sat down and looked up at them and began rubbing her fingers over the surface of the card table.

"My name is Zamilia," she said. "I'm known as Prophetess Zammie and I know why you're here."

"We need your help," said Bo.

The woman's eyes brightened for a heartbeat, then lost their glimmer. The milkiness seemed to spread over the irises.

"It's coming," she said. "Do you know what's out there?"

To Jacob, her voice sounded soothing like the purr of a cat.

"We know about the Tracker vampires," said Bo. "That what you mean?"

The woman hesitated. Suddenly she stopped rubbing her fingers over the surface of the table and stared down into it.

"I see winter," she said.

Impatient, Jacob leaned forward and put his hands on the corners of the tables. He scanned the surface of the table but saw nothing.

"Winter? What does that have to do with anything? Look, I think this is a crock of shit and we could be hunting down my cousin rather than hearing you talk about winter."

Bo gently pulled him back.

"What about winter?" he said to the woman.

"I see winter," she said again. "I see winter—red and tooth and claw. Snow and ice and fire and death in life."

"But what about the vampires?" Bo pressed. "What do we do?"

She folded her hands in front of her and glanced from Bo to Jacob and back to Bo before she paused dramatically and said, "If you're a Tracker, get as far away from this county as you possible can."

With that, she rose from the table and left the room.

The two men looked at each other. Both were puzzled. Jacob was angry.

And when they stepped from the house of Prophetess Zammie out into the night, they were met by a cold wind and a starless sky.

Chapter Twelve

Winter Blood
Part I

At fifteen minutes before midnight it began to snow in east Alabama.

Normally, residents of the region could expect a light dusting of snow perhaps once every three years. Snows of three to four inches had been recorded as often as once every five years, and the freakish storm of 1993 dumped over ten inches creating havoc in an area virtually unprepared for such weather.

The Groundhog Day storm of 2000 was a monster never seen before.

No forecaster saw it coming.

The snow swirled in a gentle breeze for the first hour, but then the wind, blowing out of the north, found its voice and began to gust, reaching velocities of thirty to thirty-five miles per hour. Visibility fell quickly to nearly zero. The Alabama Highway Patrol closed the interstate that snaked close to Soldier's Crossing. By 3:00 A.M. the snow was drifting along every roadside, and in the downtown area streetlights burned an eerie amber. Traffic, meager at that time anyway, ceased.

Soldier's Crossing became a ghost town.

In this scene of wind and snow and cold, a man in a long, dark coat continued walking, for he had a mind of winter and he had been walking since the moment the snow began and he had rounds to complete. People to see. It was his visiting time of day.

He knew death. He knew life. He knew blood.

He would walk until the world he used to know was no more.

As 3:30 A.M. approached, Winston "Blink" Tracker was still waiting for the meat truck to roll in from Tuskegee, though he had assumed more than an hour ago that the unusual snowstorm would prevent it from making a stop in Soldier's Crossing. Likely, it hadn't even left Tuskegee, and just as likely, no one would call to let him know. This particular midnight shift at Piggly Wiggly, he was doubling as assistant meat department supervisor and shift manager. Because several of the stock boys had expressed concern about whether they would be able to make it home on the snowy roads, he had sent them on their way.

At 3:35 A.M. he thought he was the only person in the store.

Munching on a glazed bear claw and sipping coffee, he sat on a stool at the meat counter and stared out over the lit display of steaks and chops and hamburger toward the darkened aisles. Beyond those aisles he could see the sodium lamps in the parking lot. He could see the snow filling up the world. It was a bizarre sight. Good sense prodded him to lock

up and go home. His daughters, Janie and Mattie
Lee, would be stirring, preparing to meet the news-
paper truck and begin their deliveries. He reasoned
that he should head them off and encourage them
not to get out on the roads. Get back in their bed.
The good citizens of Soldier's Crossing could go one
morning without their newspapers.

Those daughters. Good girls. They treated their
father well. They called him "Pops." He liked for
them to call him that nickname. He thought of them
nestled warmly together, and he knew he would not
resist when they invited him into their bed. As a
threesome they had decided long ago that it wasn't
wrong—a loving father and two willing daughters—
because intimacy is what calls you like a daimon,
calls you in a voice that does not know sin or evil.

But though the promise of the flesh of his daughters beckoned, Winston Tracker did not leave right
away. Something held him.

A memory to begin with.

Of blood and destiny. Or, more specifically, of the
day that changed his life, the day that forever diminished him as a man. He could remember it as clearly
as if it had happened yesterday. He was fourteen and
his younger brother, Calvin, was twelve, and they were
at Sweet Gum shooting their pellet guns at tin cans
they had set on a huge granite rock. He was a much
better shot than Calvin. He liked to rag on Calvin for
not being a better shot. And he remembered dis-
tinctly the moment Calvin began aiming at the row
of cans; he remembered saying to him, "You can't
hit shit. You couldn't hit the broad side of a barn."

He remembered the *psst* of Calvin's pellet gun being fired.

He remembered hearing the whining trail of the

pellet ricocheting off the granite rock and then, of
course, the stab of fire into his right eye—as if a
burning stick had been thrust into the ball. In the
months and years following the loss of his eye, he
endlessly contemplated whether the occurrence was
purely accidental or was it somehow the hand of
Fate at work. Lately he had begun to reconsider
whether he really ever forgave Calvin for what happened. Or could.

Blink couldn't decide what it all meant.

He only knew that the blinded eye explained his
life. Because of the blinded eye, he had not been able
to go to Vietnam and fight for his country, as his
brother, Calvin, had; and he had not been able to
go to college and had not been able to get a better
job and had not been able to generate enough self-
confidence to move up on the managerial ladder at
Piggly Wiggly. It didn't stop there. Because of the
blinded eye, his wife, Tilly, had left him—what other
reason could there have been? She had found a man
who wasn't a cripple, who could see her beauty with
both eyes. And because his wife had left him, his
daughters had felt obligated to tend to him; as a
result, they had not married and raised families of
their own. They clung to him for their every need.
And for his. Had he been an educated man, he would
have sensed a mythic dimension to his blindness.

Blink sat and peered into the soft darkness of the
store.

As he peered into it, it became an abyss and he
continued peering into it until . . .

Until suddenly it began to peer back at him.

Blink was startled. He squinted.

"What the hell is—hey, Rex, is that you?"

Someone was standing in aisle six—paper products on the left, pet food on the right—just standing and staring at him. He could see the eyes. Glints of red. And he thought it might be Rex Compton, his best stock boy, having returned because he forgot something. But then he heard a voice.

"Uncle Winston, I've come for you."

And suddenly, Blink could feel cold air. The automatic doors had somehow slid open. The cold wind was rushing in, whining, whining like . . . like a ricocheting pellet, and snowflakes, like feathers from a torn open pillow, were dancing over the aisles creating an eerie, muted brightness, and the brightness was falling around the figure who was approaching him and saying such soothing things to him about forgiving and being whole and walking in beauty.

Blink did not move from the stool.

The body of Franklin Tracker seemed to resonate with a curious warmth as he stepped up to Blink and reached out toward the man's face, toward the black patch that he'd worn for over forty years.

"I can give you the eyes of an eagle," Franklin whispered. "Eyes that will make you see life as you have never seen it. And you will see Calvin with new eyes and you will forgive him and you will give him another life, and your daughters will have another life, too."

Blink tried to speak, but at first he could not. He felt the warmth of Franklin's body as he edged closer and closer. Then he felt the patch being removed and he felt the feathery touch of Franklin's fingertips on the proud flesh covering his eye socket, and it felt so glorious that he wanted to sing or shout. He cried out from his heart. Not words. But the sounds of release from years of living half a life and seeing half a world.

The patch of flesh split open and fell away, and Winston "Blink" Tracker saw fully again for the first time since the day he taunted his brother. He cried out again and clutched at Franklin, and Franklin took him into his arms and they embraced and held the embrace for a long time.

"My God," whispered Blink, "it's a miracle. How did you—what did you—my God, you gave me my sight back."

"And now," said Franklin softly, "give your life to me."

It was all over in less time than a dozen heartbeats.

Confused, Blink momentarily tried to pull away, but when his throat was punctured and pain exploded there, and when Franklin's fangs sank deeper and bliss poured through every cell of his body, he relented and his thoughts plunged into a delicious blackness, and in that blackness beautiful flakes of snow swirled and gamboled and he felt a peace come over him he had never known.

His old life fell away like skin molting.

And when Franklin had finished feeding, he sent Blink Tracker home to his daughters.

Daddy's girls.

Mattie Lee Tracker was painfully shy, but she enjoyed being naked as long as no one other than Janie or her father saw her. She loved the feel of her loose flesh; she loved the pillowy feel of her stomach and bottom and the deflating balloon squeeze of her breasts. She lay still listening to Janie's raspy breathing. Who had it been tonight? Garbo? Dietrich? No, neither. How could she have momentarily forgotten? It was Theda, of course, the dark-eyed, sexy vamp

Theda Bara, she of the magnificently dark and exaggerated eye shadow. But Mattie Lee had another secret fantasy: sometimes it *wasn't* a woman. Sometimes when she curled up with her sister and invited caresses that made glitter dust fall behind her eyes—when Janie, having watched all of those old movies with those marvelous actresses, spoke in Dietrich's smoky, cabaret voice Mattie Lee would imagine it was someone else.

A man.

Not just *any* man. Not the crude men of Soldier's Crossing.

No, it had to be someone classy. A *shining* man. That's how she thought of them. A man with a certain aura about him. One who exuded light and strength and . . . passion. A man whose hands could melt her. Not that Janie's hands couldn't, but Janie liked being rough and she, in turn, wanted to be treated roughly. And sometimes to be hurt. Pops could do that. His hands were hard. They handled meat. But Clark Gable or Gary Cooper—men like that—had gentle hands, or so Mattie Lee imagined. They were men who had shine and who could bring light to a woman's darkness.

Light and the right kind of warmth.

She tugged the top blanket up to her chin.

She debated whether to get up and check on the heat. It had gotten colder in the night.

The wind shrieked like a demon.

Mattie Lee was comforted by the thought that her revolver was on the nightstand.

It was within easy reach. In case the *wrong* kind of man ever broke into the house.

There was just enough light from the clock radio to allow her to see through a crack in the blinds, and so when she lifted her head and rested it on Janie's shoulder, she saw something that amazed her: a snowstorm. And when she saw the swirling snow, she gasped and shook her sister.

"Janie!"

Her sister groaned and rolled over to face her, her hands automatically groping for Mattie Lee's breasts. She groaned again when she touched them, but Mattie Lee pushed her away.

"No, Janie. Not that. Get up, dear. Get up and see this."

Moments later, they were both up, their robes thrown on. A lamp sprayed a low light near the bed, and they had gone to the window and parted the blinds. Janie made a funny sound in her throat and then she said, "Somebody's messin' with Nature. Somebody surely is. Never seen it like this. Have you, Mattie?"

As usual, when anything unnerved Mattie Lee, her thoughts flooded with questions.

"No. You think Pops can get home OK? Should we call him? Will our papers make their run? What about the roads? Won't we get stuck if we get out there with our deliveries?"

"Shush," said Janie. "Just shush a minute. No, we won't go until out our sweet Pops is here. We'll see what he has to say. Is that agreed?"

"Yes, Janie. Should we make breakfast? Should we make coffee for him while we wait?"

"We will. Yes, that's a fine idea. We'll make coffee, and when our sweet Pops comes, we'll give him whatever he wants."

They made coffee and they waited. Janie threw together a ten-minute coffee cake and stuck it in the oven to bake and they waited. They talked about old movies and they waited. And Janie fell to talking about the weather—the effects of global warming and El Niño and the stuff of cosmic dread—and it sent Mattie Lee back to her nightstand for her revolver.

"You never know what might be out in that kind of storm, do you?" she said to Janie.

And Janie observed that with the storm Jessie Tracker's funeral service would have to be postponed, and Mattie Lee said, "We're not going to talk about suicide, are we?"

"No," said Janie, "but I've heard of people getting snowbound and going loony and killing each other."

"We don't have to talk about that either, do we?"

"No," said Janie. "All we have to do is wait for our sweet Pops and think about making him warm all over."

So they did.

As the snow continued to accumulate, it wasn't much longer before someone trudged up the steps to the screen door leading onto the back porch and threw it open. At first, Mattie Lee couldn't tell who it was—the glass panes of the kitchen door did not give her a clear view: it was as if the visitor were invisible. So she held her revolver in a two-handed grip and said, "Is that you, Pops?"

"Of course, it is," said Janie. "Who else could it be?"

And yet the man hesitated at the kitchen door before stepping through and saying, "I've come for you."

Stunned, Mattie Lee and Janie looked at each other and then back at the man who so closely resembled their father, and what they saw was extraordinary.

"Oh, Pops," Janie whispered, clasping her hands as if beside herself with joy.

"Pops, your bad eye," said Mattie Lee. "What happened? How did it get well?" She lowered her revolver and stared.

"The power of the blood, my dear sweet Mattie," said the man. "It's all in the power of the blood. Tracker blood."

"Oh, Pops, it's wonderful," said Janie, and she went to him and hugged him and then raised her face and kissed the healed eye, and Mattie Lee rushed to him as well and the threesome knotted and held as if some new bond had been forged.

"Leave the door open," said their father. "Let the night come in and the cold and all the beauty of the darkness."

"Pops, we've never heard you talk that way," said Janie. She was beaming. "The storm. We were getting worried, and we needed you here."

"Did you have trouble making it home?" said Mattie Lee.

"No, sweet girls. No trouble. Nothing could have kept me from the children of my blood. Nothing."

"We have coffee and cake, Pops. We made you breakfast," said Janie.

"Would you like some hot pecan syrup on your cake?" said Mattie Lee.

Their father chuckled warmly. He sat them down at the kitchen table, and though a cold wind pushed into the room, the heat surrounding his body kept the chill away.

"This morning you don't have to feed Pops, because he wants to feed you."

He hunkered down in front of them and rolled

up one sleeve, and as Mattie Lee watched, she thought to herself: *Our Pops is a shining man.*

His wrist was pale. Blue veins webbed up to his elbow and beyond. He raised his other hand and smiled at them. He concentrated on Janie, locking eyes with her. Janie swooned slightly; her mouth fell open lazily. The man who was their loving father lowered his index finger to his wrist. Mattie Lee gasped when a three-inch fingernail flicked into place.

"I have what you need, sweet Janie, my eldest, my chubby angel. I have light for your darkness and strength for your weaknesses."

The nail cut across his wrist as neatly and properly as if he were slicing nut bread at a tea for the Daughters of the Confederacy. The blood oozed and bubbled like fudge coming to a boil before it cools and thickens.

"This is for you. This is my blood. This is my life."

He took her by the back of the neck and lowered her head to his wrist. At first she resisted, but when his grip tightened, when his manner showed edges of roughness, she gave in and began to suck at the blood and to issue soft, gurgling noises from her throat. Seconds later, the man took her by the hair and raised her face.

Mattie Lee winced at the sight of the blood around her sister's lips, all messy and starting to drip down her chin, and yet her sister bore an expression of unadulterated gladness. And when her father offered Mattie Lee his wrist and the blood seeping from it, she held back only for an instant, reaching for his eyes, burning, *shining* eyes—two whole eyes, the blind one healed—and she whispered, "Pops, is this what you want?"

He smiled and his fangs rested on his lower lip.

The blood tasted warm and salty, and she drank; and the more she drank, the more she wanted, and the more her senses filled with . . . with light. A pure, bright light that pulled her through a dark tunnel until she could not distinguish between herself and the surrounding light.

They were one and the same.

But a voice beckoned her to return.

It was Pops. This new, shining Pops. And Mattie Lee thought: isn't it just too bad that our mother couldn't see this shining man, this husband she left—now if she could see him, she would worship him.

Her father was talking so soothingly.

"Now you will feed *me*," she heard him say.

They clung to one another all the way to the bedroom and then undressed and climbed eagerly into bed, pressing flesh against flesh. Mattie Lee felt something taking place in her body, something totally unexpected. Even though it wasn't her time of the month, her menstrual flow began, and when she sniffed the air, she knew that Janie's had, too. And then Janie was kissing Pops and then he pulled away from her lips and sank his teeth into her throat, and the moans of ecstasy filled the partial darkness. Mattie Lee felt the tingle of her emerging fangs, and when they were fully extended, she wrenched back her head and moved toward her father, her sweet Pops. As he was sending her sister into paroxysms of delight, she bit into his shoulder and she could not merely *hear* his heart beating, she could *feel* it as his warm, shining blood filled her again.

They fed until the daughters sloughed off, satiated and drowsy.

Their Pops rose from that bed of dark delight.

Naked, he walked out into the deepening snow.

To visit a blood relative.
To offer forgiveness.

Calvin Tracker watched the boy sleep. The small one cast an angelic image curled on the small cot in the corner of the Airstream trailer—innocence haloed him; Calvin had to catch himself because he had an urge to check the boy's back to see whether wings grew there. He almost feared that the boy would take flight toward Heaven or some ethereal realm beyond earthly reach. Calvin wanted him close; the boy was the only connection with Jessie he had, the only tangible means of assuaging his guilt over her apparent suicide.

Could I have kept her from doing it?
Didn't she know I loved her? Wanted her?
What drove her to do it? Roy Dale?

So much strangeness. And now this storm.

The snow was accumulating at an alarming rate. Tucking the blanket up over Jeremy Tracker's shoulder, Calvin was bitten hard by the issue at hand. He had kidnapped this boy, and the authorities might well put two and two together and come searching for him. So, storm or no storm, there needed to be a new hiding place. Bracing himself, Calvin glanced one last time at the sleeping boy, left the Airstream and entered the rear of the Hollow Log Lounge. From its back door he watched the snow swirl below the only streetlight. From his vantage point he could see his Ford tractor, now mostly covered with this snow, He hoped that if spring ever came again he could crank it up and plow garden plots for extra cash. Snow blanketing it gave a dead and abandoned and useless look to it, but he knew that it would be the one vehicle he could count on, the one allowing him to get out on the road without getting stuck.

It would allow him to move Jeremy to another hiding place.

Inside, Calvin made coffee and waited for dawn. He said good morning to the snarling fox, adding, "How's it hangin', ole friend?" But the fox was silent. Calvin sat at one of the tables with his coffee and thought about how much he had enjoyed making love to Jessie, the fire she generated within him. He thought of how much he had always enjoyed watching her undress—the way her fingers worked so matter-of-factly on buttons and hooks and how skillfully those same fingers would caress his erect penis and hold it in place as she lowered her eagerly warm and wet mouth onto it. He thought of that magical first rush of heat when her breasts touched his naked body. He thought of how entering her, of how being deep within her, had been a sensation that meant more than self-worth, more than life and more than death. And too far beyond sin to be reflected in her eyes. He missed her more than he could bear—not just the sex, but the brash and lively presence of her, the snarl and snap and sweetness of her. She had made him feel so alive. And now she was gone. And there was only Jeremy as a visible reminder of the sacred fetters of love with which she had bound him and he had willingly accepted.

Jeremy. What to do with him?

For several minutes he thought about new hiding places. He even considered Sweet Gum—its promise of a blood sanctuary—but then quickly rejected it. Eventually he thought of Warren's Auto Salvage and was cheered by the thought. But would Warren help him? Wouldn't it be abetting a crime? And yet, he believed that if he turned the boy over to authorities things would not go well. Jeremy would be sent to an orphanage or children's home or some foster home, and who could say what would happen. Wasn't he better off with blood?

Even if I don't have a claim on him I love him.

I love his mother.

Calvin had lost himself in those difficult musings when a brace of cold air swept across him causing him to start. When he glanced up, he saw something incredible: a naked man walk through one of the walls.

"Holy Christ," Calvin whispered. He recognized his visitor, or thought he did. "Shit, Blink, is that you?"

Something in the moment spoke of the irresistible thrall of madness.

"You're not seeing things, brother. It's me. I've come for you."

As Blink approached the table, Calvin felt blood rushing to his head. He feared he might pass out, or that his heart might fail, or that he'd gone completely bonkers. Or that somehow, in his lingering funk of grief and his angst over the fate of Jeremy, he had peopled the air with a phantom, and it caused flashes of insight to burn across his thoughts: we don't know what's in us, what demons are in us, what might step through the walls of our sanity and invite us to leave our comfortable sense of self.

"Come for me?"

"To make you whole. Yes, to give you the power of the blood."

"Oh Jesus, this can't be real."

"It is, Calvin. Very real. I've been given the power of the night and the power of the blood. The power of Tracker blood. I walked here through snow and the freezing air, and I did not get cold."

Calvin looked closer.

"My God, Blink, your eye. My God, how'd that happen?"

And in Blink's expression Calvin thought he saw peace but thought also that he saw a hunger that bubbles in the blood and hides out in some secret cell of the heart pretending to be imprisoned.

"Franklin healed me with his touch—the beauty of his touch, and now I've touched my daughters. Not the way you've always suspected, Calvin. This was more. I've made them strong. Strong women filled with blood. We've shared blood, and now we're powerful. See what I can do, Calvin?"

With that, the man stood on his tiptoes but then lifted slowly from the floor and hovered five or six feet in the air. Calvin shut his eyes and trembled, and his brother laughed warmly and benignly.

"This will all make sense to you when I release you from all the horrors of living. But I've also come to forgive you, Calvin. I've hated you for so long, but now I can forgive your transgressions. I forgive you for taking my sight, and I forgive you for all that happened between you and my Tilly."

"No," said Calvin. "There was nothing between us. She came to me. She threw herself at me, but—I swear to God, Blink, I never touched her. Never."

"It doesn't matter now. Nothing matters except your new life. I'm going to give you a new life and a new family. Not the old Trackers. But the new Trackers with power in the blood. In the blood, Calvin. We have power in the blood. We have forever in the blood. You'll join me and my daughters and Franklin, and then we'll walk out into the storm and give life to all the other Trackers. We'll be the Tracker family we've always been meant to be. And we'll return to Sweet Gum. And it will be glorious once again. How does that sound, Calvin?"

Calvin pushed himself to his feet.

"Goddamn it, stay away from me. And stay away from Jeremy, too, Goddamn you. I don't want this. You hear me? I don't want this."

Blink dropped softly to the floor, and when he started to approach, Calvin grabbed a chair and held it out in front of him like a lion tamer.

"Go after the rest of them—I don't give a damn— but leave me alone. I don't want this, you bastard."

"Yes, you do. You've been wanting me to forgive you for years. And you've been wanting to feel the blood of a new life in your veins. Jessie gave you that, a taste of that, but I can give it to you for lifetimes upon lifetimes. You want this, Calvin. You want to be strong to protect Jeremy. I'll make you strong. And no one will take from you what you love, unless you want them to."

As Calvin listened to the words of his brother, he could barely hold up the chair. It grew heavy. He could not muster the will to resist.

"Jeremy? I can keep him safe?"

"Yes."

"I want him safe. For Jessie."

"And you want to be forgiven, too, don't you, Calvin?"

Lowering the chair, Calvin heaved his upper body, moaning from his depths.

"Yes," he said.

Blink stepped forward.

"I'm going to kill you, Calvin. But I won't hurt you. When I finish, you'll feel more alive than you've

ever felt. You'll see and feel and hear and touch and
smell the world for the first time. And every dark
memory you have—Vietnam, the death of Jessie, all
of them—will be erased. And you'll be like a child
of the night."

Calvin couldn't move. He didn't want to move.

He felt lost and found in the same instant.

He stared down at Blink's razor-sharp fingernail
as it sliced away the pocket of his shirt and then
penetrated his skin—just a sting of pain, no more—
and his blood spilled down over his stomach, and
he met Blink's eyes and felt dizzy. But he held firm
as Blink cut deeper, exposing Calvin's beating heart,
blood gurgling and then splashing like rain onto the
floor.

Blink's fangs bit into Calvin's heart as if it were a
ripe piece of fruit.

Calvin gasped.

The pain was consuming for only a beat; bliss almost instantly replaced the pain. And as his brother
fed upon him, as the heart pumped directly into his
brother's hunger, Calvin reached out and lovingly
caressed the back of his brother's neck. And he felt
forgiven. And he felt whole and complete.

And strong.

"Thank you," he whispered.

The hour for fright.

The tractor lights punched ineffectually at the
blinding snow. If anything, the intensity of the storm
had increased. There was no one else on the roads.
Two city trucks filled with sand had gotten stuck in
drifts. A police patrol car was likewise stuck and aban-

doned. Soldier's Crossing seemed to cower like a frightened animal.

Calvin, his blood warm, his thoughts neon-bright and pulsing, hugged the blanketed body of Jeremy to him with one arm as he steered the tractor with the other. He was on his way to his brother's auto salvage, a graveyard, ironically, that promised refuge. And a place where still other Trackers could be transformed just as Calvin had been transformed.

It is a lust, he thought as the storm howled around him.

The blood lust of the body, a lust so strong that the body chooses not to listen to the heart, because the heart whispers of feeding gently, of feeding the soul. But a vampire wants more—this new being wanted more. This new being had a lust for life he had not imagined possible. It pleased him that he now shared it with other Trackers—with Blink (no longer blind in one eye, no longer harboring hate) and Blink's daughters and Franklin. And the others to come.

And Calvin knew that he had come to the right place.

Sacrifice.

That concept suddenly blossomed in his thoughts. He only vaguely understood how it connected with his new life, a life in which he no longer mourned the death of Jessie, the loss of the intimacy they had shared. Now he needed no living thing.

He only regretted that Jeremy could not know this new life, for he was not a Tracker. But the boy could live within the powerful circle that would be created, couldn't he? He would be safe from the outside world, safe from those who would weaken him with thoughts of guilt and remorse, with admonishments about the wages of sin, wouldn't he?

Sacrifice.

The boy remained silent.

Calvin held him, but not as tightly, and not as if he were his own flesh and blood.

He drove on along the preternaturally quiet road. He could hear his heart beat; he could hear the boy's heart beat; he could hear the heart of the night beat as well. And a world that few could possibly know was suddenly alive to him, a world powered by blood.

He turned in at the entrance to the salvage. Spurred on by the sound of his tractor, the junkyard watchdogs scurried out from their shelter to cry out at his arrival. They charged the tractor, but finding no safe way to challenge it, they kept their distance. Perhaps the fire in Calvin's eyes and his wild, feral aroma, wolflike and dangerous, held them at bay as well. They parted for the tractor to push forward, and they did not pursue him when he got down from the machine and, carrying the boy, set out in the darkness into the ruins that his brother Warren had created.

And Calvin knew that he had come to the right place.

Sacrifice.

Was it a notion that a man could understand?

But I'm more than a man.

Intuitively the creature that was once Calvin sought out the Blue Bird. It was cold inside the bus, and yet it was at least out of the jab of the wind, and there the creature and the boy settled in to wait for whatever wanted to come.

* * *

The dogs woke him. As did the sound of a machine, Or had it been the dream?

He had dreamed of wading in a river of blood.

The river of the blood of life?

He had waded halfway across and had found that he could not return.

My God what is going on?

Warren "Brother Man" Tracker bolted awake. The house was cold, but Ruby slept like the dead. He didn't rouse her. He dressed quickly and stopped at Royal's door and peeked in; his son was sleeping, and he prayed he was not dreaming.

At the front door he was astonished at the strength of the storm; perhaps more so, he was puzzled that it hadn't awakened him. He had slept through most of it, and the snow was burying the land, but the driveway showed the tracks of a vehicle and a few dozen yards beyond was a small tractor. He recognized it as Calvin's.

"What's going on?" he whispered to himself.

He pulled on his boots and found his flashlight. In an instinctive move, he tucked his Bible under his arm and braced himself for the first stab of the wind. Once out in the driveway he noticed that Royal's dogs were curiously quiet and subdued. They whined around with their tails between their legs and whimpered as if they'd just been whipped or beaten or kicked.

"Hey, pooches," he said. "Hey, what is it?"

He sprayed his light out over his welding and repair shop, and snowflakes danced weirdly into view. He saw no one, but he knew he had a visitor.

Somewhere out there in the darkness.

"Calvin?" he shouted.

The wind batted the word aside.

And he thought that perhaps it wasn't Calvin. In his shop he picked up his sharpest sling blade and held it against his chest along with his Bible. He was scared. He considered going back to the house. Beyond the shop he began to follow tracks in the snow. Not ordinary tracks. Or an ordinary stride. It looked as though whoever or whatever made the tracks was taking unnaturally long strides.

"My God, now, what is this?" he said softly to himself. "What in Heaven's name is out there?"

He followed the tracks to the Blue Bird. At the door to it, his every instinct told him not to enter, heeded him to return to the warm bosom of his home and family—to Ruby, dear, broken Ruby who loved him, and to Royal, his mind shrunk like a rotting cantaloupe, yet someone who needed him.

There's power in the blood.

The voice emerged in his thoughts like a radio suddenly being turned on. It seemed a preacher's voice, the tone of one blessed with the truth, a truth that would set him free. He listened and the voice continued, just snatches of words, phrases, not quite comprehensible, and yet somehow irresistible.

Words of invitation.

He stepped onto the bus. He heard whimpering. Soft crying. And thought at first that it was one of Royal's dogs. Then he sprayed the light down the center aisle of the dark bus and was startled to see the boy crouched there on his knees, a blanket wrapped around him.

Jessie Tracker's boy.

He held the light on the boy's face and saw that his mouth was wide open, his expression one of abject horror as if he were screaming except . . . except that no sound other than a whimper or a muted sob issued forth.

Put down the book.

The voice was there again, commanding his thoughts—a voice seemingly impossible to ignore or disobey. But where was it coming from? He saw no one in the bus other than the frightened, cold child.

Reluctantly he placed his Bible on the closest seat, and when it was no longer in contact with his fingers, the boy found his voice and his loud cry exploded:

"Stay away!"

Then a dark figure rose from the shadows and stood behind the boy, and the boy continued crying out until the figure closed a hand across his mouth and the boy went mute.

"Sacrifice."

The word rang in Warren's thoughts, a word sent by the dark figure who when speared by the light became recognizable.

"Calvin?"

And then something more. The boy. And Royal's dream, the dream he had shared with his father. A dream about a child covered in blood in a night of fire and ice.

Sacrifice.

Paralyzed with fear, Warren stood there, his light shining onto his brother's face, stood there unable to move because the flame in his brother's eyes was mesmerizing.

"God in Heaven, save me. Washed in the blood of the Lamb—save me."

"You are saved," said Calvin. "That's the beauty of the blood. Of Tracker blood."

"My God, no. What is this? The boy. Let the boy go."

"We can't do that. If we let him go, this boy would hate us, hate who we are. So he must be sacrificed to the cause—Tracker blood. It's about forever, my brother. It's about being immortal and being forgiven and forgiving himself and being whole. You're not washed in the blood of the Lamb, my brother. Your religion hasn't brought you peace, has it? But I can. We can. Your family. Tracker blood."

Warren quaked as he gripped the sling blade more tightly. Something in Calvin's words touched him like a lover, like the moments of intimacy he had experienced with Ruby years ago. He wanted peace. The promise of it felt warm. But he had killed, and though he had paid his debt to society, and though he had asked his God for forgiveness, he had never forgiven himself.

"How do I forgive myself?" he said.

He began to choke on his tears.

"Cross the river, my brother. Cross that river of blood and join your family. Leave this other life—it's nothing."

"How? Dear God, how?"

"Sacrifice," said Calvin, and he tapped on the shoulder of the frightened boy.

"Oh God, no . . . no, if you mean . . . no, I couldn't kill again. Never. Please. Not that."

"Look into the eyes of this boy. Come closer. Look. What do you see?"

Reluctantly, Warren approached. He was fighting back tears. What he saw in the eyes of the boy was sheer terror.

"He's . . . he's just a scared little boy."

"No, my brother. Look again."

Warren swiped at his tears, and it seemed to him that the shadows thickened and suddenly he couldn't see clearly. He dropped his flashlight and it rolled to one side.

"I don't know what I see."

"I'll tell you. Listen and you'll know. Look closely and then defend yourself."

Confused, Warren shook his head.

But then he heard it: a low, throaty growl. It seemed to come from the boy. There was movement, a menacing snarl, and then the boy was no longer a boy but some kind of animal.

"God, no," said Warren. "What's happening?"

He could hear Calvin's voice filtering through that of the growling animal.

"It's a wolf, my brother. It's a wolf. Use your blade. Use it now."

Warren looked again, and it was. Was *something*. A wolflike creature leaping up at him.

"God, no."

He swung with all his might. And then he swung again.

The blade sliced, and flesh and muscle and bone split and snapped, and blood splattered him. And he imagined the head of the wolf creature thudded to the floor and he cried out, a release of his fear, a release of all the energy fueling his survival instinct. Then he retrieved the flashlight and shone it onto his kill.

He crumpled to his knees.

And the anguish rushed from him like the shriek of demons.

The boy's headless body was dark and still.

"I'm coming for you," said Calvin. "Now I'm going

to give you the peace you need. Here I am, brother. Here is what you need."

He knelt on the floor with him as Warren sobbed. He leaned forward as if to give him a loving kiss. When he sank his fangs deep into his brother's throat, the wind suddenly gusted with a ghostly rage, and no one in the world could have heard Warren Tracker's cries of pain and cries of joy.

Chapter Thirteen

Winter Blood
Part II

Prophetess Zammie had been right.

Was she also right about Trackers needing to leave the county? Was it possible to turn one's back on blood and not see one's self as a coward?

At the kitchen table Jacob nervously buckled his overboots as the wind kicked up, almost playfully tossing handfuls of snow against the back door. He had few answers and many fears. Of two things, however, he was certain: first, that Franklin Tracker, exercising his vampiric powers, had generated the strange winter storm that now held Soldier's Crossing in its grip; second, that Brianna and Em needed to be protected. Because they were blood. More so, because he loved them. And in some corner of his thoughts a potential narrative was being written in which he rescued them, in which he swept them into his pickup and drove them as far and as safely away from this town as possible. Away from blood.

"Shouldn't you wait for the storm to let up?"

Jacob's mother, lines of anxiety etched at the corners of her mouth, stood in her housecoat by the kitchen sink drinking a cup of coffee and looking alternately at the blowing snow, beyond the window, and at her son.

"It might go on this way all day," he said.

His mother was silent for a moment or two. He sensed that she was reading import into his actions, and, as always, she was harboring secrets. It was her way.

"I 'spect you're going to Brianna's trailer," she said.

Jacob felt heat rise into his cheeks.

"Maybe, yeah. If my truck can make it down the roads. I don't know—I might have to walk. But, yeah, I could check in on her. On Sharelle, too, and Miriam and Tyler and Aunt Mollie. Do we need groceries while I'm out?"

"We're fine. I just hope they get the phone lines back up and working soon. Makes you feel cut off."

Jacob reasoned that his mother knew about his attraction to Brianna—thankfully, she didn't press him on it. No sermons. But what else did she know? Was she, for example, remotely aware of Franklin Tracker's role in turning Nature upside down? Could she know how much danger the Trackers were in?

Shouldn't he tell her even though she wasn't blood?

"This thing caught about everybody by surprise," he said.

He stood up to go. His mother's worried smile reached out to him.

"Jacob?" she said. "You still have the family Bible, don't you?"

"Sure. Yeah." But when their eyes met, he felt the

lie begin to crumble. He looked away. He felt a momentary flash of anger, sensing that she might be testing him, might even be toying with him. "No. It was . . . it's gone. I'm sorry. I should have taken better care of it."

She nodded.

"I think I understand," she said, "what likely happened. Will you be seeing Orpheus?"

"Probably."

"It would ease my mind," she said, "if you'd stay close to him because . . . whatever's out there, you shouldn't try to face it alone."

. . . *whatever's out there.*

They stared at each other as if they were communicating telepathically. Jacob could see that there was something more his mother wanted to say but was choosing not to. Secrets. Whispers in the blood. And he couldn't hear them.

Four-foot drifts angled against his truck. He managed to push his way behind the wheel, but then he found that it wouldn't crank. Part of him wanted simply to go back inside and crawl in bed and wake up when the snow had melted and the vampires had somehow disappeared as a threat.

He thought of Brianna and Em. And that's all it took.

Leaving his truck to be buried deeper under layers of the storm, he headed out through the surreal, snow-flecked morning light, trudging silently, determinedly, wishing he knew where Bo was and what he was thinking and doing. And he thought again of whisking Brianna and Em away from all the evolving terrors. Maybe he could make it happen. Maybe he could.

He walked east along Soldier Road. Like smoke,

the cold air curled into his nostrils and filled his lungs, and he looked around at the quiet, almost preternaturally serene, snow-covered landscape and was struck by the beauty of it. A monster had raised the storm, and yet, nevertheless, the unusual phenomenon touched Jacob with awe.

And as he continued walking, he was seized by the inviting sensation of letting go. How easy it would be to lie down in one of the snowbanks and let go, fall asleep in the arms of the storm. Forget the world. And enter another one. What would that be like? he wondered.

    . . . it's a strange and wonderful adventure.

The voice was in his thoughts as if a gust of warm wind had blown it there.

He knew that voice. It belonged with the face of a fallen angel. It belonged to blood.

It's moment-to-moment beauty. It's going home to a place you've never even dreamed of. It's an intimacy you would die for.

"I don't want to die," Jacob whispered into the surrounding silence.

Be on our side.

"Stay away from me."

But Jacob could feel himself edging into a dark surrender. A promise of blood that would solve all his conflicts, erase all doubts and fears . . . and loves. He felt suddenly that he needed to be savage to resist; he needed a legitimate savagery capable of taking him beyond himself to do what he must do.

"Oh God."

Jacob stopped. He shut his eyes tightly.

And when he opened them, he looked out north of Soldier Road toward downtown, and there, perhaps a quarter of a mile away, he saw a lone figure walking. He saw the figure slow down, then hesitate, then turn and look over his shoulder.

Jacob could feel the pull of eyes upon him.

The eyes of a nearly irresistible darkness and heart-easing warmth.

It was a transforming moment, and in it Jacob felt his blood turn to wine—the dialectic of comfort and despair was intoxicating.

Then a release as the arresting, distant figure of Franklin Tracker started moving again.

It was a call to blood.

And Franklin Tracker vowed that before the day ended every blood member of the family would hear it and heed it and be changed.

Forever.

Anyone who got in the way would suffer.

He walked through the storm and felt a kinship with it. He walked through the cold and felt fire in his veins. He was headed downtown. He would cross the railroad tracks and reach out with his mind of winter for his next victim.

No, not *victim*.

But rather "chosen one."

One called to the bliss of darkness.

One invited into the family of blood.

The Cause.

Yes, he knew where to find her. She would be waiting for him. She would want him and need him. They hungered for each other. Because they were blood. Because something in the blood cried out for wholeness. For a new humanity. A new bond of blood.

He walked and he felt the dragonfire of joy burning in his heart.

And the sight of Jacob walking in the distance, walking with temptation heavy in his heart, made the morning perfect.

He felt fire in his fingertips. When he held both hands up in front of his face, he marveled at the tiny flames pluming from the sharp nails. Never had *his* God given him such power, such total peace.

"Thank you, brother."

With those words, Warren Tracker turned and smiled into Calvin's face.

"You've traded your river of biblical blood—that nonsense about the Lamb—for a river of fire in a night of ice," said Calvin. "This is why I came for you."

Warren embraced him.

"What about the corpse of the boy?" he whispered over his brother's shoulder.

They pulled apart, and Calvin gestured toward Warren's fingers.

"Burn your false temple," he said. "And let the boy's body be your sacrifice to a new self. A new self born into Tracker blood for a second time. You've died and come back. You are whole and complete, and there is fire in you. Use it."

It was more than a surge of adrenalin. Warren had never experienced anything like it. Standing twenty yards from the Blue Bird bus, he aimed his fingers at it and sent flames spearing toward it like breath from the mouth of a dragon. The bus erupted; it quickly fireballed into the snowy, predawn sky.

Warren roared with the exhilaration of the moment.

He stood there and felt as if he were being swallowed by the billowing flames and the smoke. The reverie held him, warmed him, and he understood that he had been called to the blood. Tracker blood.

"Thank you, brother," he said again.

But when he turned away from the burning bus, no one was there.

Calvin had disappeared.

Opened some door into the night and closed it behind him.

"Thank you, brother. I'll be with you soon."

Snow swirled around him, and he felt intensely alive. And, more than anything else, he wanted to share that feeling with his son—the man with the mind of a boy. His broken toy of a child.

The dogs gave Warren a wide berth. Their pathetic, low-in-the-throat growls sounded cowardly. It was as if they were giving ground to some fabulous beast, primitive and bloodthirsty, eager to hunt and kill and claim any new territory as its own. Once inside his home, Warren felt like a stranger. He didn't recognize the place. He went from room to room searching for his son until he found him curled asleep in his bed, dreaming of being tossed by the world like a leaf in the wind.

Warren loved his son.

I love him so much, I'll give him a new life.

He leaned down over him in the darkness and whispered, "Royal, it's time."

The boy shook awake.

"What's wrong with my dogs?" he said. "I dreamed something came and tried to eat 'em. What's out there?"

"Shhh," said Warren, and he sat down on the bed and reached out and touched the boy's face. "Your dogs are fine. You're going to be fine, too. You're going to be different. New. I'm going to give you a new life."

"Could I have a motorcycle, too? Like Ben's? I could ride it fast."

"You don't need a motorcycle, son. No, you need something better than a motorcycle."

"Better than a motorcycle? What is that—maybe a jet plane?" The boy giggled. He was blinking his eyes rapidly, trying to adjust to the darkness.

"Better than a jet plane," said Warren. "I'm going to make it so you can fly."

"Like crows and pigeons, you mean?"

"Yes. Fly like a bird. Your own bird. A Royal bird." The boy giggled more loudly.

"A Royal bird. That's my name—Royal. I wanna fly like a real bird."

"You will."

"Could I do it right now?"

"No," said Warren. And he lowered his head closer to the boy, close to his lips, and he kissed his son at one corner of his mouth. Then he said, "First you have to die."

Confused, the boy held his breath.

And his father, sharp fangs extended, his hot breath warming the boy's throat, fell upon him and the cry that issued from the boy was plaintive and sad and filled with blood. It speared into the night, piercing it and rousing his dogs to bark excitedly. It woke his mother two rooms away, and alarm thickened her voice.

"Royal? Royal, honey, did you have a bad dream?"

Warren reluctantly pulled away from the warm pulse of his son.

"Ruby, I'm coming for you," he said.

He glided to the bedroom he had shared with her

for years. She tried to switch on a small lamp by the bed as he approached, but it wouldn't come on.

"Warren, I believe the power's off. Did you just come from Royal's room? How is he? I thought I heard him. I thought maybe he was upset. Maybe had a bad dream. Is he all right?"

"He's wonderful," said Warren.

"Wonderful?"

He knew that Ruby was squinting hard into the darkness. He could taste her apprehension.

"Yes, he'll never be the same."

"Never be the—Warren, what are you talking about? This house is getting cold. I'm cold, Warren. Get back in bed and keep me warm."

"Ruby, if you're cold, I can make it much warmer for you. You've had to suffer. I know that. You only have to suffer a little more."

"Warren, you're talking kind of strange. Get a blanket from the hall closet, and I'll be fine. Just get another blanket and come on back to bed before we both freeze to death."

Standing there in the darkness, he felt sorry for her, sorry for the hardness of her life, the disappointments, the yearnings unmet. And, most of all, he regretted that she wasn't blood. Not a Tracker in the blood.

"I wish you could come with us," he whispered, more to himself than to her, for she had rolled away from him and was punching at her pillow to make it more comfortable. She muttered something more, and he left the room and then walked out of the house with Royal, his son, in tow. And then he turned and raked his fingernails across the front door and it sprang into flames.

"Daddy, when do I get to fly?" said Royal.

"It's almost time," said Warren.

"Daddy, you made fire."

"I know, son. We have to burn away our past."

He guided his son away from the burning house and they stood and watched the place of their old lives catch a fury, and over the crackling of the flames, they faintly heard the screams of a wife and a mother, the woman who could not be called to the darkness of forever.

She was floating in a sea of candles and singing snatches of a folksy lyric from the 1960s. They were her companions, these tiny flickers of light and heat; they were alive and stayed by her with the loyalty of small animals and somehow expressed a similar, unconditional love. Candles made her feel closer to her spiritual essence. Yet, they were only candles. Some were scented candles—fruity aromas, though some were musky and some, according to Kitt, smelled like blood. Candles. And they, too, would die. Something else in common.

And as just beyond the storefront window it continued to snow, and the dawn held back as if hesitating, Sharelle's thoughts drifted to blood and family, thoughts of her mother, whom she missed, and to her father and to her brother, Ben, and to her sister, Brianna, and her niece, Emily. She sat in the display area of the window that looked out from Mixed Bag, her place of employment in the same building that contained her upstairs apartment, where even now as the unexpected snow fell, her friends, Kitt and Cardinal, slept an oblivious sleep. And next door to them the proprietors of Mixed Bag, Jerry Garbo and his wife, Big Eva, would also be sleeping.

"But I'm awake," Sharelle whispered to herself.

Her body was humming. That was the only way to describe it. She felt it begin to stir not long after midnight when she was on the edge of sleep and found, to her surprise, that her period had started. A heavy flow. Nothing quite like she had known before. And now sitting and staring at the loveliness of the storm. The awesome beauty of it. And waiting.

Waiting for what wanted to come.

She had fixed herself a cup of herbal tea, and she had allowed her thoughts to range freely as a CD of Peter Gabriel's *Passion* slithered through the deserted coffee shop. Then the pieces from a 1960s lyric had flowed out of her. She had finished her tea and slipped another CD into her portable player—something dark and enchanting, something to match the strangeness of sensing that someone was coming for her.

Someone.

The haunting music of Danzig's *Black Aria* coiled around her like a snake of sound.

"What's out there?" she whispered.

There had been no movement on the snowy streets: no cars, no people. But she imagined that just across the street, standing there alone and looking very cold and very sad, was the ghost of Josh Tracker. Staring at her.

What could he want?

Wanting her?

She closed her eyes and Danzig carried her away, swept her up and up into a dark thrumming of sound: drums and bass guitars and soprano voices wailing—up, up, up, until she was falling, falling, falling—like the first rebel angel. The CD spun to an end. Her world was almost total silence.

Back in herself she was sexually aroused. She thought of how Kitt wanted her that way. Kitt, so proud of his penis. Cardinal too—she, so proud of her breasts. To share passion with both. Should it matter? Or maybe there was someone else. Maybe it was Josh. Maybe it had been Josh all along. But no one could approve of such a longing. A longing for blood? No, that was a transgression.

She closed her eyes again. And waited. And behind her, on every table, candles burned down, flames flickered and danced and waited, too. And when Sharelle finally opened her eyes again, she gave a sudden start and clasped her hand over her mouth to keep from screaming.

Because just beyond the window stood a man.

He smiled.

To Sharelle, he looked completely at peace with himself. She returned his smile, then felt a blush of embarrassment for not recognizing him immediately. It was Franklin Tracker.

She gestured for him to come in and was about to get up and go to the door and unlock it when he tapped on the glass as if to say: "Wait, look here."

She hesitated, then blinked in wonderment as he reached his hand through the glass without breaking it, without cutting himself. He reached out for her hand. She grasped it, and he held it for support as he stepped up and through the window.

"O-o-h my-y-y God!" she exclaimed softly.

He sat down across from her and rubbed the back of her hand and stared into her eyes, and she forgot what she had seen—or perhaps she knew what it all meant even then.

"Do you know what's out there?" he said.

She glanced out the window and nodded.

"Yes," she said. "Beauty is out there."

"I knew you would say that. I've come for you because you understand what it means—what it *really* means—to have beauty in your life. Do you know who I am?"

"Yes. You're Franklin. You seem different, but I know you're Franklin."

He smiled.

"No longer. I left Franklin behind. Back in your world, a world without peace or power, without holiness or freedom. Everyone in your world is a captive. You run around as if you're free, but you're in one huge cage. People are dumb animals in cages. Less than animals. So do you know what I'm doing out in this storm I raised?"

She shook her head. She had never been so mesmerized by another human being. She had never found a man with so much sexual allure. One so breathtakingly beautiful. He reached out and touched her cheek and she feared she would swoon.

"I'm letting them out," he said. "I've come to let all the animals out. And they, in turn, are letting the other animals out. But just certain ones. Just members of *our* family," he said, and poked at his chest and then at her. "Just Trackers. Just family. Just blood. Do you understand?"

She was having difficulty breathing. She could feel blood trickling down her inner thigh. She could smell it.

"I thought I saw Josh," she murmured. "The ghost of Josh. I think he wanted to tell me something. Did you see him, too? Are you a ghost, too?"

"No. And I'm not like Josh." He turned his face away, but she could see his fine jaw stiffen, could see anger rising within him. "He liked his cage too

much. His father gave him a chance for another life
and he chose not to take it. He chose death instead.
He chose ugliness instead of beauty. He hated blood.
He hated life."

"No," she said. "You're wrong—he . . . he was gentle and humane. There was a grace about him."

"Blood is a state of grace. He didn't seek grace. He
asked for love instead of lightning. He had no real
passion. He didn't listen to the call."

"But I felt that he and I—our souls—we sought
out peace and goodness."

"You don't understand anything about the soul.
You have to die first. Not like Josh did. You have to
die in the life. You have to die in the blood."

His voice, his eyes—Sharelle felt herself floating
like a boat toward a raging waterfall. Felt she could
not resist, though part of her wanted to.

"I have a soul," she whispered. "I don't want to
lose it."

"You don't have to," he said. "At the core of yourself your soul is hotter and heavier than anything
you can imagine. It burns there as a central fire."

"What do you want of me?"

"I want you to surrender to that fire."

He leaned forward and kissed her very softly on
the cheek and then he tugged at the flannel night-
gown she wore and she met his signal and peeled
it over her head and propped herself on her knees
before him, naked. He undressed and touched her
face and her shoulders, and she had never experienced such a touch and yet she pulled away.

"But we're blood," she said.

"Everything important in life is."

She held firm, but the confusion within her was
thick. She smiled nervously and pushed at his chest

with her fingertips. "I thought you didn't prefer women."

He shook his head. "This is not about sex. Sex is just another cage. I'm beyond sex. And what we are doing is beyond sex. This is about blood and beauty. And forever. How does forever sound to you?"

"Like everything I've ever wanted to hear." She closed her eyes. "Like candles burning within. Like flying away with Peter Pan." She giggled. "Like reefer made in heaven. Like peace on earth. Like the kind of kiss you could only have in a dream."

Her eyes still closed, she felt him lean closer. Felt his lips in her hair and then down her face to her chin and then to her throat. She moaned, anticipating where his desire would take them.

When his fangs tore into her throat, she knew.

"Go deeper than love," she whispered.

And he did.

The second he stepped into her trailer, she threw herself into his arms. To him, she was heavenly there: the warm firmness of her breasts, the perfume in her hair, the feel of her fingers locked around his neck, her lips brushing against his ear.

"I'm so glad you came," she said. "It's the strangest storm. The wind woke me and I thought of you."

She was trembling. He had held her more tightly and wanted the moment to last a lifetime. Then he leaned away and her beautiful face swam there close enough to kiss. *I love you. My God, I love you much.*

"Don't be frightened," he said, swallowing back the words he truly wanted to say.

"I'm trying not to be."

In the kitchen there was laughter—Em's.

And a man's voice.

Jacob steeled himself.

"Is that Spence?" he said. The image of her former husband ghosted into his mind.

"No, of course not. It's Daddy."

"Oh."

While he was glad it wasn't Spence, he couldn't hide his disappointment over someone being there. He had needed to be alone with her. Just before he had reached her door, he had decided to tell her everything and to encourage her and Em to leave with him. For the sake of safety.

Brianna softly pulled free of his arms and led him into the kitchen.

"I bet you could use some hot coffee," she said.

"I wouldn't turn it down."

"Uncle Jacob, look at my fingers. See what Grandpa and I are doing?"

Em's tiny fingers, nearly every one tipped with a miniature marshmallow, wiggled up at him, and when he swung her into his arms, she laughed and poked a finger in his mouth.

"Mmm, good. That was a tasty finger," he said.

She cackled. "No, that was not my finger. That was a marshmallow. You couldn't eat my finger."

"Says who?"

She grunted. "Says me."

Then another voice. "Hey, little brother, I've cooked up a serious batch of hot chocolate. Want some?"

Jacob wheeled around to meet Danny's crooked smile and weary face.

"Believe I'll go for the coffee instead." He paused, then added, "What do you think of our Dixie-style blizzard out there?"

His brother's smile dissolved momentarily before flickering like the flame of a cigarette lighter.

"It's a jewel. I think maybe we need to talk some about it, don't you?"

"I'm with you," said Jacob. "We definitely do."

Brianna picked up the signal.

"Em, why don't we take our hot chocolate in the front room. And maybe later we can go out and build a snowman."

She flashed a look at Jacob that he read as questions: Would it be safe? What's going on?

Jacob had no answers. He nodded appreciatively, and once Brianna and Em had left the kitchen, he helped himself to the pot of coffee and sat down at the table with his brother, and for a score of seconds neither spoke. Jacob guessed it was because neither knew quite what to say. Then Danny began to chuckle.

"Damnedest thing, I was on the graveyard shift and hit a patch of ice and snow and put my patrol car slap in a ditch. It's still there. My replacement put chains on his tires, but I doubt he's out in this. I decided to walk over and see how Brianna and Emily were doing. It's a mother of a storm."

Jacob searched his brother's face.

"He raised it. You know that, don't you? Franklin. It's something vampires can do—raise storms, affect the weather. He did this to make it easier for him to attack other Trackers and harder for us to stop him."

Danny looked down. He shook his head.

"Maybe so, Jake. But, you know, it hit me this morning—it 'bout knocked me over—that nothing else but my family means anything to me. My children. My grandchild. You understand what I'm sayin'?"

"Some of it, sure. But we've got a problem with Franklin and—"

"Fuck Franklin. I don't give a shit about all that. Because you see, Ben came back home. Said he'd seen you. He came back and I told him things were gone be OK. And we . . . Christ, it was the best moment we've ever had. I held my son and he cried like a little boy, and I was thinking 'bout that this morning and that's when it hit me that Ben and Brianna and Sharelle and Emily—hell, they're what really mean something to me. They're what I love. They're who I love."

"I know that," said Jacob. "Of course, you love them, but don't you get it? Every member of the Tracker family is in danger this morning. Serious danger. We've got to get out there and stop Franklin, or else we've got to get our asses outta this town. Right away."

Danny waved him off.

"You sayin' I can't protect my family?"

"Jesus, no, Danny. I'm not saying that."

"You can't know this feeling, Jake. There's no way till you get to be a father. You can't know this feeling." He hesitated and pressed a fist into his chest. "No way in hell you can know what it's like to be a father and a grandfather. It's something nobody who's not a father can know—it's like there's something inside you that's more alive when you realize how much you love your kids. I can't explain. It's there. Inside. It's like something in the blood."

Jacob watched as his brother's eyes teared.

"No, I guess you're right. I can't know what you feel. Someday I hope to. But right now there's someone out in that storm who threatens everything you're talking about. Everything you love. What's out there wants blood. It wants to change every Tracker into a monster. And no one in this family is safe from it—not you or me or Ben or Sharelle or Brianna or Em—or any other Tracker. You got to see that, Danny. We got to find Bo and fight this thing. And maybe we'll have to get a lot more help."

"No. We're not goin' that way. We can handle this ourselves. Keep it blood. You go on and find Bo. I'll stay here with Brianna and Emily. I'll go downtown later and see how Sharelle is doin', too. Ben, he can take care of himself at home." He glanced down at his watch. "Bo's probably at Mr. Pancake. Not likely he has much business this morning. He's not blood, but he seems to know what we need to know."

"Yeah, he knows," said Jacob.

He didn't want to leave. He wanted to be the one staying with Brianna and Em. He thought about hearing Franklin's voice ghosting into his mind— how seductive it was. How it caused him to doubt himself. To doubt blood. And every thought about going back out into that storm to prepare to battle monsters made him shiver.

Made him cold to the bone.

He had taken her deeper than love and then he had left her with puzzling words: "I have to find the missing piece," he had said. "The blood sacrifice that will anneal us as a family and make us stronger than the world. I have to find the one thing more that will make us gods." And she was lifted up by those words.

. . . *the missing piece.*

She wanted to go with him, to search with him for that missing piece.

Suddenly she was alone, and she could not remember his leaving. It was as if he had drifted away
like smoke or had dissolved into a mist. He had left
her satisfied and yet hungry for more life. More
blood. She looked around the darkened coffee shop
and saw and heard and tasted and felt and smelled
it all as never before. She was experiencing everything as if for the first time. She had been reborn.

Resurrected in the blood.

Tracker blood.

It was cause for celebration. It was like a gift—yes,
that was the word: "gift." She needed to share her
good fortune with someone. With her friends. And
so, naked, new blood in her veins, she glided up the
stairs to awaken Kitt and Cardinal. Wouldn't they be
surprised to see the new Sharelle—no longer the quiet,
timorous Sharelle, the flower child, but a Sharelle who
walked like an animal, like a beautiful panther.

That had been let out of its cage.

Would her friends be pleased to meet this new
creature?

But before she could ride upon that thought, she
heard something painful to her ears. Something rasp-
ing out from the first bedroom at the top of the stairs:
snoring. The Garbos. A disgusting sound. Disgusting
people. They didn't deserve to exist in a world of
beauty—a hidden world that Franklin had opened
up to her.

With silent footfalls she entered their bedroom.
She went immediately to the sleeping form of Jerry
Garbo, his graying beard and mustache bent and mis-
shapen. Next to him was Big Eva, curled up facing
away from him, though her weight tended to tilt the
mattress toward her. Jerry himself was lying on his
back, his mouth open rather like a gigantic goldfish

working its lips as it breathed. The snoring punched at Sharelle's ears—such an ugly, ugly sound coming from an ugly man, a man she had once thought was cool, a hippie in a hippie-less world. An antique. Charming and even interesting when he wasn't so high he was incoherent. But not now. There was nothing cool about him. No charm. No cool.

She went to him and gently pulled back the covers from his upper body. He was wearing a dingy, sleeveless T-shirt. He smelled of garlic and marijuana and urine. She couldn't stand the sight or smell of him—nothing beautiful about him. She flicked up one of her long nails like a switchblade, waited a moment and then, just as his snoring almost woke him, jabbed the fingernail deep into his heart.

A choke of breath caught in the man's throat; he thrashed once or twice, then stiffened like a board.

"J.G," Big Eva whispered, "you OK, baby?"

She stirred, rolled over, causing the springs to screech and Sharelle to hold her ears. Then Big Eva squinted at her husband in the partial darkness, at the blood bubbling from his chest, but before she could scream or cry out, Sharelle raked a nail across the woman's throat, slicing through several layers of fat, slicing deeper as she stabbed and worked her weapon from ear to ear. Big Eva bucked and flung herself helplessly toward the corpse of her husband and then, in a matter of seconds, was still. As Sharelle glided from the room, the Garbos were heaped upon each other like a pile of dirty, bloody laundry.

She felt good. She felt beautiful. She had eliminated two pieces of ugliness.

She knew that violence wasn't Franklin's way.

But she had discovered that it was hers.

In her own bedroom she remembered the odor of

her former self and did not like it. She stared down
at two pallets on the floor—her sleeping friends—
and it struck her that they, too, were ugly creatures—
false creatures playing at being vampires. Poor
children. They could never know true beauty or true
freedom. They were not Trackers. She believed they
would worship her when they found what she had
become. If she allowed them to live.

Cardinal was sleeping soundly. There was something arrestingly sweet about her face, a child's face
behind the exaggerated makeup—black eye shadow
and lipstick—and the ridiculous hair, but when
Sharelle noticed what lay next to the young woman's
pillow, she felt her jaw tighten.

It was a small black whip, and it was coiled there
like a serpent.

Like Cleopatra's asp, Sharelle mused to herself.

Lately, Cardinal had taken up sadomasochistic
practices. She had asked Sharelle to whip and spank
her, but Sharelle had refused. Kitt had obliged.
Sharelle had left the room during that activity, finding it disgusting and yet reminding herself to be tol-
erant of the stimulation needs of others.

Now, as a new self, as a powerful, beautiful creature,
she found the whip to be ugly—an object of cheap
cruelty and false stimulation. Anyone who would par-
take of it was then, accordingly, also ugly. Like the
Garbos. And, like the Garbos . . .

Sharelle nestled under the covers with Cardinal,
who was naked and radiating warmth despite the cold
air in the room. Careful not to wake her, Sharelle
began to kiss her very softly: on the forehead and
cheek and lips and throat—and then on her breasts.
Cardinal stirred with the feathering of arousal.
Sharelle took the whip and gently lifted Cardinal's

head and wrapped it around her neck and began to
tighten it even as she returned to the breasts and
began to suck at them. Cardinal moaned and whispered Sharelle's name. Then Sharelle locked her
fangs into one breast and let the warm blood flood
her mouth, and the whip tightened, and it was almost
as if it tightened on its own, a supernatural snake
coiling and constricting, animated with a life of its
own.

Cardinal tried to cry out, a frantic effort born of
both pain and pleasure.

But the whip crushed her throat before she could
emit more than one strangled utterance. Just
enough to awaken Kitt on a pallet twenty feet away.

"Hey, what is it?" he said. "Cardinal? Sharelle?"

Sharelle drank a few moments longer, then lifted
her mouth free of Cardinal's breast.

"Shhh," she said. "Cardinal's dead to the world.
You need company?"

She heard him breathe out with anticipation of
what the offer meant.

"You know I do."

She slipped in under his blankets and discovered
that he, too, was naked.

"Are you really a vampire?" she murmured. And
her hand slid down across his chest and stomach to
his penis, and she began to fondle it.

"Would you like for me to bite you?" he said.

"Yes, very much. If you'll let me bite you, too."

He chuckled, but then as he became more aroused,
his breathing thickened and his words slurred.

"You go first," he said.

And she did.

Her fangs tore deep into his crotch. His screams,
his pain, poured into her ears like heavenly music,

like a symphony of joy. She shifted her bite to the large artery in his inner thigh and drank as if her thirst were unquenchable. Kitt struck at her feebly. And only for a few seconds before his body surrendered.

And then his soul.

When Sharelle had satisfied herself anew, she rose. Kitt's was not a soul she wanted; nor was Cardinal's. She wanted only the company of Tracker souls. Quietly she went back downstairs, dressed and repositioned herself in the front window. She thought about Franklin's search for the missing piece and yearned to be with him.

And she listened.

And began to hear a call.

Franklin's call to every Tracker vampire.

A call to gather and embrace the blood.

To feast at a family reunion.

A reunion of the dead living life more fully than anyone else possibly could.

Chapter Fourteen

Talking After the Feast

The air tasted like sour milk, coating her lips and the roof of her mouth and the back of her throat so that wherever she placed her tongue she was met with another swatch of the unpleasantness. Perhaps it was the late-morning mist that carried the sensation or perhaps it merely lingered from the "snow-cone" Emily had made for her—and demanded she taste—from what had been her snowman's arm. Her daughter had been enchanted by the idea that one could eat snow, that one might dine upon one's snowman, feasting upon its limbs.

Her gloveless hands freezing, Brianna watched as Emily patted eager fists full of snow onto her snowman's head, adding another inch or two of height to the creation, making it as tall as she. The tiny girl was happy; though a half an hour earlier, she had cried when her grandpa had left. More accurately, Brianna had sent him away, pointing out that he needed to get back to work or get some sleep and that they were perfectly fine, perfectly safe. The snow

had called them out—snow being such a rare event
and it was, in fact, Emily's first snow ever—called
them into a commons area of the trailer court, where
the white stuff was at least six inches deep. More was
falling, not heavily, and yet enough to add to the accumulation. There was no sun. Only the big flakes
of snow and the curious, gray fog or mist sticking low
to the ground reducing visibility to fifty yards or less.

Visibility.

The notion stuck in Brianna's mental filter.

She was having trouble seeing. If images from
smarmy poetry had leaped to mind, she might have
concluded that her heart was blocking her vision.
Or maybe she had simply been too long without a
man—she had to smile at that thought. Maybe guilt
and shame played a role, too. It was all much too
complicated playing out against a backdrop of darkness gathering for the Tracker family—the nature
of that darkness was being withheld from her,
though she had pumped her father, to no avail, for
more information.

The more personal angst was no secret to her.

She couldn't stop thinking about Jacob.

"Mama, my snowman's gettin' real big. Look at it."

"I see it, sweetheart. Yes, it's going to be taller
than you."

Am I in love with him?

In a sense the answer could only be "yes," she
reasoned. A niece would naturally love her uncle.
One loved one's relatives. A Tracker loved every
other Tracker. It was a matter of blood.

But this is different.

And one thing more—an emerging thought that
made her smile.

Jacob loves me.

Jacob wants me.

"A woman knows," she muttered.

"What did you say, Mama?"

"I said, 'The wind that blows is all that anybody knows.' "

"No, Mama. What did you say really?"

"Something about your uncle Jacob."

"Oh, that's good. Wait'll he sees my snowman."

Brianna felt a blush spreading across her cheeks. Just mentioning Jacob's name to her daughter made her feel oddly ashamed—and yet excited.

I'm being very foolish.

She shivered and hugged herself and said, "Em, are you getting cold?"

"No, Mama."

Her daughter said something more, but the words were blotted out by what Brianna guessed was the tolling of a bell, distant and yet seemingly quite close, Or had she only imagined it?

"I'm going back inside to get some gloves, sweetheart. You stay right by your snowman, OK?"

"I will, Mama."

The warmth of the trailer tempted her to curl up with a cup something hot and daydream about impossibilities—such as a life with Jacob. She was pleased that she had hidden her feelings for him so effectively; she believed he was completely unaware. As she slipped on a pair of gloves, she thought suddenly of Jessie, who had given her the gloves as a gift. Poor Jessie—her relationship with Roy Dale couldn't have been a good one. Why did relationships tend not to work out? Why couldn't people recognize that they need intimacy and that they should commit themselves to finding it and keeping a hold of it?

Most of the time, weren't men to blame?

Spence McVicar ghosted to mind. He was scheduled to visit Em that day; Brianna hoped the storm would delay him, for she had a vague fear of him and what he might do. He was there momentarily, reflected in the mirror of her consciousness, before she exorcised any further thoughts of him except to contrast him with Jacob. The thought of Jacob led her into a lingering terror: what if something happened to him? Something dreadful. Or what if he disappeared as suddenly as had John Taylor and Douglas and Roy Dale?

What would I do without him in my life?

When she stepped back outside, another thought seized her attention: why aren't there other children out playing in the snow? The trailer court had dozens of them—it was almost as if they were too frightened of something to come out. Then she glanced in the direction of Em's snowman and her breath caught in her throat.

Her daughter wasn't there.

"Em! Em, where are you?"

Frantically she looked around.

Then a distant voice reaching out from the mist: "Here, Mama. Here I am."

Brianna trained her vision straight ahead and what she saw drove her to the edge of panic: Em was holding the hand of a strange man in a dark overcoat.

"Em, come here this instant." She couldn't see the man clearly, but she assumed there was only one possibility. "Spence, you're not welcome here. You're supposed to call ahead. What do you think you're doing?"

"Mama, it's our cousin, Franklin. He made my snowman talk. He really did, Mama."

Then the little girl dropped the man's hand and ran to her snowman.

Brianna stared at Franklin as he approached her and he, in turn, was gazing intently at her. She had the unsettling impression that he could read her thoughts, that somehow he and his voice were inside her head.

"Hello, Brianna. What do you think of my storm?"

"*Your* storm?"

A wary smile flickered at one corner of her mouth. She glanced over her shoulder to see how far she was from the house, because she was suddenly afraid of this man—this Tracker—and anticipated grabbing her daughter and running for safety.

"That won't be necessary," he said. "Whatever gave you the idea that I would hurt you or, especially, your beautiful little daughter? She's the missing piece, you know."

"Missing piece?"

Brianna felt dizzy.

He was near, quite close actually, before she could compose herself. He was remarkably handsome, she realized, with fiery, mesmerizing eyes—eyes like fire in the night—and an indestructible air. He held her with those eyes.

"She's protected," he said.

She shook her head. "I don't know what . . . I don't understand."

"That's because you don't know what you have, and you don't know what I've become and what I've been doing. You see, I've been feasting, feasting with blood. With Trackers. And they have been feasting with other Trackers and now something wonderful is gathering and everything is going to be perfect— except that one piece is missing."

Brianna was trembling. She could feel tears threatening at the corners of her eyes.

"What do you want with us? Please, leave us alone."

"What do I want?" The man paused as if deliberately trying to create a rhetorically dramatic moment. Then he glanced toward Emily, who had busied herself again with her snowman. "I want your daughter. *We* want your daughter. But your love for her keeps us from having her. That love, and your love for Jacob, and his love for you and your daughter—a love to be envious of, and yet it's a human love, and you're not aware that there's something deeper than love. But I am, and so are other Trackers."

She found that his words virtually paralyzed her. Her mind raced for some response, some rebuttal or denial of what he maintained, but all she could say was, "How could you possibly know about Jacob and . . ."

She clasped her hands to her face and began to tremble uncontrollably, but Franklin reached out and gripped her by the shoulders, and his touch made her fears, her confusion, begin to melt away.

"I know everything I need to know. But I need your help."

"I won't help you. Stay away from me and my daughter. I'll tell my father. I'll call the police."

"Don't you understand what it means to be blood?"

"No. No, please. Just leave. Now."

He released her shoulders and lifted his hands so that they hovered near her face. When she saw his daggerlike fingernails, she tried to scream, but somehow he prevented it.

"I could make you one of us," he said. "But I would need Jacob, too."

"Why can't you . . . just . . . go . . . away?" she whimpered.

"Something in the blood won't let me," he said. She couldn't pull back from his hand reaching out, reaching tenderly toward her cheek, and when he laid that hand upon her skin, she shrieked with the pain, the pain of flesh searing as if having been branded.

Brianna felt the sensation of the afterblow of a semi passing near her. She staggered, and when she managed to tear free of his touch, she was flooded with the feeling of being dirty, of somehow no longer deserving to be Em's mother or to love and be loved by Jacob. She began to sob.

"Stop hurting my mama!"

Em was there beating her tiny fists at Franklin. He turned and lifted the little girl into his arms and chuckled at her brave defense of her mother.

"You see, Brianna, this is the love that protects. We have limited powers against this."

"Please don't hurt her. Please," Brianna cried.

Em squirmed in the man's arms, and he gently handed her to her mother.

"The rains will come next," he said. "For cleansing. Trackers reborn will gather to wait for what will give us the empowerment we need. You have until midnight. Deliver your daughter to us at Sweet Gum. She's the missing piece. Do it or we will find a way to make you suffer more than you can possibly imagine."

Clutching her daughter tightly to her, Brianna felt a fury course through her. "Jacob will fight you. He's a Tracker, too, and he loves his family, and he won't

let you destroy it. The love he feels for me and for
Em is the love that comes from the bond of family.
Something has happened to you—you don't feel
that kind of love, and I pity you."

"Pity yourself, instead. Pity Jacob. His capacity for
love is why he's such an enemy. We could destroy
him, but . . . we want him on our side. And you're
wrong about something." And his words took Brianna out of herself. They stunned her as only the
most personal revelations can. "Brianna, Jacob is not
blood."

She stared into his eyes, and a cold wind gusted
and tiny flakes of snow flecked her face.

"What do you mean? Of course he is. The son of
Clarence and Gladys Tracker. You're crazy to say
something like that."

But she knew suddenly, locked into his gaze, that
he was speaking the truth.

"No, and what I'm telling you changes everything.
Jacob is not a Tracker."

Chapter Fifteen

Cold Heart of Day

"It's where he touched me," she said.

Ghosting through foundation makeup, the hand-print on Brianna's cheek fired Jacob's anger. In the cold heart of day he vowed revenge. And he was disgusted with himself for leaving her and Em earlier, and disappointed with Danny for, likewise, abandoning them.

"What else did he do? Tell me what Franklin did."

He wanted, needed to hear it all in order to see where the battle lines had been drawn. It was terrifying to anticipate an enemy whom he had, in many ways, always known and yet now, suddenly, an enemy as mysterious as the freak storm.

"He threatened. He wants . . . oh, Jacob, he wants Em."

She moved into his arms and held on tightly, her body trembling—it was as if she were shivering from the cold, but they were on the sofa in the cozy warmth of her trailer, the power having not gone down in that area of Soldier's Crossing.

"I won't let anything happen to Em, you know that."

Holding her in his arms felt good beyond words. "I'm glad you came back," she whispered.

Images of a blaze flickered in his thoughts. Why had he returned so soon? Something intuitive. He had left her trailer intent upon finding Bo, whom he assumed would be at Mr. Pancake. He needed to hear what was on Bo's mind, how he read the storm, what he believed that Franklin would do next. But at the entrance to the trailer court, Jacob had been drawn to the sight of smoke in the distance, to an area beyond the railroad tracks and beyond the community college. He started walking toward the smoke, believing that it might be coming from his uncle Warren's auto salvage yard. No fire trucks would likely be able to plow their way down the hazardous roads to put out a fire, so he reasoned that Warren and Ruby and Royal could be in harm's way. When he was within a quarter of a mile of the salvage, he stopped.

Warren's house had burned to the ground.

And there was another blaze out deeper in the salvage.

The scene felt wrong. Jacob thought perhaps he knew why. Purely a hunch, but whatever it was, it made him turn and begin to race back toward Brianna's trailer. Those were vampire fires—he simply knew they were. He knew that Franklin had been at work. He assumed that under the cloak of the bizarre snowstorm, Franklin had been negotiating in blood.

How many Trackers had he hit?

Winston and his daughters? Warren, Ruby, Royal? Dear God.

Fear brought him back, and now, in the arms of the woman he loved deeply, he thanked whatever powers-that-be that he was there to try to protect her and her daughter and to hear about her encounter with Franklin.

"I need to go check on Em," said Brianna, reluctantly unclasping herself from him. "She was playing in her room—I'm sorry, I just start to feel freaky when I'm not right by her."

"Sure, go on."

When she returned, satisfied that her daughter was fine, Brianna began to tell everything. Almost everything. Jacob listened, imagining the scene, reliving with her the fear of seeing Em holding the hand of a stranger.

"Jacob, he said that our love for Em protects her. I guess it protects us, too, but I don't even know what we're being protected from. What has happened to Franklin? What is he talking about with his threat about midnight? What has he done to himself? And to other Trackers? Is he just crazy? Was he on something? You can't keep secrets any longer, Jacob. Please."

He sighed. "All right, yes. You need to know. I'm sorry. I should have explained some things before now."

He drew his knees up and tried to get comfortable, and she rested a hand on his knee and leaned toward him, giving him her full attention.

"Don't hold back anything," she said. "And when you've finished, I have more to say. Things that will change lives—ours especially."

Puzzled by her comment, he nodded. He could hear his heart beating. He could hear the wind howling outside, and he wondered how his life could possibly change any more than it already had.

"Well, here goes," he said. "Just remember: what

I'm about to share with you is the absolute truth, as unbelievable as it will sound to you. It all started the final midnight shift I worked at Jimmie Jack's—and it began when Josh showed up."

When he reached a stopping point, when the narrative found the present tense, he paused, waiting for the inevitable expression of disbelief. Vampires? No, that couldn't be. The Trackers—a dysfunctional family in many ways, yes, but one living out a supernatural fable in the blood? No. You must be wrong.

Instead, the woman he loved said quietly, "What now?"

"I don't know. I want to get together with Bo and Danny—see what's possible. We need to protect each other. Mostly, I want to protect you and Em."

"Can you do that?"

It wasn't an expression of doubt, merely an honest question voiced in a context where answers were not readily apparent; where one, in fact, had to live the questions—one in which everything important went deeper than words.

"We have to try. And those of us with Tracker blood can't let Franklin have his way. We have to fight him even though there's something in our blood that makes it very hard to resist him."

She nodded.

"Jacob," she said, "there's one thing more. Franklin claims . . ."

In her hesitation was a world of significance. He held her hand, and she leaned down and kissed his fingers.

"What does he claim?"

Her eyes searched his intently. It was as if she hoped she could transmit to him what she planned to say without having to speak a word.

"He told me . . . he told me you're not a Tracker."

Jacob heard her words and yet did not. A sudden wave of confusion caused him to laugh softly.

"Well, not the same kind of Tracker he is. I mean, I'm sure as hell not a vampire if that's what he means."

Brianna shook her head.

"It's not . . . I don't think so . . . no, you see . . . no, that's not what he means. I know it's not."

"Then just what do you think he means? Jesus, Brianna, I wasn't left on my mother's doorstep with a note safety-pinned to my blanket. I mean, come on. Someone would have told me before now. My folks . . . no, what he told you is bullshit. Don't listen to that. I'm a Tracker. Same as you."

"But, Jacob, what if you're not?"

"What if I'm—no, this is crazy. He's trying to mess with your mind. Don't you see that?"

She shrugged. "I suppose you could be right. The way he talks . . . it's all so . . . convincing. And frightening." She reached out and touched his cheek. "Hold me, OK? Hold me and don't let go."

And he did.

"Listen," he whispered, "I don't know exactly what Franklin's up to, but it'll be easy enough to settle whether I'm really a Tracker. In the meantime, what we have to do is find Bo and Danny. I believe I'm a Tracker, and I know that everybody who is, is in danger."

She pulled away and once again searched his face.

"But don't you see, Jacob, if you're not a Tracker, that changes things."

They looked deep into each other's eyes, embracing with their eyes, and Jacob saw something in hers that he had only dreamed of seeing until that moment.

"Brianna, this is all so . . . I mean, there's so much I want to say to you and I—"

"Wait," she said, and pressed her fingers onto his lips. "Let me say what I have to say first." She slowly, gently traced a fingertip to one corner of his mouth. Then kissed him warmly on his lips, a brief yet romantic kiss. And he felt that he had become someone else, someone he wanted to be, and he kissed her cheek where the handprint shadowed forth and then he moved to kiss her more deeply, more passionately.

"No, wait a moment," she said, "I have to say this."

He felt a smile warm his face.

"OK, go ahead. Just don't wake me from whatever kind of dream this is."

"No dream, Jacob. This is real." She gathered herself to speak and when she did, it was as if she had been holding her breath: "I love you, Jacob. I always have, but now . . . it's going to be—"

"My turn," he said quickly, gesturing for her to stop. "Whatever the truth is about me. About blood. I love you, too, Brianna. With all my heart and soul, I love you and want you and need you."

"I know you do. I've known for a long time."

They kissed like lovers separated by a war or by years or by distance. It was a kiss that broke through barriers and plunged them deeper into the heart of day, momentarily lifting them out of a growing darkness into a realm of light.

Chapter Sixteen

Deadrise

"I wish you could feel what I feel, Bonnie Gayle. I can't put it in words, you know. The best feeling— like what I felt when we first met and fell in love and I wanted you so much I couldn't eat or sleep— and being with you was a better feeling than I ever imagined I could feel."

Danny Tracker trudged through the snow and leaned into the wind, and as he talked to the ghost of his wife, his breath billowed out and was tossed aside and the eerie, muted brightness of the snow was blinding. But he felt alive, and it felt good to be alive despite the storm and despite whatever was happening to the Trackers.

"It's all about family," he said. "Just like you was always saying, only I never realized it until now. The biggest thing about it is Ben and me. It's like a fogged window that's cleared. We can finally see each other, and we can see that we care about each other. Oh, I don't know how to say all of this, Bonnie Gayle. Hell, it's like I got my son back. Like he was gone somewhere and he's come back. Come home."

Walking faster, he angled toward downtown. There was no movement on the streets and, curiously, no one even out looking around. No kids out playing in the snow. It had a bad feel. But he pushed that feeling aside. His wife was listening.

"Brianna's fine. Spence was supposed to hit town today. I reckon she's hoping the storm holds him up. He's as no good as ever. I can't bring myself to hope things go well for him, but then he's Emily's daddy and some of his blood is in her. I think Brianna's lonely. She'll find somebody else one of these days. I keep hoping she will and that she'll be as happy as you and me was. That little Em of hers—she's really a doll. She's a pistol. We made hot chocolate this morning and had the best time. I wish you could see her." He drew in his breath sharply as a stab of regret struck near his heart. Then he turned his face away from the wind. "Jake came by Brianna's trailer while I was there. A good guy. Worried 'bout what's going on with the Tracker family. Good reason to worry, too. But all this bad stuff is gonna pass—I know it will."

He crossed the tracks and glanced to his right. In the distance plumes of smoke broke through the fog. It was impossible to tell what might be burning, and he reasoned that someone, doubtless, had reported it. He continued on.

"I'm going to see Sharelle," he told his wife. "Wish she had someone in her life, too. You know, a good man. She needs that. The male friends she's had up to now—Christ, I don't know. But maybe somebody will come along. It'd make a different woman out of her is what I think."

Mixed Bag was oddly lit as Danny approached it. With a cop's cautiousness, he glanced around again, sensing that maybe someone was watching him. Then he dismissed it as he looked straight ahead, and there was Sharelle, camped in the window, waving at him. At the sight of her he felt his blood leap.

"My God, Bonnie, I love our kids. Never knew till here lately just how much I loved 'em."

The door to Mixed Bag swung open on its own. When it did, Sharelle pounced upon her father, laughing, smiling, obviously glad to see him.

"Some kind of storm, huh?" he said, puzzled by the opening of the door.

"It's a fabulous storm," she responded, and he chuckled at her characterization of it.

"Don't know 'bout that. It sure brought this little pissant town to a dead stop, didn't it?"

"But, Daddy, this town always was a little dead."

The interior of Mixed Bag was a sea of lit candles. Danny surveyed the empty area and felt a shiver volley between his shoulder blades.

"You got the place lookin' like a church, sweetheart."

She seemed pleased by his observation.

"This morning's holy. Yes, I see it in a different way this morning. You're right. It is like a church. And I've found something to worship. And I'm glad you came. So much is going on."

He held her at arm's length and began to look more closely at her. She seemed different. More animated. Older. Even her voice sounded deeper. Above all, she seemed more . . . "womanly" was the word that occurred to Danny.

"So, how you been?" he said. "You holdin' up OK?"

"I'm wonderful, Daddy."

"Wonderful? Geez, listen to you. You didn't win the lottery or somethin', did you?"

"Something better."

Danny laughed. She offered him a chair and some coffee, but he declined it, explaining that he had been drinking hot drinks at Brianna's. It was warm in the room, and it felt good to sit and be in the company of his second daughter.

"So, guess you won't be doin' much business this morning, will you? Ole Jerry and Big Eva still upstairs sawin' logs?"

Sharelle laughed softly.

"Oh, yeah, their lights are out," she said.

"Well, thing is, it's not just the storm you need to be mindful of. It might be kind of dangerous out there this morning—so, you know, I wouldn't be letting in just anybody. What I mean is, be careful, OK?"

"Daddy, I can take care of myself much better than you realize. I'm a big girl now."

He reached over and pressed her hand. "You'll always be my child," he said, and was surprised to find her hand was, for a moment, ice cold, then it began to warm considerably. "I wish your mother could see how grown-up you are," he continued. "Wish she could see all you kids. Wish your mother could be with us. I mean, the best thing in life, Sharelle, is family. It's all about blood."

"I know that, Daddy. I believe that now."

"Did you know that your brother and I are back on good terms?"

"I'm glad, Daddy. I really am. You and Ben need each other. You're going to have a lot more to do with shaping his life—I just feel it."

"He's a good boy. He's come around, and I'm

hopin' he and I can be close, you know. I'd like to be a better influence on him. Hope you're right."

"You will be, Daddy. You will."

"And your sister, Brianna—this single-mom thing is tough for her. But she's tryin' to be a good mother, and she sure loves her little girl. I mean, that's the thing: you gotta love your kids, and it kills you when things aren't goin' well for 'em. I've found that you kids are the thing for me. I'm realizin' how much I love all of you."

"Daddy, let me help you take off your coat. I want you to stay for a while so we can talk some more and get to know each other better. I don't get to see you much."

"Thanks, yeah, I know. That's my fault."

More comfortable, he relaxed, and his daughter hunkered down in front of him and they held hands and looked into each other's eyes, and he was amazed at how different she seemed. So alive. Yet, so pale.

"Daddy, is your life really good?"

His chuckle was born of nervousness and goaded by the mildly unsettling circumstance of having one's child ask a very serious question.

"Like I said, you kids are it for me. Yeah, because I've got three good kids and a precious little grand-daughter. Yeah, it's good."

"But don't you want your life to be more?"

"Wouldn't mind having more money."

"No, not that. There's much more out there than what you have. Things deeper than love."

He frowned. "Hey, not as I see it. Nothin' deeper than love."

"Franklin showed me there is."

"Franklin?" Danny could feel saliva hardening in

the back of his mouth. "Baby, I think you need to stay away from him. Now, I don't say that because he's a homosexual—that's his own business. But somethin' happened to him. Jake has seen it, too. Somethin' bad."

"No, Daddy. Something wonderful."

He shook his head and squeezed her wrists.

"You're talking crazy. Don't talk like that. I don't think you know about him."

"Daddy, wouldn't you like to feel wonderful forever?"

"Of course, baby, everybody would, but . . . hey, is this—listen, I know about that weed you smoke from time to time. It won't get it, baby. It won't last."

She smiled. Her eyes danced, then seemed to catch fire.

"Wouldn't you want to be powerful forever? Have the power to do things nobody else can? I have a gift, Daddy, a gift from Franklin. I want to show you what I can do. Here, turn and watch the stairs."

He did.

"You gone make the candles snuff out or somethin' like that?"

"Keep watching."

A few seconds passed in which he could hear her ragged breathing. He could feel her concentration. And then he saw shadowy movement. Figures descending. Jerry Garbo and Big Eva, and behind them those two friends of Sharelle he'd seen before—Kitt and Cardinal.

They shuffled down the stairs as if sleepwalking. Danny, once again, chuckled nervously.

"This some kind of show you worked out with them? They on somethin'?"

"No, Daddy. This is deadrise."

"What the hell is that, baby? What's goin' on here?"

Then, as they emerged from the shadows into the flickering candlelight, he saw blood on each of them.

"I killed them and brought them back to life. I can do that, Daddy."

Danny stood up.

"Good Christ—this is sick, baby. This isn't funny."

"Sit down, Daddy."

She took his hand and coaxed him back down into the chair. The living dead receded into the shadows. Danny glanced at his daughter's hands and saw the long, sharp nails.

"Christ, what have you done to yourself?"

"I've come back to life," she said, slipping into his lap and folding her hands behind his neck. "Remember when I used to sit on your lap? That was when I was Sharelle. I was your little girl, and you were really my daddy. I just call you that now—but I don't mean it, because I'm not your little girl anymore. And soon, you won't be anybody's daddy."

"Christ, what are you—"

He couldn't stop her. In fact, he found he couldn't resist her. Didn't want to. When her fangs sank deep into his throat, he struggled fiercely for a few seconds. The pain shocked his senses before a soothing numbness took over. He saw the candles flicker like fireflies and he thought he heard the distant tolling of a bell or maybe a police car siren. And the last thing he heard was his blood rushing from him like a freight train.

Spence McVicar was freezing his ass off.

And he was as mad as hell about it. Partly, he had

only himself to blame, for he and he alone had made
the decision to avoid the interstate and take back
roads from Montgomery to Soldier's Crossing. But,
if anything, road conditions worsened with each mile,
worsened the closer he got to Brianna's trailer court,
where he hoped to see his daughter, Emily. A mile
and a half from Soldier's Crossing, he had swerved
to miss a deer—a doe that seemed perfectly mystified
by the unusual snowfall as well as the headlights of
Spence's car. He slew sideways before coming,
ingloriously, to a dead stop with the rear end of his
prehistoric Camaro slumped in a ditch.

Motherfuck it!

Spence's exact words as the Camaro thudded to
its resting place.

And so he had started walking, and had he not
been so furious with the state of things, especially
his freezing hands (he had no gloves) and his freezing ass (a figurative condition covering his overall
feeling of being cold), then he might have reflected
upon how beautiful the fall of snow was on those
untraveled back roads.

Pristine. A word he probably did not know.

But instead he was so angry he couldn't see
straight. His anger was mostly directed at Brianna,
who, he believed, made it as difficult as possible for
him to see his daughter, but some of his anger was
also directed at the Tracker family as a whole, a sorry
bunch of bastards according to his way of thinking.
He especially did not like Danny Tracker, the cop,
who made it plain from day one that he didn't think
Spence was good enough to marry his daughter.

Fucking bastard!

Spence's anger built as he walked along in his
sneakers, no coat, no hat, the only warmth in him

was in his gut—a raging disgust that he reasoned would probably end up giving him an ulcer. He was cold and alone and friendless—except for the revolver tucked in his belt. In fantasies that warmed him, he imagined lining up as many Trackers as he could find and summarily executing them.

The only Tracker he would spare would be Emily.

God, I love her!

She tugged at his heart.

She tugged so hard that sometimes he feared he might start crying. And wouldn't that be a fucking deal? he reasoned. A grown man crying at the thought of a daughter he couldn't be with, couldn't tuck into bed every night. Well, it was her mother's fault. As Spence slogged on, bringing himself ever closer to Soldier's Crossing, he saw things very clearly—saw his past clearly. The wheels started coming off the vehicle of his life because Brianna simply had not understood him. She had nagged him constantly about getting a better job and being more responsible and drinking less and not wrecking his Camaro and . . . Jesus, a man could only take so much.

And then he had to smack someone.

And that someone, on occasion, was Brianna.

Never Emily.

Brianna had a way of getting on his nerves so hard that he would snap, and when he snapped, he would be forced to sic his anger on her. That was the long and short of it.

Goddamn her!

Shivering, his feet having frozen into chunks of ice, Spence suddenly thought of Target.

Oh shit, I miss that dog!

It had been his boyhood dog. Just a big mutt, a

mixed breed, a Confederate stew of collie and shepherd and a pinch of pit bull for flavoring. As a teenager Spence had turned that dog mean because . . . because, well, because his father had turned *him* mean. It was his father's fault. The bastard. The loser. A loser who drank. A loser who drank and took out his frustrations on a son who was trying to do the best he could. Target was his only friend. Target understood why something or someone needed to suffer as a result of the abuse Spence had experienced. Target understood that when Spence sicced him on a stray cat it was a way of bringing a rough justice to the world. Spence's world.

But wasn't a gun better than a mean dog?

He toyed briefly with the thought before almost mentally choking on it. Up ahead he saw a fire. He was immediately gladdened by the sight of it because, unless he missed his estimate, that house was Warren Tracker's on the edge of his junkyard. Spence began to jog toward the burning house; though within a hundred yards of it, he knew it was a goner. He wondered whether Warren and his invalid wife and his retarded son had escaped.

Wouldn't break my heart if they didn't.

Because they were Trackers.

The smoke and the final remnants of flames mixed with the fog and falling snow to create a hellish scene. Out in the junkyard itself he could see an old school bus smoldering. Spence decided there was no need to investigate. He had only one thing in mind and that was reaching the warmth of Brianna's trailer, where he could hug his daughter and, goddamn it, his ex-wife couldn't do a fucking thing about it. If she tried, he might just have to pull his gun on her.

Nag at this, bitch!

He snatched the gun from his belt and waved it at nothing.

Up beyond Warren Tracker's place Spence heard dogs barking. It was a good sound. Dogs enjoying the sound of their barks, playing in the snow, maybe—or perhaps chasing something in the field right before you got to Blink Tracker's house, where that old bore lived with those two weird, cuntless daughters of his.

Spence had angled slightly off the road into the large open lot, all the while following the barking of the dogs. Above the lot the fog had cleared enough for him to see the sky, and when he chanced to look into that sky, he saw something that freaked him so much he almost shit in his pants.

It was the biggest bird—or flying creature of some kind—he'd ever seen.

"Motherfuck!" he whispered.

He heard more barking. Then he heard a man's laughter.

Another forty yards and Spence McVicar thought maybe he'd lost his mind or that he was so cold he was hallucinating.

"Damn it all to hell," he whispered. "What the fuck is . . . ?"

Warren Tracker was running across the field of snow right at him, only he wasn't looking at Spence. He was looking up at the flying creature: his son, Royal.

Spence was so amazed at the sight that his legs buckled and he sat down hard on his ass in the snow and held on to his gun with both hands as if he were holding on to the only piece of sanity left on the planet. He watched as Warren continued running—a small pack of dogs joyfully barking at his heels—and up in the air, maybe fifty or sixty feet, was Royal, his arms out stiff like wings in a glide. He was negotiating slow half-loops. It was like watching a kite that was getting too close to the ground.

Then Royal swung left, then right, dropped, hit the ground and stumbled to a landing. Behind his son a bit, Warren hollered, "See I told you I'd make you fly." But Royal's attention was being directed at Spence, who scrambled to his feet and slapped a two-handed grip on his gun and aimed it at Royal's chest.

"Stop right there, motherfucker!"

Royal laughed.

His dogs, eight or ten in number, clustered around him and began barking savagely at the figure of Spence.

"Hush, fellas," said Royal. "He can't hurt us."

"Oh, you're wrong 'bout that, friend," Spence responded. "Just don't get no fuckin' closer or you'll see what kind of hurt I can put on you."

"Is that Spence McVicar?" Warren Tracker called out.

"Yes, sir," said Royal. "He's got a gun. Nobody's told him guns aren't safe."

Royal and his dogs continued their slow, matter-of-fact movement toward Spence, who quaked in his tracks because their eyes looked funny, burning with the wrong kind of light. And it was scaring the living hell out of him.

"Stay back, goddamn it, I said!"

But Royal kept coming. Spence blinked. He blinked several times because it certainly appeared that Royal had fangs and fingernails like knife blades. And the dogs had a menacing air about them that came right out of a nightmare. Spence, too frightened even to yell again, sputtered something unintelligible and squeezed off two shots, hitting Royal in the chest and knocking him to his knees. Then he shot two of the dogs. The others held back.

"You're wasting your bullets," said Warren. He stood over the figure of his fallen son, and there was silence for a half a dozen heartbeats and then Spence flat out couldn't believe what happened next: Royal and the two dead dogs got up.

"No way in hell," Spence whispered to himself in a voice he didn't recognize as his own. And then he tossed his worthless gun aside and started running—running like little boys do in their dreams.

The next thing he felt was a hand on the back of his sweatshirt—a hand reaching down from above him—and the *next* thing he felt was losing contact with the ground, and he heard his own voice crying out with some primal utterance of total terror. He closed his eyes and then vomited on himself before Royal's voice intruded.

"Hey, man, I'm dead and my daddy brought me back to life and fixed it so I could fly."

They swung up and out and leveled off at about the height of a telephone pole, and down below them Royal's dogs circled and barked, their teeth bared, the ruffs of their necks standing up to signal their readiness for violence.

"What the hell you think of this, Spence?" It was Warren, hands cupped to megaphone his voice. "What the hell you think?"

Spence thought he was going to pass out, but he fought it. He was totally helpless, totally at the mercy of these two crazed Trackers, one of whom could somehow fly. Spence prayed that he was experiencing a nightmare. Which would end soon.

"Spence," said Royal, exclaiming into the flight rush of air, "I gotta drop you."

"No, man. Shit, no. Why you gotta drop me?"

Royal circled once more, then hovered maybe twenty feet over his father and the snarling pack of dogs.

"Because my dogs," he said, ". . . they's hungry."

Before he hit the ground, Spence's scream could be heard all the way to downtown Soldier's Crossing. His last sensation was glancing at one of the attacking dogs and thinking that it looked an awful lot like Target.

Mollie Tracker's fingers trembled as they traced the words on the page. Leviticus 7:27: "Every person who eats the blood shall be cut off from his father's kin."

The storm had awakened her, the wind howling fiercely, and to Mollie, it sounded like demons calling to her from the end of the world. She had been dreaming, as had become her habit of recent, this another vivid one about blood—peopled with faceless folks she thought she recognized.

Drinking each other's blood.

Why, she wondered, would a good Christian woman dream such a dream?

It was incomprehensible to her.

She sat in partial darkness with the Bible in her lap. She had recalled the passage from Leviticus, but found that she needed to read it again to make certain she was fully aware of God's law. And there it was. In biblical black and white. Anyone consuming blood ". . . shall be cut off from his father's kin."

So. What she needed was to put the whole matter out of her mind and think of something else or someone else—perhaps she would think of Ruby Tracker. Didn't she have a birthday coming up in the next few days? Or was it, she asked herself, next month? She made a mental note to get over to see Ruby more often. The poor woman had hardly any friends. Such a woman, an invalid woman, would receive good cheer in hearing from a Christian woman, one who could offer the hopeful words of the wonderful shepherd, Jesus.

I'm coming for you.

Mollie bolted straight up.

"Who's there?"

Her heart trip-hammering, she patted at her ample bosom; she was tottering on the edge, suddenly thinking she was going crazy—all the bad dreams—and now hearing voices. Though it could have been the voice of God. Or, no, perhaps the voice of Jesus who had appeared in several of her dreams.

"Coming for me?" she whispered.

You've suffered enough.

Much like the voice of her son Franklin, who lay with men. Would God forgive him for that?

"Oh, who are you? Where are you?"

She found herself watching the closed door to her room.

When suddenly, Franklin stepped through it.

Mollie gasped.

"Are you real? Franklin? Is that you? Are you real?"

He approached her.

"Very," he said.

He strode over to where she was sitting and took the Bible from her. He quickly scanned the passages it was opened to.

"Your book is wrong," he said.

"Franklin, no," she exclaimed. "It's the word of God."

"It's wrong," he said. "I have learned that eating blood makes us one with kin. It makes us family in a miraculous, wonderful way."

"It brings death," she muttered. "Going against the word of God can only lead to death."

"No. Blood is the life. I know this to be true."

"Why have you come? You must be under the control of Satan. You lay with men. You go against God's word at every turn."

"I came because you have suffered enough. Like Ruby. You have lost your husband and your two sons—and you cannot have another life. There is nothing more for you except the lies in this book."

He handed the Bible back to her, and she clutched it to her bosom. Tears trickled down her cheeks.

"Do you love your mother, Franklin?"

"You're not my mother, and I'm not your son. The son who had you as his mother is dead. And now alive again. But even I do not want for you to suffer."

Mollie began to quake with anger.

"Are you going to kill me? Cut me and eat my blood? Is that what Satan commands you to do?"

"No. Violence is not my way."

Slumping forward, the woman sighed heavily as her anger relented.

"I'm so tired. And I miss your father. And I have bad dreams. And I wonder if Ruby, Warren's Ruby, needs my help. Will you check on her?"

"Ruby doesn't need anyone's help. I can assure you of that. Her suffering is over."

"I don't understand. I don't understand what you want. Why have you come?"

"I told you," he said calmly. "I've come because

you've suffered enough. You cannot and will not be on our side—you cannot be a Tracker and have a new and glorious life. There's nothing more for you. Your life is over."

"Franklin, I'm so tired. I don't want any more bad dreams. I just want to sleep."

He reached out to her and placed his fingertips on her forehead.

"And so you shall," he said.

Chapter Seventeen

The Eyes of the Waking Serpents

Was it true?

Toting Em on his back through the snow as the sun peeked through the low, gray clouds, Jacob could not get the issue of his identity out of his thoughts. Was it possible? Could he have lived on the planet all these years and not known that no Tracker blood flowed through his veins? Why wouldn't his parents have told him? Why wouldn't *someone* have told him? Or why hadn't he guessed it himself?

No, the bottom line was that he rejected what Franklin had told Brianna.

No, it was a vampire's way of messing with their minds.

And yet.

If it were true, then he and Brianna were not blood related and the love they shared for each other . . . no, he couldn't let himself entertain such a dream. He just couldn't.

"Hey, you're awfully quiet?"

It was Brianna so close that the puffs of her breath were mingling with his as they slogged through the deep snow, heading for Mr. Pancake. She hooked her arm inside his elbow and it felt marvelous; marvelous, too, was the feathery weight of Em as she chortled on about nothing in particular, just giggly over the nature of her transport.

"Oh, sorry," said Jacob. "Lots to think about."

"I know. Me too. I wish I could, you know, shake the effect that Franklin had on me. It's scary."

"I won't let anything happen to you and Em. I promise."

She squeezed his arm and rested her head against his shoulder as they walked. The sun speared through the clouds, momentarily opening a scene of quiet beauty to them: the drifts of snow, its eye-blistering, bright whiteness forcing them to squint.

"Maybe this is a good sign," she said, her reference to the sun obvious.

"Maybe."

There was still only the barest trickle of traffic. They walked on in silence for a few more yards, lost in their own musings as Em sang snatches of a Faith Hill song she knew by heart. Brianna looked up and held Jacob's gaze; he couldn't help staring at the barely perceptible outline of a hand on her cheek. Made by a vampire. Like the brand of ownership. Like the biblical mark of the beast. When she spoke, her voice lowered a notch into a heart-arresting seriousness.

"We'll always have each other, won't we?"

The warmth flooding through him almost made him stumble and fall. He smiled down at her. "Yes. Whatever happens from this point—yeah, we've got each other." Then, much to the delight of Em, he started jogging. "And we've got this little cowgirl—unless she gets bucked off her horse and lands in a snowdrift and we can't find her. Hold on. Oh, this is a bad, bucking bronco. I sure hope Em's a good cowgirl."

"I am a good cowgirl," she squealed, locking her tiny arms around his neck.

And laughter trailed them all the way to the door of Mr. Pancake.

It suddenly seemed a bright and shining, joyful world—one in which vampires couldn't possibly exist.

And it felt like home inside the restaurant.

Bo had his CLOSED sign up, but when he saw the threesome approach, he scurried around from behind the counter and let them in.

"Y'all get in here outta the cold. Got my generator goin' and these folks here are fixin' to have some eats if the cook'll stay at the griddle. Better join 'em."

"Sounds good," said Brianna.

"There's gray-gran'ma," Em cried out, pointing at Jacob's mother.

Em climbed from Jacob's back and ran to a booth where Gladys Tracker was sitting with Miriam Tracker and her remaining son, Tyler. Brianna followed, but Jacob lingered at the counter.

"Looks like a Tracker reunion."

"Don't it now," said Bo. He turned to the booth area and called out, "Hey, pancakes and sausage and bacon OK with y'all?" He got a resounding "yes." Then he turned his attention back to Jacob. "I was up early. Couldn't sleep, in fact. So I slapped snow tires on the van—hadn't used 'em in years—and figured you and your mother could be trapped at home. You was gone, but I picked up your mother and headed out to Miriam's and got her and Tyler. Calvin, he wasn't home, and I didn't chance it out to Warren's and Blink's—I saw smoke out there."

"You think Franklin got there?" said Jacob.

"I do. Just like I think he raised this storm. He's bringin' fire 'n ice. I figured I was too late out there. That's why I came on straight here. I reckoned you was probably with Brianna."

He gave Jacob a knowing look with the squint of an eye and Jacob chuckled.

"I'm a mystery to nobody but myself," he murmured.

Minutes later, everyone was laughing and eating syrup-laden pancakes, some with orders of meat on the side, others with the pancakes smothered in blueberries or strawberries with huge dollops of whipped cream atop the berries. Milk and fresh, hot coffee to drink.

Storms and vampires seemed a million miles away.

Jacob stayed at the counter while Brianna and Em were enjoying the company of his mother and Miriam. Ben Tracker showed up as well, and after asking Jacob whether he had seen Danny, he slid into a booth with Tyler and dug into a big order of pancakes. Jacob told the boy that his father was probably with Sharelle.

"Least, I hope he is," he muttered to Bo.

"We've got one hell of a fight on our hands," said Bo. He poured himself coffee and leaned his elbows on the counter across from Jacob.

"So what's Franklin's next move?" Jacob asked. He felt a touch guilty for not coming clean immediately with Bo about what Brianna had learned, but he reasoned that he had a right to be coy, especially if secrets had been withheld from him for years.

"He'll make the rounds. Line up Trackers like dominoes. Knock 'em down one right after another till he's got the whole dang family. The snowstorm was a helluva good ploy—isolate folks and visit 'em one by one. Franklin knows it'll keep you and me and Danny barkin' up trees—barkin' but not stoppin' things. He's got us goin' pretty good, I'd say."

"It's worse than that," said Jacob.

"How so?"

"We're dealing with a ticking clock now. You see, Franklin visited Brianna earlier."

"Holy shit—what happened?"

"I'll let her tell it."

Bo issued a low whistle of fear. "Yeah, I better get an earful of this."

"Wait, Bo. There's something else. Just a question."

"Shoot it right at me."

Jacob took a deep breath.

"The Tracker vampires only prey on other Trackers. It's all in the blood—we figured that out pretty early. Like you say, Franklin's probably out there even as we speak attacking the family one member at a time and setting family member onto family member. Well, we know then why he hasn't tried to attack you—you're not a Tracker. But what about me? He had a chance right here in this restaurant, and he didn't take it. What's up with that?"

Bo stared long and hard at Jacob before lowering his eyes and shaking his head.

"I don't have all the answers," Bo said. "We don't even know the rules these vampires are playing by in terms of the usual conventions. What you're askin'—I just don't know."

"I think maybe you do. But I won't press you. More important thing at the moment is for you to hear Brianna's story."

Bo nodded soberly, and the two men waited until everyone had finished eating before they cornered Brianna and Jacob's mother and asked Miriam to let the four of them talk for a few minutes. While Ben and Tyler played with a video game next to the jukebox, Miriam took Em behind the counter to make stick animals out of straws.

Beyond the plate glass, clouds were gathering. And in the west, still quite distant, rumbles of thunder.

"What strange weather," Jacob's mother remarked.

"Unnatural, that's for sure," Bo added.

Jacob and Brianna sat on one side of the booth with Jacob's mother directly across from him, and Bo across from Brianna. After an awkward run of seconds Jacob said, "Brianna's got something I'd like for you to hear. Some things we need to be aware of."

He gave her a reassuring hug, and she began.

Jacob's mother and Bo listened intently, alarm spreading across their faces when Brianna narrated Franklin's threat regarding Em. When she had mentioned everything except Franklin's comments about Jacob not being a Tracker, Jacob broke in.

"Could be we've learned something about their weaknesses. And I'll go ahead and say this: I'm not ashamed of my feelings for Brianna, and I don't think she's ashamed of hers for me."

"No reason that you should be," said his mother.

She smiled and reached across the table and lovingly touched the hands of both her son and Brianna. But Jacob didn't meet her smile; instead, he and Brianna gazed into each other's eyes, and Jacob picked up her invisible signal to have courage for what else needed to be explored.

Bo nodded.

"Absolutely no shame," he said. "And what you've told us makes me think as long as Franklin hasn't converted too many Trackers yet, we got a good chance to fight 'im. You and Brianna and that little Emily need to stay tight together. Might be the key to stoppin' all this."

Outside, the wind kicked up and large drops of rain were tossed against the glass. It was the kind of change in weather that made one shiver involuntarily. Jacob noticed it and felt the inevitable questions surging forward.

"There's one thing more," he said. "Something Franklin brought up—something I'm not ready to believe."

"What is it?" said his mother.

And he found there was no easy way to couch his remarks. They had to be spread on the table like a hand of poker that had been called.

"Franklin claims I'm not a Tracker. He's wrong about that, isn't he?"

His mother's eyes held with his momentarily. Then fell. She glanced at Bo, and his eyes shared something with her, and the silence surrounding the foursome was like a low-grade static, like radio reception that did not promise to clear up readily. Jacob knew what their reactions meant.

When his mother reached for his hand again, he pulled it away.

"Why?" he said. "Why in the hell didn't you tell me?"

His mother straightened, brushed at the tears seeping from the corners of her eyes, and choked out a few words.

"Because. Because I've never thought of you as anything else but a Tracker." She paused, and her voice strengthened. "You fit into our family perfectly. You've loved being a Tracker—your love of family has always been right out where everyone could see it. Your father and I talked many times about telling you—but, oh, there's no excuse. Not telling you was a mistake, and I'm deeply sorry, and I hope you'll forgive me. Please, Jacob. Please."

He swallowed and felt as if his head were filled with air and might detach and float up away from his body at any moment.

"I don't know what to think," he said. "I don't know enough to decide that."

"Gladys, we better tell the whole story," said Bo.

Jacob glared at Bo.

"Then you knew, too? I thought so. Jesus, this is incredible."

"I had an infant son die," his mother began again, her voice distant and seemingly disengaged. "And it threw me into a depression. And my doctor—my doctor was Orpheus's brother, James, and he . . ."

With a shallow desperation in her eyes, she let her voice trail off as she glanced searchingly at Bo.

"I'll go on with this from here," he said. He hesitated, working his hands together, wetting his lips and frowning, and Jacob saw how much the lives of his mother and Bo were tempered by secrets. They were of a generation in which secrets remained secrets like something in the blood. "My brother,

James," Bo continued, "well, most folks called him 'Doctor Jimmy'—you see, he never really meant to break the law or nothin' like that. But the long and short of it is that from the 1950s right on up into the 1970s he had sort of a questionable bidness on the side."

"You mean a baby business, don't you?" said Brianna. Tears were skating down her cheeks, but to Jacob, she was showing her strength, showing how much she cared for him.

"Yes, ma'am, I do." Then he looked up directly at Jacob. "Your mother never knew your real parents, son. Jimmy, he was gist helpin' some young lady who was in trouble, who probably didn't have a husband, didn't have no way to take care of a new infant and so . . . and even if you wanted to find out who that young lady was, you couldn't. When Jimmy passed in 1995, I destroyed all of those kinda records. Besides, he probably only documented what he absolutely had to. He was slick 'bout covering up a paper trail—I'll give him that. And he admired your mother and father, and he knew they'd be the best parents in the county. So there it is."

Numbing white noise, as white as the snow covering his hometown, seized Jacob's thoughts for a score of seconds before his senses kicked in once again. He felt Brianna embracing him. He felt his mother's fingertips on his arm. He heard her crying softly. And it began to rain harder. And he recalled that Franklin had claimed that the rains would come—to Jacob, a definite sign that the vampires were in control. He closed his eyes and tried to gather himself and get some kind of handle on what it all meant. His identity. The truth. But it raced past him, leaving him alone and bewildered. But when he opened his eyes, his mother's face loomed before him, and he could see the love in it and because that love was there, like something indestructible, he smiled.

"It's OK," he said. "I just need some time to think about who I am now."

Bo started to follow Jacob's comment when Ben suddenly dashed up to the booth.

"Hey, Stromile Greene's out here, and I think he's got his sister. They come up the back way. Used a pair of mules is what it looks like."

Prophetess Zammie didn't seem like the same woman.

That was Jacob's view, but then his world had been turned upside down, so he couldn't be certain he was seeing the whole reality of anything. His powers of judgment and discernment seemed to be dissolving like wet tissue.

"She had me carry her ta here," Stromile explained. "She want ta tell y'all 'bout serpents and death and the fire blazin' behind her eyes."

Brother and sister were cold from the long, damp, chilly trip into town. Zammie had ridden upon what resembled a combination sled and travois attached to two strong mules led along by Stromile. Once they were inside, Bo cleared a booth for them and made them cups of hot tea. Zammie sat with her hands clutching her cup, warming her long fingers, warming herself as her brother stood nearby taking gulps of the scalding tea as if it were only lukewarm.

Jacob and Brianna sat directly opposite the woman whose blond hair and light-complexioned face seemed darker and older than when Jacob had last

seen her, and this time, she wore no lipstick and
sported no smile, but her eyes were crossed and
milky as before. They waited for her to settle in.
Everyone else stood close to the booth. The moment
was filled both with magic and dread.

Several tense minutes passed before she spoke.

"I told you winter would come," she said in a voice
that, once again to Jacob, sounded like the purring
of a cat. "And there's been fires and death in life."
She stopped suddenly and looked around. "Where
be that little one? The bitsy girl. Let Zammie see her."

"Do you mean my daughter, Emily?" said Brianna.

"The one Nature bless to be tiny in body and giant
in spirit."

Brianna called Emily to her side, and when Prophetess Zammie beckoned for her, she went without
hesitation, as if knowing intuitively she would not
be harmed. She sat upon Zammie's lap, and the seer
woman studied her face for what seemed nearly a
minute before saying, "So you, precious least one,
so you are their missing piece."

Brianna gasped.

"That's just what Franklin called her."

Zammie bobbed her head knowingly, then
touched Emily's face much as the vampire had
touched Brianna's; but no flesh was seared, no
shadow of a print remained when the prophetess
removed her hand. "Go on and play, my child," she
said to the slip of a girl. "You are much too big for
anyone's heart to hold you."

When Emily had flitted away, Bo was quick to say,
"What have you come to tell us? You saw the storm.
What do you see now?"

As if immensely weary, the woman cradled her

chin in the palm of her hand and stared down at the top of the table as if it were a crystal ball.

"I see serpents," she said.

And her words spread chills through Jacob, and he assumed that others felt a terror blanket them as well. Then he said, "The vampire told Brianna that he was letting Trackers out of their cages. What does that mean?"

Almost as if she hadn't heard him, or, perhaps, was ignoring him, the woman began rubbing her fingertips over the tabletop. "Trackers are like serpents waiting to be awakened by fire. When they awaken, the fire flickers in their eyes and they are dead, yet more alive than any of us."

"Which ones?" said Bo. "Which Trackers have been turned into vampires? We need to know. We have to know how much of an opposition we have."

"Some things are horrible to know," she said.

"But we have to have an idea of what's out there," Jacob countered, unable to keep a suggestion of exasperation from his voice.

At that point Stromile stepped through the gathering to his sister and leaned down and whispered something inaudible to her, then he kissed her on the forehead and bowed back to his station behind everyone. Zammie's smile was suddenly more animated. She drew herself up and looked around.

"Are we ready?" she said.

There were murmurs of assent.

And then she began.

Jacob found himself trying to picture each attack and to see through to the core of Franklin's elegant design of taking lives and transporting blood beyond death. The roll call was a dark litany: Winston, then Calvin and nebulous images of his going to Warren's, and then the sacrifice of Jeremy. Warren as vampire, relishing a newfound river of blood, spreading his rebirth to his son and bringing death to his wife, Ruby.

Calvin, Warren, Royal—Jacob glanced over at Bo, who returned the glance and shook his head somberly.

Zammie paused. She was breathing out in tiny puffs, panting rather like an overheated animal in the summer sun. Once again she spread her hands out over the table, causing everyone to inch closer as if they entertained hopes of being able to see what only she could see—hoping to view the same supranormal television screen that she was watching.

"The man who worked at the Piggly Wiggly—he took his daughters, too."

Jacob could hear his shallow breathing; listening to the woman was mesmerizing. He thought of Winston and Mattie Lee and Janie and he shut his eyes tightly, cringing against the pain of two more Trackers lost to the realm of vampires. But he could not have anticipated that the real pain was just beginning and would, in fact, become even more excruciating.

"The leader went downtown," said Zammie. She was hunched over the table, peering down into its surface like someone working a huge jigsaw puzzle. "And the young woman with long hair and many, many candles was next."

"Oh Jesus," Jacob murmured. "That has to be Sharelle."

Zammie methodically described Sharelle's murder of Jerry Garbo and his wife, Big Eva, and of Kitt and Cardinal, and when she had completed that part of the vision, she suddenly slumped back in the booth and Stromile rushed forward. And Bo was there quickly as well.

"Get her a glass of water, somebody," he said.

When she had sipped at the water and recovered herself, she apologized. Bo thanked her for sharing her vision.

"What's gone on," he added, "it's worse than we expected. Calvin, Warren, Royal, Winston, Mattie Lee, Janie and Sharelle—Franklin's been busy takin' the life out of this family. I guess I mean that more than just literally."

He looked around, his countenance grave and weighted down, and then he caught Jacob's eye, but all Jacob could do was shake his head, incredulous. Stromile had stepped forward to help Zammie out of the booth, but quite suddenly she raised a hand to stop him.

"Wait," she said. "There's more."

There was a collective holding of breath by everyone who had been watching the spectacle unfold.

"But everyone else is here," said Brianna. And no sooner had she spoken those words than a choke of tears seized her. "No," she said. "No, please don't say it's—"

Zammie's concentration was absorbed in the table-top, her eyes surrendering to a milky covering, and then she began to describe Sharelle floating among candles and creating a deadrise for her father to view, then turning her vampire essence upon her father, blood on blood. Until he was no longer her father—anyone's father.

"My God," Jacob whispered.

And then a roar—"No-o-o-o!"—and Bo reaching out to stop Ben, who was tearing at the seer woman, enraged, grief ripping at him, a son refusing to believe that his father had been taken into the realm of the dead.

And had been returned from it to a life beyond imagination.

It was the legendary Ames-Dahlgren knife.

He held it up by the end of the handle, letting the blade dangle before his eyes, letting the firelight glint from it in tiny explosions of light. Light but no warmth. That was what Myron Florence was experiencing as he shivered before the fire he had kindled in the fireplace in the antique-filled living room of The Treasure House.

He was waiting for what wanted to come.

The knife was how it began. And this was not a copy, not a replica—this was the real thing. Designed circa 1856 by Admiral John A. Dahlgren, only around 1,800 of these particular knives were produced by the Ames Manufacturing Company between 1861 and 1864. Made to fit the Whitney Plymouth Navy Rifle, these knives doubled as saber bayonets.

It was the first piece he and Franklin had bought for The Treasure House.

It all started with a weapon. Now it would end with this same weapon.

Or such were Myron's projections, his wishes scripted for the plot of the day.

A light, cold rain was falling beyond the living room's picture window. On a similar day, not too many years ago, Myron had driven into east Alabama from New Jersey, where he had been teaching English at a private school. But his dream had been to move to the South and write the next great Civil

War novel—make the world forget about *Gone With the Wind*. How was he to fund his fanciful adventure? Well, that was all kudzu and moon pies in a sense. Dreams and wishful thinking usually don't have dollar signs included. And yet, in east Alabama, Myron found something better than just a place where he might launch his literary career.

He met Franklin Tracker. Young, handsome, his blood filled with the eager meaninglessness necessary to try anything—a new sexual orientation not excluded. Myron fell in love. Fell deeply, hopelessly, dangerously in love. While he couldn't literally marry his new love, he could, he discovered, marry his new love's dream. Which was to buy the old Cooperston House in Soldier's Crossing and turn it into an upscale antiques shop. And they did.

In the reverie of the flames Myron stared beyond the blade of the highly valuable knife and wondered what had taken his love from him. What beast? What monster? For, had it been another man—or, perish the thought, another woman—he could have come to terms with that; albeit suffering a broken heart in one's fifties would be the emotional equivalent of suffering a broken hip: one might figuratively "limp" the rest of his life.

Locked in his dark reverie, Myron thought about courage.

How it had taken courage to leave his position in New Jersey, move to Alabama to be with Franklin, buy the Cooperston House, start up a new business, fight a rampant local homophobia, and find peace of mind.

But how much *more* courage would it take to kill the thing he loved?

I have to see him one more time.

So he would be patient; for patience, wrote the poet Rilke, is everything.

He knew somehow that he wouldn't have long to wait, and though he tried with all his might to remain vigilant, to keep the hurt of his abandonment ready and on the surface so that he could send his onetime partner on a roaring guilt trip, he began to doze off.

He never, in fact, heard Franklin enter the room. Never heard him tread ever so softly up to him and whisper in his ear, "I've come for you. I'm here to give you what you need."

At first, Myron assumed he was dreaming.

His lover appeared to be ringed with a numinous aura.

Light but not warmth.

"I don't know who you are," said Myron. He remained seated as the man who was once Franklin, the man who was once his lover, hunkered down in front of him and glanced from Myron to the knife and back to Myron.

"And you can't know," said the vampire.

"Why?"

"Because you don't really want to know. You are trapped in a world we used to have. But I have a new world now. A new life."

"What was wrong with the old one?"

The vampire paused. He looked deep into Myron's eyes.

"It wasn't enough."

"God, I just can't. . . ." Myron choked back a rush of emotion. Tears threatened. "What more . . . what more did you want? Our business was finally doing well. This house—we had it fixed just the way we wanted it. We had intellectual stimulation—right here. Right here in front of this fireplace, how many nights did we while away talking about art or books or music? We lost ourselves examining the works of Vermeer, galvanized by the magnificent detail he lavished on domestic scenes. We read Chekhov's plays aloud, and we talked about Christina Rossetti's poetry and Oscar Wilde's 'De Profundis.' We each had our favorite music—Bach for me; Schubert for you. And we had intimacy, and sometimes it was passionate and sometimes it was something else, something companionable, but it was there. What else did you need?"

The vampire shifted on the balls of his feet and smiled mysteriously.

"I needed a new self."

"Who changed you? *What* changed you?"

The vampire shook his head.

"Don't," he said. "Don't look for a target of blame. I changed myself. I was waiting for this to come. I've always been waiting for this life."

"But what made you choose it?"

Sighing an almost human sigh, the vampire said, "Something in the blood."

"Damn you!" Myron hissed. "You're killing me. Don't you see that?"

"I do. And I regret that. I don't want you to suffer. Remember us as we were—but I'm living a life beyond what we had."

"I can't. I don't want to live without you," Myron sobbed.

"That's why I have come."

The vampire waited as Myron cried, his face buried in one hand, the other hand continuing to clutch the knife. When in control of his tears, he wiped his face.

"What happened to the love?"

"I've left it behind," said the vampire. "I've found something deeper and more meaningful."

"What? What could possibly be deeper than love?"

"Blood."

Myron gritted his teeth and shook his head, and resignation seized his body. "You have the eyes of a deadly snake," he said. "And all that remains for me is to see that you don't spread your poison more than you have."

When he lifted the knife with both hands, the vampire gestured for him to wait a moment so that he could part his cloak and bare his chest.

"In the heart," said the vampire. "Stake me here. But if you do, you will be denying me a glorious existence. Being a vampire is magic. The only magic I've ever known."

Myron shuddered as the knife, angled so that it would penetrate the vampire's heart, trembled in his hands. His body willed that he would do the deed, but something, in the end, wouldn't allow it—his humanity, his soul, his love—or maybe something indefinable and unsayable.

After a shattering passing of seconds, he lowered the knife.

And he wept again.

The vampire gently took the knife from him and kissed his forehead.

"You've suffered enough," he said.

Then, for a moment, Myron composed himself and nearly smiled. "Kiss me here," he said, "once more."

The vampire tilted his head and kissed the man coldly on his lips.

Myron shivered at the passionless gesture.

Then the vampire reached out and touched the

man's chest, and the man cried out in pain—just for an instant—as the vampire's hand penetrated flesh and bone and grasped the beating heart and squeezed it.

Until it stopped.

Jacob couldn't keep him from leaving.

Hearing that his father had been turned into a vampire, Ben had tried to tear away from the restaurant, but Jacob had caught him at the door.

"It's no use. You can't save him, and without help you probably couldn't destroy him."

"Goddamn it, I have to see him," Ben shouted. "My dad. Maybe it's not too late. I have to see him. Don't try to stop me."

Jacob held on as long as he could before the young man's strength and determination became too much. "Don't go alone, Ben," he said, losing his grip. "He's my brother. Let me go with you. And Bo, too."

Having freed himself and having climbed onto his cycle in the soft rain, Ben turned.

"No. This is what I've got to do on my own. I've got to show him how much I love him."

And then he was gone.

"Let him go," Bo called to Jacob.

Then only the ghostly shape of the blue-gray exhaust remained as evidence that the young man had been there. Jacob went back inside. Brianna rushed into his arms, and they held each other tightly. Stromile Greene and his sister, Zammie, stood quietly nearby.

Despite Bo's pleading with them to stay, they insisted on leaving.

"I'm sorry I had to be the one to bring you the truth," Zammie told all of them as she and her brother readied to go.

"We needed to hear it," said Bo.

Then Zammie crouched down and called for Emily, and the tiny girl ran into her arms.

"Little Miss, you stay close to the folks who love you. Will you do that?"

"I will," said Emily.

Jacob saw a painful frown spread across Zammie's brow and wanted desperately to be able to translate it. He had had enough of secrets. He watched then as the wise woman whispered something to Brianna, who accepted whatever was passed on to her with little emotion.

When Stromile and Zammie and their two strong mules had disappeared into the cold, wet day, Bo made fresh pots of coffee, declaring that those remaining had to make some crucial decisions regarding the future. Tyler was asked to play with Emily in the back room out of earshot of the grown-ups; he went reluctantly, and Jacob could tell that he wanted to be included among the adults.

Gladys, Miriam, Brianna, Jacob and Bo sat at one of the tables and listened to the rain intensify.

"We can't fight this," said Bo.

At first, no one else said anything. Gladys and Miriam had on their masks of motherly concern, and Brianna clung to Jacob, and he, in turn, felt a need to challenge Bo's view. But he couldn't muster the energy or the vision.

"I'm afraid you're right. If we still had Danny . . . as it is, they've got the upper hand. So then what do we do?"

"We stay together as a group and get ourselves out of town," said Bo.

"But where can we go?" asked Gladys.

"And won't they follow us?" observed Jacob. "I mean, Franklin indicated that they wanted Emily—won't they come after us, or, at least, come after her?" He felt Brianna squeeze his arm more firmly.

Bo let his eyes drift out into the parking lot, where the rain had started beating down harder, melting the snow and turning the roads of Soldier's Crossing to slush.

"They might come after us, sure, but we can't stay. My brother, Jimmy, had a cabin up near Mt. Pogahatchee in the Pogahatchee Forest. We can go there. Franklin gave Brianna a deadline of midnight. That doesn't give us much time to pack a few belongings and transport everybody up there."

"What about Ben?" said Jacob.

"If he comes back, he can come with us—otherwise, we just don't have options, and we don't have much time."

There was solemn, tacit agreement.

Alone at the table, Jacob and Brianna talked quietly.

"He'll find us," she whispered. "Franklin won't let us get away. He's in my head, Jacob. He knows what we're doing and where we are—he knows because he's in my head."

She sobbed against his shoulder, and he held her tightly.

"But remember that our love makes it difficult for them. It's our best weapon. Franklin can't take that away—he can't make you stop loving Em or stop loving me."

In a tearful whisper she responded, "No, but he

makes me feel dirty. He makes me feel that I don't deserve your love—and that I don't deserve Em."

"Don't—just don't think about it." He continued holding her and then asked her what Zammie had whispered to her just before she and Stromile left.

"She said that the vampires got Spence."

"Oh, Brianna, I'm sorry," said Jacob.

She shook her head. "I wish I could feel some regret, but I don't—except for Em. She's lost her real father; though as I see it, she's better off without him."

Suddenly, Tyler was there, close to them, pale and agitated, his eyes red and teary and his jaw defiant.

"We have to fight them," he said. "For Josh—for what he tried to do. He tried to save us. We can't just run."

Jacob stood up and Tyler stumbled into his arms.

Brianna pushed up out of her chair, alarm spreading across her expression.

"Tyler, where's Emily? You didn't leave her alone, did you?"

"No," said Tyler. "She's not alone."

Brianna began looking around frantically.

"Then who's with her?" Tyler's eyes were sad; he was the picture of a boy confused and frightened.

"She's with Cousin Sharelle and Uncle Danny," he said.

And Brianna's scream filled the restaurant.

Chapter Eighteen

Time to Set the
Night on Fire

The heaviest of the rainfall ended a few hours later.

Cold stars winked to life in the dark sky, and to Stromile Greene, it was a vampire sky, a vampire night. He was chilled to the bone. He and his sister and their two strong mules had sought shelter in an abandoned barn on the edge of Soldier's Crossing. The four of them were soaked, and a pungent steam was rising from the backs of the two mules.

"My dear brother, you ready to start up our journey again? We can make it now, I think. I want to be home in my own bed to say my prayers. I've done what I can do. The Trackers are gone suffer more—it's plain to see. They can't understand what's out there."

Patting the neck of one of the mules, Stromile listened to the calm tone of his sister's voice. He felt voices rising within him, though, and whenever that happened, he knew that danger was near.

"Yes, ma'am, we gotta go, I be packin' some of this loose straw 'round you—keep you warm. Keep the night outta you bones some. Keep you blood warm. I know that's right."

He didn't realize it, but his sister was studying him from the shadows of the barn. As he began to stuff straw around her sitting area on the sled, she said, "What are you hearing, brother? Are they out there?"

"Gist some o'bird, ma'am. That's all."

"Did I hear dogs? I think maybe I heard dogs barking. Like they're on the trail of something. Did you hear them?"

"Might be I did. Mostly a bird. Owl, maybe."

"He looking for prey?"

"Yes, ma'am. That what he be doin'. You right."

When he had created a warm and cozy nest for her, she reached out and caught his arm.

"Something has come to me," she said. "It came not long after we left the restaurant, and it hurts like fire, but there's nothing we can do."

"You got a vision, ma'am? What did it be?"

He heard her choke on a welling of tears.

"Oh, it was . . . that dear, tiny, sweet one."

"What you say 'bout her? What you see?"

"They took her. The vampires. They have her."

Stromile shut his eyes tightly, shut them as if by doing so he could keep the truth away.

"We gotta go," he said. "We got stars above us. We done all we could."

And he led the mules out of the barn. He knew of a narrow road not far from there; it would lead them the way home.

"Those stars are burning, brother," his sister called to him as she pointed upward. "Way, way up high there, the night is on fire. That's what they say about stars. Just pieces of the night on fire."

"I 'spect that's so, ma'am."

They journeyed on, and Stromile listened, and his heart thumped hard in his chest, because he knew what was out there. They were being followed. Something in flight up and to their right, winging heavily and calling distantly.

"I hear your owl, brother."

Despite the chilly air, Stromile was sweating; his throat was dry, and that fact frightened him even more deeply. Because he needed his voice.

"Yes, ma'am. He out there. I know that's right."

Another fifty yards and he slowed the mules.

"Why are we stopping, brother?"

He untied the lead reins and walked back and handed them to her.

"Ma'am, you gets'shup these here mules and stay right on this here road. I gotta step back in the woods now."

Zammie took the reins; she knew better than to question her brother. She also knew that danger was imminent.

"Be careful, sweet brother," she said.

The vampire who had been Royal swung high over the nearby pines. He hooted softly. Below him he could see brother and sister, and back a distance on the trail, he could see the man who was once his father, and he could see his dogs waiting eagerly for his command. The vampire hooted again and cut a downward angle before hearing another owl, one that felt its territory was being trespassed.

Stromile, climbing the nearest tall pine as rapidly as he could, heard the vampire's hoot. From his vantage point he could vaguely see his sister creating distance from him down the road. It cheered his heart to see it. He threw his voice again, once again perfectly capturing the sound of an owl.

The vampire swept close enough to tear with its claws the elbow of Stromile's jacket. The black man screeched like a wounded bird. Almost fell. Held on to the trunk of the big pine and trembled. Then the vampire looped and fluttered close and hovered only a few feet from Stromile, and the creature showed its fangs and hissed, but it did not attack.

It seemed satisfied just seeing what terror could do to a man's face.

And Stromile knew in the next heart-sickening instant that he had made a fatal error. For in drawing the vampire away from Zammie so she could make tracks home, he hadn't realized that the pack of dogs he had heard was under the vampire's control. But when the vampire issued an eardrum-bursting call, Stromile could not shinny down the tree fast enough.

He heard the dogs, their savage, blood-scenting barking.

Stromile ran so hard, he was certain his heart would shatter his rib cage. But he didn't care— hoped only it would beat as long as he needed blood pumping through him to reach and protect his beloved sister.

The dogs raced ahead.

Over a hundred yards behind them, he could hear the mules, terrified by what they sensed, begin to thunder down the road.

"Zammie love, Zammie love," Stromile chanted as he ran.

He knew that she was safe as long as the dogs

continued to bark, and thus the barking gave him hope, fired him to try to run faster.

And he did.

He ran until the barking ceased.

And then he slowed to listen more carefully, hoping against hope that the break in the rhythm of their barking meant that they had given up or turned off the trail. The old man was crying—crying because he was scared, crying because he could not tell what was happening.

Then Zammie's screams gathered and rumbled back toward him, knocking him momentarily to his knees. His cries of anguished denial reached her ears as several of the dogs brought down the mules and several others attacked her, going for her throat. Going for blood.

The vampires, once father and son, came upon the scene shortly after Stromile found the mangled body of his sister and sat down on the sled and held her to him. Fire flickered in their eyes; they looked upon Stromile and the dead mules with no pity.

"We would kill you," said the vampire who had been Warren, "but you will suffer more alive."

And with that, the vampires and the dogs disappeared into the cold shadows of the night.

Stromile buried his sister and the mules under mounds of straw and wet, packed snow, and though he attempted to say a few words of good-bye over his sister's body, all he could manage were the words, "Zammie love."

Then he looked up at the stars and howled like a wolf in pain.

And he struck out for Sweet Gum, seeking blood for blood.

Voices of wildness were building within him.
And there was fire blazing behind his eyes.

And fire blazed, too, in the heart of the vampire
who was once Danny Tracker.

When the rain relented, and those same cold stars
hovered above, the vampire Danny drove through
the snowy slush in his patrol car with the young
woman who was once his daughter; meanwhile, Soldier's Crossing was beginning to stir as if, bearlike,
it had been hibernating.

But Danny wasn't concerned about the sprinkling
of traffic.

Vampiric strength had allowed him to free his patrol car, and now he drove it in response, not to a
call from police headquarters but rather to one from
the vampire Franklin, who, in turn, was being directed by the Master. Tracker blood was gathering.
Gaining power. Gaining the wholeness of a different
kind of life.

But Danny, at times, was caught between that new
life—vampire in the blood—and the pull of his former life and the love he had left behind. As he ma-
neuvered along the slippery pavement, his destination
the Hollow Log Lounge (for that was where Franklin
had signaled for blood to meet), he couldn't keep
his eyes where they should have been. He was constantly drawn to the tiny girl sitting on Sharelle's
lap, and what he felt surging, coursing through him,
was an almost unimaginable desire.

He wanted to take the tiny girl's life.

And give her a new one.

But love protected her. Seemed to envelop her in
a warm golden light.

What love was that?

The love others felt for her. Brianna's. Jacob's. His own.

Still hidden somewhere in the blood that flowed through him—hidden and weakened, its energy siphoned off, yet there, causing him pain and generating guilt.

Sharelle was singing some nonsensical song and urging the child to sing along, but the child would not. The child would not even smile. The child knew. The child knew what? That she was not in the company of her grandfather and her aunt. She knew. But she was the missing piece; thus, it did not matter finally whether she was happy or not.

"Emily," said Sharelle, "our family will be so glad to see you and have you among us. Do you know that?"

The child stared at Sharelle, and the man who was once Danny cringed.

The eyes of the child were shot through with fear and distrust.

Sharelle saw the man's sad face and said, "Isn't it wonderful that we have Ben? Tyler is ours, too. And after midnight the whole family will be one. Trackers. Dead to their other lives. On fire with their new lives."

But Danny was losing touch with that new life. The more his heart ached for the distance he felt from Emily—the terror so evident in her body—the more he hated himself for what he had been forced to do to his own son; the more his new life cut him with razors of remorse, his thoughts continued to bleed and his soul grew weak.

"Ben will fight who he is becoming," he said.

"Not for long," said Sharelle. "When we have

gathered, when he feels the power of the new life in the company of his family, he will understand that blood is the life, and he will embrace it."

"I wanted it to be gentle," said Danny.

And with those words, spoken more to himself than to Sharelle, he let himself slide back in time a few hours to moments after he and Sharelle had kidnapped Emily, and they were driving back to Mixed Bag to wait to be called. Ben had found them. He had burst into the candlelight of the empty café, his anguish rushing ahead of him like a wind with no source.

"Dad! Dad! Say it hasn't happened! Oh, please, God! Say it hasn't happened!"

And Danny had met that thrust of despair in his son's voice, and he had tried to embrace him and tell him that something good had occurred—a wonderful transformation. But he could not.

Because of love.

"Dad, come back! I need you! We need you to help us fight!"

Danny was staggered by the words of his son, no longer a son.

"This is better," he said. "You don't know it, Ben, but this will be better. I promise it will."

His son began to pull on him—physically pull him out of the café into the rain. For a score of seconds it was like being on the end of a rope deep in the deepest darkness he could imagine and being rescued. Being hauled up into the light.

Then he had heard Sharelle shriek her vampire shriek of blood. A siren call back to another life, and the sound had jolted Danny and he had struck his son in the face. Ben, his flesh and blood once upon a time. And Ben's response was to wrestle him to the ground, and that was the young man's fatal mistake.

For he could not match the vampire's strength.

It was a furious struggle, but in the end it could only conclude one way: Danny's fangs puncturing his son's throat and reaching deeper than the young man's anger, deep into his blood. And when it was over, Ben had freed himself, had stumbled away, half in vampiric darkness, half in a frantic desire to remain human, and he had leaped onto his cycle and spun into the gloom.

Sharelle ushered Danny back into the present.

"It's the cops. A roadblock. Don't let them stop us," she said, and then pushed Emily down out of sight, keeping a hand over the girl's mouth.

"I'll handle this," said Danny, rolling down his window.

Two patrol cars, lights flashing, were parked hood to hood in the middle of a flooded intersection.

"That you, Tracker?"

Flashlight in hand, a young officer approached the driver's side.

"Whatcha got, Officer Milburn?" said Danny.

"Water, water everywhere. Craziest damn weather I've ever seen. You better turn around and go south on Culpepper. The whole east side of town is impassable."

"But, you see," said Danny, "it's real important I go on through." He smiled, and it was a smile that obviously made Milburn uneasy. His partner, a young black officer named Cowans, approached the passenger seat of the vehicle. He said something folksy to Sharelle—"Evenin', ma am"—and she was out of the car and at his throat before he could call for help or remove his weapon.

"What the hell is—"

Officer Milburn took two steps on his way to assist Cowans before Danny attacked him from behind and slit his throat with one razor nail; then excited by the warmth of the man's blood, he drank thirstily.

The cool, clear night had given way to a cottony thick fog.

"Goll'amighty," said Bo, squinting over the steering wheel of his van, "I can't see a blame thing. Can you?"

Jacob shook his head.

"We're close to the turnoff, I think. Watch for it."

But Jacob's attention and concern were being directed mainly at Brianna, who sat between him and Bo. She had been silent virtually all the while as they drove toward Sweet Gum, assuming as they did that the vampires would take Emily there. Her eyes closed, tiny beads of sweat on her forehead, Brianna looked as if she were in shock. And with good reason she might be, Jacob reasoned. The most precious thing in her life had been taken.

The threesome had left Gladys and Miriam at Mr. Pancake. Ben had not returned. Tyler had disappeared. There had been no word on Mollie, and there was no time even to mourn for Ruby and Jeremy and Jessie or any of the others brought down by the vampires. The only imperative was to find Emily. Find her before the vampires sacrificed her for their cause.

Bo slowed the van to a crawl.

"You think we're doin' the smart thing?" he said.

He glanced from Jacob to Brianna, then back to Jacob.

"What choice do we have?" said Jacob. "We've got to get Em back. Whatever it takes—we've got to."

"That's why I'm wonderin' maybe we should get the police and some other folks to help us. I mean, Christ, we're pretty badly outnumbered on this."

Suddenly, Brianna spoke, and the sound of her voice was unsettling to Jacob.

"No," she exclaimed. "If we brought in help, they would kill her. We can't go that way."

Jacob noticed that Brianna had raised a hand to her cheek. She seemed to be obliviously stroking the spot where Franklin's handprint ghosted through. Nothing more was said until Bo inched the van into the turnoff, and the crunch of the shell road could be heard.

"No, wait," said Brianna.

"What is it?" said Jacob.

She shook her head almost violently.

"No, wait. Wait, I hear him. He's in my head."

"Do you mean Franklin?" said Jacob.

She nodded, then pressed her fingertips to her forehead. "They're not here."

"What's she mean?" said Bo, looking beyond her at Jacob.

"The vampires—Brianna, do you mean the vampires aren't at Sweet Gum?"

"He's calling them to somewhere else," she said, continuing to press fingertips to her forehead. Her eyes were closed. "Not here. We have to go back. Go back to town, please."

Bo shrugged.

"Sure thing," he said, but he glanced at Jacob helplessly, confusion everywhere in his expression.

When they had turned around and had begun heading for Soldier's Crossing, silence filled the van for a mile or more. Then Brianna began to breathe heavily and to murmur, "He's calling them together."

"Can you see where?" Jacob urged. "Is there any indication where they are?"

Then Brianna cried out softly, as if in pain.

"No. No, I've . . . I can't . . . I've lost him. He's . . . he's out of my head. He's gone. But he'll be back."

Bo's hands tightened on the steering wheel.

"What now?" he said.

Jacob didn't know what to suggest.

"Take me back to Mr. Pancake," said Brianna quietly. "I think I'm going to be sick. Take me there, please, and then we'll try again."

She folded into Jacob's arms and he tried to assuage her pain.

"We'll find her, Brianna. I promise you we will. You're going to be OK. You're going to be all right."

But even as he said the words, he doubted them.

He doubted himself.

He doubted that there was any way to stop the vampires.

Ben found Tyler walking along the railroad tracks, and he could tell by the way the boy staggered along that the new blood, the new life, hadn't fully caught. Much inside the boy was warring—battles in his mind and heart.

But Ben wasn't sure he could help. He had felt and heard Franklin's call, and it was irresistible—it emptied him like the flush of a toilet, much of his energy swirled and drained away and he couldn't be certain what remained. Part of whatever it was thrilled him; part disgusted him.

"You wanna ride?" he called out to Tyler.

The boy turned. "Have you seen Josh?" he said.

"Josh? You mean your brother? No, man. He torched himself. He didn't want this life. He—" And Ben broke off his words because confusion was sweeping through him.

"I want to tell him I understand what he felt."

The boy stopped walking and glanced over at Ben on his cycle. The machine was idling, its metallic purr sounded eerie in the fog-shrouded night.

"Get on. We have to go where we've been called to. You have to forget about your brother, Tyler. Forget about him—it'll hurt more if you don't just forget about him."

Tyler climbed onto the bike and wrapped his arms around Ben's waist.

He was fighting back tears even as a new kind of strength was surging through him.

"I can't," he whispered.

Ben thought suddenly of his father.

"We gotta quit thinking 'bout anybody we love," he said. "We gotta think about blood."

He gunned the engine, geared, and they roared off into what was waiting for them.

Calvin Tracker stared into the flickering flame of the candle and listened as hard as he could. He was listening for voices from his old life, voices urging him to turn away from blood and embrace the past and feel guilt and remorse for his actions.

"Not to blame," he whispered. "Not to blame. I've been called to blood. I'm not to blame."

And having said those words, he felt much better.

He was seated by himself at a table in the Hollow Log Lounge; the bar was closed for business, and though the one candle flame was the only illumination, it welcomed all the shadows, just as it was about to welcome other Trackers.

Vampire Trackers.

Franklin had sent out the word.

Trackers could feel it in their blood.

And so Calvin, or the vampire who was once Calvin, waited. Restless, he glanced up at the snarling fox over the bar and snarled right back at it. And then he laughed, a high-pitched, nerve-shattering laugh endemic only to vampires.

Still, when the laughter subsided, Calvin thought he heard the suggestion of voices from the past: Jessie's and Jeremy's. Bits and pieces of their familiar voices skittered across the floor like mice. Then, moments later, they fluttered up near the ceiling like moths.

"I'm not to blame," Calvin called out.

Then he shivered involuntarily.

He did not want to be alone. He wanted to be joined by blood.

Soon. Very soon.

They clambered through the fog, hanging upon one another like drunken friends out too late. They had enjoyed each other all day. They had been in bed, in fact, when they received Franklin's call to gather at the Hollow Log.

"What does Franklin want?"

It was Mattie Lee's question—Mattie Lee, still prone to ask questions even as a vampire.

"My dear child," said the man who was once her father. "Live the questions. You don't need to keep seeking answers. Love this life you've been given."

"He's right," Janie followed. "This is a world I never dreamed was possible. We're strong and free from obligations and all the rules of society—the *sins*—we never believed in anyway, and Franklin wants to make us even stronger."

"Are you certain that no one can harm us?"

Mattie Lee's eyes lost their luster, their fire, as she spoke.

But Winston "Blink" Tracker, the man whom she had always adored, pulled her close to him and chuckled warmly.

"Worrywart. Dear, dear little worrywart. So few are brave enough to try to harm us. We are family. We are blood. Here. Here is our bond."

He offered her his wrist. She hesitated, but then he gently guided her mouth down to the raised veins. At the sight of those veins Mattie Lee's frown disappeared; hunger and need spread across her expression; fangs emerged and she trembled with anticipation.

"Drink, my dear child," said the man who knew what she needed.

And she did.

The troop of dogs heeling obediently behind the young man who was once Royal had gained in numbers; every stray, every dog that had ever thought about being a stray, every dog that still had wildness in its blood, had joined the entourage. But they had to be obedient . . . or Royal would cut their throats. Drink their blood if he felt like it. And they had to be fierce and they had to be vicious—they had to attack helpless women, and men with guns. And children, too, if their vampire master ordered them.

Their red eyes shone in the thick fog.

Their master walked beside the man who was once his father.

The younger vampire asked the older vampire, "Where are we going?"

And the older vampire said, "To a place where we can be strong. To a place where the blood of the river of life flows and we can baptize other members of our family—wash ourselves in Tracker blood and be forever strong."

"Will I still be able to fly?" the younger asked.

"You will fly. But not just like a bird. You will fly and breathe fire like a dragon, and there will be fire in your blood. And all those who are not like us will be afraid of you."

Into the fog they continued walking, dozens of dogs in tow, and the younger vampire thought about flying and breathing fire and he smiled, imagining a world of people afraid of him.

Franklin slipped out of the young woman's mind like a hand slipping out of a glove. She had experienced enough pain and confusion for the moment—she was separated from what she loved most, and he had whispered to her that the man she loved would die a thousands deaths if he continued by her side and if he continued to oppose blood and the lives of the Tracker vampires.

But she was not to tell him that.

It was a test.

Franklin would see how strong her love was.

It was the only thing he feared.

The only thing he cared for was blood—the blood of family—the power of the vampire life, the sweet, incomparably satisfying sense of self that it brought him. He could look back at his old life the way one looks back at a photo album from childhood. He could peruse images of his humanity—he could smile at how insecure and weak he had been as a human. He could even feel a pang for the human love he once had. Myron Florence had been a good man, but he was not blood. He could not cross the bridge into a new life. He would have had to remain forever on the other side. Ending his life was the only humane thing to do.

A vampire kindness.

But now as Franklin stood outside the door to the Hollow Log Lounge, he heard and felt the voice of the Master singing in his blood:

You must believe in something beyond yourself. Something larger. Or you will never be whole.

"Yes, Master," said Franklin the vampire. "I will gather blood, and I will preach your message. We have the missing piece. Blood is stronger than love. We will prepare ourselves to live the lives that have always been secretly lurking in our blood."

Somewhere a bell tolled.

And the vampire stepped through the door.

At that instant the single candle on the table where Calvin sat snuffed itself out.

Franklin raised his arm and the tiny flame reappeared, burning brightly in the palm of his hand.

Calvin Tracker had been touched by an angel.

That was the only way he could describe it—the

only way it made sense. What else could generate such heat, such soul-embracing warmth? It was the kind of touch that made one question who one was. Calvin was a vampire. Believed himself to be one. A Tracker vampire. Tracker blood. And he had been stirred by Franklin's address to all the Tracker vampires gathered at the Hollow Log Lounge.

Franklin spoke of the Master.

The Master was calling for all the Tracker vampires to assemble at Sweet Gum at midnight to become annealed by the living presence of something so powerful in the blood that it had to be experienced to be believed. Mere words could not contain it. It was in the realm of the unsayable—that's what Franklin said.

But as Calvin had sat listening to Franklin's inspirational words, the tiny girl—the missing piece—had slid away from Sharelle's lap and had gone to Calvin's side and had touched his cheek, and the look on her face said, *Why are you sad?*

The touch of that angel—for that was the only word he could think of to describe her, the only description that fit—caused him to smile. But then he had gotten control of his emotions, and he had taken her by the shoulders and pushed her away.

He wanted no part of children, because children had to be sacrificed, and when Calvin thought of sacrifices, he thought of Jeremy. And when he thought of Jeremy, he quickly thought of Jessie.

Jessie, no, I'm not to blame.

But because the angel had touched him, he had doubts.

And as Franklin finished his spiel, Calvin began to feel partly human again—his humanity was trying to reemerge, and as it welled up within him, it sent waves of uneasiness through him. Like nausea.

There was applause and cheering.

Warren "Brother Man" Tracker was patting him on the back and thanking him for the life of blood. That's what he called it: *the life of blood.* And his son, Royal, was there, too, and so were Winston and his daughters, Janie and Mattie Lee. Danny the cop was there and his daughter Sharelle, and Danny's boy, Ben, and J.T.'s boy Tyler.

Tracker vampires were forming a bond of blood.

And at the center of what they sought would be the sacrifice of the angel.

Calvin was glad when all the other vampires had left the Hollow Log Lounge; he needed to be alone; he needed to think; he needed to let his humanity sicken and die, wither on the vine. He had believed he was free of it—then the touch of that angel.

And . . .

He began to hear voices again in the empty bar.

The fox was snarling.

Calvin wondered whether the fox heard the voices, too.

The voices wanted him to say yes.

Goddamn it, no.

Calvin would not say yes to being human again, yes to living with all his dark memories again: Vietnam, the death of Jessie, the death of Jeremy.

No I'm a child of night.

Because his brother, Winston "Blink" Tracker, had called him that right before he bit into Calvin's heart and changed him forever.

But the voices persisted.

Jessie's. Jeremy's.

Dancing up in the shadows above his head until Calvin couldn't take it any longer.

"I'm a vampire!" he shouted. "The blood is the life! My life! Not yours!"

Then their ghostly faces. And, God, wasn't Jessie desirable? And wasn't Jeremy as innocent as the driven snow?

Calvin looked away from their faces. He looked down at his hands.

And he knew that it was time. He had to decide. Would he give up his new life and remain in the past?

It was time.

Time to set the night on fire.

Chapter Nineteen

Forever Sunset, Forever Blood

Over his shoulder Tyler could see the flames, and it appeared to him, with the fire licking up through the patches of fog, that someone had started the world ablaze, or that it was a sunset to last forever. He held on to Ben as they roared toward the destination Tyler had requested.

The boy could feel vampire needs and desires rippling through him, but he could also feel something else—the memory of a brother. As they pulled into the driveway of the house Tyler had lived in all of his former life, he shouted over Ben's shoulder for him to head to a weather-grayed shed out back. Ben did so, then stopped the cycle and Tyler swung off.

"Do you have a cigarette lighter?" said Tyler.

"What for?" said Ben.

"Do you? I need to know. Hurry, before I lose my nerve."

"Yeah, I got one. What the fuck's goin' on?"

Tyler stood in the spray of the cycle's single beam.

"I'm not sure. I gotta get something here. It's for Josh. I gotta do this thing for him, OK?"

"You ain't gone tell me what?"

Tyler thought for a moment.

"No. Not right now. Maybe when we're at Sweet Gum. Maybe not. God, I feel like I've got two people inside me, you know, fighting over me."

Ben nodded. "Same feeling here," he said. "Get what you're after and slap your ass back on. It's comin' up on midnight."

He didn't pay attention to what Tyler took from the shed. Ben was feeling a vampiric rush himself, and he wanted to drive fast and feel a new kind of blood in his veins, and he wanted the night to fill him and make him bigger than any fears he had ever had.

At his shoulder Tyler shivered. Then the rush hit him as well, and thoughts of blood flowed as some mysterious river held him. He glanced once more at the flames—the Hollow Log Lounge was disappearing.

And so was Calvin Tracker.

At the last possible second, he had felt the call of the new life, the vampire life, and he had run from the burning building in which he had considered offering himself to the flames and thus rejoining Jessie and Jeremy in a ghostly realm where he could know them again.

"It's not enough," he whispered to himself as he turned and watched the lounge collapse upon itself, and he was feeling good about his decision, feeling something in the blood that excited him and promised more, when he suddenly heard a cry—not a cry

for help, but rather some kind of endnote for the life
of one of Soldier Crossing's favorite watering holes.

It was the eerie, mournful, yipping cry of a fox.

But then, no, Calvin knew that wasn't possible.

That fox was dead. Stuffed. Its snarl frozen.

Forever.

It would burn along with the cherry wood of the
bar and the tables and the chairs.

And the memories.

And maybe the ghosts, too.

Calvin turned away from the scene.

He had someplace else to go. Someplace better,
he reasoned.

"No matter what happens, you'll take care of Em.
Promise me."

"Brianna, why are you talking like this?"

"Just promise me, Jacob. Please."

He slid closer to her in the booth and held her
and kissed her forehead.

"Of course I will, sweetheart. You know I will."

This was what Jacob wanted most—the woman he
loved, in his arms, and the feeling that he could
protect her from anything and everything. She was
pale and feverish, he feared, under so much stress
that he wanted to demand that she stay at the restaurant with his mother and Miriam instead of going
out with him and Bo to rescue Em. But he knew
she would want to be there. He knew that she believed her psychic connection with the vampire
Franklin might help in the rescue.

"Where is everyone?" she said, pulling away momentarily and looking around.

"Mom and Miriam are cleaning up—washing

dishes—doing whatever they can to help out. Bo, I think, is making sure we have everything we need when we go after Em. It's just a matter of knowing for certain where she is."

He studied her face because his statement held questions as well: Franklin is in your head—where has he gone? Where has he taken Em?

"Would you get a glass of water for me, please?"

"Are you picking up something? Can you tell anything yet?"

She nodded. "Maybe."

He got her the water, and as he was bringing it to her, Bo came in from the back room and Jacob gestured for him to join them.

"She know where they are?" Bo asked.

Jacob shrugged.

The two of them slid into the booth across the table from Brianna. Jacob handed her the water, and she drank it thirstily. Pain-etched lines ran down her pretty face. She had her eyes closed and her breathing was shallow. Jacob reached out for her hand.

And when he touched it, it felt like ice.

"There's fire," she murmured.

"Is that where they are?" said Bo.

She shook her head.

"No. No, I think they're being called to Sweet Gum. I see candles there. And I see the big fireplace." She frowned, and Jacob could see that she was concentrating very hard. She was listening, and she was trying to see with a sight he could not ever possess. "Yes. Yes, it's Sweet Gum and . . ."

Bo looked at Jacob.

"And what?" said Jacob, pressing. "What is it?"

"It's . . ." Brianna blinked her eyes rapidly. For a

run of seconds it appeared that she was having difficulty breathing.

"It's OK, darlin'," said Bo. "We're right here—Jake and me. It's gone be OK."

As Jacob watched, a sickening feeling swept through him: would it be? Was there any possibility that *anything* could ever be OK again?

"Brianna," he said, "what is it?"

"It's coming," she said, her voice sounding hollow, disembodied. It made Jacob feel cold inside. He and Bo waited and then pressed for something more, something that would catch in the trap of their understanding.

But Brianna said only one more thing. And when she spoke, she spoke softly, almost reverently.

"It's in the walls."

Franklin watched the walls of the old manse pulse and writhe.

The spirit of the place was alive—*genius loci*.

The Master.

In the walls.

Franklin gloried in the moment. The cavernous, dank and chilly house was dark except for the light of dozens of candles. Midnight was edging ever closer, and the scene around him was all that his dreamlike visions had promised: Tracker vampires in a semicircle, standing and staring at him mindlessly, expectantly, like zombies or perhaps like children.

Children of the night.

Trackers united: Warren and Royal and all of Royal's dogs; Calvin; Winston and Janie and Mattie Lee; Danny and Sharelle; Ben and Tyler. And there, standing like the angel of destiny in front of the mammoth fireplace in which no fire, as yet, burned, was the missing piece: the dwarf girl.

She looked frightened and alone and very tiny.

And yet Franklin could almost see a golden aura of protective light around her.

Generated by the love she engendered.

But could the child remain untouchable much longer? Against the power of blood, the strength of the vampiric will, how could her innocence stand a chance?

Franklin closed his eyes and waited for the Master to give him a sign.

His mind opened to the family history of the Trackers. He concentrated.

And then it came.

A vision.

The wounded Confederate soldier was bleeding profusely and no one could help. Hunkered down very near him was Jefferson Jackson Tracker, weary and hungry and balanced precariously on the rim of sanity. For the better part of February 1864, Sweet Gum plantation in east Alabama had served as a convalescent hospital for more than a dozen boys in gray when there was no longer room in the Columbus, Georgia, hospitals that, after the fall of Atlanta, had taken on the task of caring for many wounded soldiers.

But there was no food around Sweet Gum beyond roots, a few berries and scarce game; there was little water and few, if any, medical supplies. A doctor had been sent for from Montgomery, but he had not yet arrived, and Jefferson Jackson Tracker knew that the man on the cot could not wait much longer.

His name was Private Micah Fosser.

He was bleeding from a gunshot wound to his forearm, a wound that even when bandaged tightly continued almost mysteriously to bleed. Perhaps because Private Fosser had torn the bandage away numerous times. And what was particularly hideous—and Jefferson Jackson Tracker had witnessed this—was that to keep himself alive the young man would raise his wound to his lips and drink his own blood.

Franklin Tracker could imagine this distant scene vividly.

It was as if he were hovering above it like a balloon. He was being given, miraculously, a view of how Jefferson Jackson Tracker had become a vampire. Franklin was suddenly there, back in time, only a few feet from his Tracker relative as the man, out of his head with anguish, responded to the dying soldier's offer of the bleeding arm. Deeply moved by the gesture, Tracker lowered his mouth to the man's wound.

And drank the first blood of his vampire life.

The Master.

Who never really died, but who had been accidentally freed from the burial alcoves in the walls by John Taylor, freed, ironically, to bring new life to the Trackers who had succeeded him.

The vampire life.

Franklin opened his eyes.

It was nearing time for the Master to appear.

It was nearing time to sacrifice the child.

"Call him!" Jacob shouted into her face. "Call him out here!"

The strange wind continued to gust, making it difficult for the three of them to stand in front of Sweet

Gum within thirty yards of the entrance. Brianna had led them there. She claimed that the Tracker vampires had gathered in the mostly darkened old homestead.

They had Emily.

And the moment to strengthen the vampire blood bond through her sacrifice was approaching. Brianna was fighting to free herself from Franklin's mental control, but her consciousness was fading, and she could feel Jacob's frustration. Bo had to hold her up to keep her from collapsing.

"You can do this, Brianna," Jacob insisted. "Call Franklin out here. I'll fight him right here. Right now. For everything."

She was shaking her head, and Bo was staring beyond her into Jacob's face.

"Jake, no," he said. "You wouldn't have a chance against him. We got to try to set fire to the place and then rush in and pull Emily out of there—that's the only way."

But Jacob imagined fire in his fists. He wanted the moment—one on one.

Man against vampire.

A battle for Emily's life. A battle for the soul of the Trackers.

Suddenly the wind gusted, and they turned their faces away from it, and when Jacob righted himself, a lone, dark figure was standing directly in front of him.

"I'm here for you," said Franklin. "Forever Tracker. Forever blood."

Jacob immediately raised his fists, and the vampire smiled in the shadowy light.

"So much misdirected love in you, Jacob," he said. "If you were only on our side, you could have beauty around you eternally. If you would relinquish your love for them—for little Emily and your dearest Brianna here—you could have total bliss. And so could they. Why do you want to deny them? If you turn away from what I offer and try to fight us, you will suffer more than you can possibly imagine. Is that what you want?"

"All I want," said Jacob, "is to destroy you."

"Jacob, the Master has called. I've seen how it all began, and I know how it all must end. You can't stop it. The blood of that child will empower us beyond the reach of any humans. Her blood will light a fire in us that will be inextinguishable."

"Goddamn you," said Jacob, his anger building beyond control. "Goddamn every Tracker who wants to harm that child."

Unable to contain himself any longer, Jacob swung at the vampire with all his might, but his punch was stopped by an invisible force, and before he could swing with his other hand, the vampire reached out as quickly as the strike of a deadly snake.

And his fingertips met Jacob's cheek.

"Feel what awaits you in a world beyond the night, a world beyond your soul."

At first, Jacob felt a searing pain, like a hot poker being placed against his skin, but then another sensation dissolved the pain, and what he began to experience was a flood of pleasure, a torrent of self-fulfillment. And more. A feeling that everything in the universe made sense. Every question he had ever pondered about life had a simple answer. An answer deeper than love.

The world was based on a single premise: blood is the life.

When the vampire drew his fingertips away, Jacob

was dazed. He could sense Bo at his side; he could hear him saying something but could not make out the words. And when his head cleared, he blinked awake to see the vampire entering Sweet Gum—and then a sight that terrified him.

Brianna was running to catch up with the vampire. Jacob could hear her pleading.

"Take me instead," she cried. "Take me in place of Emily. Please. Please, I beg you—don't kill my child."

Jacob yelled for her to stop, but she had entered the old manse before there was any chance to prevent her. Bo took him by the shoulders and guided him away from the scene.

"We got to hold back," said Bo. "Too dangerous to do anything with Brianna and Emily both in there."

"But we can't just stand by and do nothing," said Jacob.

As they looked on, and as the minutes until midnight ticked away, they saw someone approaching from the shadows.

"Y'all be comin' 'round behind the house—I got me a plan, but I need your help."

It was Stromile Greene, his black face shining with perspiration, his eyes flashing fire points, and in those fire points Jacob saw something he had almost given up on.

Hope.

Brianna gasped along with the other Trackers when the rivulet of blood began to spread down the wall and out onto the floor, inching its way toward the tiny girl standing so innocently in front of the fireplace.

"It's the Master," Franklin whispered.

No one moved. There were no sounds. Barely any breathing. Even Royal's pack of dogs was silent. Brianna could only watch helplessly as the blood snaked along in a deliberate path—blood as predator, her daughter as prey.

When it reached her feet, the stream of blood began to transform into a whitish mist, which slowly spun and spread out until it enveloped the girl—and then it lifted her into the air, causing every stunned viewer in the room to look up at her.

The tiny girl screamed.

And so did Brianna.

Stromile Greene heard those screams as he skittered along the roof of Sweet Gum, maneuvering to the massive chimney, where he stopped to catch his breath. Tears welled up as he thought of Zammie, his beloved sister, and how the vampire Royal had set his dogs on her. And then he began to hear the languid, opening notes of Beethoven's *Moonlight Sonata*—it was Zammie's favorite piece of classical music, and Stromile loved playing it for her.

"Zammie, love," he whispered.

Then he wiped his eyes and climbed into the chimney opening and saw only darkness below him. Inside him there was rage and the building thunder of revenge. He cleared his throat and, bracing himself with hands and feet against the sides of the chimney, started to descend.

Crazily, a snatch of a Christmas song occurred to him.

"Here comes Santa Claus," he murmured as he lowered himself.

When Jacob and Bo heard the screams of Emily and Brianna, Jacob was on the roof watching for Stromile to reappear—hopefully, with Emily in tow. But to Bo, the moment was too much. Weaponless, he dashed into the rear of the old mansion, knowing full well that his act was foolish. And probably fatal.

The mist that the Master had become gently lowered the girl.

And the vampires roared their approval.

The time for the sacrifice had arrived.

Brianna fought to prevent it from happening, but she was outnumbered, and even a mother's supernatural strength when her child is threatened failed to win out against the Tracker vampires. They—including her father and her sister—held her, forcing her to have to watch each vampire drink her daughter's blood.

The voice of the beast filled the room just in time.

And confusion reigned.

It was the most hideous, terrifying voice that Stromile could muster. It burst upon the scene like a bomb exploding—a primitive cry replete with blood and anger that frightened the vampires long enough for Stromile to slip out of the bottom of the chimney, grab Emily and start to make an escape.

Amidst the unfolding chaos, Bo rushed in and

pulled Brianna from the vampires as they momentarily cowered in fear of the monstrous voice.

"Run out the back way!" Bo shouted at her, then stood in the way of two vampires who saw her making her getaway. Though he knew he had no chance to save himself, Bo took on the advance of the vampire Calvin and his brother Winston. It was Calvin who swung his razor-sharp nails at Bo's throat, slicing deep and bringing the man to his knees, where Winston set upon him to feed and to invite his daughters to join him.

As Bo went down, Franklin commanded the other vampires to catch Stromile and Emily before they could escape. And it was then that Tyler and Ben stole away, slipping out onto the wide porch where Ben's cycle was parked.

"This is it," Tyler called to his cousin. "This is for Josh."

Jacob could hear Stromile calling for him to reach into the chimney—Emily had been saved; Stromile was pushing her up the narrow passage. The moment unfolded in crystal clarity for Jacob: the struggle to maintain his footing on the slippery roof; the shriekings from within Sweet Gum; the feeling of extending his body as far as he possibly could, of stretching his muscles and pressing his fingers into the darkness, hoping to make contact with Em.

And thinking of how heroic Stromile had been.

And wondering what was happening to Brianna. And to Bo.

Holding his breath and reaching, reaching, reaching until a tiny finger down in the darkness grazed his hand. Feeling electrified with joy, he called out to her, "Take hold of my hand, Em. I won't drop you. Grab hold, sweetheart."

Reaching and reaching and then hearing Stromile cry out in surprise.

And pain.

The little girl was standing on his shoulders, and he was sweating profusely as he worked his way up the chimney, and he marveled at how calm the girl was remaining—or was she in shock?

He knew Jacob was reaching into the passage, trying desperately to grasp the girl and help her to freedom; he knew they were close. And that was his thought when Stromile felt something begin to twine around one ankle. Steadying himself, he looked down and saw a white mist spun smooth and tight like a rope.

Then the rope secured itself and Stromile Greene was yanked viciously.

He screamed and kicked.

And then he gave the little girl one last shove upward.

And let go.

And he knew that the darkness would claim him.

Tyler twisted open the gas can as Ben guided his cycle through the front door. The engine thundered; the tires squealed. Though confusion held sway within Sweet Gum, Franklin was succeeding in calming the vampires and regrouping them. He stood over the dying body of Bo as Ben and Tyler roared into the midst of the dark gathering, and Tyler began splashing the gas onto the floor.

"This is for Josh!" he shouted.

At first, the Tracker vampires seemed stunned by the sight of the two young men on the cycle maneuvering from room to room, the bitingly acrid aroma of gasoline trailing them at every point.

"Get them!" Franklin yelled.

Sliding and spinning into the fireplace room, the cycle lurched and lost traction, and as it did so, Ben reached for his cigarette lighter. But before he could retrieve it, he looked to see his father grabbing hold of the handlebars and wrestling at the cycle as if it were a rodeo steer. Ben's eyes met his father's. There was nothing human there. No compassion. Or love.

When the cycle crashed to the floor, Ben and Tyler were thrown off, tumbling and skidding as the vampires cried out with blood in their voices. Gasoline fumes filled the room, and the numerous candles flickered ominously.

The vampire Royal saw the moment as his.

He whistled for his dogs and set them on Ben as the young man tried to get to his feet. The other vampires parted to let the animals through to savage their prey. And Warren was there at the side of Royal, the young man who was once his son.

"Dragon!" he exclaimed to him. "Be the dragon!"

And Royal knew what that meant.

He could fly, and at that moment he believed one thing more: he could breathe fire.

The vampires urged the dogs on until they had torn away Ben's throat and had ripped the flesh from his face.

Tyler allowed himself only a second or two to stare at the attack on Ben. Then he scrambled to get the gas can. He raised it defiantly above him, hoping to catch Royal's attention.

"Burn, you bastards!" Tyler shouted, pouring the remainder of the gasoline over his head and down his face.

And Royal reared back and let his anger surge and blaze through his blood, and then he opened his mouth wide and exhaled. And spewed a spear of fire into Tyler's chest. And it blossomed in flames of fury.

The fire spread eagerly.

It raced; it vaulted; it ran with nightmarish speed throughout the rooms. The energy of the blaze built and built; the heat crackled; the noise was drowned out only by the screams of the vampires.

The old manse shook. The old manse shuddered. The old manse thundered.

At precisely midnight Sweet Gum plantation erupted like a volcano.

Chapter Twenty

Tomorrow's Sunrise

Brianna prayed.

The heat from the fireball explosion had driven her back like strong, invisible hands shoving at her, preventing her from entering Sweet Gum to try to save her daughter and to find Bo.

She hadn't prayed for years, but there, on the wet grass behind the old manse, she dropped to her knees with the billowing flames and smoke filling the moonless night, and she folded her hands and whispered, "God, please. My Emily. My Emily."

It had worked before, or, at least, she had convinced herself that when Emily was born prematurely and when the doctors hedged and suggested they couldn't guarantee much chance of survival—especially not the likelihood of a normal, healthy life—she had prayed to God to perform a near miracle for the tiny creature.

What Brianna recalled was simple.

She did not hear the voice of God—and received no warm and fuzzy feelings, no visitation from an angel or the Virgin Mary. What she remembered was sitting up in her hospital bed and being *pierced*. That was the only way to describe it: pierced through the heart by *something*—something like an arrow that couldn't be seen. It drew joy instead of blood. God's love seemed the best explanation for the phenomenon. Maybe the only explanation.

God's love had given her Emily a life.

Emily—the tiny candle flame that couldn't be snuffed out.

Inextinguishable.

Brianna prayed and longed to be pierced again. And she longed to hold her child again. And she longed to see Jacob—she had completely lost awareness of where he might be and if he was safe. She needed him. Her thoughts flitted to Bo; she assumed the worst for him, but she did not give up hope.

In her numbing anguish she thought of her mother and was suddenly glad that the dear woman had been spared all the horror of seeing what had happened to her family—what the Tracker blood curse had created—how her husband and one of her daughters had gone over to the dark side. And what of Ben?

Brianna had seen him among the vampires. One with them, no doubt.

"Dear God, please," she murmured again, her thoughts returning to Emily. Then she lowered her head into her hands and she sobbed, and as she did so, a darkness like night coming on much too quickly filled her thoughts.

It was Franklin. His psychic presence.

But she could tell that his power had been diminished somewhat.

And that possibility alone cheered her.

* * *

Jacob's ankle was on fire.

In leaping from the roof, he had landed wrong, twisting himself to try to shield Emily's body from striking the ground too hard. The little girl was crying quietly as he struggled to his feet and began to pull her away from the burning house.

He could hear the cries of the vampires.

Holding Emily tightly, he limped out from the conflagration and trained his eyes up at the roof, at the chimney area, for any sign of Stromile. But his gut feeling told him that the courageous black man hadn't made it.

"Uncle Jacob, where's Mama?"

Wincing with pain, Jacob carried the girl another twenty yards, then collapsed on the grass. He pressed her to his chest.

"We'll find her, sweetheart. We will."

But he knew that Brianna had gone into the house. Staring into those raging flames, he doubted that anyone could have escaped from them. He glanced around, hoping most of all to see her, hoping also to see Bo.

"I want Mama," the girl whimpered.

Jacob guessed that she was in borderline shock; her voice was thin and reedy, and she was quivering like a leaf in a breeze.

"I know you do, sweetheart. I know. Come on. We'll go look for her."

It felt like a dream.

Everything gauzy and indistinct and yet there was a certain penetrating clarity that staggered her. She had closed off her prayers and had stood up absolutely resolute with the belief that all she loved could not have been taken from her.

The vampires couldn't do that.

God wouldn't let them.

Off within fifty yards of her she could see someone moving as if with pain, but she could not make out who it was. Tears choked her voice momentarily—her first effort to cry out to the figure produced nothing more than a torn and nearly strangled shout.

She wiped at her tears, wiped at the smeary veil.

Because the dream was so vivid.

The figure carrying someone.

A child.

"Oh God," Brianna murmured.

And she began to run into the dream.

And when she did, Jacob turned and stopped dead in his tracks as if he, too, could not determine dream vision from reality.

"Jacob!"

At the sound of Brianna's voice, he shifted Emily in his arms and jolted into a run.

"We're here," he called out.

The darkness seemed to part for them, and as the fire burned more brightly, popping and crackling and spreading light out across their paths, Brianna began to laugh and cry at the same time and Emily screamed, "Mama!"

When they reached each other, the threesome threw themselves into a rough, joyous, speechless embrace, and tears ran freely until the darker reality of the scene caught them up.

Jacob looked into Brianna's eyes. "Bo? Did he—"

She shook her head.

"He saved me, Jacob. But I didn't see him make it out. I don't think he did."

She was holding Emily as if no force on earth could ever pry her daughter from her arms. Emily, unable or unwilling to speak, clutched at her mother's neck with every ounce of her love.

"Let's go," said Jacob. "Bo's van—just hope to God the keys are in it."

They were, and as they climbed in, breathless and dazed and numbly thankful for what seemed simply a miracle that they were together again, Sweet Gum belched fire one final time sending up a roar louder than a jet plane.

It was a primitive sound.

Blackness funneled up through the center spiral of fire. Brianna and Emily turned their faces away from the spectacle, but Jacob watched as a new resonance softened the borders of time and space, and he saw something fingering its way up through the funnel of blackness.

A writhing whiteness snaking upward like a rope trick.

He could not tell what it was—perhaps smoke or ash.

Or a fine white, ancient, deadly mist evaporating as it reached for the stars.

Jacob slugged the van into gear and sped away.

At the front edge of the burning, collapsing old manse, a lone, dark figure stood and watched them go. No one in the van saw him.

Mr. Pancake seemed like heaven to Jacob.

His mother and Miriam Tracker were there, and

though the restaurant remained closed, the two women greeted the shocked and weary threesome with food and warmth and understanding. Emily, visibly tired and shaken, was the center of attention. There was no way to tell how much psychological damage had been wrought upon her. One could only hope that she would recover from the nightmarish experience and that it would not leave too many emotional scars.

In fact, Jacob believed that Brianna was suffering more than her daughter—he could see it in her eyes: the fear, the occasional blank stares and the dullness, where there was once a lively spark.

As his mother and Miriam tended to Emily, Jacob hugged Brianna.

"I think we made it," he said.

She forced a smile. Tears threatened.

"I hope so," she said.

He wanted to ask—but dared not—whether Franklin continued to be a psychic presence with her. She must have read his hesitation and anticipated his question, because as he held her close, she whispered, "He's gone, I think. He's out of my head. I think he's gone."

And Jacob knew she was speaking of the vampire.

No more Tracker vampires.

The sun would rise on a new world—and potentially a new beginning for him and Brianna and Emily.

When Brianna slipped from his arms to get Emily a glass of orange juice, Jacob's mother and Miriam soberly cornered Jacob. He knew what each would be asking. He deflected the moment with an account of what had occurred at Sweet Gum, leaving out many specifics but emphasizing his belief that the blood curse of the family had ended.

Then Miriam spoke. "Tyler was one of them, wasn't he?"

Jacob nodded.

"I'm afraid so."

"Then he's gone, isn't he?"

Jacob's "yes" was barely audible. "I'm sorry," he added. But what he could not add—because he was not aware of it—was that Tyler had acted heroically— as had Ben and, certainly, as had Stromile Greene. The night had permitted heroic deeds.

His mother pursed her lips and tightened her jaw as if preparing for the inevitable.

"Guess there's no point in asking about Daniel and Sharelle and Ben?"

"No, ma'am."

"But what about Orpheus?"

Jacob sighed. "He saved Brianna."

Then he repeated Brianna's account of what Bo had done once inside the old manse.

"That's what he would do," said his mother. "A good man. He loved this family."

Staggered by the emotion of recalling his close friend, Jacob held his mother or, perhaps more accurately, she held him. Miriam drifted away from them, leaving them alone. Jacob's mother went to her purse and brought back a pair of keys. She held them out to her son.

"You and Brianna and Emily need to get away from here."

Looking into his mother's eyes, Jacob suddenly thought of his biological mother: wouldn't she be doing exactly what Gladys Tracker was doing? It was all about the dichotomy of suffering and comforting.

Mothers suffered—Miriam had, and Ruby and Mollie and Jessie and Brianna, too—but they generated a special energy in comforting those who needed it.

Jacob took the keys.

"What do these belong to?"

"Orpheus left them with me. His brother's cabin up at Mt. Pogahatchee—you take the ones you love up there and stay away for a while."

"It's a pleasant thought," he said. "I don't want to be around when this story breaks. All the media. All the questions. It'll be the nightmare all over again."

His mother nodded.

"Give it time for things to settle down. I'll deal with what I can. See to folks getting buried—that kind of thing. Answer whatever questions I can. I'll keep your whereabouts to myself."

It sounded good to Jacob.

"Will you and Miriam be all right?"

"Oh, sure. We're tough ole gals. I'm taking Miriam home with me. We're gone help each other grieve."

Then Jacob spoke, not the words he had expected to say, but rather words he needed to say aloud and repeat as often as possible.

"I love Brianna, and I love Em, and I want to be with them the rest of my life."

"I know you do, son. So that's what you need to make happen. Go be with them."

Brianna joined them, and Jacob told her about his mother's suggestion. And Brianna insisted, "I want us to go back to the trailer and clean up and rest first. We can leave early morning. Please, Jacob—that's the way I want to do it."

They heard sirens—probably both police and

fire—as they drove away from Mr. Pancake to Brianna's trailer.

"Nobody's going to hurt us now—right, Mama?" said Emily.

"No, baby. We're going to our nice, safe little home to rest, and then we're going to go stay in a cabin—wouldn't you like that? A cabin in the mountains."

"I would, Mama. I would like that."

"How about you?" Brianna said to Jacob, nuzzling close to his shoulder.

"Sounds like paradise to me," he said.

It was as if they had returned from seeing some intensely explosive movie, having cheered for the survivors and mourned all of the good guys who had fallen victim to the forces of evil. But Jacob didn't have to remind himself that what they had experienced was no movie. Everything about it was real. And *they* were the survivors.

Brianna's trailer seemed, nonetheless, a safe haven, out of the swing of the violence and death and loss. The Tracker family had been gutted. The curse in the blood had seized many of the members of the family and horrifically dispatched them.

So how did we survive? Jacob asked himself.

There appeared to be only one answer: love. It had to be the love that he and Brianna felt for each other, the love that they felt for Emily. Fire and love seemed the only forces capable of negating the vampires. Those were Jacob's thoughts as he sat on the sofa waiting for Brianna to return from putting Emily into bed.

"She's totally wiped out," said Brianna as she sat

down close to Jacob. "Just exhausted. I washed her
face and hands, but—oh, Jacob, will she ever be able
to get over this? Will *we?*"

He smiled as warmly as he could and pulled her
closer.

"We'll give it a damn good try," he said.

For a minute or longer they did not speak; they
held each other and listened to the warmth of
their feelings, their companionship, their love. It
was Brianna who released herself from the embrace first.

"I must smell like roadkill," she said, laughing
softly, self-deprecatingly, "and look like it, too." She
fingered an unruly strand of hair and tried to inject
some sexuality into her smile. "I need to take a
shower."

"Sure. Go ahead," said Jacob.

But she lingered, looking at him, obviously decid-
ing whether to cross a certain unmarked line.

"Come take one with me," she said.

In the bathroom she undressed in front of him.
The sight of her naked beauty made his mouth go
dry. She was even more desirable than he had imagined her to be—and he had exercised his imagination in that direction quite often. When he continued
to stand there fully clothed, she said, "You going to
shower with your clothes on?"

The teasing in her voice excited him.

Laughing at himself, he undressed, and Brianna
stepped into his arms, and the sensual heat of her
body took Jacob's breath away. She kissed him lightly
on the chin, then on the lips; then their kiss was
long and deep, a plunge into a pool of desire.

Getting into the shower together was awkward, and that in itself made the moment magical, freeing them to laugh and be tender—and to forget. The warm spray of water did something more: it washed away, or at least it did in Jacob's view, so much of the past, so much of their former selves.

They became something new as they kissed and held and soaped each other, touching, growing closer in a simple ritual that sealed their commitment to the possibility of an even more complete intimacy. When Jacob had toweled off and gotten into bed, he could hear Brianna blow-drying her hair. He waited for her, the cool air of sexual desire filling the pit of his stomach.

Wearing a fluffy white towel tucked just over her lovely breasts, she came to the edge of the bed and leaned down and kissed him tenderly. Then she whispered, "Make love to me, Jacob. It's what I want and need."

Brianna woke an hour later. She looked at the back of Jacob's head and tried to decide whether she should wake him. She was shivering, as if the sheet covering them were glazed in ice. The warmth of their eager lovemaking had faded. She felt herself sinking into a helpless state, reaching out mentally and emotionally for something to hold on to.

There was darkness in her thoughts.

Or, rather, darkness *instead* of thoughts.

She closed her eyes tightly and clenched her fists in terror.

"He's here!" she whispered.

* * *

There were tiny shadows scurrying around in her blood—that's what she imagined. They were under her skin and in her head. They were in every breath she took. She could *hear* them; they were skittering on tiny feet, racing madly as if heeding some call she herself was not privy to. Except she intuited that it was coming from the vampire.

Franklin had survived Sweet Gum.

"Jacob? Jacob, wake up. I'm scared."

She shook him, and when he had blinked awake, she watched his startled expression change the shape of his face. She fell into his arms and tried to fight back tears, fight back her terror.

"He's back, Jacob. I can feel him inside me."

She could tell by the way he held her and by the tone of his voice that he knew what she was talking about.

"I'm holding you, sweetheart. It's OK. He can't harm you."

"We need to go," she said. "We need to pack up and go right away. I don't want to stay here."

Dawn was approaching. She knew that they could be on the road quickly. Jacob had thrown together a small suitcase of clothes at his place, and they had kept Bo's van instead of opting for Jacob's pickup. All they needed were changes of clothes for her and Emily.

"Then we'll go," Jacob responded. "Get your stuff."

He scrambled out of bed and threw on jeans and a shirt.

Packing light, Brianna gathered clothes for her and for Emily. In the bathroom she hurriedly brushed her teeth as Jacob put two suitcases in the van, but when he returned, he heard the shattering of glass and ran to the bathroom.

"Jacob, he's here! Get Em! Something's happening!"

Shards of the water glass she had dropped began to transform into shadows, indistinct at first, then taking shape and becoming animated. She screamed at their movement and called out for Jacob, but he had already gone down the hall to Emily's bedroom. When he turned on the light there, he could not believe his eyes: Emily, wide awake, so terrified that she could not even cry out, was sitting up in her bed surrounded by dozens and dozens of large rats.

Yelling as loudly as he could, Jacob ran at them, scattering them with his hands; he reached for the little girl and swung her against his shoulder. As he charged back down the hallway, the walls seemed to erupt.

Rats poured out of the walls like water.

Burying Emily's face in his shoulder, he pounded through the rodents, their shrill cries almost deafening. Some clung to his legs, biting through his jeans as he headed for the front door. He called for Brianna, but he felt he could not slow down until he had gotten the girl to safety. Once outside, beyond the horde of rats, he put her in the back of the van.

"Stay right here, Em. I'm going back for your mother."

The rats were filling the inside of the trailer like a silo being loaded with grain.

"Brianna!"

He saw her as she was making her way down the hallway; she had flattened herself against the wall and was sobbing.

When her eyes met his, she cried out, "Go on without me. Go, please, Jacob. Save Emily."

But he fought through the swirling mass of creatures to her side.

"No way I'm leaving you," he said. "Ever."

He lifted her into his arms and ran as hard as he could through the ever-increasing waves of rats. Moving toward the door was like wading through a stream at flood stage; at every moment they were threatened to be pulled under.

Jacob gritted his teeth and held Brianna as close as possible.

And drew upon every ounce of courage and determination he possessed.

The sun rose on them as they drove north.

Soldier's Crossing would soon discover a strange new day of death and destruction, and then much of the rest of the world would hear about it, and Jacob knew that he would not be able to escape the narrative of the Tracker vampires for long. He and the two people he loved most were on the lam—they were running from something that would never stop seeking them. And that something was the world's curiosity about tragedies and disasters.

Jacob had a firm grasp on the steering wheel, but he could not recall how he had managed to get himself and Brianna out of the trailer. His legs were on fire from the rat bites; though a few miles out of Soldier's Crossing, they had stopped, and Brianna had tended to them and to her own as best she could. Emily sat very quietly in the backseat, sucking on two of her tiny fingers for comfort.

The drive to Mt. Pogahatchee and the cabin owned

by Bo's brother would take at least an hour; for Jacob, every mile they put between themselves and Soldier's Crossing was cause for celebration. At one point Jacob started to switch on the radio, but then he thought better of it. He didn't want to hear any news reports filtering out of the darkness they had left behind.

Brianna said little on the drive. Jacob noticed that once or twice she seemed to doze off, only to jerk awake as if the nightmarish images from hours past had flooded her mind. He held her hand and often squeezed it reassuringly and glanced in the rearview mirror frequently to see how Emily was doing. By the time they reached the cabin, she was asleep.

Mt. Pogahatchee was a tree-lined outcropping of rock, more of a foothill than a mountain. To Jacob, it seemed a fresh and inviting realm, a natural realm where one could breathe the air freely and listen to the wind and taste the sky. And no Trackers in the blood except Brianna and Emily.

And no vampires.

No horror.

No death.

And world enough and time for love.

And a new beginning.

Chapter Twenty-one

The End of Just Begun

It was the best day of Jacob's life.

Though the cabin—a genuine log cabin with cedar logs framing the abode as neatly as a model unit in a children's-toy commercial—was a bit dusty and dingy from lack of use, it was marvelously secure and comfortable. It had two small bedrooms, a kitchen, bath, plus a living room with a fireplace—plenty large enough to allow them to burrow in with their exhaustion and their secret pangs of joy and hope. No phone. No radio. No television. A *temenos* of isolation.

Before the three of them settled in for a much-needed nap, they readied the beds with fresh sheets and pillowcases, and Jacob headed for the small grocery at the entrance to Pogahatchee National Forest for supplies. And when he returned, Brianna had put Emily down. She and Jacob put away the supplies, then undressed and slipped beneath the sheets. Both had noticed something bordering on the supernatural: the wounds from the rat bites had magically disappeared—a change precipitated by more than just Brianna's medical efforts could have accounted for.

But they gave the matter little thought.

They had escaped a nightmare. Thoughts paled in comparison with that fact.

They curled their naked bodies together.

In that moment, for two of them, everything was perfect.

They woke early afternoon to cool, cloudy weather. They made hot dogs and opened containers of baked beans and potato salad and washed it all down with sweet tea. And there were chocolate-covered doughnuts for dessert. It seemed almost miraculous that their appetites had returned after the trauma of the night before. Jacob told himself that love was responsible.

"Let's go exploring," he suggested after they had stuffed themselves. He knew that he was perhaps trying *too* hard to keep everyone's mind off the horror, but he vowed that they were going to experience at least one day of normalcy if possible.

Emily, looking much better—testament to the recuperative powers of small children—squealed in delight. But before they headed off on their adventure, Brianna discovered a hunter's bow and arrow in the broom closet.

"Jacob, aren't you a pretty good archer? Look at what I found."

He took the bow and examined it. It had some age on it, but it was an expensive piece of equipment. He assumed it had belonged to Bo's brother.

"I used to be. Might be a little rusty these days. Two years ago I brought down a six-point buck with one of these."

And along the trail snaking behind the cabin, he

found a bale of straw with a weathered bull's-eye target ring.

"There," said Brianna, "you can practice."

"I'll do that. But first let's see where this trail goes."

"Em, don't get so far ahead of us, sweetheart," Brianna called after her daughter, who was running along the narrow trail crunching the fallen leaves, running with the reckless, thoughtlessly giddy abandonment that only a child knows.

There appeared to be no one else out in the woods. It was February, the slow season. Visitors would return in summer. They hiked a hundred yards or so to where the woods abruptly ended.

At the end of the trail all three of them stood in awe.

"My God, this is incredible," said Jacob.

"Emily, you keep hold of my hand, sweetheart. That's a long, long way down."

"Mama, gosh, we're up higher than all those trees. We're as high as birds."

The spot was known as Vantage Point Rock, and it afforded a magnificent view of the Pogahatchee National Forest, especially from a jagged shard of gray-glistened rock that jutted out fifteen or twenty feet from the edge of an upswept rim of land, where only the most resourceful scrub pine dared to grow.

With Brianna holding one of Emily's hands, and Jacob holding the other, the threesome edged cautiously out onto the rock, a chill wind whipping at them gently, a single, solitary hawk swooping just beyond their reach—or so it seemed. Emily giggled with queasy glee. Brianna and Jacob looked into each other's eyes, and the love they felt for each other might have lifted them from that rock out into the nothingness, where they could have danced, held aloft by emotions too deep for words.

No one wanted to leave the dizzying, soul-embracing spot.

But as twilight stole upon the scene, they drifted back to the cabin, and they sank into the evening like a happy family from a 1950s television show. Jacob built a fire in the fireplace and then built something more: a fantasy of being married to Brianna and being a father to Emily. It was all as close and as seemingly real as the flickering firelight.

As the temperature outside dropped, they huddled closer to the blaze, cozying up to it with every blanket the cabin possessed. Brianna and Emily made hot chocolate, and the threesome pulled within each other. Jacob released himself into the reverie of the fire; it was as if it awakened some primitive part of his soul. He knew what his ancestors thousands of years ago must have felt in the magic circle of nurturing flames. It appeared to him that Em felt it, too; though as the evening unfolded, she was finding it harder and harder to keep her eyes open.

On the other hand, it seemed that Brianna was deliberately keeping her distance from the fire.

"You getting too warm?" Jacob asked her.

"Oh no. No, it's . . . I'm not sure. Just a little uncomfortable being this close to the flames."

Jacob ventured a guess.

"Maybe it's because of what happened at Sweet Gum. It's understandable after that to be unsettled by the sight of any kind of fire."

Brianna nodded but looked doubtful.

"You might be right. Sorry, I don't know what it is."

Emily was tugging Jacob away from the conversation.

"Play us your guitar, OK?"

"I will if you and Mama will sing along."

And so Jacob got out his guitar and the three of them sang old John Denver hits and a few by Garth Brooks and other country-western singers. When Emily grew tired and dropped her head into Brianna's lap, and they had put her into bed, Jacob talked of trying to write "The End of Just Begun."

And of how perhaps the song was no longer relevant.

Moved by his words, Brianna kissed him and said, "I don't want this to be the end. I want forever."

The next day Jacob woke early. He decided to let Brianna and Emily sleep as late as they wanted to. In the kitchen he made coffee and settled down at the table and watched a thick foggy mist blanket the floor of the woods. He thought about what might be going on in Soldier's Crossing. He thought about his mother and Miriam, and wondered whether the authorities had been questioning them about the horrors of the Tracker family. How soon would the police and the media be looking for him and Brianna and Emily?

We can't hide forever.

But for a few days, he reasoned, they could have a taste of paradise.

Restless, he decided to haul out the bow and arrow and do some practice shooting. The air was cool and crisp, and the woods seemed to crouch in a hush as if watching an intruder. He strung the bow and gave himself twenty yards or so to zero in on the target. His first three attempts missed the bull's-eye widely.

Yet, it felt good to be shooting again. It generated memories; one in particular—of going out bow hunting with his father for the first time, of getting very tired and not seeing a deer, but hearing his father say, "Patience! You've got to have patience, Jacob! Patience is everything!"

He missed his father, and in recalling that first hunting trip, he was struck by the complexity of how to fix upon the identity of Clarence Tracker. *Not my real father.* But, no, it was impossible to think of him any other way—he would always be "Dad"—the only one he had ever known.

A dozen more attempts helped to bring back some of the prowess he once had, making it not quite so difficult to imagine having killed a large deer. He was musing upon the moment in which he had stood over that fallen deer, a magnificent creature, its blood as vivid as fire. He remembered feeling a pang of regret for having killed it.

Then, as the present returned and he was retrieving several of the arrows, the memory of the deer faded and he glanced quickly over his shoulder in the direction of the cabin. He thought of the old saying "A cat walked over my grave"—and he experienced a chill not generated by the cool air. He sensed that there was someone else in the woods.

He waited and listened.

"Anybody there?" he called out.

He concentrated, thinking he might hear the snapping of twigs.

Nothing.

If someone were out there, Jacob concluded, he had an Indian-like ability to not make noise.

On the heels of that assessment, a sudden fear seized his thoughts.

Could it be Franklin?

"The fire got him," Jacob whispered to himself. "It got all of them. Nobody could have survived."

But he could not convince himself of that.

He trekked in a circle out from the target bale. Found nothing. Saw nothing. Heard nothing. When he returned to his shooting position, he aimed at the target and pretended the bull's-eye was Franklin's heart.

To kill a vampire.

A light rain began to fall as Jacob raised the bow and imagined the dark creature was standing there looking directly at him, daring him to shoot. Jacob felt buried to his neck in anxiety. He trembled. He could not hold the bow steady.

"Goddamn it," he hissed.

He lowered the bow, then raised it again until the string almost brushed the right side of his face. He began to draw down and steady himself and the bow. Bracing his feet, he held the bow at its fullest tension.

He aimed at the vampire's heart.

Kill shot.

He held and breathed out in a puff as he released the arrow.

He knew instantly that it was off target. The orange feathers trailed the arrow like fiery sparks. Their flick echoed in his ears.

"Shit!"

He missed where he was aiming by six inches or more.

The vampire had escaped.

Or would have.

So he tried again. Four more times before he was able to hit the imaginary heart of that imaginary vampire.

"There you go, you bastard!"

Forever dead.

He quietly celebrated.

"Could you shoot a bear or a lion? Or a dinosaur?"

His breath knocked from him by the surprise of the voice, Jacob wheeled, bow drawn, to find Emily approaching on the path.

Relieved, he swallowed back his fear and smiled into her eager, questioning gaze.

"Maybe a bear or a lion," he said, "but, thank goodness, I believe it's too cold here for dinosaurs. They pretty much stay in Jurassic Park, I hear."

Emily giggled and leaped into his arms.

And he shivered at the realization that such a precious child had once been held captive by Tracker vampires. That she had been singled out for sacrifice. That she had nearly been lost to their darkness.

Jacob grew more worried about Brianna. She had eaten little lunch and appeared pale and enervated; every one of her smiles seemed an effort. Jacob and Emily fixed her a comfortable nest on the sofa after lunch; when she appeared to fall asleep, they slipped away quietly to explore the woods.

"Is Mama going to be OK?" Emily asked as they followed a new trail out away from the cabin.

"I'm sure she will, Em. She's just tired. She's been through a lot. Hey, you know, don't you, that I won't let anything bad happen to your mama."

"I'm glad."

"But, hey, how about you? Are you OK? You know, you've been very brave. Sometimes when people go through a terrible experience, well, they get depressed, you know. They just feel bad and feel like the world is a bad place and it won't get better. Do you feel like that?"

The tiny girl thought a moment—even raised a finger reflectively to her lip. Jacob smiled to himself at how serious she looked. He had no idea how she was processing everything.

"I think the world's a good place long as you and Mama are in it."

Jacob swung her up into his arms and kissed her forehead.

"That's a great answer, sweetheart."

Late afternoon, as the gray day was giving way to twilight, they returned from their adventure; Emily was laden with pinecones of various shapes and sizes. Back in the cabin, they discovered that Brianna had risen. Jacob called out for her, but she was not inside. He assumed she might have gone for a walk, so he built a fire, and when Emily settled in front of it to play with her new treasures, Jacob went looking for Brianna.

On the trail to Vantage Point Rock, he once again was struck with the sense that someone was lurking in the woods—a breathless, stealthy watching—but he admitted that it was probably his imagination. When he reached the end of the trail, however, a new fear seized him.

He saw Brianna.

And she was standing perilously close to the lip of the rock where it extended out over nothingness. For a heart-stopping instant, Jacob saw something

in the casually defiant way in which she had posi-
tioned herself that suggested she was about to jump.

He approached cautiously, and when he spoke, it
was soft so as not to accidentally startle her.

"Brianna? Sweetheart?"

She turned and gazed through him—that's how
it seemed.

"Who is it?" she said.

"Sweetheart, it's me."

He chuckled nervously.

"Oh, Jacob—I'm sorry. For a moment, I couldn't
tell. My head's kinda foggy, I guess."

He stepped out to her and took her hand and led
her away from the precipice.

"Looked like you were about ready to take flight."

"Wouldn't it be neat? I mean, to have the power
of flight. Not to be bound to earth. Not to have to
deal with all the difficult things."

They sat down on the rock. Jacob studied her face.
She seemed distracted, lost somewhere inside herself.

"What is it, Brianna? You haven't been acting like
yourself."

"Jacob, I've been out here thinking about things."

"What things, sweetheart?"

"Like love. I've been thinking, you know—well,
about where love goes when it dies?" She met his
eyes and tugged on his emotions.

"I don't—I'm not sure what you mean."

Tears scratched at the back of her throat, and she
looked away.

"It started with Spence . . . and now, I'm afraid.
It's . . . love is so difficult. Sometimes I'm not sure
I'm capable of loving and having a relationship. If
you love someone, can anything take that love from

your heart? Just reach inside you and steal it from you?"

Feelings rushed through Jacob, warm and powerful feelings, feelings he believed he had never felt before. He reached for her and brought her into his embrace.

"No one can take away the love we have for each other. I know it still feels awkward at times. We're so used to being, you know, off limits to each other. Changes occurred too quickly. We need time. Time to find a way to begin something new."

"But I'm afraid," she whispered into his shoulder, "there won't be enough time. I'm very afraid, Jacob. I'm afraid of what's out there."

Brianna seemed in better spirits that night.

A chilly wind buffeted the cabin, but the threesome was cozy around the fire, talking and singing and eating and caring about one another. Not really missing television or videos; not really missing Soldier's Crossing, though the aftermath of horror in their hometown was something Jacob pondered. He assumed Brianna did, too; he declined to bring it up, however.

The next morning was cool and bright; the sunlight, crystal clear, speared through the winter woods. When Jacob suggested they drive into the nearest town for breakfast, he was rewarded with embraces from his two favorite females. At a Waffle House that reminded Jacob and Brianna of Bo's Mr. Pancake, they ate a big breakfast, but they did not speak of Bo, choosing instead to keep their sadness tethered out of sight. The present moment was all that mattered—and perhaps a tentative glimpse into the future.

Brianna asked to go shopping at a mall for clothes for her and Emily. After dropping them there, Jacob decided to look for something that might give Brianna an emotional lift. He found it in a florist's shop: a dozen long-stemmed red roses. When he gave them to her in the van—and offered one to Emily as well—Brianna teared up, and both of them smothered him with hugs and kisses.

It was a moment he wanted to last forever.

When he was back at the cabin, Jacob spent several hours with the bow and arrow, honing his skill at piercing the imaginary heart of an imaginary vampire. But he couldn't erase from his thoughts Brianna's comments about love.

Where does love go when it dies?

Was her love for him diminishing? Would it still be impossible for them to have a relationship despite the fact that he was not a Tracker? Would there always be a barrier to their love?

It rained hard during the afternoon.

The three of them were restless and bored. Jacob tried playing word games with Emily, and they told each other stories. Brianna grew distant once again. She seemed sad. She seemed almost unreachable in some mysterious way. Jacob wanted to ask her what was wrong, but she appeared to need to be alone. She seemed not to want to talk.

By that evening Jacob feared he was losing her.

Was she still under Franklin's spell? he wondered.

During the night Jacob was awakened by thunder and lightning and a wind that fisted against the cabin. When he rolled over, he discovered that Brianna was not in bed. Instinctively, he went to Emily's room next door, but she was sleeping soundly, angelically. He went from there down the hallway to the front room; the sour, sweet aroma of the fireplace greeted him, along with a sight that took his breath away.

Candles.

Seemingly dozens of them.

Arranged in a circle. And there, sitting on the floor in the center of the circle, naked and staring straight ahead, was Brianna.

Jacob was momentarily speechless; then he grew frightened, as only a dark jab of confusion and puzzlement can frighten one. He swallowed to find his voice.

"Brianna? What is this? What are you doing?"

When she heard his voice, she appeared to snap out of a trance. She blinked and glanced around at the candles and then at herself and seemed surprised. When her eyes met Jacob's, she began to cry.

He went to her and hunkered down and held her.

"What's going on?" he said.

"Help me," she said in response. "Oh, please help me, Jacob. I need you. You don't know how much I need you."

He put out the candles and took her back to bed. She did not want to talk—just to be held and reassured. But of what, Jacob couldn't be totally certain. By morning he had decided that they needed to spend most of the day away from the cabin. Brianna woke in a good mood. She seemed not to recall the night before. Jacob let it drop. In a brochure about the national forest, he had seen a map and a description of Pogahatchee Falls, a natural wonder just over a mile from the cabin.

A plan unfolded. They packed a picnic lunch.

Jacob took the bow and arrows. A cool, sunny, lovely Southern winter day opened before them. Although they were tired by the time they reached the falls, the sight of the water purling down over polished, rounded rocks reinvigorated them. They waded in the cold water that pooled at the final plunge of the falls and sat on the rocks. There, they gave themselves up to the reverie of water moving endlessly, dancing in the bright-eyed morning. And they devoured their picnic lunch as if it were their final meal.

They lingered into the afternoon.

Emily was beside herself with glee, collecting tiny, water-smoothed rocks and oddly shaped pinecones and as many different kinds of leaves as she could put her tiny fingers on. But though Brianna had seemed to thoroughly enjoy herself, Jacob noticed that as she sat on a magnificent rock and let her eyes drift up into the canopy of pines and hardwoods, she appeared to be somewhere else.

Listening to a voice he could not hear.

Seeing her like that made Jacob's heart sink.

It was an exhausted threesome that returned to the cabin.

They made tentative plans for dinner—steaks and some substantial vegetables and perhaps ice cream for dessert—and then they retired for a nap. Jacob slept soundly with Brianna in his arms.

And he dreamed.

And the dream was a collage of dark scenes beginning with the horror of watching Josh Tracker pour gasoline over himself and ignite it, becoming a dragon to save himself. And then the killing of J.T. and Roy Dale and the burial of those two and Uncle Douglas in the snakehole. And more. A fast-forward of moments until the final conflagration of Sweet Gum and the evil legacy of the Trackers rising as a white mist and dissolving.

But was it really the end?

When Jacob woke from the nap, he knew it wasn't.

Brianna was not in bed. Emily was not in her room. Jacob called out for them, and yet he was not surprised when he received no response. He grabbed the bow and arrows and ran out of the cabin into a gorgeous twilight, the sun slanting down in the west and filling the woods one last time before sunset.

Jacob headed for Vantage Point Rock.

As he did so, he could hear his heart beating in fear. He didn't know what he would find, but he knew the vampire had returned. And he knew that one more act of violence would be necessary.

He prayed that Brianna and Emily could be saved.

When, in the distance, he heard the tinkle of Emily's voice, he ran harder—he ran as if the very movement itself might prevent something, might stave off the inevitable. He knew he must face the vampire.

One more time.

To end the horror.

He ran on, and where the woods bordered the rocks of the magnificent vista, the vampire Franklin was waiting patiently, expecting the arrival of Jacob. Dressed in a dark cloak, the vampire had his arms raised as if about to take flight. In his eyes was the oncoming darkness.

As Jacob approached, he shouted, "Where are they? What've you done with Brianna and Emily?"

Calmly, precisely, as he had anticipated Jacob's demand and had rehearsed an answer, the vampire said, "I have prepared them."

Jacob was within twenty yards of the vampire.

The ideal distance for a kill shot. One arrow through the vampire's heart.

"Prepared them for what, you bastard?"

Jacob raised the bow and drew down.

He imagined the vampire's heart in the crosshairs of his aim.

The vampire smiled, continuing to hold his arms aloft with nothing but the nothingness of sky beyond him.

"For life after life," said the vampire. "Life everlasting."

Jacob pulled to the final notch of his strength.

"You're not taking the ones I love," he said, "because I'm taking you down."

The vampire moved more quickly than Jacob could blink. He swung the edges of his cloak aside, and what Jacob saw generated ice around his heart.

Beyond the vampire stood Brianna holding Emily.

When Brianna saw him, she hissed, and Jacob saw her fangs emerge.

"My God, no," he muttered.

The vampire Franklin seemed to have dissolved, leaving only the newest vampire clutching the innocent child. And the woman who was once Brianna, once mother to Emily, flashed hatred in her eyes at the sight of the raised bow. Then she returned her attention to the child, and with a sweep of her hand across the child's face, the tiny girl who was once her daughter appeared to fall into a trance. Gently the female vampire lowered the limp body of Emily to the surface of the rock and stood again to face Jacob.

And he knew what he must do.

But he could feel the strength escaping from his

arms like air from a balloon. Tears began to blur his vision, and the vampire lifted her arms and spread them as if inviting (or daring?) him to shoot.

To pierce her and give her a wholly new life.

The moment fixed itself out of time and out of space.

Twilight thickened and eternity waited.

"I loved you," Jacob whispered.

And the string twanged hard like the final note of a song, and the arrow stitched a nearly invisible line of fire into the heart of the vampire. Her cry of pain was flung into the evening sky. Her face was twisted with that pain.

And yet before she died to life, Jacob saw her smile.

Chapter Twenty-two

The Inextinguishable

He dug the snakehole by moonlight.

He chose a spot off to one side of Vantage Point Rock so that he did not have to move Brianna's body far.

Not Brianna. This creature is not my Brianna.

After killing the female vampire, piercing her heart and bringing her a moment of joy before she surrendered her body, Jacob carried Emily back to the cabin and put her to bed.

Tomorrow he would try to find the right words to tell her what had happened to her mother. Tomorrow. Tomorrow the words might come to him.

He dug the snakehole as deep as the ground would allow.

He did not grieve for the female vampire; he grieved for his lost love.

A lost family.

A lost future.

When he had completed his digging, and as sweat commingled with his tears, he paused and looked at the sky beyond Vantage Point Rock—the splash of moonlight inviting him to end his suffering.

What's the point of going on? he silently asked himself.

Then he thought of Emily.

And his emotions surged.

She was the answer: *his* missing piece.

Without further hesitation he buried the female vampire, tamping the mound of dirt with the back of the shovel. He wiped the sweat from his forehead. Then the wind gusted high in the nearby trees; the scene darkened curiously.

He heard the tinkle of a familiar voice, and when he did, he looked back immediately toward the cabin, then back to Vantage Point Rock, where the vampire Franklin was holding Emily in one arm. In his other hand he held a single long-stemmed rose from the dozen Jacob had given to Brianna.

"Don't you want to leave all the suffering behind?" said the vampire. "You had to kill the woman you loved, the mother of this precious child. That's what living in your world demanded."

Jacob was breathless with terror.

His mind scrambled to think of some way to get Emily from the vampire before she would be lost forever.

"She was no longer the woman I loved," he said, making eye contact with the vampire, facing him as bravely as possible. "And she was no longer the child's mother."

"But aren't you," said the vampire, "weary of being so helpless, so powerless?"

"I don't want your kind of power."

Then Jacob watched in horror as the vampire, still holding Emily, stepped to the edge of the rock and then out beyond it—and hovered with nothingness beneath him.

"Are you certain?" said the vampire. "The earth has chains for human beings—you can't live life more livingly. You have no choice but to follow laws that are foreign to you."

"Please," said Jacob. "Please don't hurt her."

For the flash of an instant he thought that he saw in the eyes of the vampire something of pity. The creature returned to the rock, and Jacob felt he could breathe again.

"Your love continues to be strong," said the creature. He lifted the rose and sniffed at it. "There is beauty in your love, but beauty fades and love dies."

Jacob shook his head.

"You're wrong. Not my love for the woman who was Brianna. Or my love for that child. Or my love for my family."

"A pretty speech," said the vampire. "But that which is deeper than love is beyond death. It's the darkness within, the shadow calling us to be more than human. To become transcendent. It's in the blood, Jacob, and it burns there. And it's inextinguishable."

Jacob lowered his head.

He knew that he was at the mercy of the vampire. He saw that he must accept losing the child to the powers of darkness. Emily: the last Tracker. He could not save her.

"What I feel," he said, "is another kind of fire in the blood. It's love for that beautiful child—I'll do anything if you'll only let her go and let her live to know how magical, despite all the suffering, human life can be."

For what seemed, to Jacob, an endless run of seconds, the vampire merely stared at him, a hesitation meant to torture him before the final horror was played out. Then suddenly the vampire moved toward Jacob, moved past him to the snakehole, hunkered down and placed the rose on the mound of dirt. He stood and darkness pooled in his face. And Jacob trembled. Emily, still in the creature's arms, reached for him, and something tore in Jacob's chest.

"Please," he said. "Please don't take her into your world. Please."

But the vampire turned and carried the child again to the edge of the precipice.

"Your love astounds me," he said. "How much more pain would you bear?"

"Whatever is necessary," said Jacob. "Do what you will to me—take *me* instead of her."

The vampire carefully lowered Emily to the surface of the rock. He put his hands on her tiny shoulders, his sharp fingernails close to her throat.

"Would you die for her? Right here in the sacred moonlight? Would your love give you the strength to do that?"

"Yes. Yes, if that's what I must do to save her. Is that what you're asking of me?"

Something unsayable, something deeper than words could possibly convey, seized the vampire. Jacob could not tell what it meant. He crouched down and smiled at Emily, and the little girl returned that smile.

A primitive sound escaped the throat of the vampire. Jacob looked up into those fiery eyes and said again, "Is that what you're asking of me? My life for hers?"

Slowly the vampire lifted his hands from the girl's

shoulder. Then he gently pushed her toward Jacob, and as she rushed into his waiting arms, he heard the vampire say, "No, you have suffered enough."

And with those words the vampire turned, raised his arms and took flight, swinging up in a magnificent arc until his dark form blotted out the full moon.

Jacob watched for several seconds, then looked away, pulling Emily closer, covering her with his arms as one might shield a tiny flame to keep it from flickering out.

ABOUT THE AUTHOR

Stephen Gresham lives in Alabama. He is currently working on his next horror novel, which will be published by Pinnacle Books in 2002. Steve loves to hear from readers; you can write to him c/o Pinnacle Books. Please include a self-addressed, stamped envelope if you wish to receive a response.

Feel the Seduction of Pinnacle Horror